PERSONA NON GRATA

A Novel of the Roman Empire

RUTH DOWNIE

B L O O M S B U R Y
NEW YORK • LONDON • OXFORD • NEW DELHI • SYDNEY

Bloomsbury USA
An imprint of Bloomsbury Publishing Plc

1385 Broadway
New York
NY 10018
USA

50 Bedford Square
London
WC1B 3DP
UK

www.bloomsbury.com

BLOOMSBURY and the Diana logo are trademarks of Bloomsbury Publishing Plc

First published 2009
This paperback edition published 2010

© Ruth Downie, 2009

All rights reserved. No part of this publication may be reproduced or transmitted in any form or by any means, electronic or mechanical, including photocopying, recording, or any information storage or retrieval system, without prior permission in writing from the publishers.

No responsibility for loss caused to any individual or organization acting on or refraining from action as a result of the material in this publication can be accepted by Bloomsbury or the author.

ISBN: HB: 978-1-59691-609-8
PB: 978-1-60819-047-8
ePub: 978-1-60819-111-6

Library of Congress Cataloging-in-Publication Data

Downie, Ruth, 1955 –
Persona non grata : a novel of the Roman empire / Ruth Downie. — 1st U.S. ed.
p. cm.
ISBN: 978-1-59691-609- 8 (alk. paper hardcover)
1. Physicians—Rome—Fiction. 2. Murder—Investigation—Fiction.
I. Title.
PR6104.O94P47 2009
823'.92—dc22
2009006767

4 6 8 10 9 7 5 3

Typeset by Westchester Book Group
Printed and bound in USA by Strategic Content Imaging, Secaucus, NJ

To find out more about our authors and books visit www.bloomsbury.com. Here you will find extracts, author interviews, details of forthcoming events, and the option to sign up for our newsletters.

Bloomsbury books may be purchased for business or promotional use. For information on bulk purchases please contact Macmillan Corporate and Premium Sales Department at specialmarkets@macmillan.com.

To the excavators of Whitehall Roman Villa

Do not heap up upon poverty, which has many attendant evils,
the perplexities which arise from borrowing and owing.

—Plutarch, *Moralia*

The love of money is the root of all evils.

—The Bible, 1 Timothy 6:10

PERSONA NON GRATA

A NOVEL

IN WHICH Gaius Petreius Ruso, our hero, will be . . .

Lied for by
Valens, a fellow medic

Harassed by
Marcia and
Flora, his half sisters

Organized by
Arria, his stepmother

Put straight by
Cassiana, his sister-in-law
a cook

Complained at by
Lucius Petreius, his brother

Intrigued by
Lollia Saturnina, a neighbor

Puzzled by
Justinus, his brother-in-law (missing feared drowned)
A very short letter

Insulted by
Claudia, his former wife, daughter of Probus (see "thrown out by")

Informed by
A security guard whose name he cannot remember
Flaccus, a kitchen boy
Galla, a servant
Valgius, a snake charmer
Attalus, an undertaker

Solicited by
Gabinius Fuscus, a politician and cousin of a senator
Tertius, a gladiator
Diphilus, a builder

Confused by
Polla
Sosia
Little Lucius
Little Publius, and
Little Gaius—his nephews and nieces

Pursued by
Calvus, an investigator
Stilo, his sidekick

Annoyed by
Brother Solemnis, a follower of Christos

Threatened by
Severus, the agent in charge of the senator's estate (see "in debt to")
Copreus, a sea captain
Ponticus, a shipping agent

Thrown out by

Ennia, sister of Severus
Zosimus, a house steward
Probus, a banker, Ruso's former father-in-law

Employed by

Gnostus, an old colleague with a new name

Almost poisoned by

A stable lad

In debt to

Many people, including:
Probus (see "thrown out by")
Gabinius Fuscus (see "solicited by")
The senator, a character frequently mentioned but never appearing
Assorted tradesmen

Argued with, slept with, and abandoned (again) by

Tilla, otherwise known as Darlughdacha of the Corionotatae among the Brigantes

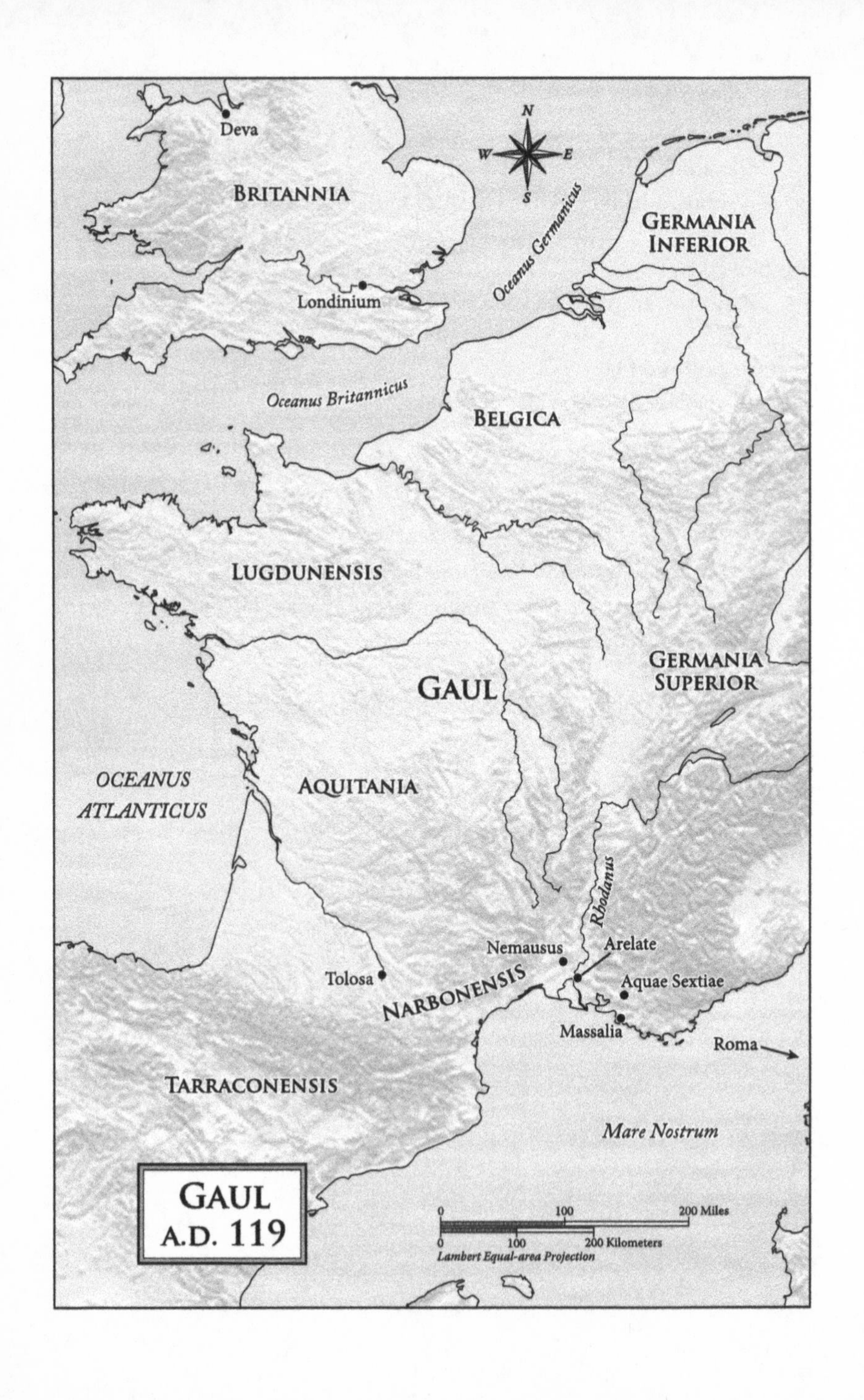
Deva
N
W
E
S
BRITANNIA
Oceanus Germanicus
GERMANIA
INFERIOR
Londinium
Oceanus Britannicus
BELGICA
LUGDUNENSIS
GERMANIA
SUPERIOR
GAUL
OCEANUS
ATLANTICUS
AQUITANIA
Rhodanus
Nemausus
Arelate
Tolosa
Aquae Sextiae
NARBONENSIS
Massalia
Roma
TARRACONENSIS
Mare Nostrum
GAUL
A.D. 119
0
100
200 Miles
0
100
200 Kilometers
Lambert Equal-area Projection

1

JUSTINUS WAS LYING in the stinking dark of the ship's hold, bruised and beaten, feeling every breath twist hot knives in his chest.

The light that trickled in through the worrying gaps in the hull showed the angle of the ladder above him. Beyond it, thin bright lines betrayed the position of the hatch. He remembered the slam, and the rattle of the bolts. Now he heard the sharp yell of a reprimand over the thumps and footfalls up on the deck of the *Pride of the South*, a ship that could hardly have been less appropriately named.

Whatever they were up to, it seemed he didn't need to die for it. If they planned to kill him, they could simply have thrown him overboard. Perhaps they would maroon him on a remote island somewhere while they sailed off to enjoy spending his master's money. He would eat berries, spear fish, and wait to be rescued. Sooner or later he would return home, thinner and browner and with a well-rehearsed apology to his master.

He forced himself into a sitting position just as the ship heeled to starboard. Cold bilge that should not have been near the cargo sloshed over his legs. Beneath him, he felt the stacked amphorae slide out of position and begin to tip and roll with the movement of the ship. Dark shapes swarmed out from among them and ran squealing along the sides of the hold.

"Hey!" he shouted, grasping at the ladder to steady himself and wincing at the pain in his chest. "Captain!"

No response.

"Copreus!" He banged on the ladder with his fist before he shouted the words that should bring the crew running. "The cargo's shifting!"

There was a muffled shout from above, then something thudding against the side of the ship, scurrying feet, and the bark of orders. Between the other sounds, he was almost certain he could hear waves breaking on a shore near enough to swim to.

"Hey!"

Struggling over the rolling necks of the amphorae, he pressed his face against a gap in the planking of the hull. Outside, he could see nothing but brilliant blue. He crawled back and smashed two of the loose amphorae against each other. Nothing happened. He heaved one up—thank God, for some reason this one was empty and relatively light—and swung it against the other. The heavy pottery cracked. Praying he could make a gap big enough to escape from before the sea started pouring in, he began using a broken handle to batter ineffectually at the worm-eaten hull.

"Let me out!" When he stopped to catch his breath he heard footsteps retreating across the deck. There was a series of small bumps against the hull before the shout of an order and the irregular splash of rowers getting into rhythm. After that there was nothing but the creaking of wood and the slop of water.

Moments later, he smelled the burning.

For a moment he could make no sense of it. Then, ignoring the pain in his chest, he took a deep breath and shouted through the gap, "You bastards! Get me out!"

Only the sound of water. The scuffle of a rat.

"Fire! Don't leave me here!"

Still no reply. The *Pride* lurched violently, rolling him up the inside of the hull and drenching him with more cold water as the amphorae crashed and tumbled around him.

"Don't leave me!"

Smoke was seeping down into the hold, forming ghostly fingers in the thin shafts of light. The water was rising. The *Pride* was listing badly now, as if she was settling down on her side to sleep.

"Help me!" he screamed, the pain stabbing his chest with every movement as he struggled to get upright. He cried out in panic as he felt himself slip down toward the water. Seconds later he came to rest against a fallen amphora. An expanse of long pale cylinders was shifting about in front of him.

He realized suddenly that every one of them was empty. That was why they were all bobbing about on the surface of the bilge. The cargo he had authorized, and seen loaded, had vanished—probably while Copreus had been buying him drinks back in Arelate the night before they sailed.

One of the amphorae gurgled and sank out of sight. The others rolled in and closed over the gap. Justinus shut his eyes. He prayed for strength. Then he edged along the ladder, which was now lying sideways, and aimed a kick at the hatch. Nothing happened.

He kicked at it again. "Let me out!" he screamed. "I won't say anything!"

A rat swam past him, scrabbled to get a grip, and finally managed to hook a paw over a handle and pull its dripping body out of the water.

Justinus closed his eyes again. "You can forgive them if you like," he growled to his god. "But they don't deserve it."

He said a prayer for his sister and his many nephews and nieces in case he did not see them again in this life. Then he began to give a last account of his sins and stupidities, all the time kicking at the locked hatch, because anything was better than listening to the creaking and splintering of old wood and the crash as something else gave way out there. Anything was better than noticing the way the cold was creeping up around him, and seeing the fingers of light in the smoky air being extinguished one by one by the rising flood, and coughing, and knowing that, drowning or burning, the end would be the same.

He was still praying and kicking the hatch when the *Pride of the South* vanished below the surface of the sunlit water, its passing marked only by a thin drift of smoke and a swell that was barely noticed by the men hastening away in a distant rowboat.

2

THE LEGIONARIES WERE still in full kit but presumably off duty, since they were swaggering down the street outside the fort with the belligerent cheer of men who had been sampling the local brew. Ruso, never keen to meet one loud drunk in possession of a sword, let alone five, walked past and ignored them. The light was fading and there was hardly anyone else about. The trumpet would sound the curfew in a minute. If this bunch didn't get themselves in through the fort gates soon, their centurion would be out to round them up.

He was halfway up the wooden steps to his lodgings when he heard the cry. He paused. The raucous laughter told him some silly girl hadn't had the sense to steer clear. The gang had found a victim.

The night guards who patrolled the streets to frighten off scavenging wolves and marauding Britons would not be on duty yet, and none of the civilians living out here would want to tackle a gang of legionaries bent on mischief. Ruso didn't want to tackle them either, but he supposed it was his duty to go and take a look. He clattered up the steps, assured Tilla, who was waiting for him, that he would be back to eat in a minute, and left before she could ask where he was going or—worse—insist on joining him.

The soldiers were not difficult to find: He only had to follow the sound of overexcited young men urging one another to do stupid things. Instead of making their way back to barracks, they had drifted down toward the river. Despite the noise—or perhaps because of it—Ruso seemed to be the only other person on the streets. The snack bar had put up its shutters for the night. The tenants of the nearby houses had chosen to bar their doors and mind their own business.

The men had their victim pinned against the wooden parapet of the bridge. None of them seemed to notice the army medical officer making his way toward them through the rough grass of the riverbank. As he drew closer he was surprised to see that the small figure was not a woman, but a native boy of about nine or ten. His captors, jostling around him like crows squabbling over a corpse, were accusing him variously of thieving, of spying, and of being a sniveling little British bastard.

Ruso strode up onto the bridge and adopted a friendly tone for "Where did you find this one?" just as a couple of the men hoisted the boy up onto the parapet, seized his ankles, and tipped him backward. The boy's shrieks of terror provoked more laughter as they dangled him headfirst above the rocky bed of the river. Someone shouted above the din, "Shut up or we'll drop you!"

Ruso vaguely recalled a couple of the faces but could not name them. Perhaps they had been patients. There were thousands of troops in the north of Britannia and there had been so many casualties at the height of the rebellion that he could remember only a blurred succession of mangled bodies. He raised his voice. "What's going on here?"

The shrieking stopped. There was some confused shuffling as the men realized they were being addressed by an officer. One of them attempted a salute, with limited success.

Finally the man holding the nearest foot announced, "We caught a spy."

The man's upper lip was distorted by a fresh red scar that reached to the corner of his eye. Ruso recalled stitching one very much like it. Probably neither of them had been in a fit state to remember the other.

He glanced over the parapet. The captive was a skinny creature whose ragged tunic had fallen over his face. Tails of mousy hair were dangling just clear of the water. "That's a spy?"

"What's he doing snooping around at this hour, then?" demanded the scarred one.

"Let's get him up and ask him."

The man looked askance at Ruso, as if he was wary of being tricked. A voice behind him hissed, "Let him up, mate. You'll get us all in trouble."

Ruso said, "He's only a child."

"They use kids," said the man.

"And women," chipped in somebody else.

"Yeah, kids and women. Don't ya?" The man gave the bare foot a shake, as if its owner was responsible for the unsporting practices of the British rebels.

The child responded with a howl.

"He's frightened enough now," said Ruso. "Get him back up."

From somewhere behind the man came, "Come on, mate, that's enough!" to which he hissed, "Shut up, I'm dealing with it!" He turned back to Ruso. "We're not finished yet. It's no good being soft on 'em. You think he's scared? This is nothing. If you knew what his lot did to our lads on the pay wagon—"

"I saw exactly what they did to the lads on the pay wagon," said Ruso, not wanting to be reminded of it. He had ridden out with the rescue expedition in the forlorn hope that some of the victims of the ambush would still be able to use medical help.

"You'd best stay out of this, sir," suggested one of the men Ruso had seen before somewhere.

"He can't," prompted the man holding the other foot. "He's got a native girlfriend."

Ruso squared his shoulders. "My name is Gaius Petreius Ruso, senior medical officer with the Twentieth Legion, and I'm taking that Briton into custody. Lift him back onto the bridge. That's an order."

"We already got him where we want him," growled the man.

"Now," said Ruso. At that moment the blare of the trumpet from the fort announced the curfew.

It was never clear whether they dropped the boy on purpose or by accident. One second his arms were dangling above the water, the next there was a scream and a splash and the thin body began to slide downstream between the rocks while his captors shouted at him to swim and quarreled about whose fault it was and who should rescue him.

The last thing Ruso wanted to do was haul several none-too-sober men out of the river. Ordering two to fetch help and the rest to stay where they were, he placed one hand on the parapet and vaulted down onto the bank.

The river god was kinder to the boy than the army had been: His body had wedged against a boulder and was being held there by the force of the flow. Ruso stepped into the rush of peat brown water that, even in late July, still carried the cold of northern hills. It was not deep but it was moving swiftly and he felt the tug against his legs. The only way to reach the boy was to wade out to where he was marooned. Ruso slithered and splashed, trying not to lose his footing on the slippery rocks, occasionally bending to grab at the top of a boulder to keep his balance. Yells of encouragement and advice came from the bridge. Ahead of him, the boy lifted his head and began to move.

"Stay where you are!" Ruso shouted over the sound of the water, afraid the child would dislodge himself and be swept farther down. There was a channel at least four feet wide between him and the boy. Now that he was closer, he could see that the river, thwarted in other directions by the boulders, flowed through the gap fast and smooth and deep. A tentative step told him that as soon as he let go, the force of the water would sweep him off to be battered against the rocks downstream.

He should have told those men to fetch a rope. He turned to call to the others, but they were so busy shouting suggestions, bawling, "Man in the river!" and warning him to be careful that nobody was listening. The boy called out something in British and tried to pull himself up. The only effect was to shift him closer to the deep channel.

"Don't move!" called Ruso, holding up one hand in a "stop!" gesture. He added, "I'll come and get you," with more confidence than he felt. He could make his way back to the bank, cross the bridge, and try from the other side, but the boy might be swept away in the meantime. He could try to get a grip in a crack in the rock this side, and reach across . . .

It almost ended in disaster. He managed to haul himself back and clung to the nearest boulder, gasping with the effort and the cold, vaguely aware of more cries from the bridge as the boy's body slid closer to the channel. He dragged himself upright and struggled to unfasten his belt with stiff fingers. It was not the form of rescue he would have chosen, but it was the boy's only chance. He pulled the belt tight around his wrist, prayed the buckle would hold, gripped the rock behind him again, and flung the loose end of the belt toward the boy.

The child managed to grab it on the third attempt. "Wrap it around your wrist!" yelled Ruso, hoping the boy was stronger than he looked and waiting for him to get a good hold with both hands. He was about to shout, "Ready?" when the boy launched himself into the flood and was instantly swept down the gap. Ruso felt the jerk as the belt tightened. The force of the water on the child's body dragged at his arm. His grip on the rock began to slide, and he felt himself being pulled into the flow.

Suddenly there was a hand clamped around his arm. Someone else was dragging at his tunic, wrenching him back up and out of the power of the water. He felt the blessed scrape of dry rock beneath him.

Miraculously, the child had managed to keep hold. He scrabbled up onto the boulder, then got to his feet and fled across the exposed rocks while Ruso's rescuers were still congratulating one another and telling him he didn't want to go in the river by himself like that, sir—what was he thinking?

If they had left him to recover at his own pace, the accident would never have happened. But his rescuers seemed determined to make up for their earlier misdemeanors. Having pulled him to safety, they now decided to form a human chain across the rocks and hustle him to dry land as fast as possible. The moment he attempted to stand on feet numb with cold, the nearest man grabbed him and pushed him toward the bank. The movement pulled Ruso off balance. His foot caught an uneven ledge of rock, bent sideways, and gave way beneath him in an explosion of pain.

3

BROKEN METATARSAL?" SUGGESTED Valens, leaning farther over his colleague's misshapen foot to view it from a different angle.

"I think I felt it go." Ruso, whose rescuers had carried him up to the fort hospital as if they were heroes, shifted himself to a more comfortable position. The movement sent fresh waves of pain crashing up the outside of his leg.

"Interesting. You've probably done a lot of other damage as well. What happens if you try to put weight on it?"

"I don't want to find out."

"Well, you know the drill."

Ruso sighed. "This can't be happening."

"No food tonight, fluid diet till the swelling goes down, and you'll have to go easy on it for a good six weeks. No wine, of course."

Ruso eyed the vanishing dimple that had recently been his ankle. "Could you try and sound a bit less cheerful about it?"

"Well there's no point in both of us being miserable, is there? Want me to help you hop down to the dressing station?"

"Who's on duty?"

Hearing the name, Ruso winced. "Bring me the stuff and I'll do it myself."

"Poppy?" offered Valens.

"Lots." There was no point in bothering with bravery.

Valens returned a few minutes later with a tray bearing a large bowl of cheap wine mixed with oil, and a smaller cup. Reaching for a wad of linen from the shelf, he said, "So tell me. How exactly did you manage to fall in the river and break your foot at the same time?"

Ruso took a drink of bitter poppy from the cup. "Long story," he explained. "But I'll be making a full report, believe me. There are five men who are going to be very—" He stopped. "Oh, gods. I told Tilla I'd be back in a minute. She won't know where I am."

"Ah, yes," said Valens, dipping the linen in the bowl. "The lovely Tilla. I should have said. She came to the gate a while ago. Your dinner's gone cold." Valens wrung out the compress. "And she's been called out on midwifery duty and she's not best pleased that some of our boys threw the messenger in the river before he got to her. So you might as well find a bed here tonight because there's nobody at home to kiss it better."

Ruso reached forward and grabbed the compress. "Let me do that," he insisted, draping it gingerly over the swollen foot and wrapping it around. So that was why the boy had been lurking around the houses at dusk.

"One more thing," said Valens, reaching for a bandage. "She left a letter for you."

Since Tilla could neither read nor write, this seemed unlikely.

"From your brother," explained Valens, nodding toward a sealed writing tablet behind Ruso on the desk.

The word *urgent* scrawled across the outside of the letter suggested that the latest financial crisis at home was even worse than usual. Ruso snapped the twine, flipped open the folded wooden leaves, and braced himself to face the details.

To his surprise, the letter said very little. On the inside of one leaf, in his brother's writing, was the date on which it had been composed: the Kalends of June. On the other, the briefest of messages:

Lucius to Gaius.
Come home, brother.

Ruso frowned over it for a moment, then passed it to Valens. "What do you make of that?"

Valens studied the carefully inscribed letters and observed, "Your brother is a man of few words."

"But what am I supposed to do about them?"

"Go home, I suppose."

Ruso grunted. "Hardly convenient, is it?"

Valens stepped back to admire his bandaging. "It could be arranged," he said.

4

"THIS IS RIDICULOUS," growled Ruso, eyeing the cup of milk he had just insisted on pouring for himself and wondering how he was going to carry it across to the bed so he could sit down and enjoy his late breakfast. He had already discovered this morning that since the lodgings he shared with Tilla were upstairs, the only safe way to reach them was to hook the crutches over one arm and hitch himself upward on his bottom.

She stepped forward and took the cup. "Go and sit."

Ruso adjusted his grip on the crutches, assessed the distance to the bed, and swung across to stand in front of it. Then he hopped and clumped until he had turned around, stuck his bandaged foot out in front of him, and collapsed backward onto the blankets.

"Gods and fishes!" he muttered, dropping the crutches on the floor and swiveling to swing his feet up onto the bed, "What am I supposed to do for six weeks like this?"

Tilla handed him the cup and retrieved the crutches. "Go home."

"It's too far," he explained, realizing a Briton would have no concept of that sort of distance. "The south of Gaul's over a thousand miles away, Tilla. Imagine how long it takes to get back down to Deva from here. Then imagine you've only done about a tenth of the trip."

Tilla yawned and sat beside him on the bed with her back propped against the wall. He realized she must have slept even less than he had last night. "I know how to do adding up," she said. "What I do not know is why your brother says to come home."

Ruso retrieved the letter from beneath the pillow and examined the leaves on both sides. The outsides bore nothing beyond the usual to-and-from addresses and the alarming URGENT inked in large letters thickened with several strokes of the pen.

Lucius's letters usually held either a desperate request for money, or a fresh announcement of a happy arrival for him and his wife, Cassiana. Sometimes both. There were times when Ruso had wondered whether the family fortunes—precarious at the best of times—would finally be ruined not by demands to repay his late father's massive borrowings, but by the need to feed and clothe all his nephews and nieces.

Lucius's requests for cash were always couched in careful terms, lest they should fall into the wrong hands: the sort of hands whose owner would blab about one creditor to another. He usually gave just enough clues about the latest crisis to spur Ruso into doing something about it. But this latest message was exceptionally cryptic.

Was the date a code? Was there something significant about the Kalends of June? If so, he could not think what it was. He turned the leaves upside down to see if there was some message concealed in the script that was only visible from the opposite direction. He tried warming the letter over a lamp flame in search of secret ink. He succeeded only in scorching the wood.

"It's no good," he conceded. "I don't know what it means."

"It means," said Tilla, "come home."

"I wouldn't get there before mid-September," he pointed out. "By the time I wanted to come back I'd be lucky to find a captain willing to take a ship out. I might not get back till the seas open again." He lifted his foot in the air. "This isn't going to earn me that much leave."

"It is a very big bandage. Valens can tell lies about what is underneath."

"But I've got patients to see, men to train . . ."

"Other doctors can see the patients and train the men. There is not so much for you to do now, and you have a broken leg."

"Foot."

She did not reply. *There is not so much for you to do now* was one of the rare occasions on which either of them had mentioned the army's apparent success in crushing a native rebellion far more ferocious than anyone had expected. The casualty figures had been kept secret, but while Ruso was on duty behind the battlefront she must have seen the wagonloads of Roman wounded arriving back at the fort. More than once during the worst of the fighting she had disappeared for days at a time and returned with sunken eyes and dried blood beneath her fingernails. He had asked no questions. That way, she did not have to pretend she had been away delivering babies and he did not have to pretend he believed her.

As if to reassure him, she said, "The baby was a girl. Born at first light. She is very small, but I think she will live."

"What did this lot pay you with?"

Tilla's smile was triumphant. "Guess."

He glanced around the bare little room. Tilla's skills as a midwife had been less in demand since the start of the rebellion. Most of the sensible locals had fled at the height of the troubles last year, dragging their wide-eyed children by the hand, burdened with cooking pots and blankets and hens in baskets. Those who remained paid her in whatever way they could manage. Eggs and apples were always useful. The first smelly fleece had been bartered for a new pair of boots; the second was still stashed away in a sack under the bed. There were no new offerings on display.

"It's not another goat, is it?"

"No, but I can buy a goat if I want. Look!" She untied her purse. Shiny copper coins cascaded onto the bed. "All earned by working!" she added.

He was pleased. Tilla had never fully subscribed to his own view that it was wrong to help oneself to other people's property, but at least she seemed to have learned to respect it. The money was only small change, but he picked up one of the coins to admire it all the same. Within seconds all thoughts of congratulation had gone. He said, "Oh, hell."

"No, they are real."

"I don't doubt they're real." He passed her the coin. "Look at the back of it. Not Hadrian's head, the other side."

"Is that supposed to be a woman?"

"It says 'Britannia.' Have you ever seen a coin like that before?"

"No."

Neither had he. It was very obviously fresh from the mint, and the only way it could have reached here was on the ambushed wagon.

He cleared his throat. "It's my duty to ask who gave you this money, Tilla."

There was no need to explain: The news of the stolen pay chest had been impossible to suppress. Finally she said, "What if I do not tell you?"

He had to say it. "If you refuse to tell me, it will be my duty to report this to HQ."

A cart with a squeaking wheel was passing outside the window. When the sound had faded down the street she said, "I will not tell you."

"I never thought you would." He reached for the crutches. "I'm going to talk to Valens. When I get back, either you or that money will have to be gone. If you're still here, we'll start packing to go home."

5

RUSO STRETCHED OUT his legs, leaned his back against the rail of the ship, and gazed up at a seagull perched on the mast. He felt queasy. The roll of the vessel did not combine well with the smell of the fleece Tilla had insisted on bringing with her, and which she was now contentedly spinning beside him in the afternoon sunshine.

How, he wondered, did seagulls keep themselves so clean? Compared with the bird, the white bandage that encased his leg from hip to toe was disgustingly grimy. It was also much bigger than necessary, and Ruso had wondered as it went on whether Valens was going too far. What he wanted was convalescent leave, not an irrevocable medical discharge from the army. Valens, however, had been confident.

"Three months to recuperate, two months' winter leave, that takes you to . . . sometime in December. And don't worry about leaving us in the lurch: I've said I'll do extra nights if they need the cover."

Ruso blinked. "Really?" He could remember only one occasion on which Valens had offered to do extra night duty, and that was because he was trying to hide from a fierce centurion with a grudge. "Can't they get one of the new men in?"

Valens tied the end of the bandage and tucked it in. "I'm a married man these days. You must remember what it was like."

"I try not to."

"It wasn't too bad when it was just her," said Valens. "But now she's got the twins."

"Well, that's your fault."

"Indeed," Valens agreed. "But a chap has to sleep sometime, doesn't he? And it's not as if she's on her own with them. That nursemaid cost me a fortune. I'm not the sort of husband who shirks his responsibilities, you know."

"So you come to work for a rest?"

"Just as well, now that you've gone and let everybody down by dancing about in the river. Did you know your rescuers have all been put on latrine duty for a month? Drunk and disorderly."

Ruso was about to remark that they had got off lightly when there was a knock at the door.

"Ah, here's the chap who's going to sign for you." Valens retrieved a writing tablet from the desk and handed it to a fresh-faced young doctor who must have arrived with the latest batch of reinforcements. "Here you are. Sign in the space at the bottom."

The man glanced at the impressive bandaging, ran one finger over what had been written on the document, and signed without making any attempt to verify it. "Sorry I can't stop to chat," he said to Ruso. "I have to go and take a leg off. Oh, and thanks for the chair."

"Chair?" inquired Ruso after he had gone.

"Well, you won't be taking it with you, will you?" said Valens. "So I assumed you'd be offering it to me, but as you're in need of a favor I've told him he can have it."

"My chair? The one I've had since Antioch?"

Valens's handsome face looked pained. "I could hardly ask him to sign without offering him something, could I? Don't worry, I've told him you'll need it when you get back."

"I'm not sure I'll be coming back. It depends on what's going on at home. My contract with the Legion runs out in January."

For once Valens looked genuinely shocked. "You mean you've got me arranging all this just so you can desert me?"

"I might decide to sign on again."

"You will," Valens assured him. "You'll miss all this fun when you're down on the farm, you know."

At the time Ruso had insisted he would be glad to get back to a civilized country. It was something he had been saying ever since he'd arrived in Britannia. But now, sprawled on the deck of a troop ship that had brought over reinforcements and was now carrying back wounded, he realized he would miss Britain's misty green hills and the chilly streams that never ran dry. There had been many times during the horrors of the rebellion when he had wished himself almost anywhere else, but he knew now that he would be sorry to leave the army.

He shook his head. At this rate he would soon be imagining he missed Valens.

The seagull launched itself off the mast, gave one lazy flap, and was soon left behind by the speed of the ship. Beside him, Tilla's left arm rose to draw out the brown fibers while her right thumb and forefinger set the spindle twirling.

Ruso allowed himself a brief moment of self-congratulation. He had removed Tilla from the control of an ignorant oaf back in Deva in the full expectation that even if she survived, the injury the man had inflicted on her arm was so serious that he would have to amputate. Instead, she had surprised everyone, not only by surviving but by dragging Ruso into an investigation of the mysterious deaths of the local bar girls.

As he watched the hand that he had saved twist the woolen fibers into a neat thread, it occurred to Ruso that Tilla was about to become a surprise once again. He really should have found a way to mention her to his family while he was serving in Britannia. It was too late now. A last-minute letter could travel no faster than they were traveling themselves. He would have to make some hurried explanations when he arrived.

Perhaps the one good thing about this mysterious family crisis was that nobody would have time to worry about the arrival of an unexpected Briton.

Seeing him watching, she said, "The wool will be a gift for your stepmother. Does she like to weave?"

"I don't think so," said Ruso, imagining Arria's horror at the prospect of making her own clothes. "But I'm sure one of the staff will be able to weave it for her."

"What does she like to do?"

Ruso shifted to get a better view of the horizon. "She's very keen on home improvements."

"Ah."

"It's a big house," he added, not feeling well enough to explain that to a woman like Arria, "home improvements" involved far more than a pot of wildflowers on the table and a patched scarlet curtain between the bed and the cooking space.

Tilla said, "It is good she has your sisters to help her."

Ruso grunted something noncommittal. It was hard to imagine his sisters helping anyone, but perhaps they had improved in his absence. He tried to take his mind off the way his stomach was moving independently of the ship by telling Tilla about brilliant blue summer skies and air filled with the song of cicadas. About the olive grove and the vineyards. About his brother's precious winery, and about his sister-in-law, the one who sent presents from home and produced all the nephews and nieces.

Tilla said, "I think I will like your home."

Ruso felt another pang of guilt about his failure to mention her to his family. "To be honest," he said, "I don't know what we'll find after that letter. Something must have gone terribly wrong."

"How wrong can it be? There is sunshine, and trees that grow oil, and no soldiers."

"Soldiers are one problem we don't have at home," he agreed. "Narbonensis has been practically part of Italy for generations." A thought occurred to him. "You've never really seen what peace is like, have you?"

When they docked on the west coast of Gaul, the last of the genuinely maimed veterans who had traveled with them left for their own destinations. Ruso removed the extra dressings. He gave one of the crutches to a surprised beggar and then regretted it when he realized how feeble his leg muscles had become during their enforced rest. Still, it was a relief to feel the fresh summer breeze on his chafed thigh and to see the limb that had been the color and shape of a giant maggot return to a normal-sized leg. He now wore only a long sock of bandage and, provided he was careful, could put his heel down to the ground without instant regret.

He clambered without assistance onto the river barge that would take them on the next stage of their journey. The joy of independence was only slightly diminished by Tilla's observation that he now had one brown leg and one that looked as though he had just got it out of winter storage.

Following the river as it wound its leisurely way across the flat lands of southwest Gaul, their lives settled into a pleasant rhythm. He taught her to play board games, and discovered she was a shameless cheat who laughed when she was caught. At last he made a serious effort to learn to speak British, and she discovered that there was a language that resembled it called Gaulish, which he tried to teach her in return. They squabbled over space in the tiny bunk, tried sleeping top to toe, and quickly decided that was worse. He bought her a straw hat to keep the sun off, and she adorned it with the wildflowers she picked on the riverbank.

As they left the barge behind in Tolosa and climbed into the carriage to make the last stage of the journey through the mountains by road, it occurred to Ruso that there were whole days now when he hardly thought of the dreadful events they had left behind in Britannia. He abandoned the last crutch for a stick as his body began to heal along with his mind. He could not remember a time when he had been happier.

It was a pity he knew it wasn't going to last.

6

BROTHER! WHAT ARE you doing here? What's the matter with your foot?"

"Aren't you supposed to be in the army, Gaius?"

"Uncle Gaius! Did you kill all the barbarians?"

The greetings and hot embraces filling the painted hallway gave no hint of the crisis that had brought him home.

"Gaius, dear, is it really you? What a surprise!"

"Mother!" he said to Arria. He had practiced the word until he no longer had to grit his teeth to say it. He thought it came out rather well.

"You're wounded!"

"It's nothing much," he assured her, and took Tilla by the arm. "Arria, this is—"

"Uncle Gaius! Uncle Gaius, I've got a loose tooth!"

He bent awkwardly, leaning on the stick. "Want me to pull it out for you, Polla?"

His niece frowned and backed away. "I'm not Polla, Uncle. That's Polla." She pointed at an older sister. "I'm Sosia."

"Sosia? Gods above, you've—" He stopped himself just in time. "Of course. Sorry, Sosia. Good to see you. Everybody, this is—"

Someone was prodding his shoulder. "I'm Marcia," put in a girl who looked alarmingly like a young woman. "I'm your sister. Remember me?"

"No, really?" said Ruso, who remembered only too well. Her embrace warmed slightly when he murmured, "I haven't forgotten about your dowry, you know."

"I need it now," she hissed. "And I'm not going to marry some rich old goat with spindly legs and hair in his ears, understand?"

"I'll bear it in mind," he agreed. "Marcia, where are Lucius and Cass?"

His sister shrugged. "Doing something boring on the farm, I suppose."

Still no clues. Evidently Lucius had not told their sisters about the letter.

He correctly guessed the names of two nephews and limped across the hall to greet the row of waiting staff like a general addressing his troops at a surprise inspection.

"Hello, Galla." The nursemaid's hair had turned gray in his absence. The kitchen boy had expanded upward, the laundry maid widthways, and Arria's personal maid in all the right places. The cook's apron was now being worn by a sour-faced man, the stable lad still smelled the same, and the bath boy, who had been ancient when Ruso was a child, managed to impress simply by remaining alive. "It's good to see you all," he said.

He was dredging his memory for names when his stepmother's voice rang across the hall in a tone he remembered only too well.

"Gaius, dear, who is this?"

Glancing around at the assembled company, all now surveying the slender blond figure just inside the doorway, the absurdity of the notion that he would be able to slip Tilla into the household almost unnoticed became clear.

A small voice at nephew level announced, "She's got a red face."

"She's got blue eyes."

"Why is her hair like that?"

"Because she's a barbarian, stupid!" explained one of the nieces.

"She's British," said Ruso, as if that explained not only her appearance but her presence. "Everybody, this is Tilla. She's our guest, so I want you all to make her welcome."

This had the unfortunate effect of unleashing more curiosity.

"Can she talk?"

"Can we touch her?"

"Is she fierce?"

"Aaah!" This last was from a dribbling toddler who had evidently learned early that he had to speak up to be noticed.

"Yes, she can talk," said Ruso, looking around in vain for his sister-in-law to get the small interrogators under control. "And no, you can't touch her. We've had a long journey and she's tired."

One of Ruso's sisters whispered something to the other and they both giggled. Tilla's expression was one he could not read and dared not speculate on, but the child was right. Her cheeks were even pinker than the sunburn on her nose. Tendrils of hair, dark with sweat, were stuck to her forehead. "Sorry about this," he murmured to her.

Tilla grasped his hand and whispered, "What did you tell them about me?"

"I'll explain in a minute," he assured her.

The hastily assembled greeting party was evidently expecting a formal speech. *Those eyes aren't really blue*, he wanted to tell them. *Not up close.* "Well," he said, searching desperately for something more appropriate. "Yes. Hello, everybody. It's good to be home." He was not sure it was true, but it was necessary to say it. "You all look very, uh . . ."

The eldest nephews had lost interest and begun to roll across the floor punching each other. A niece shouted, "Stop it!" while Galla made a futile attempt to intervene. Ruso glanced at the bust of his late father, impassively surveying the chaos from its niche beside the garlanded household shrine, and wondered what the old man would have made of this performance.

"Children!" Arria's voice rose again over the babble. "Your kind uncle Gaius has brought a real barbarian home for us all the way from Britannia. Isn't that nice of him?"

There were confused murmurs of assent.

Ruso tried again. "Tilla," he said, gesturing toward Arria, "this is my stepmother, Arria—"

But Arria had not finished. "We must all set her a good example and look after her," she continued. "Galla, go and tell the driver to bring in the master's luggage. Children, why don't you all go and take—what do you call her?"

"Tilla."

"Take Tilla to the kitchen and Cook will find her something to eat and drink. I expect she would like that." She turned to Ruso. "What do they eat, Gaius?"

The words, "Small children," were out before he could stop them. "Arria, where's Lucius?"

★ ★ ★

The nieces and nephews were finally ushered away to the kitchen, taking both of Ruso's half sisters with them to protect them from the child-eating barbarian. Ruso, faintly ashamed of himself, was left alone with his stepmother.

"Gaius, dear, what are you doing home? Are you on leave? What's wrong with your foot?"

Evidently Arria knew nothing about Lucius's letter. "Home to convalesce," he explained. "I need to see Lucius."

"I've sent one of the servants to fetch him. I must say, that's a very strange young woman you've brought with you. Why is she dressed like that in this weather?"

"Because those are her clothes." As far as Ruso was aware, Tilla had two sets of perfectly adequate second-hand clothes. These, if pushed, he could describe as "blue." He could differentiate between them only as The One She's Wearing and The One That's Being Washed.

"She can't wear heavy wool like that here. I'll ask one of the staff to find her something else."

"Is everything all right here? Where's Cass?"

Arria sighed. "Who knows? As you see, the children are quite out of control. It's such a relief to have you home, Gaius. Poor Lucius really has no idea. He's letting everything go to waste— Gaius, dear, are you listening?"

Ruso rubbed his tunic against the small of his back to wipe away a trickle of sweat. "No."

Arria sighed. "You must be tired after traveling. But I have to tell you this while I have the chance. You see how things are here. Your father would be so disappointed, after all that he did. I was hoping we would have your sisters married by now—Marcia, at least—"

"I'll sort out the girls' dowries now I'm home," promised Ruso, hoping Lucius was not going to tell him there was nothing to settle on either of their half sisters.

"In the meantime your brother and his wife do nothing but breed children who run around making sticky fingerprints on the furniture. The smallest one has no idea what a pot is for and the staff are constantly sweeping up what they've broken. They've driven away three tutors already. Cassiana just indulges them and Lucius is too taken up with his vines and his legal squabbles to notice. Galla's worn out, and—"

"What legal squabbles?" said Ruso, suddenly paying attention.

"He keeps telling me we can't afford to replace Galla, but I'm sure we could—"

"What legal squabbles, Arria?"

"Do talk to him about it, dear, will you? It's such a wretched nuisance. And now he's got your sisters involved in it."

"Involved in what?"

"Oh, something about a—seizure order, is it?"

"Holy gods, Arria! There's someone trying to auction off everything we own?"

His stepmother put one manicured finger to her lips. "Please don't shout, dear. We're not supposed to talk about it. Do what I do—just pretend you don't know."

7

THE SHUTTERS OF his father's old study opened with a screech that briefly silenced the chirrup of the cicadas outside. Sunlight spilled across the floor and threw the iron studs on the old wooden chest into sharp relief. Ruso crossed the room and slid one hand under the rim of the lid. Locked. Of course. Lucius would be wearing the key around his neck, just as their father had.

Ruso lowered himself onto the trunk and sat tapping out an impatient rhythm on the lid with both hands. He had traveled a thousand miles to find out exactly what sort of crisis his family had fallen into. Now the details were only inches away, but he had no access to them. Just as there had been no access to the details of the horrendous debts his father was incurring in a misguided attempt to bolster the family's good standing and satisfy Arria's demand for a nice house. Those too had been locked away in the dark secrecy of the trunk.

He got to his feet and limped across to the window. The air outside was no cooler. A couple of the cicadas had started singing again. He gazed north across the green of the vine trellises to where distant wooded hills were dark against the sharp blue of the sky. Closer, something was shaking the leaves of the vines. He heard voices. Someone laughed. The top of a ladder appeared above the green, then sank away again. The farm slaves would be scrambling up amongst the trellises, cutting the grapes with curved knives and tossing them into baskets.

Three fat bunches dangled almost within reach of the window. Ruso wondered whether it was a good year for the vines. Lucius would know. Despite having spent most of his childhood here, Ruso had deliberately avoided learning anything about farming. It was an obstinacy of which he was no longer proud. Still, no amount of farming lore would help if the family really were about to be the subject of a seizure order.

He had once accompanied his father to the auction of a bankrupt neighbor's property. It was like seeing an old person stripped naked in the street: All the neighbor's battered pots and pans, ancient bath shoes, blankets and bedsteads—even a baby's discarded feeding bottle—lay shabby and exposed in the sunshine, while strangers glanced over them, wrinkled their noses, and walked away. His father had stayed, bidding much too high for an old cart and a couple of hoes with worm-eaten handles while the neighbor stood grimfaced and his wife wept. At the time, Ruso had been too young to understand that his father was offering them the only kindness that was then possible.

His thoughts were interrupted by a soft knock at the door. He had given orders that he was not to be disturbed, unless Lucius—

It wasn't. It was his sister-in-law.

"Cass!"

"Gaius! They told me you were here. What a lovely surprise!"

Surprise? Evidently Lucius had not even told his wife about that letter. When Ruso managed to extricate himself from the hug he said, "Thanks for all the parcels."

While Lucius had sent urgent appeals for cash, his wife had softened them with gifts of winter woolens and jars of food from home and pictures drawn by the children.

She stepped back. "You look tired. I've told the bath boy to light the fire. Lucius will be home soon. He's doing some business in town. How are you? We heard about that dreadful rebellion in Britannia. Is that how you hurt your leg?"

"Not exactly," confessed Ruso. "It was an accident."

"Oh, you poor thing! But is it true they had to send extra troops in?"

"It's mostly sorted out now," he assured her. He was not sure whether he was allowed to reveal that Hadrian had sent in the fresh troops not just as reinforcements but as replacements for serious losses. "I haven't seen you to congratulate you on, uh—" He suddenly realized he did not know the name of the dribbling toddler.

"We called him Gaius, after you—didn't you know? Everyone says he looks just like you."

"Do they really?"

"Oh, yes!" Cass beamed at him, evidently thinking it was some sort of compliment.

"The children seem very . . . lively."

"They're dreadful, aren't they?" she agreed, as if it were something to be proud of. "But we're so fortunate. Five healthy children! Every day I give thanks for them. You never know, do you? Polla had a terrible fever a while ago, then little Lucius broke his arm, and last month Sosia was ill—Arria was so cross about the cushions but she couldn't help it, could she? We tried everything. It was a pity you weren't here, Gaius."

"Mm."

"They'll be so glad you're home. They do miss their uncle Justinus terribly."

"Justinus? Is he away somewhere?"

She stared at him. "But Lucius told you, surely?"

"The letter must have got held up. What's happened?"

She shook her head. "We don't know," she said. "That's the worst part. My brother went on a merchant ship from Arelate down to Ostia back in June and . . ." Her voice trailed off. "The ship never arrived," she said. "They could be shipwrecked on an island or something, couldn't they? Waiting to be rescued."

Since it was now September, Ruso could not pretend that this was likely.

"If it was pirates . . ." Her voice trembled and faded away.

Ruso hoped she was not going to cry. He was never sure what to do with women when they cried.

She swallowed. "We would just like to know."

"I'm sorry." The last time he had met Cass's brother was in the house of Ruso's former father-in-law, where Justinus was a respected if somewhat put-upon steward. "What was he doing at sea?"

"Probus sent him to oversee some sort of business deal. You probably heard about it. The *Pride of the South*." She paused, evidently expecting this would mean something to him.

Ruso did not want to tell her that ships went down every day. That unless the *Pride* had been carrying something valuable, or somebody famous, it was unlikely that anyone except her owners and the families of the crew would mourn her loss or even bother to remark upon it.

"We were on a different sea," he explained. "He'd have been going south. We came down the west coast and across."

"What about the men on the river barges? Didn't anybody say anything at all?"

"They might have thought it was bad luck," he said, trying to soften the blow of public indifference.

"He was so excited about seeing Rome," she said. "He had some wine from the senator's estate to deliver. He dropped in on the way to Arelate to say good-bye."

"I'm so sorry," said Ruso, and meant it. "I liked Justinus."

She hesitated, as if she was wondering whether to continue. "Lucius says I ought to give up hope," she said. "He says we should build the tomb and call his spirit home and let it rest."

Ruso, scenting a marital dispute, said, "He's probably worried about you."

"He's right, isn't he? If we don't do it . . ." She did not need to explain. Her brother's spirit would be left wandering lost and alone, unable to find peace.

"There really aren't many pirates out there these days, Cass. If there's been no word in three months—"

"I know! I know all that. I was going to say yes to having the tomb built, but . . . oh, now I don't know what to do!" She glanced around to make sure the door was closed. "Gaius, you know Probus better than any of us. If I tell you something, will you promise to keep it a secret?"

Ruso hoped his face did not betray his rising sense of foreboding at the mention of his former father-in-law.

"Probus came to see me a couple of weeks ago. He wanted to know whether I was sure my brother was dead."

Whatever Ruso had been expecting, it was not this. "Why?"

"I don't know. He seemed to be angry about something, but he wouldn't say what."

Ruso refrained from pointing out that in his experience, Probus usually looked angry about something.

"So I said to him, You were the one who told me the ship was missing in the first place, and all he said was *Yes*. When I wanted to know why he was asking, whether he'd heard something, he just told me to forget all about it and not say anything to anybody."

It certainly seemed odd, not to mention deeply insensitive. "Do you want me to talk to him?"

"No! He'll know I've told you. What's the matter with him, Gaius? Why would he ask a question like that? It was as if he thought Justinus might have run away. So now I don't know what to do. If we call his spirit to a tomb and he's still alive somewhere—what would happen to him?"

Ruso, who had no idea, said nothing.

"I wanted to go into town and ask Probus what he meant but Lucius says fussing won't bring my brother back and if I'm not careful I'll upset Probus and then we'll be in more trouble."

Ruso reflected that Lucius was probably right. The familial ties with Probus might be severed, but they still owed him money, and the last thing they needed was a hostile creditor.

"I was hoping you might know something."

"It's not unusual for ships to vanish, Cass," he said, realizing she had probably never seen an expanse of water bigger than the swimming pool at the town baths in Nemausus. "You can't imagine how vast the seas are if you haven't seen them. It could have been hit by a freak wave, or gone too close to the rocks, or . . ." Catching the expression on her face, he realized this speculation was not helpful. "There are lots of things, really. Nobody would know until it didn't turn up at the other end."

"I tried asking the fish sellers in town," she said. "They said perhaps it was sunk by a falling star. They didn't want to talk to me."

"I don't know about the star," he said, "but I'd imagine people who earn their living on the water don't want to spend too much time discussing shipwrecks."

"I don't want to cause trouble, Gaius. I just want to know what's happened to my brother. There's nobody else left to look after him."

"Of course." Ruso was wondering whether he was witnessing the obstinacy of hope or whether there really could be something odd about the disappearance of the *Pride of the South* when a masculine voice out in the hall bellowed, "Gaius! Where are you, brother?"

Cass put a hand on Ruso's arm. "Please don't say anything to him," she murmured. "He's cross enough with me already." She retreated to the door. Ruso heard a brief exchange in the hallway and a moment later she was replaced by a paunchy middle-aged man with thinning hair and bags under his eyes. Ruso opened his arms and braced himself.

8

THE LATEST HUG turned out to be less enthusiastic than the one from his sister-in-law. When they had clung to each other for what Ruso felt was a decent length of time, they held each other at arm's length. Ruso politely informed the middle-aged man that he was looking well.

"No I'm not."

"No, you're not," agreed Ruso, relieved that he had not been the first of them to say it. "I got your letter."

"Gaius." Lucius's breathing was audible, as if the lungs were weighed down with the bulk of the paunch. "This is very bad timing."

"I couldn't get here any faster. I know you had to be careful, but you might have given me some idea of what the problem was."

Lucius glanced behind him and closed the door. "How many people know you're home?"

"How long has this legal business been going on?"

Lucius smoothed the top of his thinning hair. "We could probably keep it quiet. The staff won't talk. Did you see anyone you knew on the road?"

Ruso frowned. "You didn't say anything about coming home in secret."

Lucius subsided onto the chair that Ruso still thought of as belonging to their father. "I don't know what we're going to do now. Not now that you've turned up."

Ruso stared at him. "But you're the one who wrote and asked me to come home!"

The tired eyes that reminded him of his own seemed to be displaying equal bafflement. "No I didn't. That's the last thing I would have done."

Ruso pondered the remote possibility that the letter had said, 'Do not come home.' Surely he could not have misread it? Tilla's views were of no help since Tilla could barely read her own name. But Valens had interpreted it as 'come home' too. "It was in your writing."

Lucius shook his head. "The only things I've written to you about lately are Cass's brother being drowned, and Marcia's wretched dowry."

"That's not the letter I got."

"No, you'd probably already left by the time it arrived. Are you sure this 'come home' was addressed to you?"

"Of course I am! And it looked exactly like your writing. You don't think I'd travel a thousand miles on crutches because of a letter to somebody else, do you?"

"I suppose not." The tone was reluctant rather than conciliatory.

Ruso sat on the trunk, propped his stick against the wall, and scowled as it slid sideways out of reach and clattered onto the floor. "This is ridiculous."

"Did you bring this letter with you?"

"I burned it. So if you didn't send it, who did?"

"I've no idea. I wish they hadn't."

Ruso shrugged. "Well, I'm here now."

"Yes." Lucius cleared his throat. "I suppose we'll have to make the best of it. You're looking well, anyway. How was Britannia?"

"Messy. Is it true someone's trying to bankrupt us?"

Lucius leaned back in their father's chair and folded his arms. "If I were to say no," he said, "and ask you to go straight back to Deva for the good of the family, would you do it?"

"I can't," Ruso pointed out. "I had to wangle months of leave to get here."

"So you can't go back to the Legion." Lucius managed to look even more depressed.

"Arria says somebody's applied for a seizure order."

Lucius let out a long breath. "There's a law somewhere," he said, "that says you can't take out a seizure order against someone who's away from home on public service."

Ruso began to grasp the nature of the problem. "Does that apply to an ordinary man in the army?"

"The last thing I would have done, brother, was to ask you to come home."

"So it's true then? We have a legal problem?"

"We do now," said Lucius.

9

FINALLY, TILLA WAS alone with her headache. The Medicus's nephews and nieces had been rounded up by their mother. The older girls had grown bored with her and gone about their own business, and the cook, eager to get this stranger out of his kitchen, had handed her a cup of water and suggested that she go and sit in the garden.

She glanced both ways down the long stone porch that shaded the front of the house. There was no sign of the man whom she called the Medicus, everyone else called Ruso, and now his family—confusingly—seemed to know as Gaius. She supposed he was somewhere talking to the brother, finding out at last why they were here.

She crossed the porch and went down the steps into a garden where roses and lavender grew in beds corralled by little clipped hedges, as if they might otherwise make a dash for freedom.

The path led under the dappled shade of a long wooden frame that she thought might be called a *pergola*. The word was one of the many new things she would have to learn here. She already had the word for the insects hiding up among the leaves. Cicadas. The Medicus had promised her she would grow to love the song, but so far the terrible grating screech made her feel as though she was having her back teeth sawn off.

Tilla sank onto a stone bench that looked out over a cracked concrete pond. The water had evaporated long ago, leaving a black flaking coat that might once have been algae. She gazed at a plinth where a rusted bracket reached for a statue that wasn't there, and tried not to think how far she was from home. Everything was as the Medicus had described it: the sunshine, the olive grove outside the gates, the tall vines, the winery . . . but her mind had taken his words and painted its own pictures. In those pictures nothing was quite as big, or as hot, or as foreign. Or as badly maintained.

The people were not what she had been expecting, either. The fine fleece that had taken much of the journey to spin would stay bundled up in the luggage. She did not want the humiliation of presenting it as a gift and having to watch the stepmother find something polite to say about it.

While they were traveling she had tried to understand exactly how the Medicus's family had managed to get itself into such debt, but his attempts to explain how loans worked had only caused more confusion.

"Imagine," he had said, "that you borrow a cow for a year. You drink the milk every day. When the time comes to give the cow back, you give back the cow and the calf it's produced as thanks for having had the use of it."

She had said, "What if there is no calf? What if the cow dies?"

"That's the advantage of money," he said, looking as though he thought he was clever. "It doesn't deteriorate."

"Then what is the problem?"

He had scratched one ear as he did when he was thinking, and admitted that borrowing money could not really be explained in terms of cows. "Basically, you have to make the money make more money," he said. "Instead, Arria and my father chose to spend the money on a temple to Diana and on home improvements."

"So it is as if she slaughtered the cow before it calved, ate the meat and boiled the hooves down for glue, and now she has no meat or a calf to give back."

He had pondered that for a moment before agreeing that it was near enough.

Now that she had seen the house, she understood at last what "home improvements" were. Mosaics on the floor. A hall for welcoming guests that was painted with pictures of pale women with skimpy clothes and vacant faces and muscular men leading bulls to be sacrificed. Cupids dancing around the dining room. Then there was the carved head of the

Medicus's father set on top of a lump of marble, and lots of silly little polished tables with spindly legs. What could you do with things like that? You could not milk them or eat them. They would not keep you warm in winter. She could not understand how anyone had the energy to bother, or indeed why.

The water was cool on her throat. She dipped her fingers into the cup and wiped them across her forehead. Then, since nothing seemed to be moving out here except a few bees, she tipped the rest over her head, unpeeled the tunic that was stuck to her damp back, and stretched out along the length of the bench. She put her fingers in her ears and closed her eyes. She wished she could close her nose to the smell as easily. The scent of the flowers could not disguise the fact that something seemed to have gone wrong with the drains. Just as the children's excitement at her arrival could not make up for the shock of realizing that nobody here knew who she was. In Britannia, she had thought that she was an important part of the Medicus's life. Now it was plain that even though she had been in the room with him when he wrote many of his letters home, not one of them had mentioned her.

Letting one hand trail down, she ran a finger over the parched lichen that had formed on the stone leg of the bench. She found herself picturing the brittle thorns she had seen by the roadside, offering nothing but crops of white snails so maddened by the sun that they climbed up nearer to it to bake themselves under the brilliant sky. She pushed the picture away. It was making her feel hotter. Instead she tried to imagine herself paddling in the willow-fringed shallows of the river at home. It did not help.

Arria's insistence that she be led away to be fed and watered had probably been kindly meant. The half sisters had taken the trouble to show her around the umpteen rooms of the house, dutifully pointing out decoration and glass windows, and she had done her best to think of a new way of admiring each one. She had wanted to ask about the farm: Are you worried that the soil is baked so dry? When does it rain? How many cows do you have? What else can you grow apart from grapes and olives? But the girls did not seem interested in the farm. When they were not showing off the house they seemed to do nothing but talk about clothes and boys and get in the way of the staff.

Tilla was reflecting that at least the Medicus had found time to warn her about them, if not the other way around, when she felt a painful jab in her ribs and opened her eyes to see those same half sisters standing over her.

"She's awake!" exclaimed Marcia, who had no right to be surprised since she was the one who had just poked her.

Tilla blinked as her eyes adjusted again to the glare filtering through the leaves.

"Good news," announced Marcia. "Mother says you can chaperone us into town tomorrow."

"It's not our turn for the tutor tomorrow," said Flora, the younger of the two. Then, as if Tilla might not know what a tutor was, she added, "In our family you have to learn poetry, even if you're a girl. And music."

"It's a privilege," put in her older sister. "But we won't have to put up with it much longer, hopefully. Anyway, after we've bathed and had dinner you can spend tonight unpacking, or whatever it is you do for our brother. Then if you get him to give you some money we can all go shopping."

Tilla sat up, rubbing her eyes. "Shopping?" she repeated, wondering why anyone would want to tramp around buying things in this heat. Surely the family had enough servants to fetch whatever they needed?

The girls looked at each other. Marcia said, "What did I tell you? She doesn't understand."

"Don't you have shops in Britannia?" asked Flora.

Marcia said, "They probably don't have money either. Come on, Tilla. We'll show you what a bathhouse is before the others get in there and mess it up."

10

RUSO DROPPED THE lid of the trunk and sat on it as if he could keep the family's troubles trapped inside. He said, "I might have guessed the Gabinii were involved in this somewhere."

Gabinius Fuscus and his cousin had been friends of their father: the sort of friends who insisted on lending him large sums of money. Their offers were so cordial that Publius Petreius had failed to extract any details about when they would want the cash back, or how much interest they were expecting. Since his death, their unpredictable demands for repayment had been causing the Petreius brothers major headaches. While the brothers had struggled to remain solvent, Fuscus had risen to become a senior magistrate on the local city council and his even wealthier cousin was now a senator down in Rome.

"Is it just one of them, or both?" asked Ruso.

"Neither," said Lucius, propping his elbows on the worn surface of the desk and cradling his head in his hands. "Well, both. Indirectly."

Ruso waited, wondering if Lucius's inability to define the problem might be part of the reason he had failed to solve it.

"At least the senator won't be bothering us," said Lucius. "Not in person. He's too busy down in Rome, trying to find ways of undermining Hadrian."

"Good."

Lucius looked up. "No it isn't. In the meantime he's let a shark called Severus loose to manage his estate."

"Who's he?"

"Some distant relation from Rome, apparently. Everybody reckons they've sent him and his sister up here to get rid of them."

"And this Severus is the one who's trying to get the seizure order?"

"Severus," said Lucius, snatching up a stylus and emphasizing each word with a stab of the point into the desk, "is a Devious, Vindictive, Lying Bastard."

"Ah."

"That money was all there, whatever he says. I put it in front of him myself."

Ruso decided not to interrupt. If he listened long enough, Lucius would start to make sense.

"I know what you're thinking," said Lucius. "You're thinking, Why didn't you wait while he counted it?"

"You know what the Gabinii are like."

Lucius tossed the stylus aside. "When your wife's in floods of tears and your son's howling in pain, Gaius, it's hard to care what the Gabinii are like."

Lucius had been sitting where he was sitting now, counting the money for the latest installment of the loan repayment, when there was a commotion in the entrance hall. News had arrived that Cass's brother was drowned. While everyone was absorbing this shock Little Lucius, aged four, wandered into the yard, climbed up a ladder, and fell off the roof of the stables.

"His arm was bent the wrong way at the elbow. The doctor thought he might have to amputate."

"Nasty," agreed Ruso. "Nobody would blame you if you miscounted."

"I didn't!" snapped Lucius. "Severus took advantage. We rushed into town to find a doctor and I just stopped off at the estate to dump the cash on his desk. The evil bastard must have been able to hear the child crying, but he left me standing there while he chatted to his steward. When I told him I was in a hurry, he took the money and said, 'Don't let me hold you up; I'll send the receipt over later.'"

"Ah," said Ruso.

"And he smiled when he said it."

"Ah."

"Only instead of a receipt we got a demand saying it was two hundred short, and when I didn't fall for that, he said he'd take us to court."

"I see."

"I thought the senator might want to know he had a crook running his estate, so I went and told Fuscus what was going on. Fuscus told me to go home and not to worry about it, so I didn't." Lucius cleared his throat. "Only he didn't do a thing. It should never have come to a court hearing, Gaius. Severus was lying. I thought if I called his bluff he'd back down."

"Ah."

"Don't keep saying *Ah* in that tone of voice. You weren't here. And anyway, you'd think local magistrates would back a decent farmer against some fly-by-night from Rome, wouldn't you? Especially since half of them used to spend the evenings lolling around our dining tables pretending to be Father's friends."

Ruso was less surprised than his brother seemed to be. Their father had probably borrowed money from most of the local dignitaries at one time or another. Still, no matter how annoyed they might have been, he could not understand how a small squabble had led to bankruptcy proceedings. There was something else that Lucius was holding back. "Just tell me the rest and get it over with, brother. I've had a long day and my foot's aching."

The pitch of Lucius's voice rose, as it always did when he was lying. "Tell you what?"

"Whatever it is that turned a row over the cost of a decent amphora of wine into an attempt to ruin us."

"It's not my fault, Gaius!"

Ruso shifted sideways and stretched his leg out along the trunk. "I didn't say it was."

"Now you're thinking, Why the hell didn't he just pay up immediately when we lost the court case?"

"Why didn't you?"

"Because we didn't owe him the money! I'm not rushing around paying people twice just because they lie to us: What do you think I am?"

"Ah."

"Stop saying 'Ah!' "

"What do you want me to say, Lucius? Never mind? Well done?"

"How about thank you? How about, Thank you, Lucius, for running the farm and looking after the family while I was off playing soldiers and picking up women?"

Ruso leaned back against the wall. Somewhere beyond the study door, he could hear the sound of children laughing.

"If you'd sorted out this dowry business when you were asked," persisted Lucius, "both the girls would be betrothed by now and we wouldn't have had half this trouble."

Ruso, wondering why they were now talking about dowries, said, "I was waiting till we had some money."

"By the time that happens, nobody will want them," retorted Lucius. "If they haven't already died of old age and frustration, as Marcia points out to me several times a day. And I don't suppose you've brought home any spoils of war apart from the girl?"

"There might have been time to get some if I hadn't come rushing home to help you." Ruso stopped. Arguing with his brother would only waste more time. "Sorry," he said. "Finish telling me what's going on."

"You keep looking at me as if it's all my fault."

"I'm looking at you in the hope that you'll get on with it."

Lucius scrutinized him for a moment, then grunted what might have been assent. "The magistrates gave us thirty days to pay," he said. "I was going to scrape together the cash and pay at the last possible moment, on principle."

"I would have done the same."

Lucius seemed surprised by this unexpected support. He said, "I was about to go over there with the money when he turned up here with a greasy grin on his face and said if we couldn't pay, he was prepared to come to an arrangement."

"What did he want?"

"Access to Flora."

Ruso stared at him. "Flora? She's thirteen!"

"Fourteen, brother. Keep up. He said at that age in Rome she'd be married. I told him he wasn't in Rome now, and to get out before I set the dog on him."

"Right," said Ruso. Presumably Severus had no idea that the only way the Petreius' farm dog would injure anyone would be to lick them raw.

"After he'd gone I realized he hadn't taken the money with him." Lucius ran one hand over his thinning hair. "I know, I know. I should have chased after him and made him take it. But frankly, I didn't want to go near him. I took it over there the next day, and that was when he said it was too late, he was calling in the whole fifteen thousand and applying to Rome for a seizure order."

"Because it was one day late?"

"One day."

"Surely he can't do that?"

"He can do whatever he likes. He's one of the Gabinii. Things have gotten worse since you've been away. These days half the town's scared of Fuscus and the other half's probably on his payroll."

"Even so, there must be a loan agreement—"

"Severus promised me an extension on the loan months ago, but he never put it in writing. Now he can claim that we're behind with the payments."

Ruso shook his head. "This is unbelievable."

"He was enjoying it," said Lucius. "I could see it in his face."

"And Fuscus knows about this?"

"Fuscus knows everything."

"We need a lawyer."

Lucius shook his head. "I've tried. We need a miracle. None of Father's so-called friends can help even if they want to. Seizure orders go up to the praetor's office in Rome and it's way over their heads. The only thing the lawyer could think of was that since you're technically Father's heir, and you're—well, you were—sort of away on public service, that might hold everything up."

It was not difficult to guess now who had forged that letter. Severus had found a way to bring him back so that they could be sued.

Lucius said, "Are you sure you can't pretend you're not here?"

Ruso put his foot back on the floor and reached for his stick. "I'm going to clean up and have dinner," he said. "In the morning I'll go and pay a visit to Fuscus." He held up a hand to forestall his brother's objection. "I know you've already tried, but if he knows I'm home and I haven't called, he'll be insulted, and that'll make everything worse. Then I'm going to find this Severus and ask him what the hell he thinks he's playing at."

"It won't do any good."

"Have you got any better ideas?"

11

RUSO LEANED ON the balustrade and stood taking in the view from the front porch. The lanky shadows of the pergolas had swung away from the walkways they were built to cover and were now stalking the flowerbeds. He sniffed. The drains needed to be flushed out. Lucius had been letting things go. A bird fluttered out from the ivy covering the wall that Arria had insisted on having raised to separate garden from working farmyard, and swooped to stab at an insect in the dry fountain. Even from this distance, the crack in the side of the pool was obvious, as were the failed attempts to patch it. It was an uncomfortable reminder of the emptiness of the family coffers.

Pretend you don't know.

That was what he had been doing in Britannia. Lucius was right. He had been finding ways to distract himself from his responsibilities back at home.

A waft of smoke was rising from behind the bathhouse. In a moment he would go and sweat out the dirt of traveling. Then, newly clean, he would submerge himself in the cold plunge and hope for inspiration about how to tackle the Gabinii's plans to extend their empire across his own small farm.

His musing was interrupted by a roar of, "Sit down!" from inside the house.

"From now on, you'll all sit still and eat with your mouths shut!" bellowed Lucius, with more fury than logic. "The next one to speak will be whipped!"

There was a brief pause, followed by an exasperated, "You know what I mean!" Then louder, as if someone had opened a door, "Because I've had enough! If you won't discipline them, I will."

Ruso sighed and told himself it was no use feeling nostalgic for the army. He supposed he should go and find out what his sisters had done with Tilla, and whether he needed to rescue her from it.

He was reaching for his stick when he detected a waft of perfume and heard the ominous words, "Gaius, dear! We must have a little chat!"

"Little chats" with Arria usually consisted of her telling him what she wanted him to do, followed by him explaining why he was not going to do it. "Before we start," he said, leaning back against the balustrade as if it would support his arguments, "have you seen Tilla anywhere?"

"That girl?" said Arria in a tone that suggested Tilla was of no more importance than a piece of luggage. "Oh, your sisters are showing her around. I don't expect they have houses like this in Britannia, do they? It must be quite exciting for her."

Ruso motioned his stepmother toward the stone bench, where they sat side by side in an atmosphere of lavender and drains.

"I've been talking to Lucius," he said, "about the way things are."

"It's really too dreadful, isn't it?"

"It's very worrying," he agreed, relieved that she had at last begun to acknowledge the seriousness of their situation. "I'm going to see what I can do to sort it out tomorrow."

"Oh do, please," she said. "Diphilus says it's because the man who put the fountain in did something to the water. He offered to send somebody to look weeks ago. But no, your brother wanted to do it himself. I said, Lucius, dear, you're very good at making wine, but what do you know about plumbing? So he lifted some stones up and had a poke about with a stick, but it did no good and now he says he's too busy. How can I invite people into the garden? It gives such a terrible impression."

Evidently his perception of the family's main problem did not coincide with Arria's. "Who's Diphilus?"

"The builder, dear. You remember. The contractor who helped us with the Temple of Diana."

Fleeced us might have been a better expression, but Ruso was determined not to get into an argument. Not yet, anyway.

"He's nearly finished the mausoleum he's working on," she said. "If we let him know quickly, he can fit us in for a summer dining extension before he goes onto a big villa contract."

"We don't need a dining extension."

"Oh, not a big thing. An outdoor room. You know, with stone couches around three sides and a nice table or two in the middle. Diphilus says it wouldn't take more than a week to put up. Your father always said we should have one. Over there, so we can listen to the fountain. When Diphilus has found us someone to mend it, and seen to the drains. Wouldn't that be nice?"

"Why don't we ask the original plumber to come back and fix the fountain?"

"Because he's gone off to join the army, dear."

Ruso hoped the army had posted him somewhere deeply unpleasant.

"Diphilus is doing us a favor offering to look at it. I'm sure he'll be very reasonable."

"We'll have a better idea of what we can afford before long," said Ruso, determined not to be sucked into discussing details. "If anything." He knew from watching the way she had worked on his father that Arria would interpret any interest as agreement.

"We don't have to spend on cushions for the couches yet," she assured him, as if that would make all the difference. "The staff could bring the old ones out from indoors just to tide us over. I'm sure nobody would mind."

A picture of a siege engine floated across Ruso's mind: a great tower lumbering relentlessly forward, its covering of animal hides impervious to all weapons hurled at it by the beleaguered defenders.

"Actually," he said before Arria could start again, "money is what I wanted to talk to you about. I haven't forgotten about the girls' dowries—"

"Oh, the girls can wait."

"But we can't make any decisions till—what did you say?"

"The girls can wait, dear. Young women are too impatient these days."

Ruso blinked. Arria had first started harassing him about the dowries over a year ago, and nothing Lucius said had hinted that she had changed her mind. "Well," he said, aware that his sisters would be furious, "I'm glad we're agreed."

"I've had a much better idea about how to get you boys out of trouble."

As usual, Arria was not put off by a wary silence. For some reason she was extolling the virtues of the amphora factory whose land adjoined the eastern edge of their own. "It's a marvelous business, you know," she said. "All the farms need them and nobody ever brings the empties back." When Ruso failed to enthuse she added, "Do they?"

"Not often," he said, careful not to show any interest until he knew where this was leading.

"Well, he's dead now, so it's all hers."

Ruso realized that something relevant must have drifted past him. "Who's dead?"

"Lollia Saturnina's husband, dear. Do try and listen. At least a year and a half ago. Now here you are, a handsome young officer, single, just home from the Legions. What could be better?"

There were many things that could be better, but Ruso could not think how to explain what they were.

"Don't scowl, Gaius, please. You would be such a nice-looking boy if you tried to look more cheerful. It would be quite a reasonable house with a little care and attention, and it's not far to move. I was thinking—"

"What about Tilla?"

"The barbarian?" Arria glanced around in alarm, as if Tilla were about to pounce on her from behind one of the legs of the pergola. "I know you didn't want to be lonely over there, dear, but really—is it fair to bring people like that back to a civilized place?" Leaning closer, she added in a stage whisper, "And especially not home with you, Gaius! What were you thinking?"

"I was thinking you'd make her welcome."

The painted eyes widened in alarm. "Gaius, you haven't done something very silly, have you?"

"Frequently."

"Tell me you haven't married her."

"She wouldn't have me," he said. "She says I'm too foreign."

"Foreign? You? Well, thank goodness for that. Now then . . . I'm sure we can find a nice family to take her on if she doesn't want to go home."

"She doesn't need a nice family, Arria. She's got me."

Arria let out a long sigh that seemed to express weariness not only with her stepson's present stance, but with past years of argument, obstinacy, and mutual incomprehension. "Gaius, dear, please try and be sensible."

She turned away and wiped at an invisible tear with her middle finger. "If only your poor father were here to talk to you!"

Ruso folded his arms, "Even father couldn't imagine that the widow next door is going to welcome the advances of a bankrupt."

"But you're a war hero, dear!"

"Of course I'm not! You haven't gone around saying that to people, have you?"

"Please try, Gaius. It's for the sake of the family. Poor Lucius has gotten us all into a dreadful mess and I can't think what else we can do, can you? I suppose you could try talking to Claudia, but she doesn't have much influence over him, anyway."

Ruso was not sure how or why his former wife had appeared in the conversation. Suspecting he was about to be scolded yet again for not listening, he asked, "Over who?"

"That Severus, dear."

When his face remained blank she said, "But surely Lucius told you?"

"Told me what?"

"Claudia is married to Severus now."

Ruso's astonishment was such that all he could say was, "Oh." He scratched his ear with his forefinger and pondered this unexpected complication. It was, of course, completely irrelevant. It was also . . . he was not sure what it was. His own former wife was married to an unscrupulous business agent who was related to the Gabinii. Surely even Claudia had more sense than that? Surely she had more taste?

Surprise was followed by a brief moment of smugness. He had demonstrated—according to Claudia—many faults and failings during their marriage, but wresting land from innocent families and doing deals for the fourteen-year-old sisters of men who owed him money were not among them.

"Claudia was never the right girl for you, anyway," continued Arria. "I always said so. But Lollia is a nice woman. She could run her business—everyone says she's far better at it than he was—and you could still carry on with your doctoring. She has some very good connections, you know. People who could pay you properly for a change."

Ruso recalled Valens once suggesting back in Britannia that what he needed was a rich widow. The thought was no less appalling now than it had been two years ago.

"I've told her all about you," continued Arria.

"I see. And have you told her I'm looking for a wife?"

She winced. "Oh dear. I suppose this is what happens when you mix with soldiers all the time. You will have to learn to be more subtle, dear. Now, I've invited her for dinner tomorrow night, but when you meet her you mustn't say a word about what we've discussed. We don't want to frighten her off."

"I think it's more likely to be the other way around."

The paint on Arria's lips stretched across a smile. "You'll like her, Gaius. Trust me. I wouldn't suggest it if I thought you weren't suited. Now, before you disappear into the bathhouse, you must help me choose a menu."

You must help me choose a menu. Claudia had said that once, early in their marriage. He thought he had done rather well until she told him she would do it on her own the next time.

"I really don't think this is the time to be holding dinner parties."

Arria sighed. "Gaius, you're not going to be awkward, are you?"

"I'm not being awkward, I'm being practical. And I'm never any good at this social chit-chat business, anyway."

"Never mind, dear. We'll blame that on the army. I'll invite Diphilus; he's good company. You can ask Lollia about her cough. And do try to look a little happier. She won't be interested if she thinks you're sulky. I'll have your clothes brushed and pressed, and promise me you'll have a shave and a haircut in the morning. You're not in Britannia now, you know."

"I'm beginning to wish I was," said Ruso, remembering with fondness the little room at the top of the steps, with the pot of wildflowers on the windowsill and the mystery products of Tilla's cooking on the table.

Arria was promising, ". . . chicken in dill sauce, of course, your favorite . . ."

Was it? Perhaps it had been, once. Doubtless she would be able to tell him exactly where and when he had expressed this rare burst of enthusiasm.

"—and I'll ask her to have her cook send over the recipe."

"Good," said Ruso, having no idea what else Arria had just proposed, and no interest in finding out.

"You like them too? Lovely! You see, already you both have something in common."

"Do we?"

"Oh, Gaius! Are you listening to anything I'm saying? Roast testicles!"

"Roast testicles?"

"With pepper and pine nuts."

"Ah," said Ruso.

12

RUSO LAY BACK, feeling a faint breeze from the window cool his skin. This was the first night for weeks that he had gone to bed alone. Tilla had been sleeping when he checked her room an hour ago, but his resolve to let her rest was weakening.

He had planned to introduce her properly this evening when the family gathered for dinner, only to be informed as the salad was served and the girls turned up without her, that she had "gone to play with the children."

He had found her sitting on the floor of the children's room having her hair combed by the nieces. A cheerfully naked toddler was sprawled across her lap, ignoring Galla's attempts to interest him in the pot.

Tilla took the pot from Galla and set it between her feet. Then she grasped the toddler under both arms, lifted him up, and set him on it, facing toward her. "There!" She leaned forward and said to the toddler, "We will both sit here and see who can do it first."

The girls giggled.

"Ready?" Tilla asked Little Gaius. She screwed up her eyes, bared her teeth, clenched her fists, and made a straining noise that sounded like, "Nnnnnnnn!"

Little Gaius shrieked and bounced with delight on the pot while the girls cried, "She's making a poo noise! Uncle Gaius, listen! Listen, Galla!"

Ruso was no longer sure she deserved an invitation to dinner, but he was not going to be ignored in favor of his small namesake. "Dinnertime," he said, realizing that she was still clad in her hot British wool. "Didn't the girls lend you something cooler to wear?"

Unable to turn her head without having her hair pulled, Tilla said, "Your stepmother has something yellow for me tomorrow."

He raised his voice. "That'll have to do, girls. She's mine now." To Tilla he said, "Come and get something to eat."

She stilled the efforts of the nieces by grasping the comb. "I have just had a big bowl of broth and half a loaf at the kitchen table. Then they gave me stewed apple and wine with water. What must I eat now?"

"Dinner. Whatever the cook was making while you were in there. Didn't anybody tell you?"

The eyes that were not really blue widened in alarm. "Nobody said I must eat again! It is too hot!"

"Just come in and have a little. I want to introduce you to the family."

"I do not think they want to meet me again."

"Of course they do."

"No they don't, Uncle Gaius!" put in one of the nieces helpfully. "Grandmother Arria said—"

"Never mind what Arria said," interrupted Ruso, knowing full well who must have instructed the cook to cram Tilla with food. "You're welcome to join the family for dinner."

"I will come if you want, but I am tired, and hot, and full up." There was a rare note of anxiety in her voice.

To his shame, he felt relieved. As far as he knew, Tilla had never attended a proper dinner before. In Britannia she was officially his housekeeper. It had never occurred to him to invite her on the rare occasions when he dined with other officers. He had never discussed it with her, but he was certain she would not have wanted to go. That was just as well, because he would no more have been expected to bring her than he would be expected to bring the family dog.

When he returned to the dining room he admitted none of this to Arria, to whom he explained that there had been a misunderstanding, that Tilla was weary from the journey but that in future she would be eating with the family.

He was glad she was not there to see the expression on Arria's face.

By the time dinner was over, Tilla had already gone to bed.

Something creaked out in the corridor. Footsteps passed by. Somewhere at the far end, a door clamped shut.

Ruso wondered whether to go and fetch her. He really should let her sleep. He really should sleep himself, instead of lying here going over the events of the day and wondering what he could do tomorrow to stop mess sliding into disaster.

He rolled over and scowled at the old cupboard in the corner. It reminded him of the childhood nights when Lucius had refused to let him snuff out the lamp until he had checked that those cupboard doors were locked. It was vital that they were locked after dark, because of the monsters.

Until now he had never thought to wonder how the monsters had installed themselves in the cupboard—or in Lucius's mind—in the first place. They even had names: Gobbus was a male monster with matted hair, green teeth, and breath that smelled of rotten eggs. Mogta was his sister, or perhaps his wife—their precise relationship, being of no interest to seven- and nine-year-olds, was never defined. What was clear was that Mogta liked to slide her sharp fingernails into the soft flesh of small boys in the night, and then skin them alive while they cried for their mothers.

As he watched the shadow of the cupboard breathing against the pale wall with the drifting of the lamp flame, it occurred to Ruso that the monsters must have appeared at around about the time a winter fever had taken away their own mother. Lucius had lain in this room with the same fever for what seemed like weeks, although it had probably only been a few days. The house had been full of weeping and strangers. Adults whom Ruso did not recognize, but who knew his name, told him how sorry they were and how brave he was being.

Nobody except Ruso had time to listen to a small boy's tales of what he had seen coming out of the cupboard in the fevered night. To Ruso's shame, he had found it funny—until Lucius kept him awake, crying and cuddling up to him for comfort. Then he veered between sympathy—now their mother was gone it was his job to protect his little brother—and exasperation. In fact, he had felt then much as he felt now. Except that this time the monsters were real.

Gobbus no longer lived in the cupboard, but on the senator's estate down the road, and there was no locking him away now. Ruso wondered if even Lucius appreciated just how serious this seizure business was.

If the praetor in Rome ruled in favor of Severus, the household would be turned off the land they had worked for decades. The men who had been cutting the grapes this afternoon would be put up for auction. Galla, the new cook, the ancient bath boy who had been stoking the fire since Ruso was a child . . . all would be sold off to the highest bidder along with Arria's treasured tables and couches and cushions.

As for the family—his sisters would have to find husbands where they could: old goats perhaps, but unlikely to be rich ones. Lucius would have to look for work as a farm manager, one step up from slavery.

After the sale, the profits would be divided between the creditors. Given the size of the debts, it was obvious that no one would get as much as he was owed—and that was when the real trouble would begin. Lucius might be able to wriggle out of it, because technically it was Ruso who was their father's heir. It was Ruso who would fail to pay off the balance of the debts. It was Ruso who would be declared *infamis*: the disgraced man with no rights, no legal standing, no money, no good name . . .

Despite the warmth of the room, Ruso felt a sudden shiver run down his back. No good name . . . how could a man who was *infamis* serve as an officer in the army?

He lay back, eyes wide, staring at the shadowed ceiling as if he had never seen it before. His contract with the Twentieth ran out in January. The Legate would never bring shame upon the Legion by reappointing a dishonored man. If Ruso could not persuade this Severus to drop the case, he might never get another posting back to Britannia. If Tilla wanted to go home, he would not be able to take her. Severus had not only enticed him home: He had trapped him here.

He tensed, sensing movement outside the door. The latch clicked and someone entered the room.

"Your stepmother does not like me," announced Tilla.

One of his hands made contact with hers in the dark. He heard a shuffle of fabric. When she slid into the bed and pressed her back against his chest, she was naked.

"I thought you were asleep," he murmured, sliding one hand around her waist.

"Your stepmother is spying on me," she said. "There is a slave sleeping outside my door."

He shifted one leg so it lay between hers and said, "Perhaps in case you need anything."

"I do not think so."

"No," he agreed.

She wriggled. "You are too hot."

"You're lovely and cool."

"You did not tell them about me."

"I should have," he said. "I'm sorry."

She rolled over to face him. "Are you ashamed of me?"

"No."

"I have wrong clothes and funny hair."

"So do I."

She said, "Your sisters are taking me shopping tomorrow. They said I must ask you for money."

"Your hair can't be that funny, then. They're very particular."

She seemed to think about that for a moment, then she said, "What did your brother say about the letter?"

He had expected her to be angry when she found out about the forgery. Instead she said, "I think the gods have made this wicked man write to you. Now you are here, you can help your brother to fight him."

If only it were that simple. "He's from a powerful family," he explained. "And he can use the law to back him up."

"I will help you."

He was not going to tell her that there was nothing she could do to help and that bringing her here had been a huge mistake. She did not need to know that if the wicked man won, they would not be able to return to Britannia together. Instead he bent forward to kiss her, feeling her hair brushing against his face in the darkness, and tried to think of something else to talk about.

Only as he was halfway through "Arria thinks I should save the family by marrying the rich widow next door" did he realize that Tilla might not find it funny. When she said nothing he added, "But I said, *What about Tilla?*"

The silence from the other side of the bed told him that he was digging himself deeper into a hole.

Outside, he heard the faint cry of a child and more footsteps. He had a sudden memory of Cass's brother scrambling down that corridor on all fours with two of the nephews on his back squealing, "Faster, faster!"

"Tilla," he said, clutching at a new subject, "while we were traveling, do you remember anybody saying anything about a ship called the *Pride of the South*?"

She did not, nor did she seem interested until he explained about Cass's brother. "She is the one who sent you the gloves and the socks and the olives?"

"Yes." Justinus's ship had vanished back at the beginning of the summer. Cass was right: It was very odd that Probus had turned up here just a couple of weeks ago to ask if he was still alive. Perhaps Probus had heard some kind of rumor about his lost ship and was trying simultaneously to follow it up and keep it quiet. It was typical of the man that he had not considered the effect of his inquiries on the dead man's sister. He said, "Probably nobody will ever know what happened to him."

"It is a sad way to lose a brother, far from home."

"I'd like to get over to Arelate and ask around, but I need to get into Nemausus first thing tomorrow so I can try and stave off this bloody court case." He sighed. "Then I need to find some work. Even if this Severus is prepared to settle, we'll have next to no cash left for the rest of the bills. The whole thing is a mess."

"You are tired," she said, slipping her hand into his. "Everything will seem better in the morning."

"Perhaps." Perhaps not.

She moved his hand up and placed it on her breast. "I have told that slave she can sleep in my bed," she said, wriggling closer to him. "That way, she will not tell your stepmother what I am doing."

"Good," murmured Ruso, bending forward to nuzzle her ear. "Neither will I."

13

ACCORDING TO ARRIA, the family carriage was being repaired. According to Marcia, it had been being repaired for the last six months, because Lucius was too mean to pay the wheelwright, and that was why Ruso was having to drive them and Tilla into town this morning in this awful embarrassing *thing*, and why they were so hot.

"You can't blame Lucius for the weather," he said, reining in the mules so that they were not trotting straight into the dust kicked up by the carriage that was currently speeding past the smoking kilns of Lollia Saturnina's amphora factory. "Why don't you both sit under parasols instead of wrapping up like dead Egyptians? I'm surprised you can breathe under all that."

Marcia gave an exaggerated sigh that said she thought her brother was extremely stupid, but she was not foolish enough to say so. "Because someone might see us, Gaius. Riding around on *this*." The cart juddered as she emphasized the final word with a thud of her sandal against the footboard.

Ruso remembered the faces of legionaries who had struggled miles across the wet British hills carrying wounded comrades: faces he might never see again if he could not find a way to get the farm out of Severus's clutches. He said, "You could always walk."

She snorted. "I might have known you'd take Lucius's side. And I don't suppose you've done anything about the dowry, have you?"

"Not yet," he agreed.

"But I need it!"

"Not this morning."

"When, then?"

"I'm going to talk to someone."

"What? Lucius said you would sort it out! Who else do you need to talk to? You're supposed to be my guardian!"

"And you're supposed to do what I tell you," he pointed out.

Marcia flung herself against the wooden backrest with a cry of "Ohh! What is the matter with this family? Nobody else has to put up with this!"

"No, they don't!" chipped in Flora from behind, where she was sitting with Tilla. "They don't, Gaius. Really. If you weren't off marching around with the army, you'd know."

"Over in Britannia," observed Ruso, "the men pay a bride price to marry the women. Maybe I'll ship you across there and sell you."

"How much did you pay for Tilla?"

"I'm not married to Tilla," said Ruso, who had no intention of admitting that he had bought her as a slave in the back streets of Deva.

"There are girls my age who have been married for years," continued Marcia.

Ruso said, "Not from ordinary families like ours."

"At this rate I shall be as shriveled as a prune by the time you get around to it. And there'll be nobody nice left to marry."

They were approaching the vineyards that fringed the entrance to the estate of the absent senator. Marcia's hand on his arm was a welcome distraction from the tricky meeting he would face later with the senator's devious lying bastard of an agent.

"Gaius, you wouldn't make me marry somebody repulsive, would you?"

There was genuine anxiety in the hazel eyes, which were the only part of her face that was visible and which seemed to be blacker around the edges than was natural. "No," he promised, wondering if he was about to shut off a useful source of income. "I wouldn't make you."

"Good!" The note of triumph in her voice alerted him to the fact that he had just helped her score some sort of point.

"Of course," he said, "I might ask you to volunteer."

"Oh!" With this final sigh of exasperation Marcia leaned back, folded her arms, and lapsed into a sulk.

Marcia and Flora disembarked at the roadside, rearranging their stoles around their elaborately pinned curls and shaking off the dust of the road. He had offered to drive them right up to the Augustus gate, whose broad stone arches were now visible in the town walls, but they had refused. Evidently the girls would rather traipse the last few hundred paces along the tomb-lined road in stifling heat than suffer the shame of being seen dismounting from a farm cart outside the gates.

Ruso considered asking them who was likely to care what vehicle they arrived in. Then he remembered Claudia demanding to know why he always had to argue with people like some bearded old Greek philosopher: a complaint that was especially memorable since it had been preceded by a loud howl and the use of a makeup pot as a missile.

So instead he limped quietly aside as Tilla refused his help to climb down from the back of the cart, then murmured, "Sorry about my family."

She plucked at the fabric of the pale yellow tunic Arria had insisted on lending her and which did not suit her. "Your stepmother says I must wear this while I look after your sisters. I am going with them to see all the things my people are not foolish enough to want." Reaching up to adjust the brim of the battered straw hat, she added, "Perhaps I shall bring some of these things back with me."

"Please don't," he urged, and raised his voice for the others to hear. "I've got business to see to. I'll have one of the men meet you at the seventh hour outside the Augustus gate."

"Come on, Tilla," urged Marcia, pausing to push one of Flora's hairpins back into place and then flinging the green linen stole over her shoulder. "Leave our boring brother to get on with his business. We're going shopping!"

Ruso parked the cart under a tree and left it in the charge of a small boy who promised to keep the mules in the shade. As he headed toward the town on foot, he caught a glimpse of green stole vanishing under the pedestrian archway of the Augustus Gate. For the first time in his life, he wished he were going shopping.

14

THE BUILDINGS WERE grander than anything she had seen before, but the streets smelled just as powerfully as every other town of fish sauce and fresh bread, frying, warm dung, sweaty bodies, and brash perfume.

"Come on, Tilla, or whatever your name is," urged Marcia over the clatter of a passing handcart. "We've got something to show you."

The something was a temple, its stone pillars still new enough to glare white in the sun. Marcia pointed upward. "See those marks?"

Tilla shaded her eyes and squinted at the roof that projected out over the high base of the building. "What marks?"

"Those gold marks are called writing," explained Marcia. "I don't suppose you have much of that where you come from."

"We do not need it," said Tilla, who had heard enough inscriptions read aloud to know that they were usually full of lies and showing off. "My people have good memories."

"You're not just staying with any old family, you know," Marcia continued, undaunted. "That says, 'This Temple was built by Publius Petreius Largus'—that's our father. It was hideously expensive. So everyone can see how generous we are."

"This," murmured Flora in Tilla's left ear, "makes it all the more embarrassing that Gaius won't give us a dowry."

"What's that about dowries?"

"Shh!" hissed Flora, glancing around. "We don't want everyone to know."

"As if they don't already," retorted Marcia. "And Gaius isn't even embarrassed about it, is he?"

Tilla said, "Your brother is a good man who is doing his best."

Marcia sniffed. "Is that what he told you? I bet he's bought himself a nice house in Britannia."

Tilla opened her mouth to say, "No, just a rented room," then thought better of it. Discussion of where the Medicus lived might lead to questions about herself, and she was not going to tell them that back at home she was his housekeeper.

"Huh!" said Marcia, taking her silence for assent. "I knew it!" She grabbed Flora by the arm. "Come on. I want to see if those earrings are still there."

"Mother said we had to give her the tour."

"Oh, never mind about that." Marcia turned to Tilla. "You don't want to see a whole lot of boring old buildings, do you?"

"No," said Tilla, who did not want to see a whole lot of boring old shops, either.

"See?" demanded Marcia of her sister. "She won't know the difference, anyway. They live in mud huts over there, you know. With straw on the roof."

Tilla wondered if the girl's rudeness had something to do with the heat inside her unnecessary layers of clothing. "Are we going to look for earrings?"

"Oh, yes!" Marcia's smile was surprisingly childlike. "The most beautiful earrings you've ever seen!"

They had hardly gone ten paces when there was a yell from farther down the street. An announcer had stationed himself at a crossroads and was shouting something about games being given to the people by the generous benefactor the magistrate Gabinius Fuscus. After more nonsense about how wonderful this Fuscus was, the man unrolled a scroll and read out a list of attractions that could be seen at the amphitheater in five days' time.

Several passersby paused to listen: Most carried on about their business while the man announced the promised horrors as if he were personally proud of them.

"And you think you are better than me!" Tilla murmured, ashamed that she did not dare to say it loud enough to get herself into trouble. She wanted to do as she had always done back in Deva: to cover her ears and walk away. She did not want to hear what this Fuscus—one of the Medicus's people—was planning to inflict on men and animals in the name of entertainment. But what difference would it make? One foreigner's disgust would change nothing, and sympathy for the victims would not alter their fate.

It was Marcia who caused the commotion. It was Marcia who screamed, "No!" and flung herself at the announcer, trying to grab the scroll and shouting, "It's not true! Show me where it says that! You're making it up!"

The announcer backed away and made feeble attempts to beat her off with the scroll, clearly worried about doing too much damage to a well-dressed young lady. Finally Flora and Tilla hauled her back, Tilla seizing one end of the green stole and wrapping it across Marcia's face so she was left floundering in the middle of the street as the announcer retreated and Flora shouted, "Just leave her to us! She's mad!" to the surprised onlookers.

"What on earth is the matter with you?" hissed Flora as they hustled her sister around the corner and thrust her into the shade of a doorway.

Tilla released the stole and Marcia snatched it away from her face. "Sharp weapons!" she cried. "He said they were using sharp weapons!"

"Oh, of course they won't!" Flora reassured her. "It's fixed. Gladiator fights are always fixed. Everybody knows that."

"They are not fixed!" retorted Marcia. "The best fighters win. On merit."

"Then he'll be all right, won't he?"

"You don't understand!"

"Tertius will be all right," insisted Flora. "He'll make lots of money and buy himself out. Come and look at the earrings."

"This is all Gaius's fault! If he had arranged the dowries, none of this would be happening."

"You can't do anything about that," pointed out Flora while Tilla wondered what dowries had to do with gladiators, and indeed what Marcia had to do with this particular gladiator called Tertius.

"We might as well go and look at earrings now we're here," urged Flora.

Marcia's lips pursed as if she was considering what to do. Finally she said, "All right. But I shan't enjoy it now."

15

LUCIUS HAD POINTED out last night that the bath boy was willing to cut hair, but the sight of Lucius's hair was not encouraging. They were in so much debt now that a couple of coins for a professional job would make little difference. No doubt Arria would see it as an investment.

There was no mirror at the barber's, but Ruso's chin was smooth and his head refreshingly cool as he made his way through the narrow streets. There were competing election slogans among the usual announcements and nonsense daubed on the walls of the houses, including one unlikely claim that "all the town prostitutes say vote for Gabinius Fuscus!" Underneath in larger letters was the assertion that all the followers of Christos were in support of one of his rivals. The prostitutes would have no vote, and unless the followers of Christos had enjoyed a sudden surge of popularity while he was away, their endorsement was unlikely to be welcome. Presumably each candidate was attempting to smear the other with these bizarre claims of support. Ruso was not sorry his father had never stood for election.

When he reached the house of the man supposedly favored by all the town prostitutes, Ruso found that Fuscus had discovered a new way of showing off. He had set up benches outside his house for his many clients to gather in full view of the street as they assembled to greet him each morning. Already it was standing room only, and the official exhortations to *Vote for Gabinius Fuscus!* painted in red lettering were half obscured by the hangers-on who were now blocking the pavement. If the importance of a man could be judged by the number of people who turned up at his house every morning to pay their respects—or perhaps their debts—then Fuscus was a very important man indeed.

He was certainly more important now than the previous owner of the house, a political rival who had decided to challenge Fuscus over some alleged electoral corruption. Halfway through the case, the man had been mysteriously murdered by a robber in a back alley. Within months, Fuscus had bought the house at a knock-down price from his widow. No wonder so many people took the view that it was better to be in the Gabinii camp than outside it.

Ruso approached the slave who was standing in the doorway with his arms folded and a large wooden club dangling at his side. The mention of his name left the slave's face as blank as before.

"It's about an urgent legal case," explained Ruso, not wanting to explain in front of an audience.

The slave's expression said that it was not urgent to him, and he was the one with the club.

Ruso moved closer and added in a tone that could only just be overheard, "Involving the household of the senator," he said, "and bankruptcy." He sensed movement on either side of him, as if the occupants of the benches had sat up to listen.

If they had hoped to hear something scandalous about the senator, they were disappointed. The doorman stepped smartly aside, said, "Go through, sir," and Ruso found himself promoted to a better class of waiting area. The atrium pool glistened in the sunlight, and the clients loitering in the shade of the roof that overhung on all four sides were obviously richer than those left to bake out in the street. Ruso wondered if Arria had been right: He would have made more of an impression in a toga. On the other hand a toga would look ridiculous with army boots, and the lone attempt to manage a swathe of heavy wool and a walking stick together might have ended in disaster. The few togas in evidence were so carefully arranged that it was obvious their wearers had brought slaves with them to repair any disruption caused by movement.

After the first hour Ruso concluded that they would have done well to bring a picnic too. And a few comfortable chairs. And maybe a dose of something to keep themselves calm while men who had arrived later were admitted first. As the courtyard gradually emptied around him, the occasional reassurances of the steward that "the master knows you're here, sir," only served to reinforce Ruso's suspicion that Fuscus was deliberately keeping him waiting.

When the summons finally came, Fuscus's smile was as wide as his arms, and as enticing as a crocodile's.

"Ruso! The image of your father!"

Ruso, noting with relief that the great man was not wearing a toga either, found himself squashed against a vast belly while its owner slapped him on the back as if he was a long-lost friend.

"Publius would be proud," said Fuscus, releasing the pressure and holding him at arm's length. "Look at you! Now I've got rid of the others, we can talk." He snapped his fingers and a clerk approached. "Put Petreius Ruso on the list for veterans' seats." The clerk bowed and retreated backward into his corner. Fuscus returned his attention to Ruso. "I'm giving a day of games. You'll enjoy it. My personal choice of gladiators and the best animal display the town's ever seen." Fuscus waved one hand toward another slave. "Boy! A stool for our wounded hero. Sit down and rest the leg, Ruso."

"I'm not really a—"

"So. What are you doing these days?"

"Extended leave," said Ruso, settling himself on the proffered stool and wondering how soon he could introduce the bankruptcy case that Fuscus seemed to have forgotten about. "I'm hoping to take on a few patients while I'm home."

"Of course, dear boy. Of course. Be glad to recommend you. People are always looking for doctors. Most of them to cure what the last one did, eh?"

Ruso forced a polite smile and said, "Fuscus, my brother tells me—"

"While you're home, I want you to talk to my eldest. Boys these days! No idea. Soft as butter." Fuscus reached for a grape and popped it into his mouth before offering the bowl to Ruso. "I hire the best trainers," he said, pausing to spit out the pips, "and I'm putting on the games, but . . . boys today would rather lie around playing dice and snickering over smutty poetry. They've seen too many cheap displays in the arena. Blunt weapons. No real danger. What are they going to learn from that? What we need is a few more men like you. Battle-hardened." He waved another grape toward Ruso's leg. "Hurts, does it?"

"Not now," said Ruso, catching himself about to call Fuscus "my lord," then remembering he was just an old and more successful friend of his father. "And I'm not really a hero. There are plenty of men who—"

Fuscus held out a hand to silence him. "Forget the modesty. It's no good being self-effacing these days. Boy? Fan!"

A third slave stepped forward from the shadows and began to wave a feathered fan above the great man's head. Ruso hoped the remaining figure in the background, a hefty man wearing a scowl and a large knife, would not be the next to be called into action.

"Left a bit," commanded Fuscus, and as the slave obediently moved the fan into position he leaned across the desk as if he were about to share a confidence with Ruso. "I'm told our lads took a mauling from the natives over there."

"There were losses," agreed Ruso, carefully vague. "But order's pretty much restored now. Fuscus, Lucius says—"

"Restored, thanks to men like you." Fuscus gestured toward the doors. "People out there," he said, "no idea what they owe to the army."

"True," said Ruso, wondering how much idea Fuscus had himself. Men whom Ruso admired had been cut down and died in agony. Hundreds of others had survived only to face an uncertain and painful future, mutilated in mind and body. None of them would make it here to receive the honor that they deserved and he didn't. "There were plenty of heroes," he said. "But I wasn't one of them. Medics don't usually fight in the front line."

"Nonsense. How many men did you save?"

"Not enough." Not anywhere near enough.

Fuscus scowled. "What did I just say about modesty?" He stopped. "Not married, are you?"

"Divorced," said Ruso, hastily sifting through his memory in the hope of confirming that Fuscus did not have a marriageable daughter.

"Probus's girl, wasn't it? She's done well for herself, you know. Married the agent of my cousin the senator."

"So I hear," said Ruso, suspecting that Fuscus enjoyed the sound of My Cousin The Senator. "Actually that's why I—"

"Never mind. The point is, you're single. Men will respect you and women will fight over you."

This was an alarming, if unlikely, prospect. Ruso cleared his throat. "You do know the agent of your cousin the senator is threatening me with a seizure order?"

Fuscus frowned. "Is that still going on? Your brother came to see me. I did my best for him, as an old friend of your father, but he didn't seem very grateful." He held out two pink palms. "My hands are tied, you see, Ruso. That's the burden of office." He shook his head sadly, as if contemplating the effect of the burden in his own reflection on the desk. "Leadership never wins a man popularity."

Privately Ruso doubted that Fuscus would have been popular whatever he did. At least in his current position he had influence. He could impress people by putting on games, buy them by lending them money they couldn't repay, and then employ men with large knives to demand it back.

"These are difficult times, Ruso," Fuscus was complaining. "Who'd have thought we'd live to see a good man like yourself in danger of going under? And your brother. How many children is it now?"

"Five."

"I hear those sisters of yours aren't married yet."

"No."

Fuscus shook his head. "A great shame." He looked up as if a good idea had only just struck him. "Of course, your being part of the family team might impress Severus. He's a relative of mine, you know. Very distant. He's a good man, but he might have been a little hasty. Doesn't know how we do things up here. He might take some time to think before he asks for the case to be sent up to the praetor."

"My being part of the family team?" repeated Ruso, wondering if that would add Fuscus to the list of his other inescapable relatives.

"He might be persuaded to drop it altogether. It was only ever his word against your brother's, wasn't it?"

"It was," agreed Ruso, not adding, *but that didn't make any difference before.*

"I want you with me at the games."

"As a medic?" tried Ruso, without much hope.

"I need the veterans' votes," Fuscus was saying. "They'll listen to you. Wear your armor so they can see who you are."

"I didn't bring it home." Ruso was well able to imagine what the local veterans would say if a legionary medic turned up at the games in full iron plate and helmet and tried to tell them who to vote for. "I've got an army belt."

"Will people know what it is?"

"The people who count will," Ruso promised, still not clear about what he had just agreed to and appalled to find that he was already talking like a political campaigner.

Fuscus summoned the clerk. "Forget the veterans' seats. I want the town's very own life-saving war hero sitting up with me on the balcony. Ruso, remember what I said. No pretending to be modest. Everyone sees through it these days. Did I mention that Severus is here for dinner this evening?"

"You really think you can get him to change his mind about the seizure order?" said Ruso, trying not to picture himself on the balcony of the amphitheater, hobnobbing with Fuscus's cronies.

The crocodile smile appeared again. "Dear boy, you've been away with the barbarians too long. What are friends for?"

Ruso suspected this was just the sort of equivocal answer Fuscus had given to Lucius. He said, "There is one other thing I wanted to ask you about."

The smile faded.

"On behalf of a friend."

Fuscus's expression lifted slightly at the prospect of making someone else beholden to him.

"A relative of mine was on a ship from Arelate that sank a couple of months back. The *Pride of the South*."

"Probus's man?"

"Justinus. His sister's trying to piece together what happened to him so she can arrange the memorial. If I wanted to find out, who would I talk to?"

Fuscus shrugged. "Who knows the ways of Neptune?"

"I realize it won't be easy."

"Then make up something to tell her, and don't waste any more time on it. We've got campaigning to do." He snapped his fingers and the clerk scurried forward. "Find out the names of all the local veterans with a vote, and draw up a list. Ruso, I want you back here tomorrow to pick it up, and then I want you to contact each one personally on my behalf."

The newest member of Fuscus's team should have said *yes*, but all he could manage was a strangled sound in his throat.

"One more thing, Ruso. Your little game at the gate? That's how false rumors start. You won't ever mention my cousin the senator and bankruptcy in the same sentence again. Understood?"

16

RUSO TURNED THE corner to find another election slogan—genuine, he supposed—that told him he was not the only one who owed Fuscus some sort of favor. Evidently the local silversmiths did too. He shivered, despite the heat of the day. After that meeting, he felt in need of a wash. And a drink.

There was a snack bar on the next corner. Hunched over a cup of watered wine, he ran over the conversation again. How was he going to explain to Lucius that in exchange for a vague promise of possible support, he had agreed to become one of Fuscus's yes-men? He had even managed to get himself warned off asking questions about the sinking of the *Pride of the South*.

Ruso took a long swig of the wine. He had always supposed that when a man made a sacrifice in a good cause—and his family was, he supposed, a good cause despite its manifold eccentricities—he would feel proud. But he had never imagined that the sacrifice would be one of self-respect.

He had expected Fuscus to ask for some kind of private favor. Something medical and embarrassing and strictly confidential. The last thing he had anticipated was being held up in front of the whole town as some kind of military hero. The thought of any genuinely invalided veteran seeing him showing off up on the grand balcony at the public games made him shudder.

He was not a hero. He had chosen to rush home and desert his remaining patients in the Legion. He had wriggled out of his sworn loyalty to his emperor with a half-truth. He should never have listened to Valens. He should have gone to his superior officer, explained the situation, and . . .

. . . and been told to leave his domestic affairs outside the gate and get back on duty.

Sometimes, no matter how hard a man tried, it was impossible to do the right thing.

He swilled the remainder of the wine around the cup. In Britannia, the work had been grueling but at least his duty was clear. Here, he was expected to stave off bankruptcy and ruin while helping with a political campaign and taking an interest in dowries, drains, and dinner parties. In the midst of it he had foolishly promised to help find out about Cass's missing brother.

He glanced out into the street in the faint hope that Tilla might be passing by with the girls. Tilla, the barbarian woman who consorted with rebels and thieves, believed in ridiculous gods, and cheated at board games. She had no clue about elections or dinner parties, and was unlikely to know much about drains, but he drew some comfort from the thought that he could talk to her about them later in the privacy of a shared bed. In the meantime, he hoped her morning was turning out to be more enjoyable than his own.

The barman raised his eyebrows, offering a refill. Ruso shook his head and paid up. He would go and do now what he should have done in the first place. He would bypass Fuscus and all his slippery promises and machinations. He would go and announce his return to Severus and deal with him, man to man.

17

"NOT THAT ONE. The big one on the left—no, not that big!—down a bit."

Tilla marveled at the patience of the shopkeepers. At first she had feared the girls were about to spend money the Medicus did not have. But by the time they had left a second salesman to reconstruct his disrupted display, she began to understand the game. In the faint hope of a sale, the shop staff would be obliged to pass over shoes and hairpins and earrings and necklaces and wait while the girls tried them on, craned their necks to see the effect in mirrors, giggled, and then declared that this wasn't quite what they were looking for: How about that one just above it?

"This would suit you, Tilla," suggested Marcia, holding up a delicate gold chain with blue and green stones.

Tilla shook her head. "I am not buying today." Or any other day.

"Try it on," urged Marcia, reaching across to drape it around her neck. "It's just right with your hair. Go and look in the mirror and tell me that isn't made for you."

Tilla took off her hat and picked up the shop mirror. She was conscious of the salesman's cynical gaze from behind the counter. They both knew she was only being allowed to sample the goods because he did not want to offend the young ladies. Still, it was not every day she had a chance to wear costly jewelry. She straightened her shoulders and eased down the neck of the dreadful yellow outfit with her forefinger so the stones would lie flat against her skin.

It was not a good mirror. Careless customers had damaged the polished brass surface and the serious young woman staring back at her was softened around the edges by a thousand tiny scratches.

"So," she said, watching herself frown and trying to repress the smile that followed, "you think a barbarian should wear one of these?"

"Very nice, miss," offered the salesman. The girls said nothing. She wondered if she had offended them with the "barbarian" remark. She put the mirror back on its ledge and glanced around, seeking their opinion.

They were not there. She blinked, and looked around again. It was a small shop—just a lock-up booth built into the front of a house—and there was nowhere to get lost. Apart from the man behind the counter, she was quite alone. It seemed the girls had grown tired of waiting for her and moved on.

She stepped out into the street to look for them. A heavy hand landed on her shoulder. "Forgot something, miss?"

She had not noticed the guard outside the door. His grip tightened as she squirmed, trying to catch sight of Marcia's green stole. To her surprise there seemed to be hardly anybody about. A rattle of shutters told her that the coppersmith's shop opposite was closing. "I must go," she said, reaching behind her neck to grope for the fastening of the necklace.

"Cash only," said the voice behind her. "No credit, and our master don't take offers."

"I don't want to buy it," she explained, struggling to find the fastening.

Behind her was a shuffle of leather soles on flagstones. "Let me help, miss."

She felt a hand lift one of her plaits. "That's a very expensive item, miss," said the salesman. "You don't look to me like you could afford to buy it."

"I am not stealing," she insisted loudly, wondering where the sisters had gone. How long would it be before they realized she was missing? "I don't want to steal. I forget I am wearing it. I have to go with those girls."

"Third one this week," said the doorman.

"A lot of ladies forget to take off expensive items and wander out by mistake. That's what we keep the door staff for, see?"

"Well, now I am remember," said Tilla, her frustration spilling over into a struggle with the Latin. Arguing was so much easier in British, when she did not have to think about the words. In British, she would be able to tell this man what she thought of him. But there was nobody for hundreds of miles who could translate. "Keep your necklace," she said. "Let me go."

"Funny accent," said the salesman. "Can you understand what she's saying?"

"Nah," observed the doorman. "We don't talk like that around here, miss."

"We're about to put the shutters up for lunch," said the shopkeeper. "You can stay and explain it to us."

Tilla took a long, slow breath. They were probably just teasing her, but in a strange land she had no way of guessing from their tone. Keeping her voice as steady as she could manage, she said, "Let me go. My friends will vouch for me. Their family is very important."

"Really?"

Was that a note of doubt in his voice? "Their father is Publius Petreius, who built a big temple with an inscription. When everyone hears that you make one of their guests prisoner alone in this shop, how many rich ladies will want to come here and buy things?"

She hoped the fumbling at the back of her neck was undoing the fastener and not a prelude to something worse. Moments later she felt the stones slither across her throat as the necklace was removed. "There you go, miss," said the salesman, as cheerfully as if he had been trying to help her from the start. "Try and remember next time. If your friends come back we'll tell them you were looking for them."

Tilla stood on tiptoe at the crossroads. There was no green stole in sight. Neither of the women she stopped to ask had seen two girls answering the right description.

She turned right by the shrine on the corner, hurried on to the next crossroads and then right again. She thanked whatever gods might be listening that the Romans were so fond of squares and rectangles. If she kept choosing the same direction in this ants' nest of narrow lanes, she would find herself at the other end of the jewelers' street, and perhaps meet the girls coming back to find her.

She glanced into the few shops that were open as she passed: a weaver's, a merchant selling perfumed oil, a meat stall, a scribe bent over his copying . . . no green stole in any of them. No green stole on any of the customers lolling at the shady counter of the bar, either. She passed a narrow alleyway where someone was playing a tune on a whistle. All she could see in the shadows were three curious dark-eyed children and a hen peering at her from behind a line of limp laundry.

The next open door had a picture of a smug-faced man painted on the wall beside it. The man was attached to an eager phallus that appeared to be beyond his control and, at the far end, beyond his reach as well. The Medicus's sisters definitely wouldn't be in there, and Tilla felt a momentary pity for the girls who were.

She could understand neither where the sisters had gone, nor why. It was hard to believe that they would walk off in the middle of a conversation, nor that they could vanish so completely and so quickly. She had heard tales of young women being stolen, of course: everyone had. Snatched up by gods, or ghosts, or more likely by humans with evil intent. But surely someone would have noticed two people disappearing at once? And surely Marcia would have had something to say about it?

It was hard not to conclude that the girls had deliberately run off and left her.

None of the figures chatting on the communal seats of the latrine was familiar. Back out in the glare of the street, she realized she was no longer wearing the straw hat that the Medicus had bought her. After a moment's thought she remembered taking it off in the jeweler's shop. She sighed. She was not going back there. The hat was lost.

The slave girl sweeping the paving stones in the grand square of the Forum knew nothing. The knot of women standing on the fringe of a poet's audience told her they had no money for beggars. Neither the silversmith's slave nor the boy selling fancy sandals knew anything. If Marcia and Flora had passed this way by choice, Tilla was certain they would have paused at those stalls. According to the attendant, who refused to let her in to look around without payment, they were not in the bathhouse, either.

Pausing at the next fountain, she borrowed a cup from a friendly young woman with a black eye, and gave herself a long drink. Then she asked which local god might be inclined to help a foreigner who had lost something she was supposed to be looking after.

"You could try Isis," suggested the woman, pointing across the street at a small shrine gifted with several bunches of lavender. "I pray to her for protection sometimes."

Tilla glanced at the black eye. "And does she answer?"

The woman ran her forefinger lightly along her bruised cheekbone. "Well," she conceded, "he hasn't killed me yet."

With nothing else to give, Tilla unfastened the knife from her belt and laid a lock of blond hair among the lavender before setting off again on her search.

The city slaves who had the unenviable task of dredging the Sacred Spring had no more idea about Marcia and Flora than the ducks preening their feathers under the balustrades. (Even the sacred spring, Tilla noticed, had been trapped into a rectangular stone pond. The god of the spring had taken his revenge by turning the water pea green and cursing it with a bad smell.) "Try going up the hill, miss," suggested one of them. "You'll get a better view."

The view after she had slogged up the hill was indeed better, but no more useful. The guards at the nearby tower had no information to offer except that for a special price for pretty girls, they could let her climb up to the top and enjoy a finer view still.

Tilla threw herself down in the shade of a pine tree, pausing to straighten out the creases from Arria's cast-off tunic. She surveyed the vast sprawl of red roofs stretching out in front of her. The pale oval in the distance must be the amphitheater where men would soon be trying to murder each other for the entertainment of the townspeople. Down there, somewhere in that cruel city, were two girls whose mother had sent them out under her protection.

She stood up, brushed away the dead pine needles that had made patterns on the backs of her calves, and decided there was no point in wandering about. If the girls had been taken, they would be hidden. If they had drifted off, they knew their way far better than she did. She would go back to the Augustus gate and hope they turned up in time for the cart the Medicus was sending to fetch them. If they did not, she would stay there to wait for them and send the driver hurrying home with the message that they were lost.

She could imagine what the stepmother would have to say about that.

18

RUSO TURNED THE cart left off the main road about a mile short of his own house. The slaves working in the stony vineyards and olive groves that stretched out to either side of him would all be the property of My Cousin The Senator down in Rome. The man had a country estate this size and yet his agent was prepared to seize the only home another family owned. No wonder the Gabinii were one of the richest families in town.

Ruso drove for several minutes before a graceful villa came into view. It was large enough to be grand without being ostentatious, and neatly positioned to catch the breeze and make the most of the view south across the plain. Between the house and the surrounding countryside was a long garden wall, and in that wall a pair of gates was opening to allow a carriage to exit.

Ruso narrowed his eyes and peered past the matched pair of bay horses. Someone was sitting in the seat behind the driver. Perhaps he was about to meet Severus earlier than he had expected. He wiped a trickle of sweat off his forehead and shifted his grip on the reins.

As the vehicles closed on each other he slowed the mules, then felt the tension in his shoulders ease as he realized the passenger under the sunshade in the other carriage was a woman. She was repaying his interest by staring back at him from beneath an arrangement of orange curls that seemed to be frozen to her head. He nodded an acknowledgment and returned his attention to the road just as he heard her cry, "Stop!"

The carriage rumbled to a halt and he found himself sitting no more than six feet away from its passenger. A pair of perfectly made-up dark eyes gazed at him from an artificially pale face. The reddened lips parted to emit the word, "Gaius!"

"Claudia!" Ruso was not sure how a man should address his former wife after three years of separation, but he was confident that *you've put on weight* and *what have you done to your hair?* were not appropriate.

Claudia seemed to be having the same difficulty because she repeated, "Gaius!"

She was immaculately turned out as usual, from the clusters of pearls dangling beneath her ears, down past something pale pink and floaty to the soles of her delicate coral pink sandals with matching pearls stitched at the join of the toe straps. The whole effect looked effortlessly elegant, and to achieve it she would have had the servant girl messing about with combs and tongs and pots of makeup for hours while she dealt with the strain by helping herself to a platter of cakes.

"I heard you were home," she said.

He had forgotten how she fiddled with the hair at the nape of her neck when she was nervous. He said, "You look well."

"Thank you, Gaius. I am well." She pointed to his bandaged foot. "I hear you've been in Britannia."

"I'll be fine in a couple of weeks," he assured her, realizing as he said it that Fuscus would be expecting a more heroic account of his injury.

Claudia sighed. "Well, you always did like those dreadful sort of places."

Ruso drowned out the faint echoes of an old argument with, "I hear I have to congratulate you on your marriage."

"Thank you. I take it you haven't . . . ?"

"No."

"No, of course not. Well, who would you meet over there?"

Since he was not about to enlighten her, there was another awkward pause before they both spoke at once.

"How is your father?"

"Did you finish writing your book?"

Her smile revealed one front tooth very slightly in front of the other. "You first."

"No," he said. "I gave up with the book. So how's Probus?"

"My father is very well, thank you. He and my husband are in business together."

Ruso heard the echo of another criticism: the one about his own lack of ambition. Even if he had stayed here, he knew he would never have been deemed worthy of involvement in Probus's financial affairs. He said, "I was sorry to hear about Justinus and the ship."

"Ships sink, I'm afraid. Severus has traveled himself; he understands these things."

"I see," said Ruso. If Claudia had heard any rumors about the loss of the *Pride*, she was clearly not intending to share them with him.

"Severus is from Rome," she said, as if that explained his superior understanding.

"I see." In a moment she would probably tell him that Severus was handsomer than he was and better in bed too. Not that she would be likely to recall much of Ruso's performance in bed, since it had frequently been curtailed by the room being too hot or too cold, or it being the wrong time of the month at least once a fortnight, or just, "Not now, Gaius!"

Ruso cleared his throat and reminded himself that if Claudia's husband and her father were in business together, they were not doing it to spite him. "You know he's trying to ruin us?"

The lines of her frown were deeper than they used to be. "He's only doing his job, Gaius. He has to represent the senator's interests. It isn't personal."

"Isn't it?" said Ruso. "I must have been misinformed."

Claudia pursed her lips. "It isn't up to me what Severus does."

"Lucius has children to feed," he said. "And Cass was always a good friend to you."

"I hear Lucius is drinking too much," she said. "And I haven't seen his wife for years. I hardly saw her when we were married, with all that gallivanting around the East."

Ruso took a deep breath. If he was not careful, everything would be his fault again. He said, "I'm just asking if you think what Severus is doing is fair."

He saw her shoulders stiffen. "What I think doesn't matter, Gaius. You must talk to my husband." She leaned forward. "Drive on!"

As the driver urged the horses forward she called over her shoulder, "If you've come to see him, don't bother. He's gone out. He's gone to see you."

19

THERE WAS NO time to change. Ruso pulled his tunic straight and lurched up the couple of steps toward the entrance hall. His sister-in-law was hovering by the front door in a manner that suggested she had run out of conversation and was desperate to escape.

The man seated on the stool beside the Petreius household shrine was not, at first glance, an impressive sight. Beneath a no-nonsense crop of graying hair, the pale face had large nostrils that gave the effect of a permanent sneer. Ruso judged him as nearer forty than thirty, overweight, and not in the best of health. Whatever Claudia had married him for, it was not his looks.

Severus did not bother to get up as Cass introduced him and then hurried off toward the children's room. Instead he reached for the platter that had been set on a side table at his elbow and took a drink from one of Arria's most delicate patterned glasses. "So," he said, clapping the glass back on the polished walnut table rather than the platter and spilling some of the contents, "Ruso."

"Severus. As you see, I got your letter."

The man frowned. "What letter?"

Already, Lucius's description of *devious vindictive lying bastard* rang true. "Has anyone been sent to fetch my brother?"

"You don't need reinforcements. This is all going to be nice and legal." The agent surveyed the boldly painted hall and the little wooden home of the household gods with the air of a man assessing a lot at auction. The bust of Ruso's father stared back at him from its stand. Ruso hoped that, wherever Publius's spirit had gone, he was not able to witness this meeting. Even if the whole mess was largely his own fault.

"All this and a temple too," Severus remarked, scuffing at an uneven patch in the mosaic with the toe of one sandal. "Always the same, you people. Happy to borrow and then complaining when it's time to pay up." He glanced around at the vacant-faced women on the walls. "Look at this lot. No wonder you can't pay the bills."

"We pay our bills."

"Not from what I've heard."

"What we don't do is pay them twice."

"Wake up, Ruso! Your brother's lying to you. He spent the money himself."

Ruso glanced around, wondering who was listening behind the closed doors. "Shall we talk in the study?"

Would he ever feel comfortable calling it "my study?" It was as much as he could do not to call it "my father's . . ."

Severus seemed to have some difficulty heaving himself off the stool, but once up he headed in the right direction without being told. "Hot day," he muttered.

"Want something else to drink?"

"I didn't come here to drink."

Ruso grabbed the stool and carried it into the study. He placed it where his visitor could lower himself onto it without further effort. Then he shifted his father's chair so that he could get into it without hopping clumsily along one side of the desk. "So. We owed the senator a sum of money, and—"

"Let's not dance around, Ruso. It's stuffy in here, and I'm not feeling well. Your brother's payment was short. Very short. I asked him to pay: He didn't. I got a magistrate's ruling and he still didn't. I'm running out of patience. I was thinking of bringing a few men over to straighten him out. But, since you've turned up, I'm prepared to do it through the law."

Ruso wondered what Claudia could possibly have found attractive about this charmless lout, who seemed to think he was doing them a favor by trying to bankrupt them. "Lucius tells me he paid in full."

"Course he does. Prove it."

"I can't prove anything," he said. "Neither can you. But I spoke to Fuscus this morning. He thinks you'll want to change your mind very soon."

Ruso had been hoping for a reaction to Fuscus's name, but Severus did not seem to be concentrating. He was frowning and fingering his mouth as if he was not sure it belonged to him.

Ruso said, "I'm prepared to agree to a second payment in order to get this thing settled."

Severus cleared his throat, spat on the floor, and said, "First I want an apology to the wife."

Ruso blinked. "You want me to apologize to Claudia?" That would be interesting. He could imagine what tales Claudia had told about him.

"Not you, you fool," retorted Severus. "She's not interested in you." He leaned forward to rest his elbows on his knees. "Or me. Not since that woman—what's her name? Arria. Not since Arria came around pouring poison in her ears." Ruso, who still had no idea what his visitor was talking about, thought he detected a slight slur in the voice.

"S'not my fault," observed Severus. "Stuck here in the Provinces with a complaining sister an' a bunch of bumpkins who don't know a good offer when you hear it." He looked up at Ruso as if he knew there was something else important to tell him but could not quite remember what it was. Finally he said, with more emphasis than was necessary, "Nobody upsets my wife!"

"I didn't know Arria had upset your wife," confessed Ruso, wondering how Severus was managing to appear drunker by the minute and whether he would remember any of this conversation when he sobered up. "I'll see she apologizes."

"She had no business running to Claudia like that. I made that offer in . . ." Severus appeared to be searching for an elusive word, then brightened as he caught hold of it. "Confidence! I made that offer in confidence. Confidence and good faith."

"Ah," said Ruso, reaching for a stylus and wondering whether Lucius knew that Arria had gotten herself involved in this somewhere. "Let me make a note of what we've agreed."

"I was only trying to help."

"Very good of you," said Ruso, prepared to humor him if it led to a signed agreement. "I'll just write this down and we won't need to involve Fuscus." Or too much political campaigning.

"I'm a decent man."

"Of course." A decent man who swindled debtors out of money they didn't owe.

"I knew you'd understand!" exclaimed Severus with unexpected warmth. Ruso glanced up and decided the sickly grimace was intended to be a smile. "Other men don't know what it's like," continued Severus. "Day after day. Night after night. Nothing you do ever good enough."

Light was beginning to dawn. "Claudia?" suggested Ruso.

"Bloody woman. And Daddy. And then my sister. Always something wrong. Now that sister of yours, not the loudmouth, the other one . . ."

"Flora," prompted Ruso, choosing to ignore the painfully accurate description of Marcia.

"The older one's as bad as mine. Want a nice quiet girl. Man could be happy with a nice quiet girl like that."

"You're telling me you were offering to marry Flora?"

"Nice quiet fertile girl. Thash what I need. Make some money, go back to Rome. Be a fine upstanding family man."

"Nobody here was aware that you were making a marriage offer. Or that you were in a position to do so."

Severus frowned and pondered that for a moment. "Teshting the water. Seeing how the land lies. Look before you leap. Try before you buy."

"Try before you buy?"

Severus gave a vague gesture of rejection. "No thanks. Don't feel much like it right now."

"You're saying my family misunderstood your intentions?" said Ruso, confident that Severus's intentions had been to see what he could get away with and repressing an urge to punch him on the nose.

"That interfering old cow went and told Claudia."

"Arria didn't realize the high regard you had for Flora." So high, indeed, that since the man had been refused access to her, he had decided to wreck the lives of her entire family. "We'll pay what we owe you as a result of the last judgement, and you'll drop the court case. Are we agreed?"

Severus flapped a hand toward him. "Whatever you like."

As Ruso seized a pen to scrawl out this surprising agreement, Severus added, "Nobody insults my wife! Only me."

"I'll get a couple of people in to witness it, and you can tell Fuscus over dinner tonight that it's already dealt with."

"Bloody awful paintings in your hall. Nuff to make anybody ill."

"Are you sure you wouldn't like some water?"

"I said no, din' I?" Severus rubbed a trail of drool away from his mouth and mumbled, "Feel sick."

Ruso leaped up, hopped over to the door, and shouted, "Someone fetch a bowl!"

"I'm ill!" gasped Severus, as if he had only just noticed. "Fetch a doctor!"

"I am a doctor. Have you eaten anything unusual?"

Ruso had barely established what Severus had eaten for breakfast when the breakfast itself rose up and reappeared for inspection.

"Too late," observed Ruso as Galla the nursemaid stood helpless in the doorway clutching a heavy bowl and a cloth. Severus heaved again and toppled sideways off the stool. Ruso grabbed him just in time to stop his head hitting the desk.

Severus struggled to get out of his grasp, and collapsed on the tiled floor, mumbling, "Wash matter with me?"

"You're drunk."

The man shook his head. "Not drunk." He wiped his nose and mouth with his fingers. "Everything's gone funny."

"Lie down for a moment till your head clears," suggested Ruso, motioning to Galla to keep back.

"Not drunk!" shouted Severus. He tried to get up, but his arms and legs seemed to have taken on lives of their own and skidded helplessly in the regurgitated breakfast. "Help me!"

Ruso crouched beside him and tried to help him up. Severus's legs had tangled themselves around the desk and the arm that encircled Ruso's neck almost pulled him off balance to land on top of his patient.

"Lie still," he ordered, ducking out from under the arm and mentally running through a list of possible causes other than wine. "Have you been bitten or stung by something?"

"No."

"Just lie still," Ruso urged, adding with more confidence than he felt, "It'll pass in a minute." He tried, "Did you ride over here bareheaded in the sun?" not because it was likely, but because it would buy him some time to think.

"Why's everything moving?" cried Severus, rubbing his eyes with his fists. "I can't see!"

Ruso turned to the doorway, where his servant was looking as frightened as his patient. "Galla, what did he have to drink?"

"Mistress Cassiana brought him some water, my lord."

"I can't see! The light's gone all— Help me!"

Ruso tried to detach himself from the man's terror and think clearly. He was certain this was a case of poisoning, but without knowing what the poison was, it was hard to know how best to treat it.

"Olive oil and a cool damp cloth," he ordered Galla. "Quickly."

"Just lie still now," he repeated, not knowing what else to suggest. He crouched over his patient, trying to work logically through the possibilities. The man had been fingering his mouth: presumably because the poison had entered that way. What the hell had he taken? He smelled of nothing unexpected apart from a faint trace of roses under the vomit: probably a harmless attempt to mask bad breath.

The mouth had not been dry: not henbane or mandrake, then. He was far too agitated for poppy. He had lost his coordination, but he was still able to move all his limbs. He was not choking. He had not complained of a headache, or of feeling cold. Did hemlock always paralyze? What were the symptoms of wolfsbane? There could be dozens of other poisons he had not even considered, and he could not abandon the patient while he hurried off to scrabble for clues in his medical books.

Severus was struggling to say something. Squirming around the worst of the mess, Ruso leaned down again and grabbed a flailing hand. He felt a worryingly slow and fluttery pulse.

"That bitch!" whispered Severus.

Galla returned with a jug and the cloth. Ruso wiped the sweating forehead and wished he were back with the Legion. In Africa there would have been a poisons specialist on the staff. Even in Britannia he would have been able to shout for the pharmacist. Here, there was no time to fetch even the humblest root cutter from town. He was on his own.

He turned to Galla again. "Help me prop him up," he said. "Then fetch Lucius, or one of the farm boys if you can't find him. He's to ride over to the senator's and tell them Severus has been taken ill and they need to come straight away."

He returned his attention to his patient, tipping some of the oil into the drooling mouth. "We'll get it back up, whatever it was," he promised. "Can you think of anything you've eaten or drunk that tasted strange? What about the rose water?"

Severus muttered something. He tried to push the jug away.

Ruso leaned closer and grabbed the man's arm to hold it still. "Say it again," he prompted.

"I'm dying!" whispered Severus. "The bitch has poisoned me!"

20

BY THE TIME it brought Lucius back home, the mule's coat was mottled with dark patches of sweat. Ruso watched from the porch as it was led away by the stable lad, then glanced at the horizon and saw a second cloud of dust rising from the direction of the road.

"They're on the way," confirmed Lucius, striding up the steps to the house. "Claudia's gone to town, so his sister's coming in the carriage with the household steward. I told them you were here but they've sent to town for their own doctor, anyway. How is he now? Is he fit to travel?" He paused. "Gaius?"

Ruso shook his head.

"Oh gods, he isn't—?"

"Just after you left."

"He can't be!" Lucius hurried past him into the hall. "Are you absolutely sure?"

Ruso had heard the question often enough to recognize it as desperate hope rather than an insult to his competence. He limped down the corridor after his brother. Since he was clutching the key to the study door, he was surprised when Lucius opened up and walked in before he got there. Surely he couldn't have forgotten to lock it?

Ahead of him, he heard Lucius exclaim, "Holy Jupiter!"

He should have warned him. Lucius was not used to such sights. Ruso had closed the man's eyes, but otherwise the body would be lying just as it had died.

On entering the study, though, it was Ruso's turn to be shocked. "Galla! What the hell do you think you're doing?"

Galla looked up from washing the floor. Severus's body, now naked, had been rolled over to lie against the wall. She still looked frightened, as well she might.

"She's tidying up," replied Arria, stepping forward from behind the door. "Since the family are on the way and none of you boys seem to know what to do."

"But I locked the door!"

Arria held up an iron key identical to the one in his own hand. "How do you imagine the staff get in to clean the room, dear? Galla, that'll do. The master will help you roll the body back and make it decent. You will, won't you, Gaius? We don't want to involve any more of the staff than necessary."

Ruso tightened his grip on the stick. "Arria, I told her to leave this room exactly as it was."

"I know, dear. But did you really expect poor Claudia to see him in that state? He was a dreadful man and she'll be better off without him, but at least we can show some respect."

"When I give an order in this house, I expect it to be obeyed."

Galla was kneeling motionless on the floor between them.

"You can stop now," Ruso told her. "Leave the room and don't say anything to anyone about what you've seen and heard in here, understand?"

She nodded, scrambled to her feet, and ran.

"Well, really!" exclaimed Arria. "I was only trying to help!"

Ruso took a deep breath. "Thank you," he said. "Lucius and I will deal with it now."

"I don't know why you're making such a fuss, Gaius."

"No," agreed Ruso, as calmly as he could manage. "You don't. Now if you want to help, go and fetch me a clean tunic to put on him. Then watch for his family and when you see the carriage turn in at the gates, come straight here and tell me."

"That was a bit harsh," observed Lucius after the door had slammed behind Arria. "She was only trying to help."

"She's done enough helping," growled Ruso. "Thanks to her, it looks as though we're the ones who poisoned him."

"The ones who what?"

Ruso crouched beside the body. He shifted its arm, crooked its knee to help redistribute the weight, and rolled it over toward him. "Well, somebody did."

There was a momentary pause before, "In our house?"

"Of course not. At least, I don't suppose so. But thanks to Arria, it now looks as if we've been trying to clean up the evidence."

While Lucius took this in, Ruso hauled the body over again until it was back in roughly the right place.

"He wasn't poisoned," said Lucius slowly.

"What was it, then?"

"You tell me. You're the doctor. Think of the right sort of illness and tell them that's what killed him."

Ruso was conscious of cicadas trilling outside the window. As if it were just another lovely day in late summer and there were nothing to worry about. "I can't do that," he said.

"Yes you can," urged Lucius. "And hurry up, because they weren't far behind me."

21

THERE HAD BEEN a time, early in his apprenticeship, when Ruso had assumed that breaking bad news would get easier with practice. Or at least that he would get better at doing it. The trouble was, no matter how well-rehearsed the doctor, the scene was always new to the friends and relatives playing the other parts.

Over the years he had learned only two things about giving the news of a death: first, that it never was going to get any easier, and second, that it was best to ask people to sit down first. Not that it made the shock any less, but from a sitting position it was harder for them to hit him—or more likely, outside the army, to end up clinging to him and weeping uncontrollably on his shoulder: a position from which he frequently found it difficult to extricate himself. Instead, he chose to sit and wait as words and meaning linked themselves in the reluctant minds of his hearers. He had to watch as their faces changed from fear or incredulity to realization, and to bear patiently with the occasional accusation of lying, indifference, or incompetence. But never before had he been obliged to give the news to people who, sooner or later, were bound to suspect that he had deliberately murdered his patient.

The girl with the pinched features was introduced as Severus's sister. Ennia was probably older than Marcia: something Ruso had not expected after the talk of early marriage. Unlike the steward, she did not at first seem to grasp the implications of what Ruso was telling them.

"He was all right when he left," said the steward, whose small head, narrow shoulders, and black eyes reminded Ruso of a weasel.

"It came on very suddenly," said Ruso, aware of the need not to look shifty and aware also of Lucius listening beside him. The entrance hall was really not the right place to do this, he knew. But they could hardly loll about on dining couches, and the study was occupied by a body. He should have asked them to sit out in the garden, drains or no drains. Well, it was too late now. He cleared his throat. "Would you like to see him?"

"We certainly would," said the steward, getting to his feet and offering an arm to the girl.

Ennia took no notice of the invitation to move. Both fists were pressed against her mouth, and her whole body trembled. She seemed to be staring at Ruso without seeing him.

"Would you like to see your brother?" repeated Ruso.

The steward bent forward and touched her hand. "I'll take you," he murmured.

Still dumb, Ennia nodded.

When Ruso unlocked the study door—this time he had given firm instructions to Arria about keys—Ennia hurried in and knelt beside the limp body, clutching the face in her hands and whispering "Oh, brother, brother . . ." Ruso felt a momentary relief that Arria had thought to have the scene cleaned up, and then realized he must take charge here.

He bent and put a hand on the girl's shoulder. "It might be best not to kiss him," he murmured.

"Why?" demanded Ennia.

Ruso straightened up. "I'm not sure about the cause of death," he confessed, not daring to look at Lucius.

"I see," said the steward. He was standing with his back to the door and his arms folded. His voice was thin and sharp: the voice of a man who was used to overseeing staff and knew all the tricks they got up to.

Ruso could guess what the steward thought he saw, but any attempt to put the man straight was only going to upset the girl further. It seemed she had felt genuine affection for the charmless Severus.

"He wasn't wearing that when he left the house," observed the steward, frowning at the crisp white linen that still bore the creases of being folded away in a cupboard and now also the marks of Ennia's tears.

Ennia looked up, shoved her tumbled curls behind one ear, and revealed a face blotched from weeping. "Why do you care what he is wearing?" she demanded. "My brother is dead, Zosimus, look! Have you no respect?"

The steward coughed and apologized. Lucius stepped across and murmured something in the man's ear while Ennia laid her head back down on her brother's chest and cried, "Oh brother, what will I do here without you? Severus, don't leave me! Please, brother! Who will take me back to Rome now?"

Ruso cleared his throat. He felt it was up to him to say something, although there was nothing he could think of that would be helpful and he did not want to contradict whatever Lucius had just told the steward. Finally he said, "If you'd like to be alone . . ."

"No thank you," said Zosimus, answering for both of them. "We just want to get him home and have our own doctor take a look."

"Of course," agreed Ruso. "I'll be glad to talk it over with him."

Lucius shot him a warning look. He ignored it. Severus's last words echoed through his thoughts: *The bitch has poisoned me.*

The silence was broken by a soft knock on the door. Zosimus slid aside and Cass entered the room. Without asking, she knelt beside the girl and put an arm around her, murmuring something and passing her a cloth to wipe her nose. For a few moments there was no sound but the trill of the cicadas and the occasional sniff from Ennia. Then Cass whispered something else. Ennia smoothed her brother's cropped hair and got to her feet.

"I am sorry," she said to Cass. "You must think me very weak."

"No," said Cass. "I think you show love and respect for your brother."

"I would like to take him home now."

"Why don't we wait by the carriage and the men will bring him out to us?" suggested Cass gently.

Ruso was aware of Lucius watching his wife escort Ennia out of the room.

Zosimus immediately followed Ennia into the corridor as if he did not want to entrust her to any of Ruso's family.

When they were gone Ruso pushed the door shut and hissed, "What did you say to that steward?"

"Nothing. Only that Severus had been violently ill and we didn't want the family to see him in that state."

"Just let me do the talking, will you?"

"You? You've already made them suspicious! What was that rubbish about not kissing him?"

Ruso said, "What was I supposed to do, watch her get poisoned too?"

Lucius clamped his hands over his balding head and leaned back against the wall. "As if we didn't have enough trouble with him before."

"The irony is," said Ruso, reaching down to replace the sheet over their dead visitor, "we were on the verge of doing a deal to drop the court case."

Lucius scowled. "Don't try to be clever, Gaius. Nobody's going to believe that."

"I know. Even though it's true. Have we got anything that'll do for a stretcher?"

The whole Petreius family lined up by the gates to watch the carriage pull away, with each of the children strategically placed between adults to minimize opportunities for fighting.

As the rumble of the wheels faded and Arria was saying something about upsetting Cook by canceling tonight's dinner, one of the nieces cried, "Uncle Gaius, there's your barbarian!"

Ruso shielded his eyes and squinted at the bareheaded figure in yellow making its way along the main road. "I don't think so," he said. "She's in town with the—" He stopped. "Oh, hell. Does anybody know what time it is?"

"I'll go and look!" offered one of the nephews. "I know how to tell the time!"

"No you don't!" retorted a niece.

"Yes I do!"

"He doesn't, Uncle Gaius. He can't read the numbers: He just looks at the shadow and makes it up."

"I do not!"

"Why don't you both go?" suggested Cass, grabbing a child with each hand. "I'll come with you."

As their protests faded toward the far end of the garden, the carriage bearing Severus on his last journey home turned left onto the main road and swept past the walking figure. The figure hesitated at the junction. Then it turned and began to tramp down the track toward them.

"It *is* your barbarian, Uncle Gaius," insisted a small voice.

"Yes," agreed Ruso, adjusting his grip on the stick and setting off to meet her.

"But what's she doing here, Gaius?" Arria's voice floated after him, rising in alarm as he retreated. "Where are my girls?"

22

TILLA WAS MOVING along the track with small, deliberate steps, watching her feet as if she could not trust them to obey her. As she drew closer she stumbled. He called out to her. One hand rose to flap a faint response. Cursing his lame foot, he lurched toward her in the nearest thing he could manage to a run.

"Tilla, what's happened?" He offered an arm for her to lean on. "You look terrible."

When she lifted her head her face was white. "My lord, I lost your sisters."

It was not only the weariness in her voice that told him she was almost at the end of her strength. He could not remember the last time she had called him "my lord." He said, "You look dreadful. Has something happened?"

"Are your sisters here?"

"No." He interrupted her cry of despair with, "This is my fault. We had a crisis here and I forgot to send the cart. Have you walked all the way? Where's your hat?"

She paused before replying, as if she was assessing whether it was worth using the energy. Finally she said, "The hat is lost too. My head is aching. I am sorry."

He wanted to carry her. Instead he had to ask, "Can you make it to the house?"

"Yes."

Arria was hurrying toward them, calling, "Where are my girls? Gaius? Make her tell us what she's done with them!"

"Lost," Tilla whispered, "in the shop with the jewels. I turn around, they are gone. I look for them, then I go to the gate of Augustus, but it is past the seventh hour and nobody is there. I think they are gone without me. But now they are not here."

"Gaius? Gaius! What's she saying?"

"She needs water, quickly. She's exhausted."

"But where are my girls? I should never have let them persuade me to trust her!"

"I forgot to send the cart," he explained, deciding half the truth would be enough for now. "Tilla's walked all the way home in this heat to fetch it. She needs plenty of water to drink, and tell Cook I want a jug of vinegar and a mixing bowl."

Arria bent to peer up into Tilla's white face. "Oh dear. This one's not going to die as well, is she?"

"Of course not," Ruso assured her, stifling a momentary panic at the memory of being unable to help Severus. "I know what I'm treating this time."

Tilla was propped up on his pillows wearing nothing but a cool sheet to preserve her dignity and a cold compress on her forehead. "Drink some more," he ordered, putting the cup in her hand and turning back to carry on pounding unguent of roses into a measure of vinegar.

"I am well," she insisted, although her voice was barely stronger than her pulse had been. "You must find your sisters."

"Marcia and Flora can wait," he said, tipping more vinegar into the bowl and mixing it in. "Keep drinking." He was not going to leave her until he was happy that she was recovering. This was his fault in more ways than one. He should have sent that cart, and he should have thought to warn her. In a town with a fine supply gushing from the street fountains, it had never occurred to him that Tilla might not stop for more than a couple of sips of water all through a hot morning. He had seen enough cases like this in his first post with the army, when men marching under the African sun had run short of water. It began with heat and overexertion and dehydration and, if it was not treated, it ended very badly indeed.

He dipped the sponge in the mixture and began to wipe it down her neck, across her shoulder, and along one arm.

She wrinkled her nose. "Vinegar?"

"In the army they used to complain about the roses." He turned the compress over and stepped around the bed to sponge down the other side. "Any dizziness, nausea, stomach cramps?"

"Just the headache, and I am very tired. Please. Go and look for the sisters. This is not a good way for me to start with your family."

"They should have had the sense to stay with you."

"What will I do if you do not find them?"

"I'll find them," he growled. "They'll be tired of shopping by now."

"You are not afraid for them?"

"I've got bigger things to worry about. They're not children."

She took another gulp of water. "I am sorry. You have enough troubles with that man wanting money."

"Not anymore." He explained about Severus's fatal visit.

She sighed. "This is worse. Everyone will think it was you."

Ruso hesitated. At the moment, Tilla was a patient, and a patient should be kept away from unnecessary anxiety. "Don't worry about it," he assured her, dabbing the sponge into the bowl. "I'll tell everybody what happened to him and it'll all be sorted out. Now, where exactly did you last see my sisters?"

23

ALONE IN THE Medicus's bedroom, Tilla put the smelly sponge back into the bowl and forced herself to pour yet another cup of water. Farther down the corridor, the Medicus's brother and his wife were quarreling. It was hard to grasp what the argument was about. She could hear the raised voices, but the words were muffled by the walls. Only the occasional phrase from Lucius broke through: ". . . comes back here and makes a mess of everything!" was followed by an indistinct reply. Moments later, "What do you mean, I always take the easy way out?" was clear enough. He was demanding, ". . . any idea how hard I work?" when there was a scream of, "The girls! They're home!" from Arria, followed by the sound of footsteps running along the corridor.

Wincing at the pain in her head, Tilla wrapped herself in the sheet and climbed down from the bed. She made sure there was nobody in the corridor before crossing to the window that looked out over the garden and adjusting the shutter so she could peer through the gap by the hinge without being seen. Marcia and Flora were marching up the path toward the house, looking furious. Arria hurried down the steps to fling her arms around them, crying, "Where have you been? Are you all right? I should never have left that woman to look after you. I told you I didn't trust her."

"We don't know where she went," grumbled Marcia, slapping straw off her skirt. "We've been looking for her for hours."

"But she's here!" exclaimed Arria. "She told us she'd come home to fetch the cart for you."

"We didn't know what to do," said Marcia. "We just turned around and she'd gone. We waited at the Augustus gate for hours and hours but nobody came."

"We had to beg a lift home on one of Lollia Saturnina's delivery carts," said Flora.

"Lollia? Oh, whatever will she think of us? And we've had to cancel the dinner!"

Marcia said, "Why?" but Arria was not listening.

"Your brother's gone rushing off to fetch you. Didn't you see him on the road?"

"He's a bit late," pointed out Marcia.

"We might have missed him," said Flora, picking another strand of straw out of her sister's hair. "We were so tired we had to lie down for a rest in the back of the cart."

"That woman abandoned you in town, strolled back here without you, and lied to us?"

"She probably didn't know what to do," said Flora.

"I expect she just said whatever came into her head," said Marcia. "It's not her fault. I don't suppose her people understand that sort of thing."

"This is not good enough. I'm going to have to talk to Gaius." Arria's voice grew louder as they climbed the porch steps. "You'd think if he was going to bring one home he would have . . ." Tilla missed what came next, dodging back into the bedroom as they entered the house.

Back on the bed, she lay still until the throbbing in her head subsided. She supposed the Medicus would now be hobbling around the city streets in search of two girls who were safely back at home. Nobody else seemed to have thought about that.

24

THE PAIN THAT had nailed her head to the pillow was gone. Tilla opened her eyes, gazed at the cracks in the ceiling of the Medicus's room, and wondered if he was back yet.

There were no voices outside. No footsteps in the corridor. She managed to time her ascent of the stairs so that nobody saw her slip into her stuffy little bedroom clad in one of the Medicus's old army tunics. Inside, she changed into her own clothes. On the landing she bumped into the slave who had slept in her bed last night.

"Have you seen the mistress and the master's sisters?"

"In the bathhouse, miss." The girl leaned forward to mouth across a pile of folded linen, "It is safe to come out."

It was, but now that she had the temporary freedom of the house, Tilla could not think of a single place within it where she would feel at ease. She went across to the window. Nothing was moving in the regimented garden that was still baking in the late afternoon sun. Beyond the wall, a tall gray horse was tethered in the shade of the stable building. There was some sort of compress on its foreleg. Feeling they were fellow sufferers, she went downstairs to talk to it.

When she got there, the stable lad was busy replacing the compress. His morose expression defied the jolly tangle of curls around his temples.

She said, "This is a fine horse."

"He is, miss. Pity he's not ours."

She took the animal's head to distract it from investigating the stable lad's curls. "What is the matter with him?"

"He's not looking too happy on the nearside foreleg." Glancing up, he saw she was interested. "It's an old injury. I'd have rested him for a day or two more, myself. You don't want to mess about with a good animal like this."

"Your Master has taken the mule cart?"

The lad nodded. "That's all there is now, miss. We don't have horses here no more."

She supposed they had been sold.

The lad tucked in the ends of the bandaging and added, "I wouldn't have been cleaning the harness if I'd known he needed it."

"You had the harness in pieces when the master wanted the cart?"

"I made him late."

She said, "So did I. But he was very late, anyway. Was he cross?"

Instead of replying the lad straightened up and slapped the horse on the shoulder. "Good boy."

"When the master is feeling better," she said, "he will thank you for taking such good care of this horse."

The "Yes, miss" was not enthusiastic.

"He is always in a bad temper when his foot hurts. He is not usually rude to people who do not deserve it."

The lad paused to consider this for a moment, then said, "Fair enough, miss."

"The master has many things on his mind today."

"Could you ask him what he wants done with the horse, miss? I don't want to be in more trouble. Only nobody asked about it and I didn't like to interfere."

Tilla must have looked baffled because he explained without prompting that the guest who had died—"You heard about that, miss?"

"Yes."

"It was the horse he come over on. I was going to give it a rest and take it back over in a day or two."

Tilla felt sorry for the lad, who was obviously desperate to get his hands on a high-class animal again.

"But if the master thinks it ought to go back now, I could walk it over. I don't want to get him in no more trouble."

"You think he really is in trouble?"

The stable lad reached up and pulled a section of mane straight. "I wouldn't know, miss."

"Did you see the man who died yourself?"

The lad explained that he had heard the dog barking and realized nobody was around. He had opened the gate himself to let in the visitor and his horse, and gone to fetch someone—Mistress Cassiana was the only one he could find—from the house.

"I'll say the man was ill when he got here if that's what the master wants me to say, miss," he offered. "But it's not true. Like I told the master, the horse was lame but I didn't notice nothing wrong with the man on top."

25

WANT, WANT, WANT!" exclaimed the cook, waving a vegetable knife toward the kitchen ceiling. "Always somebody wanting something. You don't need a cook, you need a magician."

"That's the nature of cooking, I believe," said Ruso. He had arrived back from town hot and tired, and banished the protesting Marcia and Flora to their room. He was not in the mood for another argument.

"First, mistress wants a grand dinner," exclaimed the cook. "With what, I'd like to know? I can't show my face in town till the bills are paid. Then after I've gone to all the trouble she decides everyone's too upset to eat it, and she just wants a tray in her room." The knife sliced down through the air and stabbed into the tabletop, narrowly missing the startled kitchen boy. "How can I work if nobody makes their minds up? The fire's gone out . . ." In case Ruso could not see this for himself, the point of the knife was now jabbed toward the dead coals under the grill. "And we've washed up. If you've changed your minds again, it's no good. It's too late."

"All I'm after is something simple and quick to eat," said Ruso, leaning back against the doorpost and folding his arms. "And some information about what happened to our visitor this afternoon."

"I see. Blame the staff, eh?"

"Information," repeated Ruso. "And put the knife down first."

"I don't know a thing about it." The knife flashed toward the kitchen boy, who was cowering in the corner. "He doesn't know a thing, either. It's no good asking him."

"The knife?" Ruso reminded him, wondering if the man was genuinely deranged or just an out-of-work actor.

The cook looked at the knife as if it had just appeared in his hand, turned it over to inspect it, then wiped it on his apron and put it back down on the table beside the sharpening stone. "We don't know anything. We were getting ready for a dinner. We didn't have time to hang around gawping. Try asking the cleaning girls."

"When the visitor arrived this afternoon, someone gave him a drink."

"That one with all the children—Mistress Cassiana. Not us."

Ruso frowned. "She must have got the crockery from here. Where is it now?"

The cook gestured to the kitchen boy, who stepped forward and pulled a stool out from beneath the table. He clambered onto it and reached up to a shelf that housed a set of slender glasses and a matching jug wisely stored out of harm's way. He retrieved the jug and one glass.

"You've washed them?" asked Ruso.

"Straight away," said the cook. "The man dropped dead. I'm not letting somebody else drink out of that glass without washing it first. If they dropped dead too it'd be my fault, wouldn't it?"

Ruso turned to the kitchen boy. "I suppose you washed the jug as well?"

His pessimism was justified. Apparently keeping the crockery clean was all part of maintaining standards in the modern kitchen.

Ruso examined the glass and the jug. He sniffed them. He ran his forefinger along the smooth inner surfaces, peered at the finger, and then gave it a tentative lick.

"Clean?" demanded the cook, as if he were daring Ruso to say otherwise.

"Pristine," agreed Ruso, unhappily. His household's cavalier attitude toward evidence was not going to look good. "What was in it?"

Apparently the visitor had wanted nothing but water. The boy had been dispatched to the well to fetch a cool supply, but he had not seen the visitor. Mistress Cassiana had taken it to the hall herself.

"So there must have been a time when she was waiting here for the water and Severus was alone?"

The cook looked as if this was a trick question. "I don't know. I've got enough to cope with in here, without worrying about everybody else. It's not my fault."

"I didn't say it was," said Ruso, wondering how many times he had heard that phrase since he arrived home. He put the glassware back on the shelf and helped himself to some sort of pastry from a baking tray on the table. "Sorry about the mix-up over dinner. We'll try not to have any more visitors drop dead. In the meantime, what else is there to eat?"

The cook looked around at the barren surfaces of the modern tidy kitchen. Then he lifted the lid off a clay pot. "Testicle?"

"I hope he came cheap?" inquired Ruso, meeting Lucius in the corridor outside the kitchen. "What happened to whatshername?"

"Part exchange," explained Lucius. "Whatshername went to the contractor as payment for the paint job in the dining room. Don't look at me like that, Gaius. She was quite happy to go."

"I'd rather have whatshername in the kitchen than a bunch of cupids dancing around the walls of the dining room. Can't we sell him and get somebody more suitable?"

Lucius sighed. "Gaius, when was the last time you bought a cook? Have you any idea how much a good one costs?"

"No," conceded Ruso, who had only discovered what Tilla's cooking was really like when it was too late to get rid of her.

"He's perfectly all right if you don't upset him," said Lucius. "You haven't been in there accusing him of poisoning Severus, have you?"

"No," said Ruso. "And now I'm going to go around not accusing everybody else. Including you. Did you see or hear anything of Severus between the time he arrived and the time he was taken ill?"

"I was busy in the winery. I didn't even know he was here. Cass dealt with him."

"I'll talk to her later." Cassiana had gone to fetch the children from one of the neighbors. "In the meantime we need to get all the servants except the kitchen staff and the stable lad lined up and I'll interview them in the study one by one."

"You mean I need to get them lined up so you can interview them?"

It was exactly what Ruso had meant, but only now did he realize how it sounded. He said, "This sort of thing seems to be part of my job over in Britannia."

"Poisoning people?"

"Investigating unexplained deaths."

"If you'd listened to me in the first place, nobody would be investigating anything."

"What would have happened if Severus's own doctor discovered he was poisoned and I'd said he wasn't?"

Whatever Lucius might have said in response was lost below a clatter of footsteps along the hallway and Arria's cry of "Oh, Gaius, this is dreadful!"

"We'll sort it out," he promised. "We just need to stay calm and—"

"Oh, never mind that! I mean, nobody's been to tell Lollia we've canceled dinner and she'll be getting dressed!"

26

Lollia Saturnina's establishment was a model of neatness. The drying amphorae were laid out in military ranks to catch the late afternoon sun. The fuel was in stacks of uniform height. Vegetables were standing at attention in their beds and beyond them, past a row of freshly painted outbuildings, a slave was stationed by the entrance of a kiln that towered above two blackened fire holes. She was busy emptying a trolley of wide-shouldered amphorae, heaving them up to a man whose voice boomed around the hollow oven in which he was stacking them ready for firing.

Ruso approached the woman and indicated the house on the far side of the yard. "Do you know if your mistress is in?"

"No," said the woman, wiping her fingers on her worn brown tunic. "I'm here."

Ruso swallowed. "You're Lollia Saturnina?"

"Yes."

He had not made a good start. Ruso took in the ancient tunic, the battered sandals, the hair tied back in a simple braid. She was wearing neither jewelry nor makeup, but neither did she need them. To his consternation, beneath the pale smears of dried clay was a very attractive woman.

The woman leaned forward, called, "Just a minute!" into the entrance of the kiln, and was rewarded with an echoing, "Right-oh, mistress!"

"Perhaps," she prompted, moving away from the entrance, "when you've finished staring, you could tell me who you are and why you're here."

"Ruso," he explained. "I live next door."

"Ah, Gaius Petreius the famous medic! Your stepmother's very proud of you."

"Really?"

"Don't worry, she did warn me."

"About what?"

"That women make you nervous. But apparently you're a nice chap underneath. So could we get underneath fairly soon, do you think? I'm no good at social chitchat, either, and I need to get this finished and clean up."

Ruso cleared his throat. "Do you need a hand?"

"No, I do this all the time."

"I just wasn't expecting you to be so . . ."

"Scruffy? Don't worry, I will dress up for dinner."

Ruso bit back the honest but inappropriate "attractive" and substituted "forthright."

She smiled. The gap between her front teeth only added to her charm. He wondered why nobody had told him, and then remembered that Arria had tried: He just hadn't believed her.

"Now, what did you want to say to me?"

Ruso had practiced various ways of describing the problem on the walk through the olive grove that adjoined Lollia's property. All explanations of the afternoon's events sounded either evasive or callous. In the end he settled for, "Arria's sorry but we can't do dinner tonight because a man who came to see us this afternoon died in my study."

"Oh dear."

It was not clear whether she was expressing regret about the death or the dinner.

"He wasn't a patient," Ruso added, then wished he hadn't. "Not that that matters, of course."

"No. Who was it?"

He explained.

Lollia said, "Poor Claudia."

"Poor Claudia," he echoed, silently recalling *The bitch has poisoned me.*

There was an awkward pause, then Lollia bent to heave up the next amphora.

"I expect Arria will want to rearrange," he said.

The gap-toothed smile appeared again. "I expect so."

"You might as well know," he said, "I think he was poisoned. But it wasn't us who did it."

"I don't doubt it."

"That he was poisoned, or that it wasn't us?"

"Both," she said, looking at him over the neck of the amphora. "I met Severus several times. Frankly, Claudia's made some very bad decisions in the last few years. Now if you'll excuse me, we need to get this fired up before it gets dark. Ready, Marius? Next one coming up!"

27

WHILE TILLA SLEPT beside him, Ruso lay staring into the darkness and wondering what he was supposed to do with *The bitch has poisoned me*. Despite consulting his medical textbooks and questioning most of the household, he was no further forward with finding out what had killed Severus, nor how it had been administered. Everyone had been going about their usual business and hardly anyone had noticed the visitor before he drew attention to himself by dying. Arria had been having her hair done in her room and was only disturbed by the commotion in the study. Ruso could find only one additional sighting of the live Severus, but the laundry maid had paid little attention as she passed through the hall and noticed him sitting on a stool. In reply to "How did he look?" she said, "I think he was wearing a brown—"

"I mean, did he look well?"

The girl thought about this for some time before venturing the opinion that the visitor had been looking hot and cross.

"But he didn't look ill?"

"No, sir. Just hot and cross, like you."

The only person he had not yet questioned was Cass, who had arrived home late with the children, organized the farm slaves' supper, dealt with a tantrum from Little Gaius, and invited Tilla to join her in a late retreat to the bathhouse. He would talk to her tomorrow.

The bitch has poisoned me.

At the time he had assumed that Severus was accusing either his wife or his sister, but now he realized those words could equally well have been directed at Cass. Of course it was ridiculous to imagine that Cassiana would poison anybody, but . . .

"I know you are not asleep," came a voice from the other side of the bed. "Are you angry with me about your sisters?"

"Uh? No. It was obvious they were lying."

"You are thinking about the man who is dead," she guessed. "How everyone will think you killed him because you owe him money and he married your old wife."

"Everyone would be wrong."

"I know this."

"Good. Go to sleep, Tilla."

"I know, because killing him here would be very stupid."

"Killing him anywhere would be very stupid." He sighed, rolled over, and reached a hand around her. "I'm glad someone married my old wife," he murmured in her ear. "Go to sleep."

She shifted to get comfortable against him. "What sort of poison is he dead from?"

"I don't know."

"Did you catch his last breath? What did he say?"

When he did not answer she said, "You are still not asleep. Are you?"

"Yes."

"Tell me what he said."

"Did Cass say anything about it while you were in the baths?"

"We talked about her brother. She does not know what to do. Her husband says she must make her mind up."

He said, "I promised her I'd try to help, but I haven't had time."

"She understands. What will happen about the money you owe, now the man is dead?"

He said, "While you were over at the baths I went through the chest in the study. There's a stack of bills from traders in town that haven't even been opened. And a tax assessment. None of them's big enough to prompt a bankruptcy, but word gets around. Some of the bigger creditors might start calling their loans in."

He felt the tremor of a giggle. "Not if they think you will poison them."

"It's not funny, Tilla. Yesterday I was just threatened with disgrace. Now if the Gabinii turn nasty they could have me tried for murder."

"That is not funny," she agreed. "So, what did he say?"

"Go to sleep, Tilla. It's the middle of the night. I have to go and see Claudia tomorrow."

"Claudia the old wife." Tilla kicked away a tangle of sheet and pulled it straight. "Will you tell her what he said?"

"Yes. It's only fair that she knows first."

She fell silent.

He was drifting away from the worries of the day when he heard, "Cass says the rich widow next door is very pretty."

"Yes, she is. Go to sleep."

"If all those people want their money back and you are not accused of murder, will you try to marry her?"

"Go to sleep."

A cool draft forced him back into consciousness as she flung back the bedding. "I will go to my own bed."

"No!" He grabbed her arm and pulled her back against him.

Far beyond the open window, some small night creature shrieked as it fell prey to a larger one.

He said, "I need you."

28

TILLA HAD ONCE seen a picture of grape treaders painted on the side of a fancy wine jug. It had seemed a delightful job: a jolly group of slaves dancing in a sunlit trough to the music of a flute. There were mountains behind and, in the foreground, shining juice pouring from the trough into a vat.

The reality was not jolly at all. They were working in the shade of the winery, it was true, but even at this hour of the morning it was hot with the sun baking the roof tiles and the walls holding back the breeze. It was surprising how quickly the thighs began to ache from trampling up and down in the shallow basin. Nor was it kind to the arms. To stop herself losing her footing in the warm slop, Tilla was having to change her grip ever more frequently on the rope that dangled from the rafters.

They could get a donkey to do this, she thought, pausing as a shadow fell across the rows of fat jars set in the floor and one of the vineyard workers strode in with another basketload to upend all over her feet. They could attach a donkey to a pole and make it walk around and around. And around. And around. Although she supposed a donkey might relieve itself all over the grapes. She was tempted to pee in that horrible woman's grape juice herself, except that it would not be fair to Galla, who would also have to stand in it.

At least the other workers had left them alone. The men were convinced that having women's feet crushing the grapes this morning would bring bad luck on the precious vintage. Instead of telling them not to be so silly, the Medicus's brother had said he would find them something else to do.

"He is being kind, miss," explained Galla after he had gone. "All the other jobs he could give us are out in the sun."

Privately Tilla thought he was being cowardly. Surely the stepmother could not tell him who should work on his own farm?

Galla's face was still red on one side where Arria had slapped it. Tilla suspected she herself had only escaped being struck because Arria was afraid of what the Medicus would say about it when he came back from consoling the old wife.

She had expected that yesterday's fuss over the runaway sisters would be forgotten this morning, eclipsed by the mysterious death of the man in the study. She was wrong. The girls, finally released from their room, had emerged to offer Tilla a sulky apology for getting lost. Immediately after the apology was accepted, they proceeded to blame her for their woes. Why had she made such a great fuss about nothing, running all over the town "instead of waiting for us like Galla does?"

At this moment Arria, who must have been listening inside the hall, marched out onto the porch and demanded, "What do you mean, 'like Galla does'?"

Summoned, the terrified slave had finally confessed that yes, when she chaperoned the girls into town, they did sometimes go off on their own.

"Where do they go? Who with? You stupid girl! How long has this been going on? Why didn't you tell me straight away?"

The girls were sent back to their room and told that Arria expected to hear some music practice. Galla was informed that since she could not be trusted to look after the family, she was now to consider herself a farm laborer.

When Tilla intervened to say it was not fair, Arria snapped, "And you can go too. Don't think I don't know what you're up to, young woman!"

"Why did you never tell her that the girls ran away from you?" asked Tilla, changing hands again on the rope.

"Because I am more afraid of them than of her, miss."

"You do not have to call me 'miss,'" Tilla reminded her. "We are in the same trough."

"No, m—Tilla. If I had known they were taking you to town, I would have warned you."

"Where do they go?"

"I told the mistress. I don't know."

"But you can guess," said Tilla, who had spent enough time as a slave to know that servants knew far more than they dared tell.

Safe from the wrath of Arria and her daughters, Galla did not need much prompting. "I think they hang around the gates of the gladiators' barracks."

Tilla paused to scoop a drowning beetle out of the pulp. She set it on the wall of the trough, shook off the slimy grape skins that were clinging to her fingers, and said, "Is it something to do with a fighter called Tertius?"

"Tertius is a very stupid boy," said Galla. "Marcia thinks he is going to marry her." Leaving unspoken the obvious conclusion that Marcia was not very bright, either, Galla added, "Did she wear the green stole?"

Tilla gripped the rope again and swung around to face her. "How did you know?"

"They did that to me too. They wear something bright on top. Then when they run away, they take it off. So you are looking for a girl in a green stole . . ."

". . . who is nowhere," said Tilla, realizing how they had made a fool of her. Marcia had deliberately wrapped her in that necklace like a chain. She spotted a pristine bunch of grapes, took aim, and splattered it with her left foot. "How do you put up with this?"

"I have never done it before."

"I mean the family."

"I pray to be able to forgive," said Galla unexpectedly.

"I wouldn't."

"Some days it is easier than others," Galla agreed, shuffling sideways. "And at least I am not often beaten."

"She hit you today."

"Today is a bad day. So was yesterday."

Tilla pondered this for a moment. "Were you there when that man died yesterday?"

Galla trapped a stray grape between her toes and squelched it before answering, "I'm sorry, miss—"

"Tilla."

"I'm sorry, Tilla. The master told me not to speak of it."

Tilla had to admire the girl's loyalty, but it was frustrating to find Galla just as reluctant to reveal the last words as the Medicus had been.

She tried, "Do you know the master's old wife?"

"Not well."

The slave was both loyal and tactful. It was very annoying.

"Severus's sister cried when she came to fetch the body," Galla said suddenly, as if she had finally thought of something safe to talk about. "I felt sorry for her."

"It is a terrible thing to lose a brother." They stopped trampling. Tilla could hear the juice trickling down into the vat. She said, "My brothers were killed by men from another tribe." Here, surrounded by high walls and sunny vineyards, gardens and olive groves, it seemed almost impossible to believe that such things could happen.

"Mistress Cassiana's brother is dead too. He went on a ship and drowned." Galla pushed back a strand of hair that was stuck to her forehead and moved to an untrodden corner of the trough.

"I heard. I am sorry for her."

"When the man came with the news he sent me to fetch her. While I was gone little Lucius climbed up the ladder and fell off the roof and broke his arm. So it was a bad day for everyone." She sighed. "The mistress is right, she can't trust me to look after the family."

"Maybe the mistress needs to learn to forgive," suggested Tilla.

"It is the only way," Galla agreed, not sounding very hopeful.

"It is one way," said Tilla. She had never forgiven the raiders from the North who had killed her family and at the moment she was not eager to forgive the Medicus's stepmother and sisters, either. "Do you think Severus's family will forgive whoever killed him?"

"I hope so. It is the only way to stop things from getting worse."

"But there must be justice. A man who has done wrong must be made to pay the price, or there is nothing to stop him from doing it again." Tilla swilled the juice around with one foot, searching for strays. "Or her," she added.

"I'm not saying his family should not have justice," said Galla, "but justice may not come in this world."

Here was something Tilla could grasp. Her own family were waiting for her in the next world, although the shortage of druids at home meant that no one was able to explain that world to her in a way that made sense. It had already occurred to her that if she were to die here, her spirit might not be able to find its way back to them any more than the lost spirit of Justinus could return until someone built a tomb and called him home.

"So," she said, pushing further at the door Galla had begun to open, "who do you think should be forgiven for killing this Severus?"

"I don't know."

"I am not asking you to know. I am asking you to guess."

Galla pursed her lips. "He never seemed like a nice man."

"Somebody must have been very angry with him. Perhaps his wife?"

"Oh no, Claudia's very respectable!"

Tilla changed hands on the rope and said nothing.

"Really. That would be terrible, a woman—"

"Terrible," agreed Tilla. "It must be somebody else."

"Perhaps Claudia's father."

"Because he did not like his son-in-law?" Tilla prompted.

"Or because of the ship," mused Galla.

When Galla seemed disinclined to continue, she prompted, "The ship?"

"The ship where Mistress Cassiana's brother was drowned." Galla paused.

Tilla took a long, slow breath. Getting this story was like pulling teeth. She was about to prompt again when Galla said, "I heard something in the market the other day. After the mistress asked the fish sellers if they had heard of the *Pride of the South.* I said nothing because it wouldn't bring her brother back and I thought it would upset her more."

"Go on."

"They told her they didn't know anything. But after she had gone I heard one of them tell his friend that the *Pride of the South* was so rotten he was surprised it had made it out of port."

Galla stopped, and looked at her as if waiting for reassurance. It seemed this was the climax of the story. When Tilla did not reply she said, "Do you think I will be in more trouble for not saying this before?"

"I will tell the Medicus," Tilla said. "But at the moment he is busy trying to find out who killed Severus."

"That's why I'm telling you!" exclaimed Galla. "It was Severus who chose which ship to invest in."

Tilla thought about that for a moment. "That would be a good reason for Cass to want revenge on him."

"Oh dear!" Galla looked as though she was about to burst into tears. "No, no. I'm sorry. I'm not very good at explaining. Severus chose which ship to invest in but he had no money. That was why Justinus was on board.

He was there to make sure everything was done properly, because the money all came from his master. Probus. Claudia's father."

Tilla swung around to face Galla with her weight resting on the rope. "And when this rotten ship disappeared, the father lost his steward and his money, and it was all the fault of Severus?"

"I suppose so."

The crunch of footsteps outside spurred them back to work before a bulky silhouette appeared in the doorway. The Medicus's brother grunted a greeting and approached with, "The lads want to be in here before long to set the press up."

Tilla guessed from the abruptness of his tone that he was not sure how to address them. He bent to peer at the green slop, grunted again, and stirred it around with a stick. "Every single grape," he reminded them. "I don't want any still whole when they come through the press."

Tilla did not dare to ask how something as soft as a grape could possibly emerge whole from beneath the massive press beam built into the wall of the winery. Instead she groped dutifully in the mush with her toes, hunting for escapees and wondering whether a man would really murder his son-in-law for making a bad choice of ship.

29

RUSO TRIED TO imagine what he would do if Claudia were not his ex-wife or, conversely, if the woman he was about to visit were not Claudia.

What was the correct course of action if a husband who was intending to be unfaithful to his wife arrived at someone else's house, collapsed, and then died with the words, "The bitch has poisoned me!" on his lips? Should his host keep these words a secret and then go immediately the next morning to reveal them to the widow?

Probably not.

The trouble was, he could not picture Claudia poisoning anyone. Shrieking at them, yes. Throwing things, yes. Sulking, yes. Poisoning—no. Why go to that bother when, as they both knew, one could simply get a divorce?

On the other hand, if not Claudia, then who? He had still not managed to question Cass, but it was inconceivable that his sister-in-law, a woman so tolerant with her children and so generous with her time, would have murdered somebody.

The gatekeeper of the big estate was a fearsome creature with only one eye. He went to consult the steward, leaving Ruso to guess whether man and guard dog had gained their scars in a fight with each other, or whether there had been others involved.

Ruso was wondering whether the gatekeeper had wandered off and forgotten him when the heavy gate finally swung open on silent hinges to reveal the weasel-faced steward. He announced, "The agent's widow will see you now," in a tone that suggested he had to obey his instructions but he didn't have to like them.

Ruso followed the man in through the gates. The white roses trained around the pillars of the house contrasted with the dark cypress branches of mourning hung above the front door. From somewhere within came the sound of wailing. Ruso was relieved to be led away to the right, where a walled garden dotted with statues separated the house from the farm buildings. The garden occupied the sort of space the army would have deemed adequate for five hundred infantrymen, their stores, their officers, and all their officers' friends, relations, and horses. As he crunched along a shaded pathway past a fishpond the size of a swimming pool, Ruso suspected that the slaves currently hoeing the flowerbeds were waiting to pounce on the gravel and rake away his footprints.

The place radiated the genteel elegance to which his stepmother aspired but which she would never achieve. And access to this was what the charmless Severus had to offer that he himself didn't, and never would have. The words of Lollia Saturnina came back to him: *Claudia has made some very bad decisions in the last few years.*

Oh, Claudia, he thought, you fool.

The steward motioned him to wait and approached a high-backed wicker chair set with its back to them beneath the shade of a summerhouse. All Ruso could see of its occupant was one slender foot in a gray sandal. After a brief and inaudible conversation the man beckoned him forward.

Ruso was appalled to find himself wondering whether, if he hobbled fast enough, he could be out of sight behind the hedge before she turned around. Instead, he took a deep breath and approached the throne.

"You can leave us, Zosimus," she told the steward. "I will ring if I need help."

Ruso blinked. Between them on the little stone table there really was a brass bell.

The steward gave Ruso a look that said he had better not try anything, and walked away.

Claudia's skin looked waxy. Her eyes were puffy below the makeup, and the dark hollows beneath them matched the murky gray of her outfit. She said, "Zosimus thinks you poisoned my husband."

Ruso shifted the bell to one side and sat on the table since there was nowhere else and he was not going to hover like a servant. "I know."

"Well, did you?"

"No. Did you?"

A crease appeared between the plucked brows. "Still as tactless as ever, I see."

Ruso had wondered how this would go, and so far it was going just as he had expected. "Let's start again, shall we? Hello, Claudia. I'm very sorry about Severus."

She groped down in the side of the chair and drew out a fan. "Thank you," she said, wafting cool air across her face. "I'm sorry too. Surprisingly."

He wanted very much to know what that meant but knew it would be a mistake to ask.

She said, "Did he suffer?"

He told her the death had been very quick. He was not sure she believed him, but she seemed grateful. It occurred to him that he could not remember seeing her dressed without jewelry before.

"I'm supposed to be up at the house receiving condolences," she said, "but if I have to stay in that room with Ennia much longer I shall strangle her. I don't care who's going to take her back to Rome now, so long as somebody does. Preferably very soon."

"Did your husband have any other close family?"

"No, thank goodness. Can you imagine what it would be like with a whole bunch of them, weeping and collapsing all over the place? All this is just a pantomime, you know. She did nothing but whine when he was alive."

It seemed to be the way with sisters. He said, "I suppose there'll be an investigation."

"Eventually."

"Had he been ill recently?"

"I thought you said he was poisoned?"

He took a deep breath. "I'm just trying to make sure of the facts. I've had some experience with things like this over in Britannia. Let me see what I can find out for you."

"You?"

Ruso could not think what he could say that would change the opinion Claudia had formed of him during three years of marriage, so instead he said, "I'd imagine Severus had enemies."

"Of course he did. It wasn't his job to make friends, it was his job to manage the estate. As you know."

"I'll need names. Details."

She shook her head. "We don't need you, Gaius. Daddy's gone to see Fuscus to ask him to send a message to his cousin the senator."

His cousin the senator. Even Claudia was doing it now.

She said, "We expect he'll send one of his own men to investigate."

"From Rome? That'll take forever."

There was still a hint of superiority in her tone as she said, "The message will go on the official dispatch service."

"Even so, it'll be at least two or three weeks."

Claudia patted her hair. A couple of strands dislodged themselves and tumbled down over one ear, making her at once half as formal and twice as attractive. "Daddy said that's what we should do," she said. "When he finds out I've been talking to you, he'll be furious."

Ruso knew better than to argue with Daddy. He got to his feet and stepped across to check that there were no gardeners lurking behind the neatly sculpted cypress hedges before saying, "This probably isn't the right time to tell you, but you need to know. I was alone with Severus when he died. His last words were, *The bitch has poisoned me.*"

She fell back into the chair as if he had struck her. "What?"

"Don't make me repeat it."

"But I—that's ridiculous!"

"If I thought you'd done it, I wouldn't be telling you."

"Well you'd better not tell anybody else." When he did not reply she said, "You haven't, have you?"

"Not yet."

She began to pick at the feathers of the fan. "You may as well know. The man was a reptile."

"I'm sorry you weren't happy," said Ruso, and meant it.

"There's no need to gloat."

"I wasn't."

A spurt of gravel rose up as the fan hit it. "Stop being so gallant, Gaius! I know all about him chasing Flora. Arria came to warn me."

"So I heard."

"I'm not surprised somebody poisoned him, are you?"

"Don't let anyone else hear you saying that."

"You're the one who said I should speak my mind."

"Did I?"

"You always said you could never work out what I was thinking!"

Ruso, enlightened, bit back, "No, what I said was that I wasn't a bloody mind reader."

She gestured around her at the elegant garden. "I put up with him in exchange for all this, Gaius. In return he had access to Daddy's business advice. The local contacts were very useful for him because everybody he knew was back in Rome and he didn't want to be too beholden to Fuscus."

"I see." So Severus had harbored ambitions of his own.

"It was a business arrangement. I didn't want him dead."

It made sense, and it made sense of Lollia Saturnina's assertion that Claudia had made some very bad decisions lately. "So if it wasn't me," he said, "and it wasn't you, who was it?"

"How should I know? It must have been somebody in your house. I expect it was Arria."

"Arria didn't go near him," said Ruso, rapidly considering and dismissing this alarming possibility. "I've already made inquiries at home. How did he get on with his sister?"

"I told you. They argued."

"About what?"

"Going back to Rome, what else? As if any boyfriend would wait for her for this long!"

"These were serious arguments?"

Claudia sighed. "Don't be silly, Gaius. She didn't kill him. She was hoping he would take her back there. Promise you won't repeat what he said. You know what everyone will think."

"People will ask what his last words were."

"Then make something up."

It was the second time in two days that he had been told to stave off questions with lies.

Claudia was frowning at him. "You'll have to practice. You're a terrible liar, you know. Try not to look shifty. And whatever you do, don't scratch your—you're doing it now! For goodness' sake, Gaius!"

Ruso snatched his right hand away from his ear.

"That always gives you away," said Claudia.

He said, "I'm not prepared to wait for a man from Rome. I want this looked into now."

"But Daddy said—"

"Daddy isn't suspected of murdering him," pointed out Ruso. "And unless I tell people what Severus said, neither are you."

Her eyes widened. "Are you threatening me?"

"I want permission to talk to the household here," he said, wondering if she realized that it was unlikely to be her household for much longer. "I need to find out what Severus did that morning. What he ate, where he went, who he spoke to."

In the silence that followed he watched her fiddle with her hair.

"Think about it, Claudia. The investigator from Rome won't know any of us. As long as he can offer up somebody plausible to the court, he won't care who it is. He'll get a smooth lawyer to drag up everything that person's ever supposed to have done or said, and the magistrates will convict them. You know what happens after that."

She sank back into the chair. Behind her, a lizard skittered up the plinth of a statue, and vanished among the folds of a stone toga. Finally she said, "All right. We'll start before we get instructions from Rome. But I want it done properly."

"I know what I'm doing," he insisted, feeling old resentments rise.

"There's only one way to do this sort of thing." She lowered her voice and glanced around to make sure the garden slaves were safely out of earshot. "The funeral contractor—a horrible man, he smells—has offered to supervise the questioning."

Ruso stared into the eyes of his former wife. "You're not serious?"

"Well, you aren't going to do it, are you? I can hardly ask the staff to question one another and besides, you know what will happen. Unless you frighten them enough, they'll just all cover up for one another."

"And if you frighten them too much, they'll make up whatever you want to hear."

"That's why we need an expert. Attalus knows what he's doing, even if he does smell. He has the contract for the amphitheater."

"Just because he can shift dead bodies—"

"He's had to do this sort of thing several times before." She paused. "I know it's not nice, but he's promised to be very discreet. He'll do everything a long way from the main rooms so there's no disturbance, and his men will bring their own equipment and clear up afterward."

"But—"

"This is not the time to be squeamish! What else are we going to do? We'll tell him to stop as soon as we've found out who did it."

Ruso clamped his fingers around the warm stone of the tabletop. "No."

"Oh, do make your mind up! You said yourself, we need to question everybody. I'll get Daddy to pay him for doing the people here, and you can pay for yours."

Ruso frowned. "My what?"

"Your household, of course. He did die in your house, after all."

"No."

The painted eyes locked with his own. "I'm the family," she said. "I decide what's to be done."

"If you insist on having the staff tortured," said Ruso quietly, "I'll have to tell people what Severus said. That way at least the male slaves will stand a chance of being left alone."

"Oh, Gaius!" Claudia flung her hands in the air in exasperation. "Why do you always have to be so difficult?"

He was spared having to answer this question by the arrival of a kitchen slave with a plate of Claudia's favorite honey cakes. He wondered what the staff who had arranged this kind gesture would think if they knew she had been discussing having them questioned under torture.

"All right," she conceded, reaching for a cake. "You talk to people here and I'll ask Daddy about Severus's business contacts. But I can't see how it's going to help."

Ruso waited until the slave was out of earshot. "Yesterday morning," he said, "can you remember exactly what Severus did? Was there anything out of the ordinary?"

She hesitated for a moment. Then she said, "He'd been having trouble sleeping lately. He was like that sometimes. Business worries, I suppose. Anyway, he woke up much too early as usual, farted, scratched his privates, jumped on me, and woke me up too."

Ruso hesitated. There was nothing of any investigative value in this account of his former wife waking up with another man, and certainly nothing he wished to hear repeated, but he had to ask. "If you were asleep, how do you know what he did when he woke up?"

She sighed. "Because I was pretending, Gaius. Sometimes he didn't bother me if he thought I wasn't awake."

Ruso said, "Oh," and felt like an intruder. Then he said, "I don't need that much detail."

"Then why did you ask?"

He wanted to say, *Did you ever pretend to be asleep with me?* "What did he do after that?"

"He washed himself over at the basin, put on a clean tunic, grumbled as usual."

"About what?"

"I thought you didn't want all these silly details? About being ill."

How illness could be seen as a silly detail when the man had dropped dead the same day was a mystery to Ruso. Trying not to sound too eager, he said, "So he was already ill?"

"No worse than usual. Country air didn't suit him. He said it gave him palpitations." She sniffed. "But the headaches and the bad stomach only ever struck after a big dinner."

"If he really had trouble with his heart—"

"If it was anything serious it would have killed him ages ago. So anyway, then he put on his house shoes, shut the door behind him, and went to his office, and I never saw him alive again." She paused. "I wasn't always cross with him, Gaius."

Coming from Claudia, this was almost an expression of affection. Ruso was aware that she had honored him with a confidence and that he was supposed to respond accordingly. He coughed, urgently summoning and discarding various possible replies. *I'm sorry* was ambiguous. *I know* was untruthful. *You weren't always cross with me, either* was irrelevant, and . . .

And it was too late. The silence was growing awkward. Ruso said, "How do you know he went to his office?"

"He always went to his office in the mornings to meet up with the steward. Not everyone is as disorganized as you."

"I'll have to talk to the steward."

"Well, good luck. Zosimus is being no help at all. It's the household steward's job to organize the funeral, isn't it?"

"I don't know."

"Well, it is, I'm sure. But every time I tell him to do something he says he can't act without orders from Rome. So I said, I'm the wife of the senator's agent and part of the family, and do you know what he said?"

This sounded like the sort of question Claudia usually answered herself, so Ruso raised his eyebrows in what he hoped looked like anticipation.

"Not anymore. Not anymore! So who am I, then?"

Ruso said, "Are there slaves mentioned in his will? People who would be freed after his death?"

"I don't know what's in his will," said Claudia. "But he didn't own any of the slaves. We're the poor relations. Practically everything here belongs to the senator." She paused. "Do you think he'll pay for the funeral?"

30

ZOSIMUS TURNED OUT to be a remarkably ill-informed steward. He was not aware of Severus having any enemies. He was not aware of anyone visiting the office yesterday morning apart from the farm manager and a slave delivering a couple of unimportant business letters that he himself had taken, read out, and answered. Nor was he aware of any reason why he should answer any more questions.

Ruso might have been convinced by the man's claim of ignorance, had he not known that Zosimus had supported Severus's lie about the debt payment being two hundred short. As it was, the only thing of which he could be certain was that Zosimus did not trust him. It was also evident that any power Claudia had once been able to wield had died along with her husband. Zosimus had not hurried out in response to Claudia's repeated ringing of the bell but had eventually strolled down the garden as if he had come of his own accord. It was therefore no surprise when the steward declared that he could not allow Ruso to enter the office or question the household staff.

"I am the widow!" Claudia reminded him, raising her chin. "I insist!"

"And I'm in charge of the staff," said Zosimus with the calm of a man who knows his position is invincible. "A message has been sent to Rome for instructions."

"But the senator doesn't know we've already got somebody here who can look into it, does he? The doctor knows all about murders. He's been involved in dozens of them over in Britannia."

Zosimus's black eyes widened at this dubious endorsement. "Well, he's a suspect in this one."

"So are we all," pointed out Claudia. "And he didn't do it any more than I did, so the sooner it's sorted out, the better. Whoever did it could poison somebody else. Me. You."

"That," said Zosimus, drawing himself up to his meager height, "is a risk I'm prepared to take."

Claudia popped in the last fragment of cake. "He might poison Ennia. Then you'd be sorry."

The steward glared at her. "I came to tell you," he said, "there are guests waiting to offer their condolences."

They made their way back along the gravel pathways, Claudia and Ruso lagging behind like a pair of reluctant schoolchildren.

"When the investigator from Rome gets here," declared Claudia loud enough for Zosimus to hear, "I'm going to complain. If Severus were alive he wouldn't dare treat me like that!"

Ruso stepped closer to her and murmured, "There must be a spare key to that office. How do the staff get in to clean and fill the lamps?"

"They wait for that horrible man to let them in," said Claudia.

Evidently security was not as lax here as in the Petreius household.

31

A LARGE ROOM in the west wing had been set aside for the laying out of the body. Claudia stepped under the cypress boughs hung over the door, nodded to a couple of other women whom Ruso assumed to be neighbors paying respects, and sat down with her hands folded in her lap and her eyes focused on nothing. Opposite her was a disheveled, red-faced creature barely recognizable as Ennia. Between them, propped up against the far wall, surrounded by flickering lamps and looking a great deal calmer than everyone else in the room, was Severus.

Ruso stationed himself next to Ennia. He waited until a suitable amount of wailing had taken place before crouching to repeat his condolences and murmuring, "May I speak with you?"

When she did not seem to have heard, he leaned closer and repeated the question in her ear. Her expression did not change as she said, "You are in league with her. Go away."

He whispered, "I'm not responsible for this, Ennia."

"Then I want to know who is!"

A hand gripped his shoulder as Zosimus breathed in his ear, "You heard the lady. Go."

Ruso got to his feet and left.

As he passed the pond there was a faint "plop." Leaning over, he could make out the silver flash of a fish through the ripples. A cough sounded from the direction of the house. Ruso glanced up to see the steward watching him from the top of the steps.

As if this were not encouragement enough to leave, he now recognized the purposeful stride of his former father-in-law fast approaching along the gravel walkway.

"Probus!"

The man stopped. "Who let you in here?"

Evidently Probus had not mellowed with time.

At the reply, "Claudia," Probus's mouth turned down as if he were refusing a loan to a potential client. "I don't know what for," he said. "She's sent for the investigators, you know."

"I came to see if I could help."

For some reason this seemed to annoy Probus even further. He jerked a thumb over his shoulder toward the gatehouse. "Out!"

"On my way," agreed Ruso, indicating the walking stick. "It's just taking me a bit of time."

"If you're not gone in a minute there'll be men here to help you."

Ruso said, "Sorry to hear about Justinus, by the way," but Probus was already striding toward the west wing, calling, "Claudia? It's all right, I've gotten rid of him."

Ruso paused, leaning on his stick, to watch Probus mount the steps and give Zosimus a perfunctory nod. Then he turned and picked his way along the path toward the gatehouse with a deliberate lack of haste. It was a small and not very satisfying form of rebellion.

He told himself that at least the steward's insistence on waiting for orders would restrain Claudia's urge to call in professional questioners. He supposed that was good news—for the staff, if not for him. As he approached the gate it occurred to him that he should have told somebody that Severus's horse was being tended by the stable lad back at home. He would have to leave a message with the gatekeeper.

The gatekeeper's dog was eyeing his approach with interest when he was surprised by hasty footsteps crashing through gravel and a voice he did not recognize calling, "Sir! Please, Doctor, sir!"

A lanky youth in a grease-spattered tunic appeared from behind the gatehouse, halted, tried to decide what to do with his hands, finally clamped them behind his back, and said, "I'm Flaccus, sir. I used to work in your kitchen."

Ruso stared at him. Claudia had indeed owned a kitchen boy called Flaccus, but not one like this. Claudia's boy was small and cheery. This one had hands and feet that were much too big for him, an anxious face made out of sharp angles, and a sprinkling of acne. Ruso leaned on his stick and decided he was getting old. "I remember you," he said. "How are you getting on here?"

"Very well, sir, thank you." Having gotten that out of the way, the youth took a deep breath. "Cook said I should come and talk to you, sir."

Ruso beckoned him away from the ears of the gatekeeper and the teeth of the dog. Safely behind an ornamental hedge that more or less concealed them from the house, he said, "To do with Severus?"

Flaccus nodded.

"Speak up," he urged, warmed by the thought that the boy still trusted him. "What do you know?"

The boy looked alarmed. "Oh no, sir. I don't know anything. Nobody knows anything. Cook says to ask what's going to happen to us, sir?"

Ruso looked him up and down. Flaccus the little kitchen boy, no longer cheery—and with good reason. By law, all the household slaves who had been under the same roof as a murdered master should be put to death for failing to save him—even if they could not possibly have helped. The emperor Nero, notorious for much else besides, had once called in troops to enforce the execution of four hundred men, women, and children whose only crime was to be owned by a man who had been done away with by one of their comrades. It was a lesson not easily forgotten.

Ruso suspected that the law might not apply when the victim was secretly poisoned off the premises—a crime against which his staff would stand little chance of protecting him—but that was a fine distinction unlikely to comfort a household in fear of their lives. He said, "Flaccus, I want you to think carefully about this. Do you think anyone here was involved in the death of the senator's agent?"

"Absolutely not, sir!"

Of course not. What else could the lad say? "Did you see him on the morning he died?"

Flaccus looked uneasy.

"I need to know exactly what happened to him that morning."

The boy stared down at feet that overhung the ends of his sandals. His shoulders shifted uneasily. "Cook didn't say . . ." His voice trailed into silence.

"Just tell me what you know," urged Ruso, silently cursing Nero and every long-dead member of the Senate who had agreed with him.

"But I don't know anything, sir. I was bringing in the firewood when Master Severus came in."

"Into the kitchen?"

Flaccus nodded. "Please don't go asking them, sir. Cook will kill me."

"Just tell me what he did in the kitchen, and I won't need to." Ruso hoped, for the boy's sake, that this was true.

"He just came for his breakfast. Bread and cheese and an apple." The boy looked up. "There wasn't nothing wrong with it, sir. It was the same as what everybody had."

"Did he usually fetch his own breakfast?"

"People are always in and out of the kitchen, sir. Cook gets fed up with it."

"And did he look well?"

Flaccus, clearly regretting ever admitting to remembering Ruso, said, "He never looked well, sir."

"Who was in the kitchen yesterday morning?"

"Just the staff, sir."

"Nobody unusual?"

"No, sir."

Not wishing to imply a suspicion of the widow, Ruso tried, "How about Claudia or Ennia?"

"Oh, no, sir!" This, apparently, would have been a memorable event. Neither of these two had ever been seen in the kitchen before midmorning.

Ruso frowned. This was not proving as helpful as he had hoped. "You're sure he just had the same food and drink as everyone else?"

"Not the drink, sir. He always has—had his own medicine. The cook mixes him up honey and rosewater. Just that, sir. Nothing that would do no harm."

"And nobody else drinks it?"

Flaccus shook his head. "No, sir. Well—not usually. But after Master Severus died, the steward came down to the kitchen and asked a lot of questions. And he made us all eat the food and share out the rest of the medicine. That's how we knew Severus must have been poisoned. But nobody was ill."

So Zosimus, the responsible steward, had been making inquiries of his own. Personally Ruso would not have risked poisoning the entire staff by sharing everything out, but presumably he had been hoping to force a confession. "Well, it looks as though he's satisfied himself that none of you was involved."

"Yes, sir." Flaccus did not seem particularly cheered by this news. "But when Cook asked him what's going to happen to us he just said we've got to wait for orders from Rome."

"I'm afraid that's true," said Ruso. "Severus didn't die under this roof. That may be a good thing for you, if not for me. But I'm not a lawyer. I don't know what's going to happen to any of us."

Flaccus sniffed. "Yes, sir. Thank you, sir."

"What I do know is that it's not going to be helped by listening to worrying gossip. Now go back to your duties and try to ignore anything you hear, because if none of us knows until we hear from Rome, nothing you're told can be true, can it?"

The boy managed a wan smile. "No, sir."

A sizeable gang of dingily attired visitors was rolling up the drive as Ruso left, presumably on the way to offer condolences to the grieving widow and sister. The gatekeeper's face was impassive as he asserted that he couldn't answer questions without permission from the steward, but his one eye was bright. Ruso suspected these were the most interesting couple of days he had had in a very long time.

32

FUSCUS WOULD NOT want a suspected poisoner visiting potential voters on his behalf, but Ruso called on the pretext of collecting the canvassing list, anyway. The gods alone knew what that message to Rome had contained, especially since Probus had been the one to tell Fuscus the bad news about the murder. He needed to put his own side of the story to the nearest member of the Gabinii as soon as possible.

This time he was left to wait out on one of the benches facing the street. He was not sorry. The ache in his foot was so persistent that he was relieved to lean back against "Vote for Gabinius Fuscus!," stretch both legs out in front of him, and close his eyes.

He was conscious of the warm wall hard against his back. Of the smell of fried eggs and old vegetables. Of the passing slap of sandals and the cackle of an old woman laughing. Of a small voice at the back of his mind that was telling him he was in serious trouble.

The only way to prove to the senator's investigator that he had not poisoned Severus would be to present the real culprit. Despite his bold assurances to Claudia that he had dealt with this sort of thing before, this was a situation unlike anything he had faced in Britannia. His assertion that he knew what he was doing had been little more than wishful thinking. He did not know the proper way to conduct a murder investigation. Indeed, he did not even know if there was a proper way.

Ruso propped the heel of his sore foot on the toes of the whole one and tried to reflect on his experiences in Britannia. There must be some conclusions he could draw; some fruit of his experience that he could bring to this current crisis.

The business of the murdered bar girls in Deva had taught him that no one in authority could be expected to investigate a crime if it were not in his own interests to do so. From the mysterious affair of the antlered god who had caused mayhem on the border, he had learned . . . what had he learned? That the north of Britannia was a dangerous place. That Tilla's idea of loyalty was not the same as his own. And in both cases, that the truth only seemed to emerge after a great deal of unproductive, uncomfortable, and unwilling blundering about. Precisely the sort of blundering about that a man suspected of murder was unlikely to be free to undertake.

He had just reached this unhelpful conclusion when a hoarse voice announced, "You're that doctor!"

He opened his eyes to see the hulking figure of one of Probus's security guards, a retired gladiator whose hefty shoulders and flattened nose served to deter both burglars and clients seeking loans without collateral.

"Remember me?"

Ruso straightened his back, put both feet on the ground, and prepared to fend off whatever trouble the man had been sent to make. "You work for Probus."

"You come to the house courting Miss Claudia."

"So I did," agreed Ruso, although it was hard now to remember why. All the signs had been there from the beginning.

"I thought you might want to know, sir, my lad's done well for himself. He's in Municipal Water Distribution."

Ruso gave a smile that acknowledged the man's obvious pride, wondered which lad they were talking about, and said he was delighted to hear it.

"Not a scrap of bother with the leg, sir. Not even a limp."

Something stirred in the recesses of Ruso's memory. "Broken femur, wasn't it?"

The mangled face split into a grin. "That's the one. Only eight years old, he was. You done a lovely job, sir."

The father's delight was clear, as was his gratitude, and Ruso felt his spirits lift. It was good to be reminded of a time when he had done something right.

"I'm glad to see you after all these years, sir," continued the man. The bench swayed as he seated himself next to Ruso. "I reckon I owe you a favor." The reason for the unexpected familiarity became clear when he leaned closer and murmured, "If you don't mind me saying, sir, there's something you ought to know. But you won't have to let on who told you."

"I won't," Ruso promised, his spirits rising even further. He was not alone in the battle to clear his name. There were people here who remembered him. People who were willing to help. He had come home.

"About your sister."

Ruso's optimism collapsed. If rumors were circulating about Severus's designs on Flora, it could reflect badly on her no matter how innocent she might be. He would have to find a way to defend Flora's reputation as well as his own.

What the guard proceeded to tell him, however, was completely unexpected. It had nothing to do with Flora. It was that Marcia had recently approached Probus in the hope of borrowing against her forthcoming dowry.

"What? Are you absolutely sure?"

The man did not know how much Marcia had sought, but according to what he had overheard, she had already consulted several financiers. Probus had refused her request, as presumably had all the others.

"Good," said Ruso, wondering why nobody else had had the decency to warn the family. "I appreciate you telling me."

"Right you are, sir." The man got to his feet. "It weren't me what told you, though. I don't want no trouble."

"Of course not," Ruso agreed. And then, with foreboding, "I'll talk to her."

"Ruso!" There was no embrace this time. Fuscus remained seated. He reached for a grape, frowned at it, and tossed it aside. "I thought you'd be here before now."

"I was."

"Really? They didn't tell me. What's all this about you poisoning my relative?"

"I didn't." Ruso offered condolences on the death of Severus and briefly wondered why Fuscus was not over at the estate paying his respects. Presumably he had more important things to do. "Severus was taken ill at my house," he explained. "I did what I could for him, but it was pretty hopeless without knowing what he'd taken."

Fuscus sighed and closed his eyes. "A great tragedy. A terrible loss to our family. A man in the prime of life. Whoever did this deserves the worst possible punishment. It's a shame we won't have time for a trial before the Games. We could have had the murderer fed to the beasts. Very slowly."

"They've had other doctors look at the body," said Ruso, "but I don't think they've come up with much. His widow and his sister have asked me to try and track down whoever did it." It was almost true. Just after she had told him to go away, Ennia had said she wanted to know who was responsible for her brother's death.

Fuscus opened his eyes. "Last time you were in here asking about a ship. No wonder you don't know much about poisons if you waste all your time poking about with things that don't concern you."

"If I don't concern myself with this, people will think it was me."

Fuscus's hand paused in midair. "Probus told me it was you."

"And what do you think?"

There was a pause while Fuscus popped another grape into his mouth and said around it, "I'm reserving judgment. Until we get instructions from my cousin the senator."

"Do you still want me to talk to the veterans?"

"What?" Fuscus spat out the pips. "Of course not. Stay away from them. Don't even mention my name. I'll get my publicity men to paint the signs out and we'll find somebody else."

Signs? "But I didn't do it."

"In fact, stay out of town altogether. It looks bad."

"I had no reason to kill Severus," insisted Ruso. "You know that. You were going to persuade him not to bankrupt me."

Fuscus shifted in his chair. "I don't think you understood me there, Ruso. I said I'd do my best to support you, but if you remember, I also said my hands were tied." He shook his head. "A man in my position can't be seen to be influencing the course of the law. Not even for the son of a dear old friend. We're dealing with principles. Principles are what raise us above the barbarians."

"What if I told you Severus and I were about to do a deal and he was going to abandon the seizure order, so I'd have been crazy to murder him?"

Fuscus's eyes widened. "Why didn't you say so? If there's a witnessed and sealed agreement—"

"There wasn't time."

"Pity," said Fuscus in a tone that implied he did not believe a word of it. "You'll just have to explain it all to my cousin the senator's man. Assuming he sends one. If not I may have my own men carry out an investigation."

"I'm intending to get it sorted out before then."

"Forget it, Ruso. It doesn't matter what the widow and the sister want. The investigation has to be independent. None of the suspects must be involved. Understand?"

"Oh, yes," agreed Ruso, backing toward the door to terminate this waste of time. "Perfectly."

Fuscus gestured to dismiss him as if he were brushing away a fly. "Stay out of it, Ruso. Go home, tend your farm, look after those sisters of yours, and stay where the investigator can find you when he comes for a chat."

33

STAYING AT HOME waiting to be accused of murder was the last thing Ruso intended to do. He needed to find out what poison had been used.

Moments later he was appalled to find himself facing an exhortation from G. Petreius Ruso, veteran of the XX Victoria Victrix, urging the voters of Nemausus to support Gabinius Fuscus.

Fuscus's publicity man had been busy with his paintbrush overnight. In the next four streets Ruso saw his own name three times. He was relieved to turn left into a narrow entrance where the walls were too grimy for election slogans and the mingled scents fell over him like a curtain: spice and vinegar and mint and roses and old wine. The street ahead widened into an area where the surrounding tall apartments trapped the babble of conversation and radiated the afternoon heat. The area was lined with the stalls of herbalists and drug sellers. This was the place to find out about poisons.

The first stall had attracted a couple of women who were trying out cosmetics on the backs of their hands. Marveling at the patience of shopkeepers hoping for a sale, Ruso found himself drawn into a crowd that had formed outside a booth next door. A half-naked man lay on a table under the shade having something green and glutinous plastered on his chest by a leather-aproned physician.

One of the onlookers glanced down at Ruso's stick and the toes poking out of his dusty bandage. "You'll have to wait," she said, putting her arm around a thin child whose tunic was so big that he looked as though he had shrunk in the wash. "We're next."

"And then it's me," put in another voice, followed by a fit of coughing that did not sound as though it would have a happy ending.

Ruso nodded and moved on. There was nothing to be learned here beyond what he already knew: that if he survived to set up a practice in town, he would be facing stiff competition.

A wooden sign reading "No money, no medicine. No exceptions" was nailed to the next stall. The welcome was similarly unfriendly, the buxom stallholder asserting that she didn't sell poisons to people who didn't know what they wanted. No, not even people claiming to be doctors. Rats, eh? If it was really for rats, why hadn't he said that in the first place?

It was an admirable moral stance, but Ruso wondered how she managed to sell anything at all.

His next choice was hung with limp greenery drying in the sun and stacked with little lime wood boxes and stoppered animal horns full of powders and creams. The trader welcomed him like an old friend. Ruso understood why when the man tried to persuade him that he wanted to buy frankincense.

"Guaranteed pure, sir," the man added, handing over the box for examination. "Top quality. All the way from Arabia. Male, second harvest. Only the best."

The man watched as Ruso held the pale lump of resin up to the light, rolled it between his fingers, and sniffed.

"It's very expensive."

"I'm not saying you won't see it cheaper elsewhere, sir," the man agreed, "but you'd be wasting your money." He leaned forward as if he was confiding a great secret. "You wouldn't want to know what some of this lot around here put in theirs."

"I'll bear that in mind," promised Ruso. He closed the lid and handed the box back. "What I'm really interested in—" He was interrupted by a scream from farther down the street. He turned, grasping the other end of his stick. A man who could not run was not much use in chasing a bag snatcher, but if the culprit came this way . . . To his surprise, the scream was followed by cheering and applause.

"The Marsi are in town," the man explained.

"The Marsi?" This was good news.

"If it was up to me, I wouldn't let 'em through the gates," grumbled the man. "It's dangerous, bringing snakes into a place like this. One of these days someone's going to get bitten. Then we'll see what their cures are like. What was it you wanted?"

"It doesn't matter."

"Let me do you a deal on that frankincense, sir. I wouldn't want you to be going home with some of the rubbish they sell down the road."

"Thanks, I'll think about it," said Ruso, giving the man a smile that they both knew was no compensation for a lost sale.

Shoppers had begun to desert the stalls around him and drift toward the new crowd that was gathering. The women from the cosmetics counter tottered past, craning to see what the fuss was, clutching their baskets with pink-and-black-streaked hands.

Ruso could not move fast enough to get to the front, but the mountain man's shrill voice above the notes of the flute made it clear that the townsfolk were seeing the power of magic over the deadliest of snakes. The effect on the onlookers was conveyed by their gasps and exclamations of, "Oh, look!"

Beside Ruso, a father lifted his small daughter onto his shoulders to get a better view. "Can you see the snake?" he demanded, unable to see it himself. "What's it doing?"

"Snake!" cried the child, pointing and wriggling. "Snake!"

Ruso leaned back against the shutters of a shop selling perfumed oils and bags of fresh lavender and rose petals. He had seen too many deadly snakes in Africa to want to watch one being provoked, magic or no magic. He hoped the performance was not going to go on too long. His foot was aching. His stomach was reminding him that it had been a long time since breakfast. But he needed to talk to the Marsi.

By the time the Italian mountain men had finished their show and sold snake products to the eager crowd, several of the stallholders had begun to pack up for the day. The shoppers drifted away, headed for home or the baths, several pausing to slake their thirst in the shade of the nearest snack bar. The two Marsi, their skin already tanned to leather and their eyes as dark as those of the unblinking snake still draped around the older man, seemed not to notice the heat. The younger one was stacking boxes that could have contained the performers or the remedies that were made from them. The older man looked up, lifted a fat coil of reptile from his shoulder, and gave Ruso a gap-toothed grin before asking in a rough country Latin how he had enjoyed the show.

Ruso, unable to identify the species of snake, stepped forward to just outside striking distance. When he introduced himself as a Medicus, the man's smile widened.

"Medicus, eh? We got what you want!" The man gestured to his son to bring one of the boxes across. "A live helper of Aesculapius!"

Ignoring Ruso's protests, he lifted the lid from the top of the box to reveal a set of dark coils with no discernable markings. "You've heard the stories. Get your hands on the real thing."

"I'd rather not," said Ruso.

"Take a look. He don't bite." The man slid one skeletal hand into the box by way of encouragement.

"I think some of my patients would be frightened off."

The man chuckled and tied the lid back over the snake. "So, what else can we do for you?" He lifted one of the pots stacked beside him on the pavement. "Snakeskins boiled in wine, good for earache and toothache." He placed it in front of Ruso and reached back for another pot. "Roast viper salts," he announced, showing the pot to the snake before placing it beside the other. "Recommended by Dioscorides himself. Sharpens the eyes, releases tight tendons, reduces swollen glands."

Ruso bought a pot of the boiled skins, hoping they would not only cure earache but loosen the man's tongue. "Perhaps you could help me with something else," he said.

"Perhaps," agreed the man. "Who knows?"

The younger man had paused to listen.

"I had a difficult patient the other day. Confusion, aggression, odd feelings around the mouth, vomiting, diarrhea, loss of vision—"

"What happened to him?" demanded the younger man, stepping forward.

"He died."

"And you want my father to tell you what it was?"

"What can you suggest?"

"What I suggest," said the youth, "is that you take your skins and clear off. We're honest traders. We got nothing to do with that sort of thing."

"I didn't mean to imply—"

"That the Marsi know all about poisons? So why did you ask?"

"Stop!" The older man's hand rose to silence his son. "The Medicus didn't mean no harm. He's here to learn. He reckons his patient got bit by a venomous beast."

"Exactly," said Ruso, although Severus had denied being bitten and he had found no trace of a puncture on the body.

The youth glowered at him and said nothing.

The old man's smile was not as broad this time. "We can't help," he said. "We don't know no snakes what give them symptoms."

"Perhaps it wasn't a snake," said Ruso. "Do you know anyone I could ask?"

"No, we don't."

"I'd pay."

"And I'd take your money," said the man, "but I still wouldn't know nobody."

Ruso sighed. He was not going to argue with someone wearing a large and unidentifiable snake, even though he was certain that the man was lying. At the moment, he couldn't run fast enough.

34

GALLA WAS OVER in the shade of the stone barn, eating with the other farmworkers. Tilla had followed her across as soon as the horn was blown, picked up a wooden platter from the pile, and joined the line for bread and the strange stuff these people thought was cheese. Then she had turned to find there was no obvious place to sit. Galla, her sticky feet now dark with the dust of the barn floor, was already sharing a rough bench with the stable lad. They were too busy chatting to notice Tilla. She recognized the odd word of Gaulish, but they were speaking fast and she could not pick out the meaning. The other workers, some asleep, were sprawled across all the available space in the shade. One or two of the men were staring at her with more interest than was necessary, but no one offered to move. No one smiled and said, "Come and eat with us!" Nobody showed any concern when she wandered away.

Safely alone in the quiet of the winery, she laid the platter on the corner of the juice trough, settled down beside it, and tried to tell herself she was not miserable.

She could not expect to fit in here. She was not a servant. It was obvious that the staff knew that, even if Arria refused to understand it. She was not a member of the family. She was not the Medicus's wife. She was neither a Gaul, like the farmworkers, nor a Roman like the Medicus. She was not a Gaul pretending to be a Roman, either, which was what most of the people in the town seemed to be. In every imaginable way, she was an outsider here.

She supposed the only barbarians these people had come across were either slaves or the naked figures she had seen carved on some of the funeral monuments lining the road out of town. Warriors with wild hair and long mustaches being beaten down and trampled under the march of Roman progress. Perhaps the sight of a free Briton wandering about the place made them nervous.

She took a mouthful of bread and eyed the unappetizing green slop in the trough beside her. It had never struck her until now that the Medicus, who had been so rude about British beer, preferred a drink in which strangers had trampled their sweaty feet.

She wondered what he was doing. What he had said to the old wife. Whether he was still with her now. It occurred to Tilla that she did not know a great deal about the old wife, except that she was the one who had left and demanded a divorce. The Medicus had never seemed to want to talk about her. He had not wanted to mention the widow next door again, either, until she had asked.

She tried to cut a slice of the cheese. It stuck to the knife. How could these people be so pleased with themselves? They could not even make cheese!

She was wiping the blade with one finger when she heard movement outside the doors. Whoever it was, they must not see her alone in here feeling sorry for herself. Licking the finger, she hid behind a stack of the big two-handled baskets the men had been using this morning to carry in the grapes. She slipped her knife silently back into its sheath. She would not give them cause to say that barbarians hid in corners clutching weapons, waiting to pounce.

By the time she peered around the back of the stack and realized the visitor was the Medicus, the scrape and bang of the great door closing out the sunshine drowned the sound of her greeting.

A man who was shutting himself into a farm building in the dark was likely to want to be alone. Therefore a person who found herself hiding barely four feet away from him should immediately call out to warn him of her presence. But before she could speak, the Medicus had hurled his stick to the floor. He raised both fists and pounded the air, filling the building with a prolonged roar of something that sounded like, "Aaaargh!"

Perhaps this was not the time to reveal herself.

"Aaaargh!" bellowed the Medicus again. "Holy gods almighty! Jupiter's bollocks! Give me strength!"

This unusual prayer ended with the slamming of a fist into the nearest suitable object. Tilla could not hold in the shriek as the stack of baskets landed on her and knocked her backward against the wall.

For a moment he glared down at her as if she were a rat he had just caught trying to steal his dinner. Then, without speaking, he grabbed her arm and pulled her up.

She stood rubbing the bruise on the back of her head while he limped across to haul the door open. When he returned he said, "What are you doing in here?"

"Is your foot hurting?"

"Never mind my foot. What are you doing in here?"

"You should sit down and rest. It is making you cross again."

"I'm not angry because of my foot, Tilla! I'm angry because of everything else!" He bent to retrieve the stack of baskets. "I'm angry because—" The baskets creaked and complained as he flung them back into the corner. "Never mind. It's too complicated."

The Medicus was not the most patient of men, but she had never seen him quite this exasperated before. She was not sure what to do to calm him. "I have bread," she tried, pointing across to the platter still propped on the corner of the trough. "And cheese. The cheese is not set and it smells bad, but you can share if you want."

"Not now. I have things to do." He reached down for the walking stick, but she was faster.

With the stick behind her back, she said, "If you go now, you will do the things badly."

"I haven't got time to play games." He held out his hand. "Give it to me."

Instead she took the outstretched hand in her own. "Sit and eat this strange cheese, my lord."

He let out a huff of exasperation, glared at her, then gave in and let her lead him across to where they could sit side by side with their backs against the trough. When he had stretched out his legs between the broad shoulders of the two nearest jars buried in the floor, she handed him a chunk of bread.

He said, "D'you know, you're the only person who's offered me anything to eat since breakfast?"

"Did you see her?"

"Remind me why I thought it was a good idea to come home."

"She is not your wife now. You do not have to listen."

"It's not Claudia," he said. "It's all the others."

She held out the platter so he could pull off a blob of cheese. "Tell me about the others."

As far as she could understand, a difficult meeting with the old wife had been followed by a useless trip to town where he had been kept waiting for hours, practically accused of murder, heard alarming rumors about his sister, and found his name was "slapped up all over the bloody walls."

No wonder he was upset. Clearly gossip traveled just as fast here as at home. "You should write something back!" she said. "It is not your fault that man died."

"The writing's got nothing to do with Severus," he said, adding "at least, not yet. But if I don't find out who really poisoned him, they'll soon think of something worse to put up there. It's because of the election."

She said, "The what?" but he had moved on to complain that he had barely closed the gate on his return when he heard Marcia and Flora shrieking at him from their bedroom window that Arria had locked them in and was trying to starve them and he must get them out right now.

Inside the painted entrance hall he had found Cass and a gaggle of small loud people begging him to make Arria let Galla back into the house to look after them. When he tracked down Arria she would not talk about any of these things unless he would agree to a new date to have dinner with the widow next door. Then he escaped to the yard and found the farm slaves pleased to see him because the brother had gone out somewhere, and they wanted someone to tell him it was all wrong to have women treading the grapes.

"Actually . . ." He paused, as if he had only just noticed, "Why are you in here? You haven't really been treading grapes, have you? You don't have to listen to Arria."

"I am here because Galla is made to work in here," she explained. "And it is not fair. You must tell your stepmother."

"Ah." The Medicus closed his eyes. Then he laced his fingers together and placed them behind his head. "I think," he said slowly, "I am becoming a god."

She frowned. "It is the wine in the air." Or perhaps the smell of the cheese.

"The last reported words of the emperor Vespasian."

She wiped up the last smear of the cheese with the final crust of bread and waited for him to explain.

He said, "Do you know what emperors do, Tilla?"

That was easy. "Send soldiers to steal the land and make us pay taxes."

"They spend half their waking hours listening to people who want things. As, it seems, do gods. Maybe it wasn't as much of a transition as everyone thought."

"They all want you to be a god who comes home across the sea and mends everything."

"Apparently, though none of them invited me. How d'you think I'm doing so far?"

"Terrible. Now I have seen what peace is like, I understand why you come to Britannia."

"I wish we'd never left."

"You do not have to worry about that man," she said, reaching forward to pick a flake of bread crust from the front of his tunic. "I can tell you who poisoned him. It is the father of your old wife."

He opened his eyes. "Probus? What do you know about Probus?"

"He paid for the ship on which Cass's brother was drowned."

"But why would that make him want to poison Severus? I mean, any more than anybody else would?"

She explained what the fish sellers had said about the ship when they thought there was nobody around to hear them.

The Medicus listened carefully, then said, "I can't see Probus handing over money to a man who knew nothing about choosing a vessel, even if he was his son-in-law."

"But—"

"I'll look into it, but I'd imagine Severus only borrowed the money. If the ship sank, he'd have had to pay it back."

"Perhaps he was killed because Probus was angry at losing his servant Justinus."

The Medicus did not look convinced.

"Or perhaps because he did not pay the money back."

The Medicus shook his head. "Respectable bankers don't go around murdering people who owe them money, Tilla. It's bad for trade."

"Not even to remind the others to pay?"

The Medicus eyed her as if he was not sure where she had heard of such a thing. She said, "I understand about borrowing. I am not a stupid barbarian like you think."

"I've never thought you were stupid."

She noticed he did not say anything about her not being a barbarian.

"Probus isn't like the Gabinii," he said. "He doesn't own enough muscle to make trouble, and he doesn't have huge sums of money stashed away. He has to take in cash so he can lend it out. Nobody's going to trust their savings to a violent man."

This was something she had not considered.

"In fact, if Severus was fool enough to send Cass's brother to sea in a leaky old bucket, Cass had more reason to want him dead than . . ." His voice trailed off into silence.

"She did not know about the ship being bad."

"But she was there."

"Where?"

"She was around when Severus came to visit. She knew what he was threatening to do to the family. She gave him the drink."

This was not what Tilla had intended. It was hard to believe that such a fond mother could be a secret poisoner. On the other hand, how far would a woman go to protect her children? Tilla did not want to think about it. She folded her arms. "If you are sure it is not that Probus man, then I think you should be very careful," she said. "It could be your old wife."

"Claudia? Never."

"How do you know?"

"She's not that sort of person."

"Nobody is that sort of person all the time. Her husband is a bad man. We know he steals money from your family and he is no good at choosing a ship, and she has to live with this man every day. You think yours is the only little sister he tries to sleep with?"

"That's a reason for divorcing him," he said. "Not murdering him."

It was always hard work making the Medicus look at something he was trying to avoid. "If a wife wants to keep the husband's money but not the husband," she explained, "he must be dead. Not divorced."

Again, he looked askance at her, as if he was wondering how she had thought of something like that. "But he didn't have any money," he said. "He didn't own any of the property on the estate and after the ship sank he must have owed a huge amount to Probus."

That was something she had not thought of. She said, "Did you tell her what he said at the end?"

"Yes."

"So now you can tell me. Perhaps I can help."

She heard him take in a breath. "It's awkward."

Tilla wound a strand of hair around her forefinger. The little he had told her about the old wife had suggested he was relieved to be rid of her, but the business between men and women was always complicated and there was no way of knowing whether he had told the whole story.

Nobody here had known that the Medicus had a British woman until she had arrived. Everyone here thought he was single. Claudia, when she found out her second husband was much worse than the first one, could have sent that letter herself, waited until she had the Medicus back in Gaul, and then murdered her husband. Now the Medicus was stupid enough to defend her. It all fit together, and it made a shape Tilla did not like.

She slid the finger out and let the hair unravel into a ringlet. The shape in her mind twisted into something worse.

"If a woman poisons her husband," she said, "she must pretend that it was not her who did it. So she might wait until he is on the way to see someone else, and give him something that will not kill him until he gets there."

"Claudia wouldn't do that to me," he said.

The words hung in the heavy air of the winery.

"She wouldn't," he insisted.

The Medicus was stubborn. The old wife was an untried enemy. Trying to argue him back into his senses might well do the opposite. She said, "I am sorry you do not trust me."

"It's not that I don't trust you, Tilla, it's just . . . Look, if I tell you, you must promise not to repeat it."

"Yes."

"He was obviously confused at the end. He didn't know what he was saying."

"Yes."

"So when he said, *The bitch has poisoned me*, it can't have meant what everyone will think."

Tilla took a long slow breath.

He said, "Well, you did ask."

"This is the last thing he wants to say to the world, but the old wife tells you he is lying, so you are trying to find somebody else to blame."

"I'm trying to find out the truth."

"But you already know!"

When he did not reply, Tilla said, "Perhaps you should try and think inside your head, even if she is my old wife, should I believe everything she is saying to me?"

"I'm the only one who can help her, Tilla."

"The senator will send a man from Rome to ask questions. Then we will see whether you should help her or not."

The Medicus got to his feet. "Next time," he said, brushing the dust off the back of his tunic, "I'll lie to you. Will that make you happy?"

Next time I'll lie to you? Tilla stared at the froth winking at the mouth of one of the great jars. All the things she wanted to say tumbled over each other in her mind and ended up in a soggy tangle that came out as, "No."

She wished she had not come to this place. Nothing had gone right from the moment they had arrived at the farm. Now she felt as if some sort of unsuspected hollow had opened up underneath her. As if he had been watching her all along, comparing her with the old wife and the widow next door as a man would compare horses for a race. If she pushed him too far, he would lie to her. He had just told her so.

She put the platter aside and stood up. Keeping her voice as bright as she could manage, she said, "I will find out from Galla which fish seller knows about the ship."

"In the meantime, tell her from me to keep it quiet."

"Yes. Can she go back to the house now?"

"I don't know why she isn't in the house," he said. "What's this fuss about taking the girls to town?"

She explained. "She is here because a servant cannot do two different orders from two different people. The mother wants her to tell what she knows about the daughters, but the daughters order her to be silent. It is not her fault." She would have repeated, "It is not fair," but now she must remember to be careful not to annoy him.

"I'll straighten it out with Arria."

There were footsteps in the yard outside. A shadow fell across the rows of jars. Tilla said, "You can talk to Galla. She is here."

Galla drew back, alarmed.

Tilla beckoned her in. "The master is going to say you can go back to work in the house."

"Not yet." The Medicus was reaching for his stick. "I'll talk to Arria."

"But you are head of the family!" She stopped. Would he go back and tell the old wife about the awkward Briton who was always arguing with him? "They must do what you say," she suggested.

"I know," he agreed. "But then she'll be having two different orders from two different people again, won't she? You have to do things in the right order with servants, Tilla."

"Yes," she said, hitching her tunic up over her belt. She dipped her feet in the bucket to rinse them. Then she climbed back into the treading trough and, before she could stop herself, said, "I can see that telling people what to do all day is very hard work."

35

THE PUNGENT MIXTURE of burned walnut husks and vinegar that the bath boy was dutifully plastering across the top of Lucius's head was unlikely to cure his bald patch, but it would not help to point that out. Instead Ruso leaned back against the side of the warm bath, let his injured foot float to the surface, and observed, "I hear Tilla spent the day in the winery."

"I put them in there out of the way."

Ruso said, "Someone needs to talk to Arria."

"I know."

"Do you think Cass would do it?"

"No." Lucius reached for the wine flagon. He took a long swig and clapped it back on the tiles. Ruso retrieved it. He was ignoring Valens's advice to avoid wine and, besides, if he did not intervene soon, Lucius would have consumed the whole lot by himself.

Ruso said, "Claudia's hair has turned orange."

Lucius's eyes widened. "I'm surprised they let you in over there."

"Probus turned up just as I was leaving. As friendly as ever."

A dark drip separated itself from Lucius's hairline and began to slide down his temple. "Miserable old bugger. The last time I saw him was when he came over here to tell Cass that Justinus had drowned."

Ruso mused, "I liked Justinus."

"It's knocked her sideways. She only had one relative."

In the silence that followed, Ruso could hear something dripping. He gazed across at the crack in the plaster that ran all the way down from the window, crossed a blue fish and a mermaid's arm, and was going to cause a leak in the bath one day. He wondered if Lucius too was imagining the simplicity of having only one relative.

"She was all for having some sort of tomb put up to start with," said Lucius. "Heaven knows what it would cost, but apparently that's what you do when you haven't got the body. I was just coming around to it and now she's changed her mind. Blowed if I know what to do with her."

At last the bath boy finished pottering about and went out to see to the fire.

As soon as the door closed, Ruso said, "His household knows he was poisoned. Claudia's father has told Fuscus that I did it."

"Oh, marvelous. I knew this would happen."

"It could be worse. They've sent for instructions from the senator. We'll have at least two or three weeks to find out what really happened before somebody from Rome gets here."

Lucius smeared the drip of hair lotion across his cheek. "So it's *we* now, is it?" he said. "How do you suggest *we* go about it, exactly?"

Ruso took a swig from the flagon. "When I was in Britannia—"

"You aren't in Britannia now. You can't just get the army to go around burning people's houses down till somebody confesses."

"Claudia was talking about getting professional questioners in—speaking of which, is that one of your offspring being tortured out in the garden?"

Lucius listened for a moment, then said, "Cass will sort it out. Who's going to pay for the questioners?"

"Nobody. I've asked her to wait."

"Right," said Lucius. "I'm sure that'll make a big difference."

Ruso closed his eyes, took a deep breath, and slid down to the privacy of the bottom of the bath.

Forty-five, forty-six . . . He shot up, gasping in air and releasing the illogical panic clutching at his chest. When he had wiped the water out of his eyes and his breathing had settled down, the thought that had flashed and faded in his mind while he was counting returned. "Who, how, and why?"

"What?"

"The things we need to find out about the poisoning. Who did it, how, and why."

"I'm a simple farmer," pointed out Lucius. "And nobody trusts doctors. So how are we going to do that, who would tell us anything, and why would they want to?"

"It's like geometry," Ruso persisted, ignoring him. "Find two angles of a triangle and it doesn't matter if you don't know the third one. You can work it out."

Lucius eyed him for a moment, then reached for the wine. "If you're going to try saving the family with geometry," he said, "I need another drink."

"I haven't got very far with how," Ruso admitted. "I don't know what the poison was, and Claudia says none of the other doctors who looked at him could agree, either."

"Well I never," said Lucius, shaking the flagon and trying to peer inside it. "Doctors who don't agree."

"Who, then? It must be somebody on the senator's estate or somebody here." As an afterthought he added, "Or somebody he met on the way over."

Lucius tipped up the flagon to drain the last few drops. "Well done, Gaius. You've really narrowed it down there."

Fighting an urge to shove his brother's head under the water, Ruso said, "It's not that bad. Obviously not everybody Severus came into contact with would want to kill him."

"Oh, I don't know," said Lucius sliding down until he could lay his head back on the edge of the bath with his eyes closed. "You met him, what did you think?"

Ruso paused for a moment. "It doesn't sound as though Cass is out there."

"Somebody will be."

"We've got to think logically. The likely suspects are . . ." Ruso began to count on his fingers.

"You'll need to use your toes as well," said Lucius. "And mine."

"We'll start with the estate staff."

"Dozens of them, and I bet nobody liked him."

"Number one is the staff, collectively," said Ruso. "Taking numbers two and three together for a minute—Claudia and the sister. They won't have read the will yet because of the murder, but they're bound to inherit whatever he had to leave."

"Sisters don't murder brothers to get hold of their money. They just nag them till they hand it over."

"Actually I don't think he had enough to make it worth the bother," Ruso conceded. "Even the servants nearly all belonged to the senator, which is why Claudia's now being elbowed aside by the steward. And she wasn't a happy wife, but she didn't need to kill him to escape. She could have divorced him."

"It's not that easy," muttered Lucius.

"It is for Claudia," said Ruso. "The sister, Ennia. Claudia says she and Severus argued a lot."

"It's not her, Gaius. You saw her with the body."

Remembering the sight, Ruso said, "She was about to kiss him on the lips before I stopped her. You wouldn't do that if you'd poisoned somebody. Fourth, there are his business enemies, but unless someone intercepted him on the way over or bribed one of the servants, it's hard to see how they would have done it."

"If we start poking around, they'll be our enemies too."

"Claudia's going to see what she can find out from her father."

"Why is Claudia being nice to us?"

"Because I was a better husband than Severus," said Ruso, prouder of the speed with which he had dreamed up this answer than he was of the way he had really obtained Claudia's cooperation.

"She won't get much out of Probus if he finds out you're behind it. I still think she did it."

"Then there are the people here. Number five, we can count our stable lad out, even if he didn't approve of Severus's treatment of his horse. Six, our kitchen boy drew the water but wouldn't have a reason to murder him. I know I didn't do it, so number seven is . . ."

Lucius sat up so quickly that the water slopped over and landed with a splat on the floor tiles. "Cass has got nothing to do with it."

"I'm sure I'll be able to rub her off the list as soon as I've spoken to her."

"Thanks. Very gracious."

Ruso cleared his throat. "Tilla thought we ought to take a look at Probus," he said, not adding that Tilla too now suspected Claudia.

"So *we* includes your girlfriend as well? Why don't you invite the bath boy in to give his opinion?"

Ruso was determined not to be distracted. "She's picked up some gossip about Severus borrowing a lot of money from him to finance the ship that sank."

"Then Probus wouldn't poison him, would he? He'd want him alive to pay it back. Face it, Gaius. It's obvious. Claudia did it."

Ruso's mind was turning over a question that had not occurred to him before. "Why was Justinus on the ship in the first place?"

"Or maybe it was your girl who did it. Perhaps she fed him some wild barbarian potion, trying to do you a favor."

"Tilla was in town. You haven't answered the question. Why was Justinus on the ship?"

Lucius rubbed one ear and wiped a black smear of hair lotion across his cheek. "To keep an eye on the business, I suppose."

"But why—"

"Holy gods, Gaius! The man's dead: It doesn't matter! Stick to the point. Do you realize that if *we* don't find out who poisoned the senator's agent, *you'll* be the one on trial in the Forum for murder?"

Ruso closed his eyes and prayed for patience. "Then perhaps," he said, "since you can see all the problems so clearly, you might try thinking what you can do to help, instead of knocking aside everything I'm trying to suggest."

Lucius's hand slapped onto the surface, splattering them both with water. "I tried to help! I warned you not to drag the family into a murder case, but you wouldn't listen to me!" He shoved himself away from the side of the bath. His voice echoed from the domed ceiling. "I had all this debt business under control too, but no, you had to interfere! You've never listened to me. Even when we were children. You were always right!"

"I was older!"

"You still think I can't manage without you!"

"I've never said that."

"You didn't have to! Poor old Lucius, can't do without his big brother. You think this is all my fault and you're going to sort it out, don't you?"

"It is your fault! If you'd just stopped to get a receipt from Severus we'd never have been in this mess!"

"There never was a letter, was there? Admit it, Gaius!"

"Of course there was! Ask Tilla."

"What does she know? She can't even read!"

The boom of their voices collided over the splashing as Lucius grabbed his brother and yelled into his face, "You just came home to check up on me!"

"No I didn't!"

It was a stupid, childish fight that turned into something worse. The kicking and splashing and grabbing and grunting and yelling, "Get off!"

and "Admit it!" and "No!" and "You made it up! Admit it!" and "No!" turning into heavy punches and pain.

Lucius, shorter but heavier, had Ruso's face within an inch of the surface, yelling, "No I didn't!" when Ruso suddenly felt him slacken his grip. He became aware of another voice. A smaller, higher voice, calling, "Papa! Uncle Gaius!"

Ruso released his hold on Lucius's throat.

"Polla!" exclaimed Lucius as the brothers hastily pushed apart.

"Papa, stop fighting," ordered Polla in the brisk tone she used with her younger brothers. "Little Lucius is up the pergola and he can't get down and Publius is shaking it."

A smaller figure appeared from behind her skirt and cried, "Aah!"

Lucius wiped the thin strands of badly rinsed hair out of his eyes. "Where's your mother?"

"She's busy. Papa, your nose is bleeding."

"Aah!"

"Tell Publius I said to stop," said Lucius, wiping his upper lip and then glancing at his fingers before washing them in the bathwater. "Then go and call Galla to put them to bed."

"Galla isn't allowed to look after us."

Ruso tucked a guiltily bloodstained fist behind his back and offered, "Ask Tilla."

Polla shook her head. "I don't know where she is. The laundry girl is there but the boys don't take any notice of her. Papa, why is there black stuff on your head?"

Lucius uttered a word not commonly used in the presence of children and rose from the bath. "Tell them I'm coming." He swore again when he realized the towels had been on the floor when the water slopped over the side. He wiped his head with a sodden towel, then flung it aside and strode naked toward the door, muttering, "I can't stand much more of this. Where the hell is she now? What's the matter with this family?"

36

RUSO STRETCHED OUT on his bed, closed his eyes, and savored these few moments of privacy. One of the things he had forgotten about family life was that a man could never be alone. Of course he was rarely alone in the army, either, but there he frequently found himself in the company of men who were not expected to speak to him unless spoken to, so that despite their presence he could occupy himself with his own thoughts. In a household—at least, one as ill-disciplined as this—anyone felt free to accost and interrupt him at any time. Even the study was not safe now that he knew Arria had her own key. It was a sorry state of affairs when a man had to hide in his own bedroom on a warm evening with the shutters closed and a stick wedged in the door latch just to get some peace and quiet.

He had spoken firmly with Arria, agreed that his sisters deserved to be confined to their room until morning, and insisted that Galla must be allowed back into the house. He had also reminded her that Tilla was not a servant and would be dining with the family this evening. He had then gone down to the winery to convey this message, only to find both Tilla and Galla already eating at the long table set up in the yard for the farm slaves and sharing a joke with Cass, who was busy supervising the feeding of the staff while her children ran wild in the care of the laundry maid.

No, Tilla assured him as he drew her aside, she did not do these things just to embarrass him. Why was she sitting outside the bunkhouse eating stew? "Because I am hungry after all that work."

"But you're supposed to be dining with the family!"

"You said that last night, but then that man is dead and the stepmother says there is no dinner."

Ruso stared at her. "She meant the dinner with the neighbor was canceled. I know there was a lot of rushing about, but there was food in the kitchen."

Tilla shrugged. "Nobody tells me."

He said, "Why didn't you ask?"

"She says there is no dinner, why bother to ask?"

"Of course there was food, Tilla. You're a guest. You should expect to be fed. It's bad enough dealing with my family without you being deliberately obtuse."

"Being what?"

"Never mind. Finish your dinner here. And don't do this again tomorrow."

"Galla has invited me to meet her family tomorrow evening."

Before he could object, she added, "Cass has said she can go."

No doubt Tilla would enjoy the company of a slave's relatives far more than that of his own. Ruso, who had not even been aware that Galla had a family, said, "The evening after, then."

"Yes."

He went back to the table to inform Galla that her banishment from the house was over: She was to return to her duties as soon as she had finished her meal.

Galla was clearly delighted. "It is an answer to prayer, my lord."

"Good," growled Ruso. "It's not often I've been the answer to anyone's prayers lately."

As he limped back toward the house he found Cass beside him carrying a basket of eggs. At last, a chance to talk. He was about to broach the subject of Severus's death when she said, "It was kind of Tilla to go and work with Galla in the winery."

Ruso tried to remember if he had ever heard Tilla described as kind before. The word had never occurred to him. Perhaps he had been too hard on her.

Cass stepped ahead of him and shooed a hen away before pushing open the gate between the farmyard and the garden. "How's your foot now?"

"About the same. Cass, I need to talk to you about yesterday."

"Well, you haven't really had a chance to rest, have you? Poor Gaius. It hasn't been much of a homecoming for you. What a shame."

Ruso gave an embarrassed shrug and mumbled something about it not mattering. Indeed, until this moment, it had not struck him that nobody had bothered to thank him for coming home. Now he was about to repay Cass's thoughtfulness by questioning her as part of a murder investigation.

"Dear me," she observed before he could open his mouth, "that sage is looking very squashed. I hope it wasn't the children."

Ruso followed her gaze to the battered flowerbed at the foot of the pergola, and said, "Cass, I need to know exactly what happened when Severus came here."

"We haven't made Tilla very welcome, either, have we? I hear Arria has plans for you and Lollia Saturnina instead."

"Arria has plans for lots of things."

"Lollia Saturnina is a very nice woman, Gaius. But I don't think she's looking for a husband."

Following his sister-in-law up the porch steps, he said, "I doubt anyone's looking to marry a suspected poisoner."

Cass giggled. "Oh, Gaius. Anyone who knows you knows that you couldn't possibly have done a thing like that." They crossed the hall and she paused with her hand on the latch of the children's room. "Come in and say good night to them," she urged. "Then we can talk."

They were greeted by the sight of a naked Little Gaius beaming at them from his pot. Around him was an array of beds that were all empty except the one from which the laundry maid had just sprung up, patting her bedraggled hair back into place. Apparently Master Lucius had taken the other children to the kitchen in search of supper.

Cass dismissed the maid, inspected the contents of the pot, and informed their producer that he was a very good boy. "Isn't he a good boy, Uncle Gaius? Stand up, baby, and let's give you a nice wash."

"He's a fine little chap," observed Ruso, noting with approval that all of his namesake's parts were in the right places, and wondering if one ever got to the end of a conversation once one was blessed with children. "Cass, I need to—"

"But he doesn't talk yet," replied his mother, pursuing the toddler across the room and deftly maneuvering a tunic over his head before he could escape. "All the others did. Do you think we should do something?"

"I don't know much about children, to be honest," said Ruso. "He looks healthy enough." Judging by the all-over tan, young Gaius took frequent exercise in the fresh air, as unencumbered by clothes as any Greek athlete. "His hearing seems fine. He'll probably talk when he's got something to say."

She placed the pot on top of a cupboard beside a bowl of peaches, apparently oblivious to her son's offering within, and wiped her hands on a damp cloth. "Bless you, Gaius. I'm sure you're right. It's very reassuring having a doctor in the family. Children are such a worry. You know how it is. And Lucius is under such a lot of strain, coping with everything. I'm really glad you're home."

"Lucius isn't."

She reached toward the pot without looking, realized her mistake, and picked up the bowl instead. "He's just worried about the money. He's glad to have you here really."

Ruso marveled afresh at the way some women could interpret their husbands' statements to mean exactly the opposite of what they said.

Cass was saying, ". . . none of us wants to think what could happen if we were accused of poisoning Severus."

"That's why I need to ask you—"

"Have a peach, Gaius. Tell me something. You never really got on with Arria, did you?"

As Ruso took a peach, his namesake ran across and reached up for it, dancing on the tips of small pudgy feet and crying, "Aah!" in case Ruso failed to notice him.

"He can have a slice," suggested his mother.

"Aah!"

"In a minute," Ruso promised him, unsheathing his knife to slice around the stone and wondering whether children really should be rewarded for wandering about instead of going to bed, even if peaches were good for the digestion. "When you see what she's done to the family," he said, twisting the two halves apart and cutting a generous slice, "I think I had good reason."

"Say thank you to Uncle Gaius."

The child looked at his mother as if she had just suggested something very odd and retreated with peach juice dripping down his chin and soaking into his clean bedtime tunic.

He indicated the child. "There's no money to bring him up, nor his brothers and sisters, because she wouldn't stop spending and Father wouldn't stand up to her."

Cass weighed a peach in one hand and pondered that for a moment. "Your father once said to me that he only wanted to see her happy."

"What about the rest of us?"

"He said she had a difficult time fitting in here. Everybody was very fond of your mother."

Ruso wondered how much Cass had been told about the arguments. About the times when he had used, "You're not my mother!" as a weapon. Now he thought about it, his new stepmother could not have been much older on arrival than Marcia was now. The thought of Marcia being left in charge of two small boys was frightening. The thought of Marcia being given a limitless budget was positively terrifying.

Marcia borrowing money. That wretched rumor was another thing he was going to have to tackle tomorrow. So far he had failed to get any relevant sense out of Cass, whom he liked and who appeared to like him. How he was going to worm any truth out of Marcia, who didn't like him at all, he had no idea.

"You were asking about Severus," said Cass, unexpectedly returning to the subject she had ignored earlier.

"Yes." How did women do that, he wondered? And why?

"I won't be wasting any tears on him, despicable man. Lucius has hardly slept for weeks with all the worry."

"So yesterday . . . ?"

"He turned up not very long before you did. He said he knew you were home and not to try and make out you weren't."

Ruso nodded, pretending not to notice Little Gaius spitting a lump of peach onto the floor behind his mother's back.

"I said you were in town and we'd ask you to call on him when you got back," continued Cass, "and he said no, he'd wait. I offered to go and find Lucius, but he said no to that too."

"Did he seem ill to you?"

"I thought he might have been drinking. I fetched him some water and hoped you would come home quickly."

"Where did you get the water?"

"I called the kitchen boy to fetch it from the well so it was cold. There was nothing wrong with it: I had a sip myself before I took it into the hall. Then you arrived."

"How long was he alone in the hall?"

"Just as long as it took to get the water."

"And you were waiting—where?"

She frowned. "In the kitchen, Gaius. If I'd had some poison handy I might well have put it in his cup while Cook wasn't watching, but I didn't."

"Sorry."

"I know. You have to ask. I don't suppose you've had a chance to find out anything about my brother?"

"Not much, I'm afraid." There was no point in upsetting her by passing on the gossip Tilla had heard about the poor state of the *Pride of the South*. "Though I did wonder why he was on the ship in the first place. If Severus was responsible for the cargo, why didn't he send one of the senator's men to look after it?"

"It wasn't anything to do with the senator," she explained. "Severus was running the venture for himself. Justinus was there because his master, Probus, was the one who had loaned Severus the money."

Ruso's attempts to disentangle this were complicated by Little Gaius's efforts to climb up his leg in search of more peach.

Cass pried the child off and stood on tiptoe to kiss Ruso on the cheek. "You're a dear man, Gaius. We must all try not to worry. It's lovely to see you happy with Tilla and I know you'll do your very best to sort everything out."

Was he happy with Tilla? Tilla certainly did not seem happy with him.

Ruso rolled off the bed and shoved his feet into the indoor sandals Arria had insisted Lucius lend him. The connection between Cass's brother Justinus and Severus was bothering him, although it probably had nothing to do with the deaths of either of them. Anyway, Justinus was one of the very few people who definitely hadn't murdered Severus.

In the unlikely event that they might help him find out who had, Ruso decided to offer some of Lucius's best wine to the household gods before dinner. Then while Tilla enjoyed the company of the servants, he would eat with his family amid the dancing cupids of the dining room.

He did not feel like a dear man. He suspected that even his very best was not going to be good enough to sort this mess out. He recalled the way Little Gaius had run around the bedroom with peach juice dripping down his chin, oblivious to the fears of the adults whose duty it was to protect him.

Unless Ruso could expose the real poisoner of Severus before the investigator got here, he might be too busy fighting for his life in a court case to do anything about saving the farm. If the family were turned off the land, the sight of Little Gaius would be one of the memories that would haunt him.

37

DISASTER MIGHT BE looming, but discipline had to be maintained. The next day, as Ruso led Marcia toward the stone bench in the garden, he was silently mourning the erosion of the power of the Paterfamilias. There had been a time—he was not sure when, but he knew there had been one—when the head of a Roman household had enjoyed absolute power as well as ultimate responsibility. When orders were obeyed without question. When women were grateful to be protected—grateful, indeed, not to be left on the rubbish heap at birth—and happy to be married off whenever and to whomsoever the family deemed appropriate. When a decent man could keep his household in order by threatening them not only with a sound beating but with execution.

He had to concede that the beheading of unruly relatives seemed a little harsh, but obviously one would exercise discretion. The point was, in the old days, a man had commanded respect. What would his ancestors have done, had any of them been faced with a scowling Marcia, arms folded, demanding, "You said you were going to talk to somebody. So have you talked to them?"

"Not in the way you mean," said Ruso, lowering himself onto the bench.

"Gaius, you promised—"

"Sit down."

"But you said—"

"Sit down, Marcia."

"But you promised you would—"

"Sit down."

"I'm not going to sit down if you shout at me!"

"I wasn't," said Ruso, who hadn't been, and was not sure why he had gotten himself into an argument about sitting down when she could hear what he had to say quite well standing up. "But if you don't listen to me, I will shout like a centurion ordering his men on a parade ground. And then your mother will come out and hear what I'm going to say."

His satisfaction as she slumped down beside him on the bench was short-lived. He had, he realized, effectively promised not to tell Arria. Still, Marcia was listening now. At least he assumed she was listening, although she seemed to have found something that urgently needed gouging out from beneath one of her fingernails.

"Are you particularly short of money for some reason, Marcia?"

"We're all short of money in this family. Lucius is mean and so are you."

"Because I've been told," he said, "that you've been trying to borrow against your dowry."

"Who told you that?"

"Never mind. Is it true?"

"Is it true?" The wide hazel eyes that reminded him of Arria met his own in an expression of innocence and outrage. "Of course it's not true! How could I? I haven't got a dowry. That's the whole point!"

"That would be one of the reasons you've been refused, I expect," he ventured, still unable to believe that Probus's guard would have invented such a tale.

"I haven't—I can't believe I'm hearing this!"

"So you can assure me you haven't been trying to raise money on the quiet? Because obviously that would be very embarrassing. Not only for me as your guardian, but for the whole of the family."

"You're always trying to raise money. You and Lucius. Everybody knows."

"That's different."

"Well, I haven't! And I think you're horrible to even think I might. What would I need money for?"

"You tell me."

"Who was it? I bet it was that barber, wasn't it? I bet he said it just to stop you complaining about that haircut."

"There's nothing wrong with my haircut, and it wasn't the barber. Look, I'm sorry about the dowry. Maybe I should have explained what's going on."

"I know what's going on, Gaius. Lucius made a mess of paying Claudia's husband so he was threatening to take us to court in Rome to get all of our money—not that we've got any, according to Lucius—then he came over here and dropped dead, and now everybody's saying you poisoned him."

Ruso cleared his throat. "Well, I suppose that's more or less it."

"But I shan't believe them, Gaius. Do you know why? Because I don't go around listening to gossip." She got to her feet. "And neither should you. Can I go now?"

He watched his sister stalk back toward the house, the sunlight filtering through the leaves over the pergola and dappling the linen of her tunic. Perhaps, prejudiced by the mother's past excesses, he had misjudged the daughter. That must be the answer, because the other possibility was not fit to contemplate. Surely a veteran of his wide international experience could not have been so easily outmaneuvered by an almost-sixteen-year-old girl?

38

RUSO SEEMED TO be doing no better finding out who had poisoned Severus than he had with disciplining Marcia. Who, how, and why? might be the right questions but he did not like the answers he had found so far and he was running out of places to search for new ones. He had even toyed with the idea that the man might have poisoned himself, only to dismiss it as a sign of his own desperation.

He scowled at the crack in the side of the pond. The news of the death would not even have reached Rome yet. There was still time for him to sort out this mess. Meanwhile, he needed to clear his head. He needed a change of scene. He needed to get back to work. He might be a man hovering on the brink of ruin, but he knew how to wield a scalpel. There was one man in town who might be glad to see him, and just possibly that man might know something about poisons.

As he was reaching for his stick, a figure he did not recognize strolled in through the gate, patted the dog on the head, and made for the house. Arria appeared in the doorway and bustled down the steps to meet him, crying, "There you are!" and holding out a hand to be kissed.

Moments later Ruso found himself being introduced to Diphilus the builder, a man on the oily side of handsome. He was, as Arria announced with joy, available for dinner tomorrow evening. Ruso suspected Diphilus was the sort of man who was available for dinner any evening as long as he wasn't paying for it.

"Are you available for clearing drains this morning?"

"Gaius is just out of the army," said Arria, as if she had to excuse him. "Wounded by those dreadful Britons."

Diphilus smiled at them both and said he would be honored to look at the drains of a war hero. Arria looked delighted. Ruso, feeling outnumbered, went across to the stables. He would probably get more sense out of the mule.

Two early shoppers had paused to chat in the shade of the Forum wall. Ruso was relieved to see that the latest exhortation to support Fuscus, partially obscured behind them, was not long enough to begin with "G. Petreius Ruso, veteran of the . . ." His relief was shortlived. Glancing back over his shoulder as he rode past, he saw the wall from a different angle.

He had just made out, "The town poisoner says vote for . . ." when the shorter of the two women shouted, "Oy! Who d'you think you're staring at?"

Ruso urged the mule on down the street, pursued by a cry of, "We're respectable married women! You keep your eyes to yourself!"

The Games were not taking place for another two days, but as he squinted up at the glaring white stone of the amphitheater he could see small silhouettes moving about on the parapet, slotting in the masts for the sails that would be pulled across to shade the audience from sunstroke. Below them, other shapes appeared and vanished again, hurrying around the stone lattice of arches and corridors that formed the massive and elegant oval in which Fuscus's entertainment would take place.

A cart piled high with animal cages was being maneuvered beneath the carved bull's heads that adorned the main entrance. Whatever was in the cages was smelly but silent and hidden by a sailcloth that had been thrown over the top as a rough shade. Ruso rode on around the outside of the building. As he passed, some sort of animal noise—a roar or a bellow, it was hard to say which—echoed from deep within the arches. The mule pricked up its ears, but plodded on past the municipal slaves busy sweeping the flagstones. Presumably whatever had made the sound would have its blood mixed in with the sand of the arena in a couple of days.

Farther on, someone was applying fresh paint to the entrance numbers on the sides of the arches. Traders were unloading their vehicles. A sweet stall, a fritter vendor, and a souvenir salesman had already claimed the shade under the trees across the street, hoping to attract early trade. All were no doubt grateful to Fuscus for the opportunity to make a little extra money. As, in a roundabout way, was Ruso.

The gladiators' barracks in the building next door were marked by a gaggle of excited females clustered around the heavy gates, waiting for a glimpse of their heroes. Ruso hoped that Marcia and Flora had never stooped to cupping their hands around their mouths and yelling encouragement through the cracks in the woodwork. Still, these alarmingly forthright young women might be of use to him now. Their devotion would have armed them with the information he needed.

Ruso dismounted and led the mule into the haze of competing perfumes.

"What's the name of the doctor in there?" he asked a couple of pink-cheeked girls whose diaphanous outfits were made even more distracting by the way they stuck to their owners in the heat.

One of them seemed about to reply when a scream from a girl by the gate set off a cacophony of shrieking. Cries of "Who can you see?" merged with a chant of, "Xantus, Xantus, Xantus!" and several devotees were leaping to fling scraps of fabric and posies of flowers over the gate. Ruso wondered whether Xantus was embarrassed. A little leather bottle of something (perfume? Love potion? Magic formula for courage?) sailed over into the barracks. He tried his question again, hoping for a name he recognized.

"Gnostus," said one of the girls, not bothering to look around.

This was not encouraging. He had never heard of a doctor called Gnostus. He led the mule forward, clearing a path with the untruthful "Watch your backs, he bites!" until he was standing in front of the gates. Rapping on the wood with his stick, he shouted, "Visitor for Gnostus!"

There was a pause. A small slot in the door slid open. A pair of bloodshot eyes appeared and a voice repeated, "Gnostus?" as if wondering whether the visitor had gotten the name right.

Ruso unfastened his medical case and held up the largest pair of surgical forceps he possessed. Ignoring the mingled gasps of horror and delight from the crowd, he said, "I'm the other surgeon."

"Wait there," said the voice. The slot snapped shut again. As the girls giggled and whispered behind him, he tucked the forceps into his belt and indulged in some unnecessary straightening of the mule's headband.

His wait was rewarded with the sound of the bar being lifted out of its brackets. Girls began to inch forward as one of the gates moved back. They stopped at the emergence of a leather whip, followed by the doorman who yelled, "No admittance to the public!" and cracked the whip in the air as if he were disciplining animals. From the squealing that followed, it was hard to tell whether the girls were excited or terrified.

As soon as the tail of Ruso's mount was safely inside, the gate slammed shut behind him and the bar thudded back into position.

The dust in the center of the wide courtyard bore witness to the scuffles of a morning's training, but the battered wooden sparring posts stood deserted in the midday sun. Abandoned shields and leather jerkins and shin guards were stacked in one corner. The favors that had been tossed over the gates were nowhere to be seen. A low murmur of conversation and the scrape of spoons on bowls suggested the trainees had retreated into the shade of the low building on the right to eat. Without its occupants the courtyard, with its stink of sweat and embrocation, could almost have been one of the military training grounds Ruso had left behind in Britannia—except that one of the posts bore a set of manacles dangling from a heavy chain, and the Twentieth had more sense than to arm itself with the impractical nets and tridents he saw piled up beside the gate as he handed the mule's reins to the doorkeeper.

The doorkeeper's "First on the left, mate" was rendered unnecessary by a sudden roar of pain from that direction. Moments later a skinny man of about Ruso's own age emerged from the door wiping bloodstained hands on his apron. Ruso was convinced he saw a brief flash of recognition on the face before the man demanded, "What other surgeon?"

"Hello, Euplius!"

Euplius's face arranged itself into an expression of confusion. "Who?" He retreated back into his room, beckoning Ruso to follow. "We haven't met. I'm Gnostus, all the way from Ephesus. Doctor to the finest gladiator troupe in Gaul. Those are my apprentices. And you are?"

"Ruso, senior surgeon with the Twentieth Legion," said Ruso, glancing at a heavily muscled man who was sitting on a chair between the trainees and clutching a bloodstained rag to his mouth. Surely his memory could not be that bad? It was many years since he and Euplius had met during their apprenticeships, but could there really be two medics cursed with those ears?

"As in Gaius Petreius Ruso?" queried Gnostus, lifting the lid from a jar and pouring liquid into a wooden cup. "I've heard of you." He handed the cup to his patient.

"Not everything you've heard is true," Ruso assured him.

"Keep swilling that around the cavity," ordered Gnostus. "Slowly."

The man removed the rag, took a tentative sip, and grimaced.

"It's good stuff," Gnostus promised.

The man did not look convinced.

Gnostus offered the jar to Ruso. "Guess."

Ruso dipped in the tip of a finger and licked it.

"Bisobol gum in wine," said Ruso, identifying part of the disgusting taste. He nodded to the patient. "Good for toothache and gum disease."

"What else?" demanded Gnostus.

Ruso tried another dip. "Poppy."

"And?"

"Not a clue."

Gnostus grinned. "It's a new recipe I'm trying out. Excellent results so far."

One of the apprentices leaned forward to sniff it. The patient mumbled something indistinct, which might have been gratitude and might have voiced the suspicion that the doctors were lying to him.

As they watched the apprentices escort the shambling patient out across the courtyard with his jaw cradled in one hand and the cup in the other, Gnostus said quietly, "Sometimes I wonder why I bother. He'll probably be dead in a couple of days."

"You just have to patch them up and send them back out there," said Ruso, seizing a chance to emphasize his credentials. "Exactly what I've been doing with the Legion."

Gnostus closed the door. "You gave me a shock, Ruso. How long is it?"

Ruso felt his shoulders relax. "Fifteen years?"

"And more," agreed his companion.

"So why are you calling yourself Gnostus?"

The creases were deeper but the lopsided grin that formed them was still the same. "Bit of misunderstanding about the labels on bottles," he explained. "Angry relatives. It wasn't my fault, but you know how it is."

"I do now," said Ruso.

"New name, new town . . . I hear you've had a few problems. You should try it."

"I'm hoping it won't come to that. In the meantime I was wondering if you'd be needing an assistant surgeon for the games."

"I'll be needing a bloody miracle worker," observed Gnostus glumly, sinking down onto a stool. "But at least you'll have some idea which bits to stitch together. Unlike some. I'll say one thing for Fuscus, he knows how to draw a crowd."

"They're gathering around the gates already," observed Ruso, settling himself on the treatment table. "What is it women see in gladiators? Most of them are slaves and they're nearly all filthy ugly."

"Who knows?" said Gnostus. "You wouldn't believe the offers the gate staff get."

"They don't allow women in here, surely?" asked Ruso, hoping there was nothing else he did not want to hear about Marcia.

"Only the women who pay enough," said Gnostus. "And sometimes we have to house the ones due for execution. But they're chained up, of course."

Ruso pondered this grim prospect for a moment. He needed the work. Just as, faced with Fuscus, he had needed the man's influence. He said, "How much do you know about poisons?"

Gnostus observed that poisoning did not make for much of a show, and suggested, "The people you want to ask are the Marsi."

"I've tried," explained Ruso. "They were insulted."

Gnostus grinned. "I'll bet. Next time, ask for Valgius and tell him Gnostus still doesn't want to buy his snake." He pointed at Ruso's stick. "So. War wound?"

"Not exactly."

When Ruso told him, Gnostus was incredulous. "They let you go home with just a cracked metatarsal?"

"Long leave," explained Ruso, not entirely truthfully. He was adding, "And I was missing the sunshine," when there was a knock on the door.

The new arrival was a youth of about eighteen who might have been handsome in a thin and poetic way had it not been for the jagged scab that ran from eyebrow to hairline.

"Afternoon, Tertius," said Gnostus, not bothering to get up from the stool. "What is it this time?"

The youth glanced at Ruso and then back at his own doctor. "Please, sir, I'd like to consult doctor Gaius Petreius."

Gnostus sighed. "He'll only say the same as me."

"It's a personal matter."

"You don't have personal matters," Gnostus pointed out, ignoring the pained look on the youth's face. "You won't have any personal matters for the next two and a half years. If you last that long." He turned to Ruso, who had gotten to his feet, and murmured, "Whatever he thinks he's got, he's going in the arena. Otherwise the pairs will be one short, and the boss won't want to refund the hire money to Fuscus."

"I can't sign you off sick," Ruso explained to the youth. "You'll have to—"

"I don't want to be signed off sick, sir!" the lad exclaimed. "I just want to know if there's a message."

Ruso blinked. "Message?"

"From Marcia."

39

I THOUGHT THAT'S why you were here, sir," said Tertius, clearly frustrated at Ruso's bafflement. "She said you were coming home to settle her dowry at last so she could buy me out."

Ruso did not know which part of this sentence to pick on first. "Marcia knew I was on the way home?"

"She said you'd be back soon."

At last the mystery of the letter was solved. It had not been sent by Severus at all. Marcia had taken up forgery and then lied to him about it. Restraining a momentary flash of fury at the thought that he had been dragged into this whole mess by his own sister, Ruso said, "Why would I give her a dowry so she could borrow money to go around buying gladiators?"

Tertius coughed. "She wasn't going to tell you that part, sir. But we're running out of time. I was hoping you were here to see to it yourself."

Ruso, perched on the edge of Gnostus's operating table, looked the stringy youth up and down and wondered if young men were getting stupider or whether he had been just as much of a fool at that age. He understood how it felt to be desperate to leave home, albeit for different reasons. He had been lucky enough to have a childless uncle in search of an apprentice. Arria—equally keen for Ruso to leave—had managed to persuade his father that medicine was not such a terribly disreputable trade for a decent citizen's son, even if it was mostly the province of slaves. She had avoided adding, "and Greeks," since Uncle Theo was in the room at the time.

If Ruso had been in the position Tertius now described to him—parents honest but dead, no money and no connections—would he have considered selling himself to a gladiator trainer?

No, he would not. "You could have joined the army."

"But then I couldn't marry Marcia," pointed out Tertius, as if this made sense.

"You couldn't marry her if you were carried out of the amphitheater on a funeral bier, either," pointed out Ruso, and then regretted it when he saw the look on Tertius's face.

"I was a bit drunk at the time, sir."

"Ah."

"There were three of us."

Evidently it was true: Young men were getting stupider. "What happened to the other two?"

"When they sobered up they sent for their fathers to buy them out."

"Leaving you stuck here for three years."

"Only two and a half now. I've been training ever since."

"So this will be your first real fight."

Tertius nodded. "I'm good. Ask anybody. I'm only a Retiarius now, but everybody says I'm Samnite material. I'm fast, and I reckon I can entertain the crowd."

"I see." If Tertius was going into the arena armed only with a net and a trident, he would certainly have to be fast.

"I thought if I was good, the trainer wouldn't want to lose me." He paused. "To be honest, I always thought the fights were fixed."

Ruso wondered what Tertius could possibly have imagined would be going through the head of any designated loser in a "fixed" fight. Perhaps he had expected to be pitted against a lesser—and less valuable—man. And to be fair, many of the professional bouts in the local amphitheater ended in battered defeat rather than death. Until someone like Fuscus came along with too much money and demanded more excitement.

Ruso looked at the cracked forehead and the chewed fingernails. "You're not a marvelous prospect for my sister," he observed.

Tertius squared his shoulders. "I'm not a coward, sir. I'm a hard worker. You ask anybody here."

"But you're a gladiator."

"I love her, sir!" said Tertius, as if this made some sort of difference. "I love your sister. And she loves me." He had been standing with his hands behind his back and his feet apart. Suddenly he stood to attention. "Sir, I would like to request permission to marry Marcia Petreia."

It was like being back in the army. Except that none of the things for which he had been asked permission in the army had ever involved his sister. Ruso sighed. "Stand easy, Tertius. You can't marry anybody while you're under contract to a gladiator trainer."

"That's why she was trying to buy me out, sir."

Clearly Marcia and this youth were well suited: each as dimwitted as the other.

Ruso got to his feet. "It would have been better if she'd told me the truth in the first place."

"I'm sorry about that, sir. When I see her I'll have a word with her."

It was so cheeky that, had the circumstances been less grave, Ruso would have smiled. As it was, he said, "I don't know how much news you get in here, Tertius, but I'm hardly in a position to help you at the moment."

"You're free, sir. And nobody else is going to."

Ruso observed that his sister's beloved might not be very bright but he was certainly persistent. "I'm not going to promise anything to do with Marcia Petreia," he said. "And you shouldn't expect anything from me. But if circumstances change, and I find I'm able to help you, then I'll see what I can do."

Ruso watched the spring in the youth's step as he made his way back across to the barracks and wondered if that last vague promise made him almost as much of a fool as Tertius himself.

Gnostus had given him the key to the medical room before heading off to join his apprentices for lunch and told him to lock the door on the way out. Apparently all doors were kept locked here and sharp weapons stored out of reach. Movement around the compound was carefully controlled by the staff and a favored few among the top fighters. Gladiators might be heroes but most of them were also slaves. The veteran with the whip was there both to keep the public out and the occupants in.

Thus it was with some surprise that Ruso, turning to make his way across to the mess and return Gnostus's key, found himself face-to-face with his former father-in-law.

Probus's demand of "What are you doing here?" was an unwelcome echo of their last meeting.

"Looking for a job. You?"

"Business."

"You're investing in gladiators?"

Probus scowled. "Of course not. Here on behalf of Fuscus. You don't think he deals with these people himself, do you?"

Ruso, who had never really thought about the business side of public entertainment, said, "I thought he was supposed to have handpicked the fighters."

"Then he fixed a price with the trainer and left the rest up to me."

Ruso hoped "the rest" did not include the sanctioning of job offers to medical assistants. "How's Claudia?"

"None of your business." Probus moved closer and lowered his voice. "You had no right to ask her to look into Severus's commercial dealings."

"I thought you might know who else he'd upset."

"Do you have the least idea what releasing private information to someone like you would do for my reputation?"

"Speaking of reputation," said Ruso, "you could have told me Marcia was looking for a loan before I heard it as gossip."

"That's exactly my point," snapped Probus. "Client confidentiality."

"She wasn't a client. You refused her. Quite rightly."

Probus eyed him for a moment. "You were a deep disappointment to me, Ruso. So much ability, yet so little . . ." he paused, searching for a word. Finally he settled on, ". . . judgment."

"I didn't poison your son-in-law."

"What you've never understood is that for a man to succeed in life, it matters what people think of him. A lost reputation is impossible to recover. In my line of business, I have to be seen as utterly trustworthy."

"Mine too. What if this poisoner goes for Claudia next?"

"Are you threatening my daughter now?"

"Don't be ridiculous. And stop telling Fuscus I did it, will you?"

When Probus did not answer, he continued, "Someone knows the truth. Help me find out."

"There will be a proper investigation. We're waiting for instructions from Rome."

"I'm not."

Probus took a step closer. "You have no idea what you're doing, Ruso. Are you trying to drag me down with you? And Claudia too? Because I won't let that happen."

"Tell me something, Probus. When a man lends the money for a shipping venture, who carries the risk? The one who borrows it and arranges the voyage, or the lender?"

"A shipping loan?" The voice was incredulous. "We are discussing my daughter's safety!"

"Humor me."

"The lender, of course. High risk, high return."

"That's why you sent Justinus on the ship." Ruso moved closer and murmured, "Severus lost you a lot of money, didn't he?"

"You know nothing about my affairs."

"If someone tells the investigator from Rome that Severus sank a lot of your money on the *Pride of the South,* you might be a very plausible suspect."

"You wouldn't!"

"You know how it is. Whoever gets picked as the culprit will have all his private business pegged out for inspection in the Forum while the lawyers argue over his moral character."

A couple of thickset men dressed only in grimy loincloths strolled across the courtyard and began to sort through the pile of nets, one of them displaying a lattice of scars across his back as he bent over. Others were beginning to emerge from the barrack room. Shrieks of "Xantus!" rose over a chant of "Am-pli-a-tus, Am-pli-a-tus!" and hammering on the gates. Probus stepped aside in disgust as something that looked distinctly like female underwear landed in the dust near his feet. He glanced around to make sure he could not be overheard before murmuring, "I thought better of you than this, Ruso."

"We're caught in the same net," said Ruso. "There's nothing to be gained by fighting each other. Help me."

"If you try to take me down—or Claudia—I'll ruin you. You think I don't know you're still in far more debt than the farm is worth?"

"So. We share what we know, and we help each other."

Probus appeared to be considering his options, and not liking any of them. Finally he said, "I have to get ready for the funeral. I can give you some time tomorrow morning. Come alone, and don't tell anyone. You've caused enough trouble already."

"I'll be there," promised Ruso. Watching his former father-in-law cross the courtyard and enter a shadowed door in the corner, it struck him that if Probus was involved in the murder after all, a lone and secret visit to his house was definitely not a good idea. But the banker was also taking a risk in associating with him. They could circle around each other deciding whether to land the first blow, like the pair of fighters now donning their glittering armor in the afternoon sun, or they could try and behave like partners with a common interest in seeking the truth.

In the meantime, he was off to visit some men who claimed they weren't poisoners, either. There seemed to be a lot of that about.

40

"YOU AGAIN," OBSERVED the dark young man, pausing as he loaded the stack of snake boxes into the handcart. "Make it quick. We're going."

Ruso said, "Valgius?"

The man nestled the boxes into the straw and checked the fastening on the top lid before turning and fixing unblinking snake eyes on Ruso. "I might be able to find him."

"Gnostus still doesn't want to buy that snake."

"You're from Gnostus?" The furrows in the hard face spread around an unexpected grin. "Why didn't you say so before?"

"He said you might be able to help me with something."

The young man glanced around to make sure nobody was listening. "Your poisoning?"

Ruso nodded.

"My father said it sounded a bit like rhododendron honey."

Ruso stared at him, vaguely recalling theoretical warnings about honey from bees that had fed on the wrong plants. He had never met it in practice.

"How fast does it act?"

"Depends how much you take. It tastes fine, so you could eat a fair bit and not know."

"I thought you could tell bad honey from the color?"

"Nah," said Valgius. "Not really."

"You mean it could have been an accident?" An accident! Of course. It made perfect sense. The killers were the bees whose honey had been used to make Severus's morning medicine. The investigators could simply trace the source of the rogue honey and record the whole episode as a tragic accident. The lifting of a burden to which he had become so accustomed made Ruso feel positively lightheaded. He had solved the mystery! He was free!

He was free for the fractional moment that passed between his question and Valgius replying, "Nah. Must have been done on purpose."

"But if you can't tell . . ."

Valgius was shaking his head. "Ask yourself this," he said. "How many bees are there between Gaul, at one end of the sea, and Pontus, right up past the other? You wouldn't end up with rhododendron honey here by accident. Mind you, I've not heard of anyone dying from it, but I suppose if you ate a lot . . ."

"If a man with a weak heart," mused Ruso, "were to drink a large quantity of poisonous honey and rosewater on a hot day . . ."

"It's possible."

"So how would you get ahold of the honey in a place like this?"

"Ah," said Valgius, turning back to the cart. "That's your problem. Me, I've got to get all the boys and girls loaded up before the old man gets back."

Ruso peered at the boxes, curious. "Can you really tell the boys from the girls?"

"You can sometimes get some idea from the tail," said the man. "But if you want to be sure you need two people, a blunt probe, and—"

"Never mind," said Ruso, backing away with a hand held out in surrender. "Another time."

The man who had failed to sell Ruso the frankincense gave up pretending to be pleased to see him again when he found out why he had come. "I don't know who's been telling you that rubbish," he insisted. "I'm only a simple root cutter. Remedies and cosmetics. I don't sell food."

"That's funny," said Ruso. "Because three of the people I've spoken to around here told me you were the man to ask."

"That lot?" demanded the root cutter, glancing around at the other stallholders who were beginning to pack up at the end of the afternoon's trading. "What do they know? Like I tell them, if you want to sell as much as me, make the effort to invest in quality product. Walk the hills, find the best places, get out of bed before dawn every morning, and get cracking. But oh, no. It's easier to sit on your backside and gossip about other people."

Ruso said, "I'm disappointed. I'd have thought with your range, exotic honeys would have been a good complement."

The man upended the wooden tray on which he had displayed his produce and banged it to detach the mud and stray leaves. "Sorry."

"Pity," said Ruso. "It would have been fun. Ah well. I suppose it'll be the old laxatives-in-the-soup routine, then. Unless you know anybody else I could try?"

The man wiped the rest of the dirt from the tray and said, "What is it you're looking for, exactly?"

Ruso told him.

"You don't want to eat rhododendron honey. Send you silly."

"Exactly," said Ruso. "It's my brother's birthday coming up. We always play jokes on each other." He indicated his bandaged foot. "Look what he did to me."

"Funny kind of a joke."

"Family tradition," explained Ruso. "Point of honor."

The man looked as though he had more to say but had stifled it in the face of a prospective sale. "You'd have to order it at least ten days in advance," he said. "There's not much call for it."

Ruso muttered a curse in what he hoped was a disappointed tone and explained that the birthday was the day after tomorrow. The root cutter shrugged an apology and groped under the stall for an empty basket. He began to stack the unsold medicine pots in it.

"What about your supplier?" Ruso tried. "Could I go direct?"

The man carried on working, clearly not such a fool as to reveal the name of his source and sacrifice his profit. "Too much could make him ill, anyway," he warned. "You'd be safer with the laxatives."

Ruso wondered how much longer he could keep this up. Claudia's voice floated into his mind, reminding him that he was a terrible liar. He was probably wasting his time. He should have gone back to ask Gnostus about local suppliers of dubious substances. Still, while he was here he might as well finish the job.

"What about your last customer for it?" he tried. "When did you last sell any? Would he have some left?"

"She," corrected the man.

Ruso felt his stomach muscles tighten. Trying to keep his voice even, he said, "If I could find her, I'd make her a good offer."

"I didn't ask her name."

"What does she look like? Perhaps she's somebody I already know."

The man's eyes narrowed. "I don't pass on my customers' business. Now clear off. I'm an honest trader and I'm busy."

The man bent down to heave up another basket. The knife point pressed against his left kidney took him by surprise.

"I was lying," said Ruso, ramming the tip of his forefinger harder into the man's back and hoping he could not turn his head far enough to see the knife Ruso hadn't had time to get out still slung on his belt. "It's not my brother's birthday. It's about a murder investigation. And if you don't tell me who bought that honey, you're going to have much nastier people than me around here trying to help you remember."

Ruso's hands were shaking as he untethered the mule. It could not be true. It could not be . . .

The man had no reason to lie.

He had sold the poisonous honey several days ago to a respectable young woman who had known exactly what she wanted. A young woman with orange curls and lots of makeup. No, he couldn't remember what she had been wearing, but he remembered what she had on her feet because she had trod in something and blamed him for not keeping the pavement clean. So he had lent her a cloth to wipe the mess off her fancy sandals. Coral pink sandals with pearls set in the front.

41

SEVERUS'S FUNERAL PASSED with neither incident nor enlightenment, and if anyone thought he was being disposed of with indecent haste, they did not say so in Ruso's hearing. All the members of the Petreius family who were old enough to behave themselves had been marshaled at the little cemetery on the hill behind the senator's house. Marcia and Flora looked suitably drab and disheveled and inappropriately cheerful. A funeral meant another day away from the privilege of studying music and poetry.

Ennia spent most of the funeral weeping on the sloping shoulder of Zosimus the steward, breaking off only occasionally to glare at Claudia. Fuscus, as a respectable magistrate, stood well away from Probus, the financier, in the ranks of solemn-faced local worthies come to pay their last respects to the agent of My Cousin The Senator. Several drivers dozed by expensive carriages, ready to facilitate a quick escape for their masters when the funeral feast—to which the Petreius family had not been invited—was over.

The grief and fear on the faces of the estate staff was all too real. Ruso counted at least thirty of them, and there would be others back at the house busily cleansing and purifying.

As the burning wood crackled and the column of smoke rose into the clear sky, the smell of incense failed to disguise the stench of burning flesh.

Ruso glanced around at the mourners. Everyone he knew who might possibly have a motive for poisoning Severus was here. If he were the senator's investigator, which one would he decide to accuse?

The answer was obvious. The only certain way to save himself would be to reveal that Claudia had bought the honey. And if he did that, Probus would bring the fragile edifice of the family debts crashing down around him. He would survive as the powerless guardian of a family with nowhere to live. Tilla would have to choose whether to stay here and share his disgrace, or travel home alone.

42

THIS GOD DID not have much of a house. Fifteen or twenty of his followers were crowded into a stone outbuilding that seemed to have been hastily cleared for the purpose. There was no statue. No shrine. No sacrifice this evening, either. Tilla was relieved about that. Galla did not seem the sort to be involved in murdering babies and drinking their blood, but she had heard that this dreadful practice was the reason the followers of Christos were only marginally more popular with Rome than the Druids. Mind you, much of what the Romans said about the Druids was lies too.

When she asked about the sacrifice, Galla assured her that it had already been done. There was no sign of it. Tilla glanced out through the crack between the door frame and the wall. All she could see in the narrow streak of vision was a massive kiln and a stack of wood ready to fuel it.

There was no blood—just a motley selection of food and drink that the worshippers had brought and laid on the cloth in the middle of the floor. Galla had brought the bread she had saved from her lunch. Tilla, who had misunderstood her invitation to meet her brothers and sisters, was embarrassed to find that she had come to face a new god empty-handed. But what could she have brought? The fleece stuffed under her bed was inedible and she could not imagine a god—or anyone else—wanting the grape-and-feet juice she had helped to produce yesterday. Casting her eye over scattered loaves of bread, grapes, olives, two cheeses, small cakes, and a platter of cold chicken, she considered the offering she had made to the goddess in Nemausus. Hair would definitely be wrong here, too.

"Those who have, bring to share," explained Galla, evidently sensing her discomfort. One child had brought a striped cat, but since the sacrifice had already been carried out, it was presumably safe curled up on her lap. Two old women arrived without gifts and sat huddled under their shawls by the edge of the cloth. Moments later one of them appeared to be chewing. Either she was sucking her teeth from habit or she had sneaked something from the cloth before everyone else started.

The man who seemed to be the leader welcomed everyone to the supper, "especially Brother Solemnis, who has brought greetings from our friends by the river at Arelate . . ." Brother Solemnis was a bony youth with buck teeth. "And it's a joy to welcome two new sisters." He glanced at one of the old women. "Agatha from the town, and . . ."

Tilla said, "Darlughdacha," at the same moment as Galla said, "Tilla."

"But you can call me Tilla," she conceded. The god would not know her by her British name, anyway.

"You've come a long way."

"From Britannia."

"It's a delight to have you here, sister."

She found herself returning his smile, surprised and a little suspicious that these people were so glad to see her. This was the warmest welcome she had received anywhere since they had left home.

"You must take our greetings back to the believers in Britannia," continued the man.

"I do not think there are any," she said.

"Then the lord has a job for you!" The man seemed happy to hear this. "You will have the honor of telling them good news!"

Everyone looked so pleased at this prospect that Tilla decided not to explain how few Britons would be interested in announcements from the far end of Gaul, good or otherwise.

Someone started singing. Others joined in. Knowing neither the tune nor the words, Tilla was obliged to listen. It became clear that this god welcomed both those who could sing in tune and those who only thought they could. Things would have been much improved by a few pipes and some dancing, but the food was taking up the only space left on the floor and for some reason nobody suggested going outside. Indeed, even the singing was surprisingly restrained, although some of the participants closed their eyes and began to sway as if deeply moved. When it was over Galla leaned across and whispered, "It is safe here, but it is best not to draw attention."

By the time the leader had thanked Christos at length for the food and everyone had opened their eyes again, several little cakes had vanished from the platter and both old ladies were sucking their teeth.

Privately Tilla thought that the leader would have been wiser not to speak to Christos about eating his flesh and drinking his blood. It was the sort of thing that got people into trouble. She suspected this group had been badly advised. They did not have a proper priest: The man in charge was dressed as an ordinary worker. It was the same at home. Her mother had always said that since the Druids went into hiding, odd ideas had been allowed to flourish like weeds.

"We will eat and drink together until the lord comes," announced the leader.

"He is coming tonight?" whispered Tilla, wondering whether this was an illicit party and the lord who owned the building would expect to find his workers at their duties.

"We never know," said Galla.

No one seemed very worried. Perhaps they had set up some sort of a lookout. For some reason Tilla was reminded of a long-dead aunt who had laid out a bowl every evening for her absent husband even though everybody knew he had set up home with another woman down in Eburacum.

During the meal the leader and another man took turns entertaining the diners with Greek read from a battered scroll, while a woman translated into Latin. The story was not a patch on the stories they had at home. It was not a story at all. It seemed to be just some sort of letter urging people somewhere else to cheer up because their god was looking after them even if they ran out of food or clothes or if people attacked them. For a moment she wondered what was the point of worshipping a god who refused to defend his followers, then it occurred to her that this was uncomfortably close to the situation at home.

When most of the food was gone and one of the old women had hidden half a loaf of bread under her shawl, it was time to pray to the god again. Tilla glanced around at the faces: the two old women, five or six sun-browned men with the hard hands and patched tunics of farm slaves, the girl stroking the striped cat, the leader and his wife, three women who were not wealthy, a couple of child slaves, and the bony youth from Arelate. All had their eyes closed. She supposed they were busy trying to picture the god they could not see but who, according to Galla on the way over here, was everywhere and loved everybody. Tilla let her own eyes drift shut and tried to imagine this god, but without success. How would you recognize him? Without a statue to show what he looked like, or even a tree or a rock to mark his special home, how could anyone tell whether he was somewhere—or nowhere?

Since it seemed anyone could pray and everyone wanted to, the prayers went on a long time. Some of them were in Gaulish or Greek. One of the ones she understood was a request to the god to protect and guide the emperor.

Tilla pursed her lips. If any of them had seen what his army had done in the north of her land, they would not be praying for the emperor.

She whispered in Galla's ear, "Why are we praying for him?"

"He is appointed by god to rule over us."

"Didn't the army torture your Christos to death?" What was the matter with these people?

"We must try to love our enemies."

"But if you love them, they are not your enemies, are they?"

Galla opened eyes that shone with something alarmingly close to passion. "Exactly!"

Tilla felt herself growing impatient with this naïveté. After the punishment the emperor's army had suffered at British hands last season, the only reason a legionary would embrace a Briton would be so that he could stab him in the back instead of the guts.

As the prayers rambled on she began to wish that, since this god was everywhere, his followers would talk to him in their own time and not bore everyone else with their daughter's barrenness or their husband's bad temper, their chronic lumbago or their nephew who had been daft enough to sell himself to a gladiator trainer. But instead of wishing it was over, people seemed to be urging the speakers on with scattered cries of "Amen!" and "Yes, father!" Perhaps they were trying to keep themselves awake.

Someone thanked the god for the brother from Arelate, and prayed for the brothers and sisters facing the temptations of that wicked city full of foreign sailors. The brother from Arelate, evidently untroubled by the insult to his hometown, politely responded by praying for the believers here and thanking the god for the kind hospitality they had shown him, then prayed for willing mules and a clear road home tomorrow.

Sister Agatha declined the leader's invitation to pray, although if she had any manners she would have given thanks for all the food the god must have seen her quietly stashing away under the shawl.

"Sister Tilla, would you like to pray?"

She hesitated. "Does the god understand British?"

Eyes drifted open. Heads turned toward the leader. It seemed no one had asked this question before.

"The lord will understand," he said, "but for the sake of the brothers and sisters, Latin or Greek would be best."

Tilla nodded and stood up. "I will do my best." She closed her eyes, stretched out her hands, and took a deep breath.

"Mighty god who is everywhere!" She had never tried praying in Latin. It felt like trying to run in somebody else's shoes. "This is Tilla, Darlughdacha of the Corionotatae among the people of the Brigantes in Britannia." Nobody else had bothered to introduce themselves, she remembered now, but the god who was everywhere might have been busy somewhere else when she was named the first time. "I pray you will free my people from the army who have stolen the land that is rightly ours and hunted down and murdered our holy men and women."

She paused to draw breath. The "Amen" that filled the gap was hesitant. "I pray you will heal the Medicus's foot even though he is proud and stubborn and will not rest it."

This time the "Amen!" was fulsome.

"Make his family wise and his sisters honorable."

"Amen!" She was doing better now.

"And I ask you to reveal the true poisoner so he will not be blamed for it."

Silence. She opened her eyes and caught several worshippers swiftly closing theirs.

"Great god, make his sister-in-law strong and comfort her mourning for her brother and may she know she will see him in the next world."

There was a chorus of "Amen!" and "Yes, lord!"

"And the man or men, or woman or women who gave them that rotten old ship, may they never rest!"

A lone "Amen!" from one of the old women.

"May their crops wither and die!" Someone coughed. "May their intestines tangle and rot!" Tilla was conscious of a stifled giggle. She had to concede that traditional curses did sound rather odd in Latin.

"Give them toothache that cannot be cured," she continued. "May their eyes fail and their skin itch and flake and be covered in warts!"

A fervent, "Amen, sister!" from the same old woman.

"Amen," she concluded, and opened her eyes. Everyone seemed to be staring at her. Evidently they had never heard a British prayer before.

"Ah—thank you, sister. That was a very unusual prayer."

"I am not used to praying in Latin."

"Never mind. I think everyone understood."

"Well done, sister!" observed the old woman. "That was the best praying we've had in weeks!"

The leader gave a message of blessing from the lord who had, as she expected, failed to turn up. Evidently his people were used to it. The blessing sounded well-rehearsed.

Brother Solemnis's slack mouth dropped open when Tilla tapped him on the shoulder and whispered, "I have something to ask you, Brother. You are from Arelate. Can you tell me anything about a ship called the *Pride of the South*?"

A flush rose from his neck and began to spread up his face. He managed to stammer an apology for knowing nothing at all.

As the cloth was having its crumbs shaken off outside the door, Tilla overheard one of the women saying to the leader, "That's exactly the sort of thing I mean, Brother." The woman glanced at her before adding, "We need proper rules about who can speak."

"I'll think about it, sister."

"The believers in town have a rule that says . . ."

Tilla and Galla left the conversation behind and went outside. The sun was below the horizon and in the failing light the rows of newly turned amphorae laid out to dry behind the kiln looked like a regiment of sleeping pigs. A woman she had not seen before was walking along one of the rows, counting and noting something on a writing tablet. Remembering where they were, Tilla whispered, "Who is that?"

"The widow Lollia Saturnina," came the reply.

It was true, then. She was pretty. She owned a successful business. And she could read and write. Even worse, Galla now said, "You will meet her. I hear she is coming to the house to dinner tomorrow."

As they set out to walk back between the rows of olive trees to the

Medicus's house, Galla said, "It is as well to be careful what you pray about, sister. People talk."

Tilla wrenched her mind away from Lollia Saturnina. "Even about prayers?"

"I'm afraid so."

They were interrupted by a couple leaving the meeting who wanted to say good-bye. As Tilla stood waiting for them to finish chatting with Galla, an idea began to form. It was a ridiculous idea. It was an inspired idea. It was an idea that seemed to have come from somewhere outside herself.

As they walked between the gnarled and stunted olive trees she said, "How would you know if your god was telling you to do something?"

Galla thought about that. "Some people hear a voice," she said. "But I never have. I suppose if I had an idea about a good thing, and it would help somebody, I would try to do it."

"If your god told you to do something but somebody else might not like it, what then?"

"We must obey god rather than man." Galla sounded as if she was quoting something.

"And is it true what it says in that letter from the Greek man? Your god will protect his people whatever happens to them?"

"God loves us," Galla assured her. "If we keep the faith, there is a place ready for each one of us in heaven."

Tilla voiced the problem that had been niggling at the back of her mind. "But you meet in secret."

"That doesn't mean we have to put ourselves in danger on purpose."

"Would your god protect me in Arelate?"

Galla stopped. "Why would you go there?"

"I am only thinking about it," explained Tilla. "Arelate is the place to find out about the missing ship. I was thinking, if this Brother Solemnis has a cart . . ."

"You can't go somewhere on your own with a man. And Arelate is full of sailors, and where there are sailors there are bad women."

Tilla said, "But your god is everywhere."

"What about Master Gaius?"

"The Medicus is a problem," Tilla agreed.

"There are many things you don't understand about the faith."

"I understand what it is to lose a brother." She also understood that if she did not find a way to avoid it, she was going to have to eat her first ever Roman dinner tomorrow night in front of the Medicus's family and be compared with the rich and beautiful Lollia Saturnina, who knew how to read and write.

Before Galla could object, she gathered up her skirt and ran back down between the trees, past the squat boundary stone and the drying amphorae and into the yard where the driver was standing chatting to some of the workmen. "Brother Solemnis!" she cried. As his skinny neck reddened and his eyes widened in alarm, she said, "I may need to go to Arelate. What time do you set off in the morning?"

43

THE SURFACE OF the bench was still warm beneath her, but the late evening air was mercifully cool. Tilla wrapped her hands around her shoulders and gazed at the house that was the Medicus's home, but not hers. A yellow glow around the dining room shutters reminded her of how he had changed the subject when she asked if he was thinking of marrying Lollia Saturnina.

A shape appeared in the doorway, clattered down the steps, and hurried toward her. Resolving itself into Galla, it hissed, "Mistress Cassiana is coming!"

This was good. Cass was friendly. Perhaps they could talk over the problem.

"I think she's cross with us!"

Tilla frowned, wondering what she had done to offend now. Before Galla could explain, a second shape emerged from the house and Galla fled.

Cass seated herself on the bench, folded her arms, and said, "I hear you cursed the person who supplied the ship."

Tilla felt her stomach clench. She wished she had said her prayer to the god in private. What had possessed Galla to relay it to her mistress? She said, "I was trying to help. I know what it is to lose a brother."

"Galla told me because she is loyal," explained Cass, answering her unspoken question. "She wanted me to know before I heard any gossip."

When Tilla did not reply, she continued, her tone suddenly sharp, "What do you know about it?"

Tilla wished she could crumble away into the dry ground under her feet. Even trampling about in that slimy grape trough was better than feeling the churning in her intestines. The only people who had shown her much of a welcome since she had arrived here were Cass, Galla, and the worshippers of Christos. Galla had kept a secret from her mistress out of kindness, and Tilla had just betrayed her with that stupid prayer.

"I know Galla is a follower of Christos," said Cass. "I don't care about that. My brother was one too. What do you know about the ship?"

Tilla cleared her throat. There was no way out of this but to tell the truth. "Galla heard a rumor that it was a rotten old ship that should never have gone to sea."

Cass seized her arm. "I knew there was something! I knew there was something not right!"

"That is why I cursed the person who hired out the ship to Severus," explained Tilla. "He must have known. He deserves to die too. Your brother is dead because that person was greedy."

"What else did Galla tell you? Why would the captain try and get to Ostia on something that wasn't seaworthy? Has she heard anything else?"

"I do not know. You must ask her."

"But it means there are people who know things!"

"She overheard this from the fish sellers at the market."

Cass's face fell. "I've already tried them. They won't talk to me. Lucius won't go to Arelate and ask, and Gaius has too much to do already."

"Yes," said Tilla, wondering whether this new god could be speaking in the words of Cassiana. "I know."

44

TILLA WAS NERVOUS walking through the garden in the cool of the morning, clutching her bag in one hand and a borrowed straw hat in the other. The air around her was silent apart from the call of a bird and the plants rustling in the breeze. The screeching insects had not woken up yet.

The dog at the gate sniffed at her curiously as she slipped back the bolts, but he was trained to stop people coming in, not going out. She pulled the gate gently shut behind her and said a silent good-bye to the strange household where she had spent the last three days. She had her savings, four and a half denarii, and her comb in a little leather pouch hung around her neck. Her cloak was bundled inside her bag in case she had to sleep outdoors, and her knife was strapped to her belt.

Traveling alone and unprotected to a strange city seemed far more dangerous this morning than it had last night. She had almost lost her nerve as she watched the Medicus sleeping. She heard the steady rhythm of his breath falter. Heard him mutter something as he dreamed. Waiting, motionless, until he settled again, she told herself both their lives would be less complicated if she were away for a couple of days. Indeed, their lives would be less complicated if they had never met, but she did not want to think about that. She only knew that if she stayed, she would have to face an evening lying across a dining couch in a borrowed dress—probably yellow again, so that her skin would look gray and her hair would look dirty—while all these foreigners wished she had not come so that the Medicus could propose to Lollia Saturnina.

She had kissed him lightly on the forehead, picked up her things, and crept out of the room.

Reaching the roadside, she trained her eyes on the western approach and watched for the cart to appear. She reminded herself that she had the protection of the God Who Is Everywhere. Just in case the god needed a reminder, she lifted her hands and prayed that he would keep her safe. That he would look after the Medicus while she was away. That he would help her find out about the *Pride of the South*. That Lollia Saturnina would have a laugh like a donkey, or dribble down her chin. "Amen," she added at the end, remembering the formula. It was important to get the words right, or the prayer would not be heard. Everyone knew that, and besides, it would not do to get on the wrong side of a god who was everywhere and saw everything.

There was a great deal she did not understand about this Christos and she felt no better for praying to him. But she understood that Cass's brother had died because of someone else's greed, and that a means of getting to Arelate to find out the truth had been presented to her while she was in the presence of the god's worshippers. She had upset Cass last night without meaning to, and she needed to make amends. Besides, she was the only one who could help. The Medicus was too worried about debts and murder, and Cass's husband was of no use. Most of the household must have heard him shouting at her again last night. The Medicus, who had barely spoken to Tilla since she had returned from the meeting next door, had pinched out the lamp and observed that Lucius and wine were not a good combination.

"You should talk to him."

"He wouldn't listen."

She said, "I hear the widow next door is coming to dinner."

"And Diphilus the builder."

"She is the one who is very pretty and very rich."

There was only a brief pause before, "Diphilus isn't."

"Even if you find out who did poison that man, you will still have no money."

She felt the warmth of his sigh on her shoulder. "I'm going to have to face a difficult decision before long, Tilla."

She did not ask what that decision was. She did not need to. All she said was, "Not tonight."

"No." He nestled his head against her. "Not tonight."

A train of donkeys loaded with panniers of lettuces and onions plodded past on the way to market. Minutes later the driver of a cart reined in his mule, called, "Oy! Gorgeous! Going into town?" and pointed to the seat beside him. She told him she was waiting for someone, and he drove on.

Tilla tried to push away the memories of the last time she had been taken away on a cart from a place she did not want to be. She hoped she was not making another terrible mistake. Instead of rescuing her, that driver had turned out to be even worse than the people from whom she was fleeing. If it had not been for the Medicus's intervention she would not be alive now. What if Brother Solemnis turned out to be another crook? He had not looked like a criminal—in fact he had looked distinctly alarmed at being asked for a lift by a strange foreign woman. But she had been wrong last time. She shivered and rubbed the scar on the arm that her kidnapper had smashed when she tried to escape. The arm the Medicus had insisted on trying to mend when others would have played it safe and left her to try and survive with only one hand.

She should have said something to him about this journey. He did not deserve to be abandoned without a word. But if he had known, there would have been an argument. He would have had to pretend he wanted her to stay and eat dinner with the rich widow.

Tilla's gaze followed the track of the long shadow that stretched away from her feet in the direction of the town. There was still no sign of the man from Arelate.

At her feet, the tiniest ants she had ever seen were swarming around a dead bee, shifting first one end and then the other, nudging their charge along through the dust. Others were scurrying to and fro along an invisible track, carrying back news of the discovery to their nest.

She put on the hat she had borrowed late last night from Galla. Now the tall thin person in the shadow had a huge round head.

The clang of a distant bell made her look up. If Brother Solemnis did not turn up in a minute, she would be missed at the house. Perhaps she had said the prayer wrong. Perhaps the new god was too busy being everywhere to stop here and listen to one woman.

The bee was being hustled away into the dry grass at the side of the road.

This trip was a very big mistake. She should face up to Lollia Saturnina instead of running away. She must go back now, before someone from the house saw the family guest standing at the roadside with a traveling bag.

But then who would find out about Cass's brother?

"I am going to count to ten," she told the god. To be fair, she would do it very slowly. Then if the driver was not here, she would walk back down the track and hope the dog would not make a fuss when she sneaked back in through the unbolted gate.

By the time she had reached eight, her hopes of reprieve were rising. On "nine" they were dashed. There was a vehicle approaching in the distance. There were also footsteps running up the track behind her.

"Stop!" cried Cass, breathless, struggling with a bright blue-and-green-striped bag slung over her shoulder.

Ten. She had been caught. Feeling relieved and rather silly, Tilla picked up her own bag and turned to walk back to the house.

"Galla told me," called Cass. "Don't go without me!"

45

TILLA HAD WANDERED off somewhere by the time Ruso woke. She would be with Cass or Galla, keeping out of Arria's way. Lucius was nowhere to be seen, either: probably sleeping off last night's wine and bad behavior. Ruso was not sorry. He had nothing amicable to say to him, and he did not want any more discussions about Who, How, or Why. He knew the answers now. What he did not know was what he was going to do about them.

Before Ruso could dismount from the mule, the one-eyed gatekeeper silenced the dog with, "Oy, Brutus!" and said, "Miss Claudia's not here, sir."

"You mean she's not on the premises, or she's not allowed to see me?"

The eye met Ruso's own. "I wouldn't want to lie to you, sir."

"But you would, if you were ordered to."

The scars folded around a grin. "I would, sir. Miss Claudia's not here. Can I say something, sir?"

The man's attitude seemed to have warmed considerably since the last visit, perhaps as a result of Ruso's conversation with Flaccus the kitchen boy. "Go ahead."

"Some of us hope you get away with it."

"It wasn't me!"

The one eye blinked slowly, and Ruso realized the man was winking at him.

"It wasn't!"

"If you say so, sir. You might want to know the investigators have arrived, sir."

Ruso stared into the eye. "That's impossible. The message was only sent a couple of days ago."

"Turns out they were just down the road in Aquae Sextiae, sir. On some other business for the senator."

This was not only bad news, it was an amazing coincidence. "Are you sure?"

"One of 'em's a smartarse called Calvus," the doorman told him. "His mate's just here to provide some muscle." Before Ruso could ask how he knew, the man added, "I haven't got no instructions to lie about them, sir, see? I just let them in a minute ago. If you want to talk to them, I'll go and ask."

"No thanks," said Ruso, gathering up the reins of the mule. He urgently needed to talk with Claudia, but the last thing he intended to do was to walk straight into the arms of the official investigators.

Ruso turned the mule and was just persuading it into a trot when the man called, "Hold on a minute, sir, I was wrong. Miss Claudia's here after all."

Claudia was there, but so was the gatekeeper, and behind her he could see Zosimus the steward hurrying toward them. The conversation he needed to have with her would be impossible. The best he could do was to beckon her outside the gatehouse and respond to her frantic "Gaius, there are men here asking questions!" with "Have you been lying to me?"

"Me? No! Ennia's the one who tells lies. All this nonsense about the marvelous boyfriend in Rome? I said why doesn't he come and fetch her then, and it turns out he's been dead for years! She only wants to go back there because nobody here will have her."

"Claudia, listen. I've talked to the root cutter."

"Who?" Claudia's face was impressively blank.

He glanced over his shoulder. There was no time to be subtle. "It was you, wasn't it?"

"What? What was me?"

He was not going to pretend he had to explain.

The manicured nails dug into his arms. "Who's been telling you lies?"

"He described you."

"Who? Gaius, what are you talking about?"

Suddenly he felt weary. "Just tell the truth, Claudia. Please. For the sake of the staff. The investigators will find out sooner or later, anyway."

"But I didn't—"

Her protest was cut off by the arrival of Zosimus, backed up by the gatekeeper and the gatekeeper's dog. Ruso was not allowed onto the senator's property. An official inquiry was under way. If he had anything to say, he could say it to the investigators when they were ready. In the meantime, he was to stop harassing the bereaved family.

Ruso had never seen Claudia look so frightened as when Zosimus escorted her back toward the gate.

46

PROBUS'S SLAVE USHERED Ruso through an entrance hall that had changed little in the years since his last visit. The heavy iron-bound chests in which his former father-in-law kept other people's money were still flanked by two surly faced men armed with clubs and daggers. The man who had told him about Marcia's attempts to borrow money, now back on duty, showed no sign of recognizing him. He followed the slave out into the garden where he had once asked for Claudia's hand in marriage and wondered whether Probus knew that she had murdered her latest husband.

Probus was seated by a fountain that much resembled the one in Ruso's own garden, except that it was built properly and it worked. When the slave had been dismissed he said, "Keep your voice down. We won't be heard over the water."

Evidently Probus did not trust his staff any more than he trusted Ruso, who perched on the side of the fountain and trailed one hand in the cool water. He wondered what Claudia was telling the investigators. None of it would answer any of his own questions: questions like how she had managed to poison Severus without harming the rest of the household, and why he had been such a fool as to believe her.

Probus was still talking. ". . . but I haven't heard anything."

Ruso cleared his throat. "Anything about what?"

The corners of Probus's mouth turned down even farther than usual. "You were the one who wanted to meet, Ruso. Kindly have the courtesy to listen."

"Sorry."

"You wanted to know about Severus's business affairs."

Ruso nodded, although in the light of what he now knew, they were of limited interest.

"Everyone knows the Gabinii are hard men if you cross them, but until recently I thought he was honest. If I hadn't, I would never have loaned him the money for the shipping deals."

"Or let him marry your daughter," put in Ruso.

"Of course not."

Ruso had been considering telling Probus what he had found out about Claudia, but the arrival of the investigators had changed everything. With luck, they would find out about her for themselves. He would be clear of the murder charge without incriminating her himself or incurring Probus's revenge in the process. On the other hand, her denial had been remarkably convincing . . .

". . . whether it was Justinus all along," Probus was saying.

Ruso did not like to admit that his attention had wandered again. He said, "Ah."

"But Justinus was with me for fourteen years and was always entirely reliable."

"Like his sister," put in Ruso.

"I like to think I know how to judge a man," continued Probus, "but when the letters of credit started appearing in different ports after the ship had gone down, it was difficult to know what conclusion to draw."

Ruso frowned. "You mean things turned up later that should have been at the bottom of the sea?"

Probus gave a tut of exasperation. "You've never really understood how business works, have you, Ruso?"

"No. Did you say there was more than one shipping deal?"

"This was the third. The others had gone smoothly, so I had no reason to suspect there was anything wrong when Severus asked for a bigger investment."

Probus's voice was calm, but there was a faint involuntary flicker of the left eyelid that Ruso had not noticed before.

"When Justinus left here, he was carrying a certain amount of cash, but certainly not enough to fund him for the whole trip or purchase the cargoes. That was arranged in the usual way, with letters authorizing him to withdraw cash up to specified amounts from bankers in the various ports where I have arrangements. Since the ship disappeared, someone has been going around withdrawing the cash."

"So you started to wonder if he really was dead and went to ask Cass if she'd heard from him?"

"He may be dead," continued Probus, oblivious to any distress he might have caused. "Or he may have been part of a conspiracy to rob me. As I'm fairly certain Severus was."

"The letters could have been washed up on a beach somewhere. Anybody could have gotten hold of them."

"Justinus had orders to keep them on his person at all times and destroy them in the event of a shipwreck."

"I see."

"No you don't!" Probus seemed to startle himself with the sudden exclamation. He glanced around the colonnades that surrounded the garden, then dropped his voice again for, "I accept that you probably didn't kill Severus. I don't know who did and frankly, I'm not interested. He was a serious disappointment, he lost me a lot of money, and my advice to Claudia was to get rid of him."

He caught Ruso's eye and added, "Divorce him, of course."

"Of course," agreed Ruso. "Divorce him. Unless you and she decided to take revenge on him together."

"Don't be ridiculous, Ruso. We don't all do business like the Gabinii." Probus dismissed the possibility so summarily that Ruso was inclined to believe him.

"But if you stir up some false connection between Severus's death and this shipping business," Probus continued, "the senator's investigator will start poking around in all sorts of affairs that could have . . ." He paused. "Unintended consequences."

"There may already be a whisper in Rome that Severus was up to something," said Ruso. "Did you know that two investigators have arrived this morning? Apparently they were already up here."

Probus was as surprised as Ruso had been, and no more pleased. He leaned back in his seat and surveyed his former son-in-law. "Let's hope they can be persuaded to keep out of things that don't concern the inquiry."

"I think they'll be the ones doing the persuading."

Probus sighed. "You may be clueless about business, Ruso, but until now you were always fairly good at keeping your mouth shut."

"Thank you."

"And you do appear to have some residual sense of duty to my daughter. So I'm going to tell you exactly what I think happened, and then perhaps you'll understand why it's so important that I know if your Cassiana hears from her brother. At the same time you'll understand what a difficult position you'll put me in if you aren't discreet."

Ruso waited. If he could glean some information to help Cass, this would not have been such a wasted meeting.

"It's my suspicion," said Probus, "that the captain and the crew sold the cargo—or possibly there never was one in the first place—and then scuttled the ship, which my informants now tell me was practically worthless. Presumably Severus paid next to nothing for it, despite having taken a large sum of money from me to invest in a decent vessel. They may have done away with Justinus and stolen the letters, or he may have joined them and used the letters himself to defraud me. What matters is that this is kept confidential. If there's any whisper of suspicion that there are unauthorized letters of credit circulating around the banking fraternity in my name . . ."

"You'd be ruined. Nobody would ever trust your seal again."

"This is only a short-term problem," insisted Probus. "The letters had cash limits and an expiry date on them. All I have to do is weather the storm. But after the loss I sustained on the ship in the first place, it's a considerable nuisance."

Ruso thought for a moment. Over the years experience had formed a small clearing in the fog of his commercial ignorance, and it had revealed some of the dangerous terrain of borrowing and lending. "Who else put in money to the shipping deal?"

Probus visibly stiffened. "I was acting alone."

"I'm surprised," observed Ruso. "With that large a risk, I'd have thought you'd want to spread it. The first trips went well. Severus seemed to know what he was doing. I'd have thought you might suggest to a few clients that if they had money to spare, they might want to invest it in something that would give them a good percentage."

"I was acting alone," insisted Probus. "It was a family arrangement between myself and my son-in-law."

"Come on, Probus! Most of your reputation is built on introducing rich lenders to good borrowers."

"Will you keep your voice down?" hissed Probus, halfway out of his chair. "You have no idea how these things are arranged!" When Ruso made no attempt to argue, he settled back down again. "Even if there were other investors, I couldn't possibly divulge their names," he insisted. "No more than you would divulge details of a patient. Everyone who invests in shipping knows they risk losing their money. That's why the interest rates are so good."

"So you haven't told your investors that you think they were swindled by the man you recommended to them."

"Even if there were other people involved," said Probus, skirting around the question, "none of them has complained. So if nobody suspects anything, nobody would have a motive to do away with Severus."

"And they won't be asking you to refund their money."

Probus winced. "Ruso, try not to interfere in things you don't understand. The loss of the ship is not relevant to the murder." He leaned closer. "If word gets out, Claudia will be ruined. All she has is what I can give her. It looks as though that worthless husband left her nothing at all."

"So who's got the money? He can't have set all this up for nothing."

"I have no idea. If it's here, he hid it away somewhere neither Claudia nor I can trace it. Possibly it's all still over in Arelate with his contact there."

Ruso looked up. "He's got a man in the port?"

Probus sighed. "Of course he has. You don't imagine he made all the arrangements from this distance by himself, do you?"

"Who is he? This contact?"

"I always assumed he kept the name to himself so I couldn't deal with the man directly and cut him out altogether. I've been told since that he was called Ponticus. He must have been in one of the marine shipping guilds, but nobody seems to know how to find him now. There's a rumor he drowned on the ship with the captain and crew."

"If he's that heavily involved in a fraud, he probably started the rumor himself."

"He's not someone I want to do business with," agreed Probus. "The sooner I can wash my hands of this whole affair, the better."

"What I can't understand," said Ruso, "is how you can know that Severus was doing business with violent and ruthless criminals who did away with your own man, and yet when Severus is poisoned, you're confident it didn't have anything to do with the shipping deal. Is there something else you're not telling me?"

Probus frowned. "Obviously it wasn't the same people. Severus was on their side."

Ruso reached for his stick. "You need to go and have a serious talk with your daughter, Probus. There are things she might tell you that she won't tell me."

"What? Why? Claudia knows nothing about any of this." Probus's voice rose as Ruso stood. "I thought we had an understanding?"

"Talk to her."

"Where are you going?"

"To Arelate," he said. "There's something else going on here. Something I think the investigators might already know about. I'm going to find out what it is."

47

YOU HAVEN'T SEEN Tilla, have you?"

The slave brought his handcart to a halt on the way to the refuse heap. "I don't think so, sir."

"Never mind," said Ruso, heading toward the winery. It was a shame the boy was not a year or two older. Before long, he would have no difficulty remembering whether he had seen a young woman like Tilla.

The winery contained only his brother. Lucius did not look well enough for a trip to Arelate, even if he could be persuaded that anything useful might be found out when they got there.

Ruso leaned on one of the tree trunks that supported the press and watched the precious juice oozing out and trickling down the sides of the slats. Deliberately casual, he said, "How's the head?"

"There's nothing wrong with my head," growled Lucius, squinting at the angle of the massive main beam and checking the pulley ropes that held it in position. "Why is it if a man has a few things to say, everyone assumes he's drunk?"

Ruso moved away from the press and began to pick his way between the rows of jars set in the floor. The magic of fermentation had begun. Yesterday's juice had vanished beneath a froth that sparkled in the streak of sunlight from the double doors. By contrast, the black pitch that coated the insides of the empty jars made them look like the openings of tunnels into a dark underworld. He said, "I take it Tilla's somewhere around with Cass?"

"Cass has been avoiding me all morning. I don't know what the fuss is about. If people would listen in the first place, I wouldn't have to shout."

Ruso reached the far wall and turned. From here, his brother's bulk was dwarfed by the colossal apparatus of the press. He said, "The investigators have turned up."

Lucius glared at him across the jars. "You said we had weeks!"

Ruso explained the coincidence of them being over in Aquae Sextiae.

"Why?"

"There must be something else going on that we don't know about. Maybe the senator sent them to keep an eye on Severus."

Lucius gave a sigh of exasperation. "They'll be crawling all over us here before you can blink. How far have you got with saving the family by geometry?"

Ruso wove his way back between the jars, realizing he knew very little that he was yet prepared to tell anyone.

Lucius dipped a scoop into one of the jars and tasted the contents. "Well?"

"When I was in Britannia—"

"You told me. Gaius, does it ever occur to you to wonder why you get tangled up in this sort of business?"

"I was only going to say, things often get worse before they get better."

Lucius gave a grunt. "I hope that comes out with a bit more conviction when you say it to your patients." He took another sip from beneath the froth in the scoop. "Mm. That's about ready for the concentrate."

Ruso, feeling he should take an interest, tipped the scoop and savored the rich juice that slid out from beneath the froth.

Lucius pulled the cloth cover off a jug and tasted the contents before pouring the rest into the jar he had just sampled and giving it a vigorous stir. He said, "Let's hope they turn up tonight."

"Who?"

"The senator's men. Arria's invited that Diphilus to dinner. I'm surprised anyone dares to eat here."

"She's invited the widow next door as well."

Lucius tapped the last drops off the scoop. "Lollia Saturnina?" he said, dipping it in a rinsing bucket and wiping it dry. "Might not be so bad then. As long as nobody mentions bankruptcy or poisoning."

"Or the *Pride of the South*?"

The silence that followed revealed more about the depths of last night's marital row than the shouting had. Ruso was about to change the subject when Lucius said, "This thing with Justinus has sent her odd in the head. Your Briton hasn't helped, telling her Severus as good as murdered her brother by hiring a rotten ship. What's the matter with these women?"

"I haven't got time to speculate."

"Now she's got some mad idea about me going around interrogating sailors. As if I've got time to rush off to Arelate in the middle of the vintage!"

So that was what the argument had been about. Grateful for the cue, Ruso said, "I'll go."

Lucius looked at him oddly. "You?"

"If the investigators turn up while I'm gone, don't say anything about the ship unless they ask. If they do ask, make it clear that Cass didn't know what state it was in before yesterday, so she had no more reason to dislike Severus than the rest of us."

"You mean you knew as well? Gods above! How many other people has that woman of yours told? It's complete rubbish. I tried to explain to Cass last night, but she wouldn't listen. If you want to get rid of someone you do it secretly on dry land. You don't go paying for a ship and drowning a whole lot of sailors as well. She's not thinking straight."

"I'll try and sort it out," promised Ruso.

"I won't need the cart tomorrow," said Lucius. "You can take that bloody interfering barbarian as well."

"I could ride across this afternoon."

"Justinus can wait, brother. He's dead. And so will you be if you don't turn up tonight for Arria's dinner."

48

RUSO WAS APPLYING himself to the clumsy process of climbing the porch steps when he found himself facing his stepmother.

"There you are, Gaius! Where have you been? We need to talk about the seating plan."

"Have you seen Tilla anywhere?"

"You will shave before dinner, won't you? We want Lollia to think you've made an effort. When I think of the wonderful dinner parties we used to have when your poor father was alive . . ."

"Have you seen Tilla?"

"Now, the seating plan—"

"Tilla?"

"No, dear. I expect she's with the farm slaves."

Arria was as surprised as everyone else when he told her the senator's investigators had arrived.

He said, "They'll probably want to question us all."

"But we don't know anything!"

"We know what happened. We're the only ones who do."

She sighed. "Oh, Gaius. I do wish you hadn't made such a fuss. Why can't you just tell them you've changed your mind and you've just realized he was ill?"

"Why would I say that?"

"Well, dear, I would have thought that was obvious."

It was, but he did not want to admit it. He said, "If you were poisoned, would you want somebody to pretend you weren't?"

"Really, Gaius! There's no need—"

"I'm trying to do the right thing, Arria."

"So are we all, dear. So what shall I say to them?"

He said, "Tell them what you know."

"But what I know looks so bad! There you are, shut up in a room with him, and the next thing that happens—"

"Had nothing to do with me," said Ruso, edging past her in the direction of the kitchen. "If it did, I'd make up a better story. What's for lunch?"

Arria put a restraining hand on his shoulder. "Please don't upset Cook, dear. You can't imagine what it does to the pastry. And by the way, what did you say to Marcia yesterday? She was terribly cross."

"We talked about a dowry," he said, not in the mood to go over what he had since learned about Tertius the gladiator. "I'll explain later."

"Well, you'll have to settle something on her now, dear. Who's going to marry her when everybody thinks you poisoned Claudia's husband?"

Ruso knew quite well that the yolk of hard-boiled egg was prone to disintegration. He should have brought a bowl. Instead, he was seated in front of the pile of unpaid bills and making an undignified attempt to lick scattered gray and yellow crumbs out of his cupped hands when someone rapped on the study door.

"What?" he demanded, slapping the remains of the egg from his hands and wiping them on his tunic in a manner of which his mother would not have approved.

The end of Galla's "Please, sir, may I . . ." was inaudible.

"Open the door, woman!" he called, wondering whether her common sense had finally deserted her or whether he really was as terrifying as she seemed to think.

He slapped a bill from the wheelwright shut and looked up to see her standing in the doorway clutching a tray of dirty wooden bowls and grubby napkins. "Is this important? I'm busy."

Galla shuffled in and pushed the door shut with her foot. "Yes, sir."

He leaned across the desk and helped himself to a small loaf of bread from the corner of the tray. Failing to find any sign of teethmarks or dribble on it, he said, "Has this been anywhere it shouldn't be?"

"No, sir. Miss Polla didn't want it."

Ruso sat back and tore off a chunk of bread. "Well?"

"Thank you for letting me back in the house, sir."

"It was only sensible. Is that what you came to tell me?"

"No, sir." Galla appeared to raise herself to her full height—which was not great—before taking a deep breath and announcing to a point just below his chin, "Tilla is gone to Arelate, my lord."

"She's what?" The bread landed on top of the wheelwright's bill.

The repeat of this surprising statement was mumbled to the tray, as if Galla had used up all her courage in saying it the first time.

"Gods almighty! Why didn't you come and tell me this earlier? When did she go?"

"I couldn't find you, sir. I think she went just after dawn. She told me to say she was sorry not to say good-bye."

"But what in Jupiter's name does she want to go there for?"

Galla gripped the outside of the tray and pushed the edge back into the folds of her tunic as if it were a protective barrier between them. "I asked her not to go, my lord."

"This is ridiculous. I thought she'd got over this sort of wandering off. It'll take her all day to walk that far in this heat, and she'll probably be robbed on the way. Where's she going to sleep?"

Galla cleared her throat. "She was hoping for a lift. She talked to a man with a cart."

"Which man?"

"Solemnis, my lord."

"Never heard of him. Who does he work for? What the hell does he think he's playing at?"

Galla looked as though she was going to burst into tears. "He is . . . a friend of a friend, sir."

"Can he be trusted?"

"He is a follower of Christos, my lord."

"You mean she's run off to join some weird religion?"

"No, sir. They have gone to find out about the ship."

"They?"

"Mistress Cassiana is gone too."

Ruso stood up and flung the first stack of bills back into the trunk. "Put that bloody tray down," he ordered, snatching up his stick. "Lock the rest of this stuff away, then take the key down to Lucius in the winery. Tell him his wife's run off to Arelate with Tilla and a—no, leave out the religious bit. Tell him I've gone to get them back before they get into trouble."

"Yes, sir."

"As if we haven't got enough problems! Why didn't you send me a message? Why didn't you tell somebody?"

The girl opened her mouth as if she were about to speak, then closed it again.

"Don't stand there gasping like a fish! Say it!"

Galla swallowed again. "I'm sorry, my lord," she said, lifting a pile of documents from the desk. "I couldn't find you, and I did not know who else to tell." She knelt to tidy the jumble of tablets and scroll cases in the trunk.

She had a point. Who would she tell? Arria, who had let Tilla tread grapes? The girls, who had abandoned Tilla themselves?

"You could have told my brother."

"Mistress Cassiana told me to look after the children and not to say anything, sir."

Of course. Rocking sideways to rest his weight on the stick, Ruso said, "There must be times, Galla, when you wish you were part of a different household."

"Never, my lord."

"Really?" Swinging around to head for the door, he muttered, "It must be just me and Marcia, then."

From the top of the steps, he could see over the wall to where the stable lad was lugging buckets of water across the yard. "I need Severus's horse tacked up!" he called. "Now!"

49

BROTHER SOLEMNIS HAD hardly spoken a word since they set off this morning. Tilla watched him from her none-too-comfortable seat on a bundle of hides in the back of the cart and wondered if he was praying for the protection of his god. On top of the usual carter's worries about lame animals, breakdowns, bad roads, damaged goods, and bandits, he had now been accosted by a barbarian woman and a stranger, demanding a lift to Arelate. She suspected he had only taken them because he was too frightened to refuse.

Cass was not much better company. She had chattered nervously as the cart first rattled and jolted them away from the farm. She had never been to Arelate. It was a big and beautiful town. The river was said to be huge. This would be an adventure.

As the sun rose higher, her excitement faded. When they passed a milestone she read, "Nemausus, eleven miles," as if it were a mark of loss rather than a sign of progress.

Tilla reflected that more and more these days, she was thinking it might be useful to be able to read. Somewhere among the other letters chipped into the tall stone must be the good news of the diminishing distance to Arelate.

The milestone must have inspired Cass's sudden, "We won't be back tonight, will we?"

"We will find an inn." Had Cass only just thought of this? How fast did she imagine a mule cart could make a trip of over twenty miles?

Cass was chewing her lower lip. "What if they wake in the night?"

"Galla will deal with them," said Tilla, guessing she was talking about the children.

"I'm their mother."

"They will manage. They are used to Galla, and they are not babies."

Cass fell silent again. Tilla leaned back, closed her eyes, and tried to pretend that she was still traveling with the Medicus to a peaceful land of blue skies and gentle breezes where she would be welcomed into a new family.

"Lucius will be furious."

"Lucius will have to learn to treat you better," insisted Tilla, secretly disappointed that so far neither the Medicus nor his brother had come after them.

Cass was saying something about, ". . . divorces me?"

"Of course he will not divorce you. He cannot afford a slave to do your work and nobody else would marry him."

In the silence that followed, there was plenty of time to wish she had thought about that before she said it.

Cass said, "I hope somebody remembered to collect the eggs." When Tilla did not answer she said, "What if the slaves eat all the provisions?"

"Then they will go hungry later."

"We should never have left home."

"We are doing a good thing," Tilla insisted, pushing aside the urge to explain that if Cass had not turned up at the last minute, she would have abandoned the trip herself and been at the dinner to face the widow and all her money and watch the Medicus trying to make his difficult choice. "We will go and find somebody who knows about your brother's ship."

"But what if—"

"Most of *what if* never happens. Pray to Christos for help. Galla says you can do it anywhere."

"If Galla hadn't told you about Christos, we wouldn't be here. When I get back Lucius will have her whipped."

Tilla was glad she was not Galla. Somehow, everything was always her fault.

"Anyway," continued Cass, "I can't pray to Christos. You'll have to do it. You're not married."

"Does that matter?"

"Christos's followers are supposed to obey their husbands."

Tilla tried to picture the women who had been at the meeting and wondered if they had all been there with male permission.

"I told my brother Lucius would never let me follow a foreign religion when we've spent all that money building Diana's temple, so it was no good him telling me any more about Christos."

The cart jolted in and out of a pothole. Cass pushed back one of the bundles that had slid sideways beneath her. "I should have let Lucius build a tomb."

"You can build a tomb when you get home."

"I tried to explain to him, but he wouldn't listen."

Tilla yawned and lifted Galla's hat in the hope that some cool air might circulate around her head. She wished Cass would keep her worries to herself. It had all seemed so straightforward last night, in the enthusiasm of the singing and the cries of *Amen, sister!*

"We are doing a good thing," she repeated, wishing she was not doing it at all.

50

THE LEATHER WATER bottle thumped against his side as the horse thudded across the burned stubble of the wheat field, cutting off the corner where the track led up to the main road. Ruso jammed his fluttering hat lower on his head and glanced down to check that he had fastened the safety strap on his knife. He urged the horse to leap the ditch and flung it into a sharp turn to veer past a train of startled pack mules. Ignoring the angry yells of the driver, he dug his heels into the gray flanks and headed along the verge at a gallop.

He could hear nothing around him: only the rush of air and the thump of hooves. Ahead of him, a flock of sheep scattered at his approach. He yelled an apology to the shepherd—who should have had more sense than to use the road, anyway—and urged Severus's horse on. It responded with a further burst of speed that would have set the stable lad laughing with delight. This was as near as a man could get to flying. At this rate, he might even catch them before they reached Arelate. Whatever transport this Solemnis had to offer, it would not be as fast as his own.

With luck, all that would be needed was to make Solemnis one very sorry carter and deliver a lecture on why women should never travel with strange men, even in a civilized country. If they were unlucky . . . Severus's contact might be in the port. He did not want to dwell on what the man might do to silence two women who were asking the wrong questions.

Ruso squinted at the sky. It must be past the eighth hour by now. The sun was well over the zenith and it was appallingly hot. His eyes felt gritty. The kerchief he had tied over his nose was slipping down. He pushed it back into place, wrinkling his nose in a futile attempt to hold it there and finally yanking it down out of the way and swearing at it. He had never intended to hurtle across to Arelate at this speed. As usual, he was having to clear up somebody else's mess. And as usual, instead of talking things over in a sensible manner, Tilla had decided to make his life far more difficult than it was already. Sometimes he wondered whether she did it on purpose. A one-woman rebellion against Rome.

Severus's horse, out of condition from its enforced rest, was already beginning to tire. He would have to pick up a fresh animal halfway—and since he was not on active duty, he would have to pay. In the meantime, he slowed to a canter and swerved to overtake a heavy goods vehicle, not bothering to wonder what might be under the tarpaulin at the back. Nobody facing a journey of over twenty miles would travel by oxcart: It was quicker to walk. He was just urging the horse past a panniered donkey when it struck him that Tilla might well be doing what he least expected in order to avoid detection. On the other hand, if he paused to inspect every vehicle he might not catch up with them before the light began to fade and the town gates closed.

There was no sense in looking over his shoulder, but he did it all the same.

As he had expected, there was no blond head poking out from under the receding tarpaulin. Instead, the wagon was being overtaken on both sides. Two more riders were pounding toward him, evidently staging some sort of race.

The road ahead was clear to the next rise. Fields dotted with the orange roofs of small farms stretched away into the distance on both sides. He wondered if the shepherd had managed to regroup his flock before those two idiots thundered past and scattered it again. As he topped the rise to see more empty road ahead, he could hear the racers' hoofbeats. He nudged his own horse aside to let them pass.

Two men with kerchiefs over their faces drew level with him, one urging on a black horse and the other a big roan. Both men looked old enough to know better. The roan was much too close.

"Move over!" he yelled, just as the roan barged him. Ruso's horse leaped sideways. A front hoof slipped on the side of the ditch and he was sent lurching over its shoulder. The horse managed to scramble up and Ruso righted himself, wishing he had a cavalry mount and a decent saddle. He was still trying to calm the horse when he noticed the men were turning back.

"I'm all right!" he yelled, holding the animal steady in the middle of the road, well away from the ditch in case it decided to spook again at their approach.

They were coming too fast. Both shouting. He saw the odd movement of the hand. The flash of metal in the sunlight. For a moment he stared, unable to believe what was happening. To have survived Britannia only to be attacked by bandits here at home.

His fingers fumbled with the safety strap. They were almost on him now: the one on the black with knife raised, the other reaching forward, ready to seize the reins of his horse.

No time for his own knife. He urged the horse toward the gap between them, ready to barge the roan while hooking at the knife man's arm with the end of his walking stick. He had to get away from them and go to warn Tilla.

It would have worked. It would have worked beautifully. In fact it was on the way to working when his own mount stumbled on that front leg. He heard the rider of the roan cry out as the two horses collided. Ruso's lunge toward the knife man became a wild wave in midair as the gray horse gave way beneath him and they crashed to the ground in a crunching confusion of hooves and tail and elbows and gravel.

Ruso's first instinct was to curl up, hands protecting his head. Only when the thrashing about had stopped did the pain start to burn its way through the shock.

Someone was nudging his shoulder. He wanted to say, *Don't just poke the casualty, talk to him!* but then he remembered in whose company he had fallen. He lifted one arm—at least that much was working—and found himself staring into the whiskery nostrils of Severus's horse, which was examining him with an air of puzzled concern.

He rolled over onto his back. A shadow fell over him and an oddly shaped fist clutching a knife filled the center of his vision. Beyond it, he managed to make out that the other man had unrolled some sort of document.

"In the name of Senator Gabinius Valerius," announced the reader, "I order you to come with us. Put it away, Stilo. He's got nowhere to run."

The man backed away. As he sheathed his knife Ruso saw that someone had done an untidy amputation of the last two fingers. He sat up and began to inspect himself for damage. He said, "You're the investigators."

"Calvus and Stilo," said the knife man, who must be the one the gatekeeper had described as the muscle. "I'm Stilo."

Ruso wiped the blood off a scrape on his elbow and decided the rest of him was only bruised. Mercifully he had done no more damage to his foot. "Why didn't you say so before?"

"If you didn't know who we was," countered Stilo, "why was you running away?"

Ruso unstrapped the bottle that the stable lad had filled for him. Evidently he had not bothered to rinse it: The water tasted disgusting. "I wasn't running away," he said. "I need to catch up with somebody."

"A lot of people need to catch up with somebody when we want to talk to them."

"Get back on your horse and come with us," said Calvus, gingerly easing his shoulder backward and forward with the opposite hand and wincing as he did so. He was slightly built and several inches shorter than Ruso: a man who might be irritated by his gruff companion but who would need his bulk as backup.

Ruso stifled his professional curiosity about the state of Calvus's shoulder and moved on to examine the gray horse.

He stumbled as a hand shoved him from behind. Stilo said, "He said, get back on."

Ruso retrieved his stick and urged the horse forward a few paces. Its gait was not dissimilar to his own. He swore quietly. There was no way he was going to catch up with anyone on this animal. "I'm trying to get to a friend," he said, without much hope. "She's in danger. I need to borrow a horse."

The answer was in the looks on their faces. The best he could do was to get home and try and persuade someone—Lollia Saturnina?—to let him borrow a fresh mount. "This one's lame," he said, "and so am I. It'll take me hours to walk anywhere." He glanced from one to the other of them.

"Get on Stilo's horse," ordered Calvus. "The exercise will do him good."

The glare that accompanied Stilo's handing over of the black horse's reins suggested that Ruso would be sorry for this later.

51

RUSO HAD HOPED to leave out parts of the truth. Omission was easier than lying. As he and Calvus rode slowly back along the road with a resentful Stilo leading the lame horse, it seemed that he might get away with it.

He summarized the circumstances of Severus's death, adding that Claudia had since confirmed that her husband was not in the best of health.

"Yes, I hear you've been to see the widow," observed Calvus. "Twice."

"We used to be married," said Ruso, noticing the heavy ring on Calvus's right hand and wondering whether a stone that size was there to add a sharp edge to his punch.

Calvus said, "What was Severus doing at your house?"

"We were both involved in a court case."

"He was going to wipe you out, and you're telling me he just dropped by for a chat?"

Ruso suspected the investigator would not believe that Severus had come to discuss a settlement, and he was right.

"Why would he do that?"

They were approaching the oxcart they had overtaken a few minutes before. The driver looked them up and down, noted the lame horse, and passed by with the barely concealed superiority of one who had known that too much rushing about never came to any good in the end.

Ruso said, "It's complicated. There was a falling-out between the women in both families."

"And Severus let it affect his business decisions?" It was obvious that Calvus was not convinced.

"Judge for yourself," suggested Ruso. "You've met Claudia."

"Somehow," said Calvus, "I don't see a man like the senator choosing an agent who's told what to do by his wife."

"Severus made some remarks about my sister," Ruso explained. "Apparently he meant it as a compliment, but my brother took it as an insult and my stepmother reported it to Claudia, who gave him a very bad time about it. He was angry with my family for stirring up trouble in his marriage, and since—according to him—we owed him money, he decided to make things difficult for us."

"I see."

"Only later on, he realized things had gone too far," said Ruso. "We'd just done a deal to straighten things out when he was taken ill."

"We'll need to talk to whoever witnessed the agreement."

"There wasn't anybody," explained Ruso. "There wasn't time to get things organized. I was more worried about his state of health."

"I see."

"I know this doesn't sound very likely."

"Did I say that?" asked Calvus.

"You didn't say that," confirmed Stilo across the horse.

Ruso said, "Severus was a bully and a liar. We can't have been the only people he tried to swindle."

"The first rule of investigating," said Calvus. "Never trust a suspect who tries to blame somebody else."

"I'm trying to help."

"If Severus went around swindling people," put in Stilo, "where'd he hide the money? The wife says he didn't have a bean."

"All I'm saying is, he might have had other enemies. People with fewer scruples."

"We'll bear it in mind," said Calvus.

"If we get desperate," said Stilo.

"It could be somebody who knew he was coming to see us and who deliberately tried to blame us for his death."

"Talks a lot, don't he?" observed Stilo to his partner. "I reckon it was him."

"Before we jump to conclusions," said Calvus, frowning at Stilo across the back of the lame horse, "go through again exactly what happened when Severus fell ill."

Ruso's account was as accurate as he could make it. So accurate, indeed, that as he explained the process by which he had eliminated all the causes he could think of, Stilo began to yawn. "So you're saying he was definitely poisoned, right?"

Ruso said, "I think so."

"Well was he, or wasn't he?"

"I can't think of anything else that would make sense of the symptoms."

"Is that yes or no?"

"Probably."

Stilo sighed. "You're all the same, you medics. It might be this or it might be that, or it might be some other bloody thing altogether. Do you have a special school where they teach you how not to answer questions?"

"Yes."

Calvus said, "What were his last words?"

" 'Somebody's poisoned me,' " said Ruso.

"Hah!" Stilo raised his free hand to the sky as if imploring the gods to listen to this idiot.

"Somebody has poisoned me," repeated Calvus slowly, as if he were speaking to a foreigner who was just learning Latin. "I'd say that was a clue, Doctor, wouldn't you?"

"Perhaps."

"Hmph," put in Stilo. "For a minute there I thought we were going to get a straight answer."

"He might have been wrong."

Stilo muttered something that sounded very much like "Smartarse."

Ruso had a feeling that, had their positions been reversed, he would have felt the same way. The most convincing part of his story was the censored version of Severus's last words. All the rest—the conveniently unwitnessed offering of a truce, the victim's sudden collapse in the lone company of a man equipped with medicines and a motive—pointed in entirely the wrong direction.

"It wasn't me," said Ruso. "If I were going to murder Severus, I'd have found a much cleverer way of doing it. I'd have used a poison that wasn't so obvious, or I'd have found a way to blame somebody else right from the start."

"I see," said Calvus.

"It can't be him, boss," said Stilo. "It weren't clever enough, see?"

"I see," said Calvus again. "Tell us how you would have done it then, doctor?"

52

RUSO SURVEYED THE household lined up along the porch in an awkward parody of the welcome he had received only a few days ago. This time nobody was looking cheerful. Lucius was striding up and down and muttering to himself despite being ordered to stand still. Arria and the girls looked bewildered, Galla pale, and even the nieces and nephews were temporarily overawed by the presence not only of Calvus and Stilo, but of four grim-faced men armed with clubs. Ruso recognized a couple of them as Fuscus's men. Try as he might, Ruso could not imagine Fuscus had sent them to protect the family of his dear departed friend Publius Petreius.

Evidently the staff did not like the look of Fuscus's thugs, either. The cook was clutching a saucepan as if it were a weapon. The kitchen boy and Arria's maid seemed to be trying to hide behind him. The bath boy was a picture of drooping misery, and the cleaning girl and the laundry maid stood with heads bowed, each seemingly examining the reddened hands clasped in front of her for some explanation of why this was happening.

The stable lad scurried in through the yard gate and ran up the steps to join the others, trailing a strong whiff of embrocation in his wake. The nine farm laborers, not usually allowed to enter the house, hesitated down on the path.

"And you lot," ordered Calvus. "Up you go."

The men looked variously at Calvus, at Ruso, and at Lucius, evidently not sure whom to obey.

Ruso moved forward. "Go and stand next to the other staff," he ordered them, counting the line to make sure nobody was missing except the two women who were at this moment heading into unsuspected trouble in Arelate.

He made his way down the steps and turned to address his household. "These men have come to ask us all some questions about the visitor who died here the other day," he said. "They're representing the senator, and I want you to answer them as fully and as truthfully as you can."

He turned to Calvus, whose long dark eyes were surveying the family with an expression that reminded Ruso of a predator choosing its next meal. He said, "You can use the study when you've finished inspecting it," and, lowering his voice as he drew closer, added, "My people are witnesses. They'll do their best to help you, but most of them don't know a thing. They don't need to be frightened and they certainly don't need to be hurt."

Calvus raised one eyebrow. "What an interesting idea."

It occurred to Ruso that what the man lacked in height, he made up for in arrogance. "You didn't need to bring a bunch of thugs with you."

"The suspect telling me how to carry out the investigation."

"It'll never catch on," said Stilo.

Ruso felt his muscles tense. He made a conscious effort to relax his shoulders before saying, "I'm warning you not to do anything you'll regret later when you find out the truth."

"Nice of you to care," said Calvus. "But I've been in this business a long time—"

"A very long time," put in Stilo.

"I've been in this business a very long time," repeated Calvus, "and I don't often suffer from regret."

Ruso turned on his heel and limped away toward the garden seat. If he did not put himself out of reach of Calvus immediately, he would hit him. And that would do his case no good at all.

53

RUSO SLAMMED THE gates so hard that they rattled. He shoved the bolt across and turned to the dog. "Next time," he instructed it, gesturing toward the gate that shut out the departing investigators, "bite them."

The enthusiasm with which the dog wagged its tail did not inspire confidence.

Rubbing his sore elbow and feeling ten years older than he had this morning, Ruso turned to limp back toward the stables. Already the shadow of the pergola was stretching its legs across the garden. Tilla and his sister-in-law were somewhere far beyond the safety of the estate, and there was no way anyone could catch up with them before dark.

The crunch of footsteps announced someone behind him. "If my vintage is ruined," announced Lucius, "it'll be your fault."

"Is everyone all right?"

"If you couldn't keep that bloody woman under control you had no business bringing her here."

There was no time to argue. "We've got to get to Arelate tonight, brother. Cass and Tilla don't know what they're walking into."

"It's bad enough you getting us all accused of poisoning. Now my wife's run off because your fancy woman's filled her head with rubbish, and you send a slave to come and tell me!" Lucius kicked open the yard gate, sending a couple of hens fluttering away in alarm. "You don't know how it feels to have to lie to your own children, do you? To tell them their mother's gone for a holiday and you don't know when she's coming back? Did you see the faces on those nosey bastards just now? Even you suspected her of being a poisoner: What must they think?"

"Are the mules fast enough, or can we borrow some horses?"

"I'm in the middle of supervising the vintage, remember? Good old reliable Lucius, here every year—"

"We've been through this. We need to—"

"I stay here and work while you float around the empire picking up women. You don't have the faintest idea what responsibility really means, do you? Now I'm going to be gone for who knows how long, because somebody who can walk on both legs needs to go and get my wife out of the clutches of that woman so she can come back here and do her duty!"

Lucius paused for breath and Marcia's voice floated across the yard. "Are you two going to have another fight?"

The unified, "No!" was one of the few things they had agreed on since Ruso's return.

"I'll take the cart," growled Lucius to the approaching stable lad. "The farm will have to manage without it because my brother's wrecked the only fast animal we've got our hands on and that woman he brought—"

"Yes, all right!" snapped Ruso. "If you'd taken your wife seriously in the first place, you wouldn't need to chase after her now."

"Hah! You're advising me about marriage?"

Ruso took a deep breath, consciously unclenched his fists, and said, "Neither of us did anything to help, so Cass and Tilla have gone to Arelate by themselves to see what they can find out about the *Pride of the South*. Now I've found out Severus had a man in the port who—"

"What man?"

"All I know is that his name is Ponticus, and if he finds out why they're there, he'll try to silence them."

Lucius ran a hand through his thinning hair. "I can't believe this. You knew my wife was in danger and you didn't even tell me?"

"If we leave now—"

"Oh, no. This time *we* is just me. You've made enough of a mess."

"But—"

"I'll take the stable lad. You can stay here and do all the work for a change. You can have the old mule that's left, and that horse will want delivering back to the estate in the morning."

"But—"

Lucius's fist shot out and grabbed a handful of his tunic. "Just for once, Gaius, just once—will you bloody well let me make my own decisions?"

54

RUSO LEFT HIS brother strutting about shouting orders. He was making his way back past the dead fountain when his thoughts were interrupted by a wail of "Gaius!"

It was time to see what he could do to clear up the rest of this afternoon's chaos.

"They've been through our underwear, Gaius!" shouted Marcia, leaning out over the porch balustrade, clearly eager to get her complaint in first.

"Not while we were in it," added Flora.

"Really, Flora!" This last was from Arria, who was positioned at the top of the steps like a legionary about to defend a breach in the garrison walls. As he lurched unevenly up toward her she said, "You must send a complaint to the senator, Gaius! They've upset everybody and broken one of the best bowls."

"Only one?" asked Ruso, relieved. While Calvus questioned the household, Stilo and three of Fuscus's thugs had been searching the house for—he was not sure what. Poisons, he supposed. Stilo had emerged still clutching the knife in his disfigured hand. Perhaps he imagined that if he found the poison, someone was going to force him to swallow it.

"It was one of a set. A beautiful set. Your poor father bought them for me." She sniffed. "On our first anniversary."

As he climbed the steps, he saw that his stepmother's eyes were glistening with tears. The girls, noticing the same thing, retreated into the house.

"It's all right," he assured her, putting an arm around her shoulders and realizing this was probably the first time he had ever touched her voluntarily. "We'll get another one."

"But they've been through all our lovely things!"

The lovely things were of secondary interest. "Is anybody hurt?" The fourth member of the gang had been ordered to prevent him from leaving the garden. Ruso had been forced to wait out the questioning, limping back and forth along the gravel paths, listening for any sounds from the house and planning to beat Fuscus's man aside with his walking stick if he heard anyone scream. He had heard nothing, but he was still relieved when Arria confirmed that Calvus and Stilo had done no worse than frighten their victims.

"And they've upset Cook! I knew they would. Goodness knows what we'll get for dinner now, and we can't cancel Lollia again. Those dreadful men made him open all the jars in the pantry and then they made the kitchen boy eat something out of every one of them. No wonder he was sick."

Ruso scowled, trying to stifle the guilty awareness that he might have spared them all of this by giving the investigators the evidence about Claudia buying rhododendron honey. "What about the others?"

"Then they found some wretched dried leaves in the barn—Lucius says he uses them to get rid of wild dogs—but they've taken them away."

"Dogbane?" suggested Ruso, summoning a vague childhood recollection of watching his father's farm manager making dry leaves into cakes with suet and being told not to touch them.

"Oh, who knows what he keeps in there?" Arria sighed, letting him lead her out into the garden. "And now they've taken your lovely case . . ."

"Nothing that was in my medical case will be a problem, I promise you," he insisted.

Arria sniffed. "But it was so beautiful, with all those pretty clips and places to put the little bottles. What would your father say?"

"He'd say at least they let me keep the instruments," insisted Ruso, who was privately outraged at the confiscation. After all the arguments about duty and responsibility, the gift of the medical case had been the tacit sign of his father's acceptance that Ruso was not going to stay at home and run the farm. "They promised to release it when they've checked the medicines." As if he had been likely to believe them.

"Oh, Gaius, what are we going to do? I told that horrible man we don't know anything and it was all a silly fuss about nothing, but he still kept on asking questions and looking at me."

"A murder isn't nothing, Arria."

"But he wasn't murdered, Gaius! For goodness' sake!"

This was unexpected. "Have you been talking to Lucius?"

"I told him, you're not that sort of doctor."

"What did you say to him, exactly?"

"I told him the truth. Well, that was what you wanted, dear, wasn't it?"

"And the truth is?"

Arria paused to run her little finger along the lower lid of each eye and inspect it for stray makeup.

"You look fine," he assured her, knowing he would get no sense out of her until her poise was recovered.

Arria patted her hair. "I explained to him," she said, "that you've been away in the army." She put her hand on his arm. "Please don't be cross with me. I'm sure you're a very good doctor. I'm sure you know all about arrows and sword cuts and what to do when people get their fingers stuck in those ballista things, but really, dear—the legionaries don't go around poisoning people, do they?"

"Not as far as I know."

"So you really don't know an awful lot about it, do you?"

He bristled. "I know a lot more than most people."

"Yes, dear, but even you can still make a mistake. Can't you?"

"Of course, but—"

"And you're tired after all that traveling, and to be frank, Gaius, you do have a tendency to overdramatize."

"I have a *what*?"

"You see? I knew you would be upset!"

"A tendency to overdramatize," he repeated, deliberately keeping his voice under control. "What else did you say?"

"Nothing. I didn't even know Severus was here until after he—until it was too late. Then I just asked Galla to make him look presentable for the family."

"Right."

He sensed her movement as she straightened up beside him. "I only did it to help. I didn't mean to make you cross." She sniffed again. "I know you've never approved of me, Gaius."

"I—what?" He did not want to discuss this now. Or indeed, ever.

"I know everyone thought I only married your father for his money."

Ruso cleared his throat. "That was all a long time ago."

"I did my best, you know. It wasn't my fault I could never be your mother." She wiped away tears with her forefinger, crinkling the skin beneath her eyes. "If you could try to like me just a little bit, Gaius—"

Ruso cleared his throat again.

"All this will blow over," he assured her, feeling the graze on his elbow as he tightened his arm around her. "We'll find a way to sort out the money, Lucius will bring Cass home, the investigators will find out we didn't poison Severus, and in a few weeks it'll all be forgotten."

"Really?"

"Really," he assured her, ignoring the voices in his head that were demanding to know how all this was going to happen and pointing out that he should have told her about Marcia's gladiator.

"And you'll be nice to Lollia and Diphilus tonight, won't you?"

Ruso, who had forgotten all about the wretched dinner, managed a grunt of assent.

"Goodness knows what we'll eat: Some of the traders have been very tiresome. I wish these people would keep proper records. Of course Lucius has paid their accounts. Anyway, Cook says he's found some oysters and there's enough here to manage. Now, the next thing is entertainment. If the girls do some practice perhaps they could play their—"

"Do they ever do any practice?"

She paused for a moment. "No, perhaps we'd better just talk to each other. Seating is going to be awkward with an even number of diners, but I'm going to put you with Lollia at one corner, and then Diphilus and me at the other, and the girls . . ."

Ruso made an effort to care, and failed. He would wait till after the dinner guests had gone and then tell her about Marcia.

Arria leaned her head against his shoulder. "I am glad you're home, Gaius. I'm sorry you were let down by that girl. What did you call her? Tilla?"

"At least she and Cass are together," said Ruso.

"Cassiana is bound to come to her senses in a day or two. And that girl will find a way to survive. These foreigners are often cleverer than we give them credit for, you know."

"True."

Arria lifted her head. "After all, she managed to work her way around you, didn't she dear?"

55

THE STABLE LAD looked up from heating a potion of what appeared to be melted fat and vinegary wine, and declared the animal to be not too bad, considering. "This should fix him up, sir."

Ruso explained about the unscheduled leap across the ditch and the stable lad declared that idiots like them investigators shouldn't be allowed on the road, which echoed Ruso's sentiments precisely.

Spotting the water bottle slung over a hook, Ruso took it down. "I appreciated the drink," he said. "But this needs a good rinse through before it's used again. It tasted a bit stale."

"Oh, it's not ours, sir," explained the lad. "It was left slung over the saddle pad, so I just filled it up for you."

"It's not ours? You mean it came with Severus? The man who was poisoned?"

The lad looked sheepish. "Sorry, sir. I didn't think."

Ruso, who had drunk most of the contents on the journey back to the house, paused to ponder the state of his internal workings.

"It was pretty much empty before, sir."

"Never mind," he said, hoping that the minor gurgles and rumblings of which he was suddenly acutely conscious were nothing to worry about. "Just keep it with the saddle for now and make absolutely sure nobody uses it."

"Are you feeling all right, sir?"

Ruso ran one hand through his hair. "I think so," he said, reminding himself that the snake man had said it wasn't usually fatal and vaguely aware that he might just have found out how Severus had been poisoned after leaving home. "I'm going to go straight to the kitchen and drink a large quantity of saltwater. If it doesn't work, I want you to tell the investigators exactly what happened and who the flask belonged to. And make sure everybody knows it had nothing to do with tonight's dinner."

The stable lad's eyes widened. "I'm really very sorry, sir."

"I don't doubt it," agreed Ruso. "Hopefully, I'll be in a fit state to tell you off properly when you get back from Arelate."

56

RUSO WATCHED LUCIUS, with the stable lad beside him, driving the cart up to the main road and turning the mules toward the darkening clouds of the eastern sky. With luck, Severus's accomplice was still away in some distant port, cashing in Probus's letters of credit, and had left no one at home to mind his affairs and fend off inquisitive women. If not, Tilla and Cass's best hope was that Lucius would catch up with them before they got themselves into serious trouble. This time, Ruso was not allowed to interfere. His little brother was determined to tackle the monsters himself.

When the vehicle was finally out of sight beyond the vineyards, he shut the gate and walked back across the garden. In his hand was a list of detailed reminders that Lucius had left for the farm slaves to stop them from ruining everything in his absence, despite the fact that all of them had been working this land for most of their lives. Ruso hoped they knew what they were doing. Instructions like "Day 2, jars 3 to 8, add brine" were meaningless unless the men knew what quantities were involved, and there was now nobody left to ask. Apart from the staff, the only other adults here to consult were Arria and Marcia.

The gods alone knew what the investigators must be making of what they had found here today. A resentful farmer with marital problems, a medic with massive debts and some knowledge of poisons, a stepmother who had her staff clean up the site of a murder, and a cook who washed up the evidence. The only faintly good news from today was that so far, they did not seem to have found out that Severus had been instrumental in the death of Cass's brother. He supposed it was only a matter of time, though, before they worked it out and added her to their list of possible suspects. Once they had put all that together they would probably be able to convince themselves that the barbarian who had fled the scene with her had something to do with it as well.

He would make a final check on the injured horse before taking himself to the baths to prepare for the dreaded dinner.

"Galla!"

At the sound of Ruso's voice across the garden, the slave's body jolted as if she had been speared.

"I'd like a word. In the study."

Behind the closed door of the study he demanded to know exactly who this Solemnis the carter was and how Tilla had met him. "You may as well tell me," he insisted. "Lying will only get you into worse trouble."

"I would not lie to you, my lord."

"So. Who is he?"

Galla took a deep breath and gabbled, "He is a follower of Christos, my lord."

"I know that. Where did Tilla meet him?"

"At the meeting, my lord." The pitch of Galla's replies was rising with her terror.

"What meeting?"

"Of the Christians, my lord."

"What's Tilla been doing meeting with Christians? Where?"

Galla lifted a hand and pointed toward the window. "Next door."

"And this was the so-called family you took her to visit last night?

"Yes, my lord."

"I see."

She stood motionless, staring at her feet.

"How far has this superstitious nonsense spread? What about the rest of the staff?"

"There is only me, my lord." He could barely catch her words. "I have not been very brave at sharing the good news."

"But you have been sharing it with Tilla."

Galla lifted her chin. "She is alone in a foreign country, my lord. I—it is a comfort to her."

"Alone in a foreign country." Ruso felt his fists clench. "She was vulnerable! You had no right to prey on her like that. These Christos people are—" He broke off. "The business about orgies and sacrificing babies isn't true, is it?"

"They are kind to one another, my lord. They share what they have and feed the poor. They nurse the sick and wait for Christ to return."

"And while they're waiting, they break up marriages and run off with young women who don't know any better."

Galla's eyes drifted shut and her lips moved as if she was muttering to herself.

"You'd better not be praying to your god in here."

The eyes opened again.

"You know the sort of good news I want?" demanded Ruso. "I want to hear that the people I'm responsible for are safely back home. And then I want to hear about a religion that doesn't cost a fortune, doesn't take up too much time, and expects its followers to do what they're bloody well told."

Galla swallowed. "My lord, in one of the letters from the saints it says—"

"I don't want to know," he said, "And if you want to remain part of this household, neither should you." He paused. "You haven't got any religious stuff around the house, have you?"

When she did not reply he repeated the question. After another silence he lowered his head into his hands. "Get rid of, it whatever it is. No, on second thought—bring it to me and I'll get rid of it. I never thought I'd have to say this, Galla, but I don't trust you."

57

RUSO DID NOT normally waylay his dinner guests before they arrived, but he needed a private word with Lollia Saturnina. So private that she asked the slave who was carrying her indoor shoes to walk twenty paces behind them through the olive grove.

"We've had a slight problem at home," he said, noting with approval the simple elegance of her dress and the absence of flashy jewelry.

She said, "Severus, or another one?"

"Another one," Ruso confessed. "In the course of sorting it out, I've been warned that you have an infestation of Christians."

"Really? Are you sure?"

"A couple of our people went to a meeting on your property two nights ago."

"A meeting?"

Ruso hoped the feeling of light-headedness was the result of rushing to intercept Lollia after hastily bathing on a very empty stomach, and not something to do with the contents of the water bottle. He said, "Apparently they came across some chap there, and he's enticed them away with him."

"Are you quite sure? We haven't got anybody missing."

"We've lost two," said Ruso. "Four now, because Lucius has taken our stable lad and gone to look for them."

"I'll have a word with the staff," she promised. "I've never heard of Christians stealing people before. Aren't they supposed to look after one another and feed the poor?"

"I don't mind them feeding the poor," said Ruso, annoyed that she was failing to see the point. "Even if it does encourage scrounging. And I don't mind what rubbish they believe. I can even put up with them being a secret society and thinking their god is better than everybody else's. But they can't go running off with other people's . . ." He paused. "With other people's people."

"No, that's quite unacceptable," agreed Lollia.

"They've been hiding things in the house here as well. You might want to have a look around your own place in case there's another crackdown."

"I will." Lollia paused to inspect the olives forming among the slender leaves. "I've never understood why people make a fuss about the Christians," she said. "Surely nobody really believes they burned down Rome?"

Ruso shrugged. "Who knows? If they steal people's . . . people, who knows what they'll do next?"

58

BROTHER SOLEMNIS'S MULES clopped over the long wooden bridge into Arelate as if they had not noticed that it was held up only by a row of boats moored to two posts. His passengers were wide-eyed: Cass staring at the gleaming expanse of river flowing beneath them and Tilla wondering what would happen if the mooring ropes broke.

"Everything's bigger than I thought," whispered Cass. "We should never have come."

Tilla, who was feeling the same way, was not going to admit it. "If we had never come," she said, "we would not know about the beautiful wide river and the strange bridge that will still live in our minds when we are old and gray and our teeth fall out."

As she spoke the cart lurched over a bump and she grabbed at the side to steady herself.

Relieved to be safely across, she shook the dust of the journey off her borrowed straw hat, scowled at the sight of yet another amphitheater rising above the red roofs of the town, and observed, "My friend and I need beds for the night."

She saw a blush spread up the back of Brother Solemnis's neck. He only just halted the mules in time to avoid plowing into four slaves carrying a litter out of a side street. She tried again. "Brother, we need beds."

Brother Solemnis seemed to be having trouble speaking. Finally he blurted, "But what will Mother say?"

Cass leaned forward and explained gently, "My friend is hoping you can recommend an inn where we will be safe."

The blush grew deeper. Finally the lad managed to stammer out a name. "Run by a woman," he added, as if this might make it safe for them, although not for a defenseless young man. As if to make sure he was rid of them, he said, "I'll take you."

The woman at the Silver Star Inn seemed delighted to welcome them. She was probably bored with only a sleeping cat and cobwebs for company.

Tilla had long since discovered that the price and quality varied in a place like this but the basic offering did not. During the journey through Gaul, she had once sighed over yet another insipid cup of watered wine and asked whether there wasn't something else? The owner, who seemed pleased to be asked, took so long to list the wonders of all the other wines on offer that she wished she had kept quiet. Even the water had to be praised. It was from his own spring, fit for the gods themselves, with the very taste of ambrosia. Realizing he had not understood the question, she had asked if there might be beer or mead? How about sweetened milk?

The bartender had looked at her as if she had just insulted his children, and said, "This is Gallia Narbonensis, madam. We are not in the North now."

This rejection of beer seemed a peculiar form of obstinacy, especially now that Tilla had found out how wine was produced. But even Cass, to whom she had confided her quiet longing for a long drink of barley beer, had reacted as though her boredom with the subtle and complicated tastes of Gaul were something about which she would do well to keep quiet. So when the usual watery offering turned up in cups that were none too clean, Tilla accepted it with a smile. Then she admired the cat, kicked Cass to stop her from staring apprehensively at the cobwebs, and began to ask questions.

The innkeeper was very sorry to hear of the loss of the lady's brother.

"We are looking for anyone else whose man died on the *Pride of the South* so my friend can grieve with them. She is thinking of raising a monument to him by the river."

Cass's face betrayed surprise. Tilla, who had only just invented the monument, was rather proud of it.

"My brother was an honorable steward of a wealthy man," explained Cass.

"His master wants to help pay for the cost," said Tilla, voicing the lie that Cass had only implied. "But we want an inscription. A very long one, in big gold letters. We want to find out the date of his death and where his body might lie."

The woman shook her head. "I wish you luck," she said, "but there is a great deal of sea beyond the end of the river, and one ship is very small."

Later, when Cass had slipped out to use the latrine and probably inspect the kitchen for cleanliness, the woman leaned closer to Tilla and whispered, "Is she gone?"

Suddenly understanding that the woman could not see the cobwebs, Tilla said, "Do you want to tell us something else?"

"It is none of my business."

"I will not be angry," promised Tilla.

"The brother's master," whispered the woman. "Do not commit yourself to paying a lot for that monument on his behalf."

Tilla frowned. "You know him?"

"I know his type," insisted the woman. "If he sent that poor man to sea in an old bucket like the *Pride*, then he did not care much about him. And if he has money, he is not prepared to spend it."

Tilla put a hand on the woman's arm. "What else do you know about this ship?"

"It is a very unlucky ship."

"We know this."

"They say the dealer who bought it sailed on it and drowned with all the crew."

Tilla fingered the chipped edge of her cup and wondered if this was going to be a wasted trip. "Perhaps there is nobody left to tell us anything."

"There is someone who might know," continued the woman, "if you aren't too fussy. Go to Phoebe's Bar in the Street of the Ropemakers."

Tilla repeated the name. "Who shall we say sent us?"

The woman sniffed. "If you say it was me, she will tell you nothing. Nobody speaks to Phoebe since she cannot keep her hands off other people's husbands."

59

SURVEYING THE LAMPLIT debris of the dinner party, Ruso could not remember when he had endured a longer evening. Or a more embarrassing one.

Had he not seen it, he would never have believed that the Arria of the pinned curls and the tastefully displayed cleavage could have been created from the woman who had clung helplessly to him out on the porch not two hours before. Even her voice had changed. The tremor of anxiety had been pushed aside by a new confidence. This was Arria's dinner party, the dancing cupids were on display, and she was not going to let a little thing like a poisoning ruin it.

Even the cook had somehow managed to recover from the invasion of the investigators, and the food was not noticeably worse than usual.

Those, together with Lollia's company, had been the best aspects of the evening. As for the worst—there were plenty to choose from.

There had been Arria's cry of "How lovely of you to come! Gaius, you remember Diphilus, our nice builder? Diphilus, Gaius says we can't have the outdoor dining room!"

There had been Arria's vaunted pride in his achievements over in Britannia, and the apprehension of Lollia's "Are you going to tell us all about them?"

There had been the awful sense of doom as Marcia offered, "We can tell you something much more interesting!" followed by a glare from Arria and an unabashed "A man's been poisoned right here in our house!" and then Flora's "But it's all right, it wasn't us."

There was Arria's simpering smile when Diphilus said, "It must have been a shock for all of you young ladies," and Marcia's "Not as much of a shock as having strange men investigating our underwear this afternoon."

Diphilus had downed his wine in one gulp and held up his glass for the laundry maid (promoted to wine steward for the evening) to refill it.

Arria asked Lollia to tell them all about amphora production. Lollia had just said that she was afraid everyone would find it very boring when Flora finished draining the sauce from the lettuce leaf into her mouth and said, "Everything's gone downhill since Gaius came home."

Ruso was wondering how much wine she had consumed when Marcia stepped in with "It's not Gaius's fault, it's that Tilla he brought with him. She's turned us all into barbarians. Now she's stolen Cass."

"And our other brother has gone mad and run off after them," put in Flora.

Arria told them it was not nice to talk about family business at dinner, and Lollia attempted to come to the rescue with "I'd like to have met this Tilla. Is she someone you know from Britannia, Ruso?"

He said, "Yes."

"But now she's gone," said Arria, as if that were the last word to be said on the subject.

For a moment nothing could be heard but the scrape of spoons on bowls. The cupids cavorted silently across the walls while Ruso thought wistfully of Tilla's attempts at cookery in the little room with the flowers on the windowsill.

Moments later he became aware of a strange feeling in his stomach: perhaps caused by the contents of Severus's water bottle, or perhaps by the appearance of a bowl of reheated goats' testicles on the table in front of him. It occurred to him that there was a certain irony about being accidentally poisoned by one's own ex-wife. When he returned his attention to the conversation, Lollia was saying, "Just fifteen."

Marcia's triumphant, "See?" was wasted on Ruso since he had no idea what they were discussing.

"Lollia was married at fifteen!" Marcia was determined not to let the point go. "Lollia, tell Gaius he must sort out a dowry before I die of old age and shame."

Lollia smiled and reached for an oyster, Arria told Marcia not to harass the guests, and Ruso said, "Did I tell you I went to the gladiator barracks today?"

There was a tinkle of metal on mosaic. Marcia reached down to retrieve her spoon. When her face reappeared, it was flushed.

"I've got a job there," he explained.

Marcia's hazel eyes were locked on to his own, searching his face for some clue to what he had found out.

"I met some interesting people," he continued. "I'm not sure I can do much to help them, though."

"Of course you can, dear, you're very good at that sort of thing." Arria turned to Lollia. "It's all those years in the army, you see. Gaius knows everything there is to know about chopping off and stitching up. Will you be going to the Games?"

Ruso missed the effect of this on Marcia because he was distracted by a small arm appearing from beneath his couch. It was followed by a dark head, then the naked owner of both crawled forward and tried to pull himself up by grabbing the three-legged dining table on which sat the bowl of testicles. The table was a delicate creation in polished walnut, not intended for use as a ladder. Before Ruso could grab it, table and toddler had crashed onto the mosaic in a howling tangle of limbs and spilled food.

Cries from the surrounding diners were undercut by a screech of "Galla!" from Arria.

Ruso lifted off the table. To judge from the noise Little Gaius was making, he was not seriously injured. He swept the child up under one arm, ignoring the wails and waving arms at one end and the small fat legs kicking the air at the other. "Galla!" he shouted, swerving around the end of a couch and lurching toward the door just as Galla appeared. She reached for the child. "I'm sorry, sir. He ran away again."

"Girls!" ordered Arria, seizing her chance. "Go and help Galla put the children to bed."

The demands of "What?" were almost in unison.

"Your mother asked you to put the children to bed," put in Diphilus, with more gallantry than sense.

Marcia said, "We don't have to do what you say."

Hearing echoes of his childhood, Ruso looked into the hazel eyes and said, "You do have to do what I say. Apologize to your mother, and to Diphilus."

Marcia opened her mouth to answer, then closed it as understanding dawned. Her brother and official guardian had been to the gladiator barracks. What followed was not gracious, but it was an apology.

After the girls had gone Ruso had piled the splintered remains of the table in a corner beneath a cheerful cupid who was driving a chariot pulled by two goats. Returning to the couch, he took refuge in his wine while the staff scoured the floor for potsherds and testicles and Diphilus explained in detail to the three remaining diners why fixing the drains would involve digging up most of the garden. Arria was so intrigued that she did not notice the glass in her hand gradually tilting and tipping its contents onto the floor.

To Ruso's alarm, Lollia glanced across at him and winked.

60

ARRIA BRUSHED A stray olive aside and sank onto the couch while the cleaning girl and the laundry maid lit more lamps and bustled around her with cloths and brooms. "We can't go on like this, Gaius. Those wretched girls!"

"Lollia said it was a very entertaining evening."

"I don't want to talk about it. And that child! At this rate we shall have no furniture left."

"There's too much of it, anyway."

Arria picked at a piece of fluff on the cushion. "I know you and your brother aren't interested, but your father always wanted us to have a nice home."

"At the moment we're lucky we've got a home at all."

She looked up. "Well, I'm sorry to have to say it, dear, but whose fault is that?"

Ruso stared at her.

"Your father was wonderful with money!" she said. "And always so generous. I can't understand how you two have grown up the complete opposite. He worked so hard to set up all those investments, and neither of you seems to have the faintest idea how to manage them."

Ruso started to laugh. "Father didn't have investments, Arria, he had loans! Loans to pay for all the things you insisted on buying. All the plans that got bigger and bigger—"

"He agreed to the plans. I never bought anything without consulting him first."

"He never intended to build a temple that was going to cost a fortune to run forever and ever. And he didn't live long enough to agree to all these cupids."

"He would have liked them!" cried Arria. "Do you want us to live in a mud hut like your barbarian?"

Ruso took a deep breath and reminded himself that he was no longer nine years old. He was a grown man and he was responsible for what was left of the family. "No," he said, wondering how many times Lucius had already tried to explain this to her, "I want us to live within our means. I know Father didn't tell you all the details, because he didn't tell us, either, but a lot of the money was never really there. Now we have all this . . ." He glanced around the dining room. "We have all these things, and we have to find a way to survive while we pay for them."

Arria's hand crept to her mouth. "Are you saying your father lied to me?"

"I'm saying," said Ruso, trying to remember what Cass had told him and wishing she were here to deal with this, "he was very fond of you and he wanted you to be happy. Now you won't be ordering anything else, will you?"

Arria sniffed. The paint in the outer corner of one eye had smudged, giving her a black streak like an Egyptian. "It isn't my fault, Gaius," she insisted. "Not all of it. Not the court case and everything. And all those children!"

"We've all contributed," Ruso conceded. "But you have to listen, Arria. The only way out of this is to stop spending money."

"Not even a little outdoor dining room? It won't cost much. Diphilus is such a nice man."

"No. We have to concentrate on keeping things going while Lucius and Cass are away, and we have to get these wretched investigators off our backs."

Arria shook her head. A pin tumbled out of place and landed unnoticed on the couch. "There never was any money? Are you sure?"

"Yes."

"No more lovely things?"

"Just enjoy the lovely things you have."

She was saying sadly, "Poor Diphilus will be so disappointed," when a voice from the doorway announced, "Never mind poor Diphilus. When are you going to make Gaius give me a dowry?"

Ruso growled, "Not tonight."

"Then what about Tertius?"

Ruso said, "Tertius made a choice," at the same time as Arria said, "Who is Tertius?"

"I need money, Gaius."

"So do we all."

"Then Tertius is going to die!" cried Marcia, bursting into tears. "And all you want to do"—this was addressed to Ruso—"is to make money out of cutting him up! It's all your fault, Gaius! I hate you!"

"Then you shouldn't have called me home," said Ruso.

61

AFTER A RESTLESS night throughout which one of them waited in dread for mice and the other for spiders, Tilla was relieved to open her eyes and find she could make out the hump that was Cass's shoulder. Beyond it she could see the outline of the shutters. She closed her eyes again and slid her hands up over her ears in case the movement she was about to make should disturb anything with four paws and a tail and send it scuttling across her face. Then, with a move sudden enough to scare it away, she sat up.

Beside her, Cass muttered and groped for the blanket, pulling it over her head. Tilla peered at the floor, decided there was nothing moving down there, and padded across the room to open the window.

The chilly air out in the yard smelled of dung and wood smoke. A donkey shifted and stamped, banging its bucket in the hope of food. Somewhere beyond the walls, a bird chirruped an early call.

"Wake up!" she hissed, shaking her companion by the shoulder. "Wake up. We have to go and find Phoebe's Bar."

The sun had risen by the time they had tidied themselves, rejected the woman's offer of breakfast, and made their way through the waking streets to join the early traffic crossing back over the floating bridge. Safely on the opposite shore, they headed downstream to where the merchant ships were moored along the wharf.

A swaying crate was being guided into a hold by men shouting instructions to the crane operators. They dodged out of the path of a slave lugging an amphora just as a long train of laden mules began to pass along the road in front of them. An old man wheeling a trolley of boxes of fish plodded by in the opposite direction. As they approached, the screech of metal on stone signaled the opening of warehouse doors.

Cass was muttering something that sounded like, "Oh dear, oh dear . . ."

Tilla said, "I hope this Phoebe serves breakfast."

They were barely past the first warehouse when she stopped.

"Is it here?" Cass was gazing around her. "I can't see it."

"Something else."

The sight of chained slaves was not unusual. What Tilla had not expected was that the grimy and dejected figures slumped on the dockside ready for loading would be dressed just like the people she had left at home. She hurried forward, ignoring the guard who was busy chewing and examining his own teethmarks in a hunk of bread.

Kneeling by the nearest woman—the trader had at least had the decency to chain the men separately from the women and children—she whispered in her own language, "I am Darlughdacha of the Corionotatae among the Brigantes. What is your name, sister?"

The woman's sunken eyes held no expression.

"We are nobody," said the girl chained next to her. "We are prisoners. Leave us alone."

"You must have a tribe. Your accent is—what? Selgovae?"

"We have no tribe."

"Of course you do! Selgovae? Anavionenses?"

"What does it matter?" demanded the girl. "In a few days we'll dock in Ostia and they'll put us up for sale like cattle."

"What is she saying?" demanded Cass, crouching beside Tilla. "Does she know my brother?"

The girl looked at them both, asking in British, "What does that one want? Why are you here?"

"Tilla! What is she saying?"

Tilla put a hand over Cass's. "She doesn't know your brother. She has her own troubles." She turned back to the girl. "I cannot help you," she said, "and our own gods cannot hear you from here. But I have found out there is a great god who is everywhere, a god with no name who answers if you call him 'father.' "

Several of the nearby slaves were paying attention now. The guards were watching too.

"My friend needed to travel to this place, and straight away this father god sent a man with a cart to bring us," continued Tilla. She glanced around before adding, "He is more powerful than the emperor. He has a son called Christos and the Romans tried to kill him and he came back to life. You should try praying to him."

The girl held out both palms. "We have nothing to give."

"He does not want your gifts. He likes . . ." Tilla paused, wondering exactly what this god the father did want. "He likes songs and long prayers," she said, "and sharing food and—oh, you must stop doing sins and you have to forgive people and then Christos will come back from heaven and fetch you."

"What are sins?" asked a woman.

"Forgive which people?" demanded one of the men.

Tilla, who was not exactly sure what sins were herself, said, "People who need forgiving, I suppose." Somehow this new way of life did not seem as attractive here as it had in the company of the other believers.

"So," said the woman, "if we honor this father god and forgive the guards, will he help us escape?"

"I don't know," admitted Tilla. "But they say that if you love this god and obey him, he will take you to live with him in the next world when you die."

"Huh," retorted the man. "We'd like a bit of help before then."

Tilla got to her feet. "You will never know till you try," she said. Turning to the girl, she said, "Courage, sister. I have been a slave to a Roman. He is a good man. It may not be as bad as you fear."

"I hope not," agreed the girl, "because what I fear is very bad indeed."

As Tilla and Cass began to walk away the man called after them, "Oy! What tribe did you say you were?"

"Corionotatae. Of the Brigantes."

"I might have known!" retorted the man. "Trust a Brigante to be playing both ends against the middle."

"That's enough!" called the guard, putting his bread down. "No more talking!" He turned to Tilla. "If you're not buying, don't interfere with the stock."

Tilla sighed. "My people," she said sadly, gazing out between the masts to where a lump of driftwood was swirling on the current. "Always the same."

Cass said, "What is the matter with your people?"

"Nothing," said Tilla, setting out once more along the wharf. "They are clever and brave. But when you offer them something good they can always find a reason why it will not work. I tried to tell them about Christos."

"Justinus believed Christos would take him to heaven," Cass mused, falling into step with her. "But how will Christos find him when his body isn't buried?"

"I don't know," said Tilla. "I have only been to one meeting. I think there are some things I have not found out yet."

62

RUSO WOKE, STARED at the ceiling, and remembered why there was no one in the bed beside him. One by one, all the other things he was supposed to be worrying about sidled into his mind and drifted around it like unwelcome guests. Thus it was something of a relief to realize that he had something to celebrate. He was not poisoned.

He swung his feet to the floor, stood up, stretched, then bent and touched his toes, wincing at the stiffness from yesterday's accident with the horse. He flexed his fingers, shook his head, and spent a quiet moment assessing the state of his interior. Then he slapped his thighs, punched both fists in the air, and went in search of breakfast.

"Galla!"

She changed course, eyes wide with apprehension.

"You promised to give me something. Where is it?"

She swallowed. "I cannot, my lord."

"While you are part of this household, Galla, you are to do as I say."

She lowered her head and said, "Yes, my lord." Her stance as well as her voice betrayed her misery.

"You might think it doesn't matter," he explained. "But you see where all this secret society business has led to with Tilla. If this sort of thing carries on they'll decide to start rooting out the Christians again. Don't you think this family's in enough trouble?"

"We would never want to cause you trouble, my lord."

"Not *we*," prompted Ruso, "*they*. Now what is it, and where is it?"

Moments later Ruso was in the study with the door wedged shut, munching on an apple and running one finger along a line of Greek lettering. When he reached the end of what appeared to be the first sentence, he threw back his head and laughed.

All slaves under the yoke must have absolute respect for their masters.

What a shame it was that Galla could not read this document she had been hiding inside Little Lucius's mattress. The rest of it was a denunciation of philosophy, a shrewd observation that a fondness for money was at the root of most of the world's troubles, and some sort of rant about fighting a good religious fight in order to win eternal life.

That, as far as he could recall, was the original problem with the Christians, even before they had started enticing women away from home. They saw religion as a fight. They upset everyone else by refusing to sacrifice to the normal gods on the grounds that their own wouldn't like it, ignored polite requests to be a little more open-minded, and then refused to be coerced, in the belief that clinging stubbornly to their faith in this world would win them happiness forever in the next one.

On the other hand, "absolute respect" surely meant obedience? He would read this to her and translate it before he burned it. As an obedient slave with absolute respect for her master, Galla would do what she was told and stop fooling around with foreign religions.

63

YESTERDAY'S BREAD WAS dry, but cheaper. The two women were washing it down with a jug of watered vinegary wine, leaning over the ramshackle bar that opened onto a side street where two slaves were laying out a great length of fat rope. As Cass explained about the drowned brother, Tilla wondered how the grim-faced woman behind the counter could possibly have managed to lure away somebody else's husband.

"The only thing I know," said Phoebe, not looking up from stirring one of the huge pots set into the counter, "is that the dead don't come back."

Cassiana straightened her shoulders. "But we can remember them."

"What I'm saying," continued the woman, "is, you don't want to listen to drunks and layabouts. So if you're chasing this rubbish about ghosts, you're wasting your time."

"Ghosts?" Cass's hands on the counter turned into fists. "Who has seen a ghost?"

The woman lifted out the spoon. "They all drowned. The captain and the owner and the crew and your brother. Don't waste your time."

"Tell us about the ghosts," said Tilla.

"A couple of fools who reckon they saw the captain and the owner. Late at night in a bar, of course."

"What are their names?" Cass was almost on top of the counter now. "Which bar was it?"

"I told you, it's rubbish."

Tilla handed her too much money for the breakfast, and said, "You knew this captain and this owner?"

"I've seen them once or twice. They reckoned they were too good for us in here." The woman counted the coins and did not offer to return any change.

"And these two were the only ghosts anyone saw?" asked Cass again.

"Copreus and Ponticus."

"Tell us what these men looked like," urged Tilla. When the woman looked her in the eye she handed over another coin. At this rate they would be walking home.

Moments later a fat man who walked with two sticks rolled up to the bar and maneuvered himself onto a stool. The woman abandoned her attempts to describe the missing Copreus and Ponticus, and moved away to greet her latest customer by name

Tilla said, "One last question. Where do I find someone who has seen these ghosts?"

"One of them cheap whorehouses downstream," said Phoebe, without turning around. "I wouldn't know which. I'm a decent woman."

Evidently the time Tilla bought had run out.

Beside her Cass murmured, "How can we go into places like that? What will Lucius say?"

"It is not going in that is difficult," said Tilla, gathering up the two extra loaves she had bought to give to the chained slaves. "It is getting out. Besides, in a town this size we could spend all day finding them all." She weighed the purse slung around her neck. "We will have to buy more bad wine and make do with talking to bar girls." She glanced at her companion. "We will find out everything there is to know, Cass. Now we know that Captain Copreus is a muscly man with tattoos, and that this Ponticus wears a bronze ring with a ruby set in it. If they are alive, we will find them. I promise. Don't cry."

"I am not crying for myself." Cassiana rubbed her fist across her eyes. "I am crying for my brother, here alone with all these wicked people."

64

OUTSIDE THE GLADIATORS' barracks, groups of rival supporters had taken to trading insults and chanting the names of their favorites in an atmosphere that suggested a party rather than a fight. Inside, half a dozen men Ruso did not recognize were sparring with wooden practice weapons under the eye of a trainer. The yard smelled of beef stew, grease, and fear.

He made his way across to the surgery, where the assistants were ripping up linen rags and rolling them into bandages. Gnostus was perched on the operating table by the window, running one finger along the script of a writing tablet. At the sight of Ruso, he leaped up and thrust the tablet under his nose. "Anything I've missed?"

Sponges, plenty of ligatures, splints, needles . . . Ruso scanned the list, mentally rearranging it into a more logical order. It would be no good remembering something vital tomorrow.

"There could be as many as twenty casualties in here," pointed out Gnostus. "And we'll have to patch up the animal hunters too. But of course some will go straight to the undertaker."

Ruso nodded. "Looks fine to me," he said, handing the list back. "As long as your boys know where to find it all."

Gnostus glanced around to make sure there was nobody but the slaves in earshot, then admitted, "I've never done anything as big as this before. Any advice?"

Ruso watched a slave chase a long strip of linen along his knee until it became a fat roll of bandage, and wondered what he could possibly offer that would help. "Talk to your men beforehand," he suggested. "Make sure everybody knows who's doing what. Split the roles into examination, surgery, and dressing, get the porters organized, and delegate the simple stuff."

"That's how they do it in the Legions?"

"That's how I do it. Once things heat up, you just have to try to keep going without yelling at the staff or falling asleep over the patients. So, what do you want me to do?"

Gnostus thought about that for a moment. "Right now," he said, "look confident while I get the team together for a briefing."

"Do they know I'm the town poisoner?"

"You haven't met my lads," said Gnostus. "You'll fit in nicely."

Ruso spent most of the briefing wondering what was happening to Tilla and Cass, and the rest trying not to speculate on the tales that could be told by the half dozen scarred and ragged individuals summoned to support the medical staff. Gnostus introduced him as a veteran surgeon from the Twentieth Legion. If any of them had heard anything else about him, their faces did not betray it. Despite looking as though they had just been scraped out of a gutter, they also seemed to know what they were doing.

As the men shuffled out, Gnostus grinned at Ruso. "I s'pose this is like tying your bootlaces to you, isn't it?"

"Oh, gods above," muttered Ruso, glancing out of the door and seeing Tertius approaching across the yard. Then, in answer to Gnostus's question, "No, not really. No it isn't. I've never done anything quite like this before, either. Excuse me a minute."

Tertius stopped and stood at attention as Ruso approached.

"Tertius, I'm sorry—"

"I'd like to thank you for trying to help, sir," said Tertius stiffly. "And to request a small favor."

While Ruso was hoping a small favor would not mean smuggling him out through the gate, the lad held out one fist, turned it over, and opened it to reveal an iron ring and a couple of fat sestertius coins on his palm. "I'd be grateful if you could give the ring to Marcia, and the money to my aunt who works at the amphora factory of Lollia Saturnina."

Ruso took the ring and the coins and slipped them into his purse. "Of course." He pulled out the writing tablet that was tucked into his belt and said, "Marcia asked me to give you this."

The youth took the writing tablet that Ruso had eventually accepted from Marcia late last night and refrained from unsealing and reading. Initially she had been so unrepentant over the "come home" letter that he had refused to take it. But she had pointed out that Tertius had done nothing wrong and he might be dead in two days' time, and did Ruso want to make his last hours on earth even more miserable than they already were? Didn't he want to make him happy and confident and give him the best possible chance in the arena?

Tertius snapped the thread and ran his finger along the lines of text, his lips forming the words as he deciphered them. He swallowed hard, then held out the tablet to Ruso.

"I want you to know that your sister's letter is completely respectable, sir."

"I'm sure it is," said Ruso, motioning it away with his hand. Under the circumstances he felt the lad deserved something passionate rather than respectable, but preferably not from his own sister. "I wish I could help."

"Thank you, sir."

"We haven't got the money," explained Ruso, feeling irrationally guilty that he had not tried to raise it. "At the moment, nobody would want to lend it to me."

"That's all right, sir," declared Tertius, raising one arm in a good imitation of a military salute. "I wish you good fortune."

"And I you," said Ruso, returning the salute and noting how much more mature Tertius seemed to be now that there was no hope of escaping the arena tomorrow. He said, "I hope we'll be in a position to discuss this again in the future."

Tertius dropped his arm. "You can count on it, sir," he said, his face lighting up in a grin that would have broken Marcia's heart.

65

I HEAR YOU young ladies are looking for Copreus."

The grin was predatory and the breath stank of cheap wine and onions, but he had the deep tan and the muscled forearms of a mariner. Tilla resisted Cass's tug on her arm. There was a chance he might know something.

"We are looking for anyone who knows the crew who sailed with my friend's brother," she said, reaching along the counter and pouring him a drink from their own jug. They had worked their way down to the seediest of the side street bars now: the sort where nobody bothered to sweep up the cockroaches after they squashed them.

Cass had grown paler and quieter with every place they entered. Tilla was beginning to feel more and more light-headed despite her efforts to drink mostly water. "The brother was lost on the *Pride of the South*," she explained, glancing across to judge the distance to the door. "We want to raise a memorial."

"A memorial, eh?" Dark creases of embedded grime appeared on the man's neck as he raised the cup and took a long, slow drink of wine. "Next time I see old Copreus, I'll tell him. He'll like that."

Tilla felt Cass's fingers dig into her wrist. She tried to keep her voice calm as she said, "You have seen him?"

He held out his cup. When he had drunk the refill the foul breath wafted closer until their heads were almost touching. "Large as life," he whispered. "Sitting over in that corner there."

Both women turned to peer into the dingy corner where an old man was hopefully not as dead as he looked.

Cassiana whispered, "Real, or a ghost?"

"Ah," said Onion Breath, "who knows? It was the end of a long day, I was tired, the wine was cheap."

"Did he speak?" demanded Cass at the same time as Tilla tried, "Did you see him eat or drink?"

"No speaking," said the man, shaking his head. "No eating, no drinking." The breath surrounded them again. "Come here and listen carefully, ladies, and I'll tell you exactly what I saw that night."

Trying not to think about head lice, Tilla leaned closer. Cass did the same.

"What I saw," he murmured, "was old Copreus sitting over there where Granddad is now, just quiet, watching me from the corner. I said, 'You're drowned,' and he lifted up his arm and pointed at me." The man leaned back and extended two fingers to point first at Tilla and then at Cass, who flinched. "And then he got up out of that chair—" The man stood up. "And there was a flash of light . . ." He raised his hands in the air. "And then, poof, he vanished!"

Seeing their reaction, the man burst into harsh laughter.

The two women's eyes met. Without further discussion, they both bent to pick up their bags. For a moment they glanced around the empty floor, bewildered. Then Cass said, "Oh, no!"

"Something the matter, ladies?" asked Onion Breath. The half dozen other drinkers at the nearby tables all seemed preoccupied with their own business. None appeared to notice the distress of the two women at the bar. None was holding a blue and green striped bag like Cass's, or a plain brown one like Tilla's own that had now vanished with it.

"We have been robbed!" cried Cass.

A couple of players glanced up from a board game.

"I know how you feel, love," offered another man, raising his cup. "The prices in here, we've all been robbed."

The players resumed their game.

Tilla turned to the man behind the bar. "This sailor kept us talking while we were robbed. You must have seen! Who was it?"

The barman's face was blank. Tilla seized Cass by the arm and made for the door. One of the drinkers got up off his stool and stepped across to stand in their way. The old man in the corner coughed, opened his eyes, and went back to sleep.

Cassiana said, "We are going to report this place to the authorities!"

A large hand landed on Tilla's shoulder and the breath wafted around her again. "No need for that, ladies. We'll look after you. Won't we, lads?"

The pair at the board game looked up and grinned.

One moment Tilla was standing captive by the bar; the next moment her knife was out and Onion Breath was yelling and clutching at his hand while Cass snatched up a jug and ran to stand beside her.

Someone said, "You shouldn't a' done that, girl."

Tilla glanced around the room. The man was right: She had made a foolish mistake. She had run in the only direction open to her, and now they were cornered. They could not fend off six men for long with one knife and a wine jug. She muttered a prayer to Christos, but the Briton had been right. Heaven was not much comfort when you needed rescuing here and now.

"Help us!" she demanded, looking at the barman, but his attention was fixed on Onion Breath, who had seemed so friendly just a few minutes ago.

"You're closing early today," Onion Breath told him. "Take the afternoon off."

The barman glanced at Tilla and Cass, then dropped his cloth and fled out into the street.

"We'll have a private party." Onion Breath shut out the sunlight and swung the wooden bar up to drop it across the door. "I'm first with Blondie," he announced. "Steady on there, Granddad. You'll get your turn."

66

RUSO PRESENTED HIMSELF at the gates of the senator's estate without much hope, but to his surprise a slave escorted him into the garden where Claudia was sharing the shade of a summerhouse with her sister-in-law. Both were sitting with their hands in their laps and their backs very straight. As Ruso approached, Claudia's expression betrayed a warmth of welcome he had rarely experienced when she was his wife, whereas Ennia's pinched face grew even tighter. In response to his polite inquiry, Ennia burst out, "Of course we are not well! What do you expect? My brother is dead!" She turned to the slave who had escorted Ruso across the garden. "Why was he allowed in?"

The slave mumbled that he did not know.

"He is here," put in Claudia, "because I left instructions that if he called, I would see him."

"My brother would never have allowed him in!"

"Your brother is not here."

Ruso said, "I'd like to talk privately with Claudia, Ennia."

Claudia replied, "Of course," at the same moment as Ennia said, "Well, you can't."

In the silence that followed, the girl looked from Ruso to Claudia and back again. "Oh, all right," she said, and got to her feet.

She was still within earshot when Claudia said, "Really, she's such a child!"

Ruso waited until he heard Ennia's footsteps retreat along the gravel path behind the tall cypress hedge before saying, "She's bound to be upset."

"She doesn't have to be completely unreasonable. Even if she does think you poisoned her brother."

Ruso seated himself on the bench Ennia had just vacated and said, "We both know that's not true, don't we?"

Claudia gave a dramatic sigh. "Gaius, what is the matter with you? Daddy keeps saying do I want to tell him something, but I don't. You're as bad as the investigators, both of you."

"Claudia, I know what happened."

"They've been crawling all over us like lice. They've turned out all the bedrooms, and the farm buildings, and you wouldn't believe the chaos they caused in the kitchen. Zosimus is furious. The staff had been getting the preserves in for the autumn and that Stilo opened up every single jar and made the kitchen boy eat some."

"Flaccus?" asked Ruso. "Is he all right?"

"They even went through my makeup."

"I hope they didn't make you eat that?"

"Don't be silly, Gaius. They got one of the girls to do it. And of course she was sick too. I did warn them."

"Do you want me to look at them both?"

"They keep saying I must know where Severus kept his money. I've already told Zosimus to show them the strongbox in the office, but they keep saying there's more hidden somewhere." She gestured toward the elegant garden with its tranquil fishpond. "Severus didn't own any of this, you know. He wasn't rich. Besides, I'm the victim. They're supposed to be nice to me."

Ruso was beginning to wonder if Calvus and Stilo were reaching the same conclusions about the murder as he had himself. He said, "So they tested the honey, then?"

"They tested everything."

"They wouldn't be able to tell from the taste," Ruso continued. "And you'd need a substantial dose." He had proved that himself.

Claudia's "So you really have found something out!" seemed excited rather than alarmed.

"Of course if the victim was known to have a weak heart . . ."

"You have found something! Oh Gaius, bless you, I knew you would!"

This was hardly the reaction he had been expecting. Maybe his wife was much cleverer than he had ever realized.

It would not do to dwell on that thought. "I didn't come here to play games, Claudia. I spoke to the man you bought the honey from. He sold it to a woman wearing the same sandals as you, and she had . . ." Even now he could not bring himself to upset her by calling it orange. "She had hair the same color as yours. It's hard to mistake."

All around them the air was live with the singing of the cicadas. Claudia tightened one hand around the edge of the wooden bench, and then released it again. When she said, "You really do think I did it!" her voice was husky.

"The bitch has poisoned me."

The neatly plucked eyebrows drew closer together. "I can't understand . . ."

"You were seen buying the poison. There's a witness. If I tell that to the investigators, your father will ruin my family. Please, Claudia. You can still do something good for other people. Confess."

"But it wasn't me. I told you that."

He sighed. "I wanted to believe you."

"Then believe me! Anyone can buy a pair of shoes. Dozens of girls have hair this color. It's very fashionable."

Ruso shook his head. "It's too much of a coincidence. Severus was unfaithful, he'd lost your father a lot of money, you didn't love him—"

"I didn't love you, either," she retorted, tearing the pins out of her hair in distress. "But I didn't murder you!"

To Ruso's surprise, Claudia's strength of feeling was such that she grabbed the top of her head and began to tug at her curls. He was even more surprised when the curls came detached from the head and she flung them at him.

"There! Anybody can buy my hair too!"

He stared in disbelief at the dark cropped head that now faced him. Claudia's hair was not very much longer than his own. More interestingly, the tips of the hair were olive green. He lifted up the wig, shook it, and pretended to examine it while he struggled not to laugh.

"I had the hairdresser flogged," said Claudia. "But it won't bring my hair back any faster. Well, what's the matter with you? Haven't you ever seen a wig before? I can show you the other one if you like, still tousled from the funeral. Anyone can buy red hair too! It wasn't me."

Ruso was still considering his reply when they heard footsteps and looked up to see Zosimus striding toward them, followed by several garden slaves brandishing hoes and scythes in a manner that did not look horticultural. Ennia emerged from behind the hedge to join them. Claudia snatched back the wig and crammed it onto her head, whispering, "Perhaps it was Ennia in disguise!"

Ruso said, "Why?"

"I don't know, do I? Because she's a horrible little toad and she hates me. Shush. If you mention my hair I'll kill you."

The steward stopped at a safe distance and announced, "The investigators have forbidden any contact between the suspects."

So Claudia was a suspect. Ruso reached for his stick and got to his feet. "I was just going."

As he joined Zosimus to be escorted back to the gate, he heard Ennia say, "I told my brother he was a fool to marry you!"

Suddenly Ruso wondered how long the girl had been lingering behind that hedge. He had heard her footsteps retreat along the gravel, but that would be easy enough to counterfeit. Distracted by the arrival of Zosimus, he had not noticed the sound of her approach. How much had she overheard?

67

THE DOOR BAR had barely clunked down into its socket when Tilla heard someone outside hammering on the wood and yelling, "Open up! Man needs a drink!"

Onion Breath called, "We're closed!" at the same time as Cass cried, "Help us! We've been—" It ended in a scream as Onion Breath stepped across and hit her in the face.

Too late, he remembered about Tilla's knife. As he staggered backward, staring at her in disbelief, there was a crash from across the room. The door, frame and all, collapsed inward with two men on top of it.

The men tried to get up but were knocked aside by drinkers clambering over them to flee into the sunlit alleyway. The old man in the corner rose from his seat and staggered out after them.

Onion Breath was slumped beneath one of the tables. He was not moving. Tilla stared at him. Was that it? Was that how easy it was?

A voice was saying, "Are you all right, miss?"

She leaned back against the wall, waiting for her heart to stop thudding.

"Miss?"

She knocked the hand away from her arm, then realized it was meant in friendship. "Sorry," she said to a curly-haired youth she vaguely recognized. She was aware of a strong smell of horse as he took the bloodied knife from her hand.

The second rescuer was still sprawled along the length of the door, largely because Cass was on top of him, wiping blood off his chin with her skirt and crying, "Lucius! Oh, Lucius, my love, where are you hurt?"

Tilla rubbed her eyes in confusion. What was Lucius doing here? And was that the Medicus's stable lad?

Lucius was not so badly hurt that he could not cling to his wife and gasp, "Cass! When we saw that thief running down the street with your bag I thought—"

"Oh, my darling, you're so brave!"

The stable lad looked at the reunited couple, then at Tilla. "Master Lucius knocked the thief down and took your bags back, miss. Then he made him tell us where he got them. I don't know if everything's in them."

Tilla moved one hand to indicate the body of Onion Breath. The lad stepped across the fallen door and bent to peer at him.

Lucius lifted his head and noticed Onion Breath for the first time. "What happened to him?"

"It is the sort of thing that happens in a place like this," said Cass, suddenly decisive. She got to her feet and took the knife from the stable lad. "None of us saw anything."

Tilla was still staring at the body, vaguely aware of Cass bustling about with water and a cloth. The stable lad touched her arm. "We ought to go, miss," he murmured.

Tilla looked up. Lucius seemed to be suffering from no more than a bitten lip. His wife had a red mark on her cheek that was already beginning to swell. "That will teach you," Lucius announced to Onion Breath, "to mistreat the wife of an honest farmer."

"Yes," said Cass. She handed Tilla the knife, now clean, and picked up the striped bag that the stable lad had retrieved. "I would like to go home now, please, husband."

They stepped out into the narrow street. Apart from a long rope and a stray dog, it was empty. Evidently the rope makers had decided not to see anything, either.

68

ARRIA PAUSED ON her way to the bathhouse and informed Ruso that there was no sign of poor Lucius coming back from Arelate. No, there was no word of Cassiana or That Girl, either. "The staff keep asking me to decide things. Why don't they know how to do it themselves? What's the point of buying slaves if we have to do all the work? As if I don't have enough to do!"

Ruso, preoccupied, let the wave of complaint wash over him and only surfaced to hear, ". . . and join us in the baths. All the young people are there. The children have hardly seen you since you've been home."

"I need to go and check on the farm staff," he said, suspecting it was Arria rather than the children who wanted some adult company. "Then I've got to get ready for the Games tomorrow." He ran his fingers over the soft leather of his purse, feeling the circle of the iron ring inside. "Could you tell Marcia to come and find me as soon as she's free?"

The mindless rhythm of the iron blade sliding along the sharpening stone usually soothed whatever agitation Ruso might be feeling, but this afternoon it had not had time to work its magic when there was a knock on the study door. He laid the scalpel back in the linen roll where he now kept his instruments, and hid them behind the desk. Then he retrieved the ring from his purse and called, "Come in!"

Marcia closed the door behind her and leaned back against it. "Did you give him my letter?"

Ruso nodded, trying not to stare at the rags tied around the curls in his sister's damp hair, which gave her the odd appearance of a cavalry horse being prepared for parade.

"Did he tell you it was respectable?"

"Yes."

She attempted a smile as she said, "I knew you'd be too stuffy to read it!" but he saw the way her fingers were twisted around each other.

"He looks in good shape," he told her. "He's very confident. That's half the battle."

Marcia seemed to find that more reassuring than she would have had she realized how little her brother really knew about gladiators.

"They'll be having the grand dinner tonight," she said. "They do that, you know. Before the Games."

"I know."

"And then tomorrow there'll be the sacrifices to Jupiter and he'll be in the procession." There was no need for her to explain what came next.

"He didn't have time to write a reply," he said, holding out the ring. "But he asked me to give you this."

She took it. Instead of slipping it onto her finger she turned it around, examining it. "I have been thinking," she said. "If he is not dead, but horribly mutilated, what will happen?"

"I'll do my best. Men often recover far better than you expect."

"I mean, what shall I do? With a cripple?"

He could not answer that.

She gave a sudden howl of grief, ran forward, and flung her arms around him. "Oh, Gaius!" she sobbed, her rag-tied head pressing hard against his chest. "I can't bear it, I really can't!"

69

LUCIUS HAD HARDLY spoken to Tilla from the moment he had burst into the bar until they had turned the cart off the road to settle under the trees for the night. She knew that he blamed her for his wife's sudden rebellion. When she had said she would sleep under the cart beside the stable lad, there had been no offer of a more comfortable night with Cass up under the leather canopy.

Rolled in their cloaks on the hard ground, Tilla and the stable lad both seemed to be pretending that the other was not just two feet away in the darkness. Inside the black bulk of the cart above them, Cass was asking Lucius about the children. Had Sosia's tooth come out yet? Did Publius eat his dinner? Had they gone to bed without a fuss? When they asked where she was, what had he told them? Had they been upset?

Listening to the replies, Tilla felt sadness weighing down on top of nighttime chill and exhaustion. Cass and Lucius had a home to go to, and a family waiting for them. Tilla was no longer even sure that her family was waiting for her in the next world. It seemed that Heaven, like god, was everywhere, but not everyone was allowed to go to it. None of her people had worshipped Christos. Perhaps they had been rejected at the gates, like soldiers who did not know the password.

Even Britannia was not home. By now someone else would be renting that little upstairs room outside the fort. Some other soldier's woman, perhaps. Someone who would never be part of the army but who was no longer part of her own people, either. Someone to whom marriage did not seem important, but who might one day find herself desperate for a welcome among the family of a man who was not her husband.

Lucius had already told them about the surprise arrival of the investigators as they had driven out of Arelate. He was now giving Cass a repeat account of exactly what they had said to him and what he had said back. Lucius's part in the story was getting bigger every time he told it. She caught the sound of a yawn. Cass must be weary after all that lying awake worrying about spiders, but she was still loyally pressing her husband with questions as if he were the cleverest, bravest, and most interesting man in the world. And then what happened? And what did you do? No, really? So what do you think will happen about the dogbane?

Lucius moved on to describing his trials during his search for them in Arelate, and how he had visited all five of the marine shipping offices, "but nobody could remember seeing you." Tilla could hear the accusation in his voice. She saw now that she had gone about everything in the wrong way. She did not understand how things worked here. She had never even heard of Marine Shipping Offices. No wonder she had failed. They had found neither the mysterious Ponticus that Lucius had come to warn them about, nor any real trace of the ghostly Captain Copreus.

She was lucky they had not been pursued for knifing Onion Breath in the bar. She supposed she would have to tell the Medicus about that before one of the others did. It was not the sort of thing a Roman looked for in a woman. She was willing to bet that the widow next door had never killed a man in a bar fight. Even the old wife had used poison, so that she could pretend she hadn't done it and the Medicus could imagine that he believed her.

Tilla trapped the far end of the cloak between her feet and tugged it down. She wondered what the Medicus had said to the investigators. She saw now what a terrible mistake this trip had been. She should have stayed back at the farm, loyally supporting him as if she thought he too was the cleverest, bravest, and most interesting man in the world. That was what Roman men seemed to want. Instead, afraid of looking a fool over dinner and convinced she could do something about Cass's brother when everyone else had failed, she had run away.

Tilla yawned and shifted the bag that she had folded into a lumpy pillow.

The Medicus had once asked her to marry him. She had refused. He would not ask again now.

Lucius and Cass were still talking softly as her jumbled thoughts gradually settled into stillness. For a brief moment she was aware that something important had just drifted past her. It was the sort of unexpected clarity that sometimes lit the mind in the middle of the night: an understanding usually followed by the thought, *I must remember that in the morning*, but already when she tried to catch it, it was gone.

70

THE MORNING LIGHT was barely outlining the shutters when Ruso opened his eyes and remembered two things: first, that Tilla was not here, and second, that this was the day of the Games and he had not yet given Tertius's money to the aunt. Since he could hardly stroll onto Lollia's property without greeting her, he supposed that would mean yet another meeting. Arria would be proud of him.

Later, watching the early sun gild Lollia's hair as she took the two coins from him to give to Tertius's aunt, he wondered where that same sun would find Tilla and Cass this morning. He had already spoken to the household gods on their behalf. Since the gods could not be relied upon to act unaided, as soon as he had discharged his duties at the amphitheater, he was going to hire a decent horse and ride to Arelate.

Making his way back across the olive grove in search of breakfast, it occurred to him that until recently, if he had ever felt in the mood to marry again, he would have been searching for someone exactly like Lollia Saturnina. Now, distracted by worries about Tilla, he could not recall a single word of what she had just said to him.

71

THEY WERE ON the barge, and he was telling her she must not get her words muddled up. Calvus and Stilvicus. Calpreo and Ponto. Repeat after me. Pons, Pontis, Ponticorum, Ponticuli, Ponticissimissimus. You must learn to speak Latin properly in a peaceful country, Tilla!

The widow who had lamed his horse was catching up with him now, leaping over the rows of amphorae with her hair streaming out behind her. Tilla tried to follow but her feet were mired in the grape juice and as soon as she pulled one free she remembered the other one and found it was stuck again. She knew she should pray for help but she could not remember the right words in Latin and then the drowned ship's captain who was lying in the corner of the winery woke up, pointing at the knife in his chest with two fingers and laughing. With a huge effort, she leaped out of the trough, fled across the winery, crashed her forehead into the beam of the winepress, and found herself lying on the ground underneath a big wooden box, stunned and terrified.

A familiar voice said, "Are you all right, miss?" She tried to remember where she had heard it before.

"You forgot where you were," said the stable lad. "There's no room to sit up under here. Is your head all right?"

She ran a hand over her forehead and decided it was. Then she lay back beneath the cart and allowed her mind to poke at the edges of the fear, proving to herself that it could not rise and swallow her. It had been a dream: a confusion of all the things that had happened to her. She was getting everything and everybody mixed up, especially the nasty men. Lucius had told them how one of the investigators had frightened the children by waving the stumps of his fingers in their faces. The other one . . . had nothing to do with it. The other one was some onion-breathed sailor who thought it was funny to terrify innocent women, and who had lived to regret it, but not for long.

She saw again the twin fingers of Onion Breath stabbing toward her eyes in that horrible bar. His fingers had not been missing. Just tucked away in the palm of his left hand when he had pretended to be Copreus . . .

She narrowly missed banging her head on the cart again.

"Lucius, wake up! How many fingers does this investigator man not have?"

"Huh?"

Cass's sleepy voice repeated the question.

Lucius grunted "Two."

"Which hand?"

"What's for breakfast?"

"Close your eyes," insisted Tilla, leaning over the side of the cart so he could see her upside down. "See him in your mind. Which hand?"

Lucius yawned. She ducked out of range as he stretched his arms into the early morning air.

"Think!" she urged.

Cass, seeing the expression on Tilla's face, said, "This might be important, husband."

"Um . . . right."

"Tell me what else he looks like. And the other one."

Lucius gave a grunt of protest, then slowly described the heavy build and the cropped hair and the tattoos.

Tilla recalled the description they had been given of Ponticus by the grim-faced Phoebe. "Is the other one short, about thirty years old, with a clever face, and he wears a ring with a red stone?"

Lucius frowned. "If you already know, why are you waking me up?"

She said, "Calvus and Stilo. Ponticus and Copreus. They are not drowned,

Cass! Lucius has met them at the farm and the Medicus is back in Nemausus asking questions about the things they have done."

"Holy gods," said Lucius, pushing strands of hair out of his eyes and sitting up. At last he seemed to have understood. "Wake up, wife. We need to get back and warn Gaius."

72

THE YOUTH IN the usher's tunic stepped out in front of them. "Ladies only up here, sir!"

Ruso fixed him with a glare that suggested if he did not get out of the way, he would shortly find himself tumbling down the several flights of steps that the remnant of the Petreius family had just toiled up. "I'm escorting these ladies to their seats," he growled.

The youth glanced both ways along the corridor. Failing to spot any other officials among the spectators clambering around the stone labyrinth of the amphitheater, he stepped smartly aside with, "Of course, sir!" as if this had been his intention all along.

The crush of people thinned as they climbed the final steps. Eventually the four of them stood blinking in the morning sun, staring out across the vast oval whose circumference was alive with the hubbub of spectators settling in for a day's entertainment.

Arria glanced up at the canopy stretched out above the curving rows of benches. "Well, at least we shall be in the shade."

"I told you," said Flora. "It said on the notices. *Shades will be provided.*"

"We'll sit down here," announced Marcia, starting to pick her way along the front row before anyone could argue.

Arria called after her, "We'd be more private higher up, dear!"

"I want to see!"

Arria pursed her lips and turned to Ruso as if to say, What can I do with her?

Marcia settled herself next to an aisle on the front tier of seats, and flung the green stole sideways as far as it would reach to prevent any other hopefuls sitting too close before her family caught up. Ruso, who found the narrow space between the benches and the parapet no easier to negotiate than the stairs, edged along through the gap and finally unslung the sack of supplies from his shoulder. Arria busied herself pulling out the contents. Marcia leaned her elbows on the parapet and stared down at the small figures of the slaves raking the arena, as if glaring at an expanse of sand dotted with bushes in pots—presumably the forest for the morning's wild animal hunts—would give her some clue about how events would unfold later in the day.

"I don't know why we have to sit up here," she grumbled. "We can't see a thing."

Flora grabbed a cushion from the bag and knelt on it, scanning the tiers of seats above them to see if she recognized any of the other females edging along the rows and snatching up their skirts to scale the stone steps.

"Would you like a cushion, dear?"

When Marcia did not reply, Arria leaned around Flora and tapped her on the knee. "Do take one, dear, the seats are very hard."

Marcia snatched the cushion with an, "Ohh!" of exasperation and slapped it down on the seat as if she were swatting a wasp.

Ruso removed the food basket and two leather-covered water bottles from the sack. He was relieved to see that neither was the one that had belonged to Severus. "Anybody want a drink?"

"I don't need a drink!"

"Marcia, please!" said Arria. "There's no need to be rude."

"I want some," said Flora, seizing one of the bottles and ignoring her mother's plea to use a cup.

"I'll come and find you if I can," promised Ruso. "If I don't—"

His reply was interrupted by a shrill and slightly off-key blast of trumpets.

"I know, dear," Arria assured him over the rising noise of the crowd. "We'll make our way over to the Augustus gate and hire a carriage. Flora, really! What will people think? You really must—oh look, here they come!"

A roar rose like a tidal wave around the amphitheater. Ruso glanced down into the arena. A standard-bearer on a white horse had just emerged from one of the tunnels and was trotting around the perimeter displaying a golden image of the emperor to the crowd. He was followed by a man with the ceremonial birch rods and a chariot in which stood Fuscus, fresh from the sacrifices at Jupiter's temple, waving to the cheering spectators with one hand and clinging on with the other. The crowd yelled even louder as a parade of men marched out in his wake, their bright blue cloaks shimmering with embroidered gold.

"Tertius!" screamed Marcia over the din, leaping to her feet. "Tertius, look up, it's me!"

Arria's cry of, "Marcia, behave!" was barely audible.

The gladiators were followed by a squad of slaves displaying their armor to an audience that howled and stamped its approval.

Ruso squeezed back toward the exit past several women who looked as if they might push him over the parapet in their excitement. At the top of the steps he paused and looked back at his family. Arria had given up trying to restrain Marcia and was pretending not to notice the screaming and waving.

The last time he had been inside this place his father had been alive, Lucius had been courting Cass, and he himself had been a married man. Now his father was dead, Lucius and Cass were quarreling, his little sister was in love with a gladiator, and Claudia was at home pretending to mourn the loss of a different husband.

He glanced down over the bobbing coiffures of late arrivals still clattering up the steps and caught the glare of the usher before starting to force his way down against the flow.

Ruso had never managed to work out exactly how the honeycomb of stairs and corridors fit together to hold up the miracle that was the amphitheater. Navigating by counting the arches, he made his way past the latecomers being directed up to their seats and paused to buy an apple from a fruit seller in case there was no time for lunch. He showed his pass to the attendant, who moved aside to let him descend the steps into the area reserved for competitors.

As he went lower, the appetizing waft from the fritter sellers outside was overwhelmed by a sour stink from the condemned cells. Above him, a sudden silence from the crowd told him the entertainment was starting in the arena. He was not going back up to watch. Hidden away deep beneath the seating, he unlatched the door of the dank vault that had been reserved for medical treatment.

As his eyes adjusted to the gloom he could see that the room was more or less empty apart from a couple of tables, two chairs, an empty brazier, and some rubbish that had been cleared away and dumped at the far end. The larger of the tables was bare, ready for its first patient. The porters had stacked the other with the boxes of medical supplies that Gnostus had organized yesterday and placed several buckets of water underneath.

Ruso unraveled his roll of instruments and began to lay them out on the side table. A room without much daylight was not an ideal place to perform emergency surgery, but then, nothing about this grandiose combination of sport, warfare, and public execution was ideal.

A roar from the crowd washed through the corridors. Ruso neither knew nor cared what beasts had been winched up from the vaults for the hunters to chase around out there. He had more important things to think about.

He wished he could believe in the existence of some unknown woman with a grudge against Severus who would take the trouble to disguise herself as Claudia and had the chance to put poisonous honey in his drink, but he could not. Claudia's denial had been vehement, but she had offered no alternative explanation except the vague suggestion that Ennia might have disguised herself and murdered her brother for no reason. It was true that Ennia could fit two sides of the triangle (the "who" and the "how") but only Claudia could supply a plausible "why."

The truth, of course, could be found by dressing a selection of females in pink sandals and orange wigs, parading them in front of the man who had sold the honey, and demanding that he identify his customer. To arrange that, he would have to confide in the investigators and incur the vengeance of Probus.

Ruso seated himself on the operating table and ran his fingertips over the rough edge of the wood. He envied Euplius, who had vanished from a difficult situation and reemerged somewhere else as Gnostus. How easy life would be if a man had no responsibilities. He now saw how simple life had been in the army compared to this: just himself and Tilla.

He was not going to wait around to be arrested. If Lucius did not reappear with the women, he would set off for Arelate as soon as he had finished here. But even if he found Tilla and all this mess were magically straightened out, would they ever be able to regain the trust they had lost?

He didn't know the answer to the next question, either, which was introduced by, "Holy Jupiter, you gave me a turn sat there in the dark!" and resolved into, "Have you seen any hats with wings on them?"

Ruso blinked, dazzled by the sudden blaze of torchlight. "Pardon?"

"Mercury hats," explained the man clutching the torch as Ruso tried to remember where he had seen him before. "I've found the boots," he continued, holding up a jumble of footwear with large flaps attached in the shape of wings. "They're with the hooks in the toolroom, but nobody can remember what we did with the hats."

Ruso finally recognized Attalus the undertaker from Severus's funeral, now evidently having trouble costuming the employees who would remove the dead from the arena.

"Going to look bloody stupid out there with no hats," grumbled the man, raising the torch and peering toward the pile of junk at the back of the vault. "What's in that lot?"

"Not a clue," said Ruso. "Help yourself." He slid down from the table and held out a hand for the torch.

"If you want something done, do it yourself, see?" continued Attalus, groping his way through a pile of empty boxes and tipping a sack load of what appeared to be rags out onto the floor. "I told them to get all the gear checked over in advance, and what do they do? Leave it till the last minute and then come whining to me." He bent to examine the scattered rags and gave them a perfunctory poke with his toe. "The gods alone know what this rubbish is." He dragged out a board that appeared to be a piece of painted scenery and flung it aside. "You're the doctor everybody thinks poisoned Severus, right?"

"I didn't."

"So I hear." Attalus kicked a sack aside and yelled as a rat shot out, ran across the floor, and disappeared out of the door. "Ought to get a dog," he said. "It's a disgrace, the state of this place."

"What exactly did you hear?" asked Ruso, moving the torch as close as he dared without setting the undertaker or the junk on fire.

"Turns out it was the wife all along," said Attalus, tugging at the corner of a basket.

"Who says?"

"The investigators, or so I'm told." Attalus heaved the basket out and dropped it onto the floor before lifting the lid with his toe. "So that's you in the clear, then, eh?" He bent down to peer inside. "Got 'em!" He snatched up the basket, flung the winged boots in on top of the contents, and took back the torch. "Sorry about the mess," he said, stepping over it. "Got to run."

"Hey! How do they know it's the wife?"

"I'll send somebody down to clear up."

"But how do they—"

"Who cares?" retorted Attalus. His voice echoed down the corridor as he retreated. "Just be glad it's not you!"

73

THERE WAS A rattle and a clang as the porter tipped hot coals from the shovel into the brazier for the cautery irons. He had just glanced at the empty operating table and observed, "Not long to wait now, boss," when they heard a voice calling for the medic. The porter grinned. "There you go, boss. What did I just say? They ought to give me a job down with the Oracle." He stepped across to the door and shouted, "In here!"

Ruso reached for one of the leather aprons slung on a nail in the wall. "Tell Gnostus to send me some help up, will you?"

Squinting at the apron in search of the head hole, Ruso had greeted his first customer with, "Right, what can we do for you?" before he realized that the person who had come into the room was not a patient at all.

"Tilla!" He flung the apron aside and hugged her, shouting after the porter, "It's all right, I don't need any help with this one!" Burying his face in her neck he said, "Thank the gods! Is Cass back? You're covered in dust, are you all right? Did you see Lucius?"

"Cass is at home with the children," she said. "Lucius has gone back to make his wine and they are not shouting anymore, and I am very bruised after riding fast in that bumpy cart."

He pulled her close. "I tried to come after you," he said. "The horse fell."

"Galla told me you are working here," she said. "I have many things to tell you, or I would never come to a bad place like this."

"I have to earn a living, Tilla."

"That is what you always say."

"You shouldn't have run off like that with someone you didn't know. You could have gotten into all sorts of trouble. Why didn't you tell me?"

"I found out something important," she said, dodging the question. "The two men who have come here are not from the senator. They are not real investigators."

She stood back and waited for his response, looking very pleased with herself. Outside, there was some sort of commotion farther down the corridor.

"Not investigators?" Ruso tried to make sense of it.

"The clever one wearing the ring is a man called Ponticus who did Severus's business in Arelate. He is the one who bought the bad ship." The shouting was growing closer. "The other one with the fingers missing is a sea captain called Copreus who is supposed to be drowned."

"The captain of the *Pride*?"

"Yes."

"But what are they doing here?"

At that moment the door burst open and a voice cried, "Where's the surgeon? Injured man coming in!"

Ruso reached for the lamp and held it up to light the others in the bracket on the wall. "That's me," he said. "What have we got?"

"Huntsman. Tripped over. Tiger got to him before they could get him out."

He nodded. "Go and tell Gnostus I need a hand here. He'll be down with the fighters." He leaned across the table and held out the lamp. "Light the rest of them, will you? Then get a cloth out of the last box on the left, soak it in wine, and wring it out."

Tilla did not reach for the lamp.

"If you're not going to help," he said, placing it on the table, "keep out of the way."

Their eyes met. Finally she hooked a finger through the handle of the lamp. "I am still not glad about what happens in this place," she said.

Ruso placed one hand over the clothing shears to check that they were within easy reach. "Right now," he said, "I shouldn't think the huntsman's too happy about it, either."

74

IT WAS MIDDAY before Ruso finished cleaning up the huntsman's shredded shoulder and trying to put it back together, all the time wondering if it would have been kinder to suggest that the man were swiftly finished off. He stayed to supervise the dressing, then took Gnostus's advice and went to find some lunch. Gnostus's view, unfortunately expressed in front of Tilla, was that since the lunchtime entertainment was only a few criminals, there wouldn't be much for the medics to do unless the beasts turned on their trainers.

"What does he mean?" demanded Tilla as they left the stuffy confines of the lamplit room for the relative cool of the corridor.

Ruso muttered, "Executions," through a dry throat. "Come upstairs, we'll get something to drink and you can tell me about Calvus and Stilo."

"Executions of people *with animals*?"

"It's not much different to what happens in Deva," he assured her, realizing now how little attention he had paid to the gruesome death sentences meted out within a few paces of the fort. "Just on a bigger scale."

She gestured toward the steps that led out to the glare and bustle of the arena seating. "And all those people come here to watch this thing happen?"

"Not really," said Ruso. "It's not the star attraction." He took her arm and steered her toward a crowded exit. "Which means there'll be lines building up at the lunch stalls."

He got her as far as the exit before she stopped dead. This, he supposed, was some sort of achievement, although the man who shoved past them both with, "Get out of the way, will you? Bloody foreigners!" was clearly unimpressed.

He drew her aside. Standing in the shade of a massive pillar as the lunchtime crowds flowed out into the sunshine, he decided to cut short the inevitable argument. "I can't do anything about it, Tilla. There are twenty thousand people here who—"

"I want to see it."

"No, you don't. Come and tell me about Calvus and—"

"Do not tell me what I want!"

"Trust me. You don't." He knew it would be useless to explain to her that the victims were all criminals sentenced to death in a fair trial. Useless even if it were true, which it probably was not.

Standing close so as not to obstruct the exit, he noticed for the first time how the sun had bleached her hair. How unfashionably and delightfully freckled her face had become. He said, "Why would Calvus and—whatever their names are—why would they come to Nemausus?"

From somewhere inside the arena came a shrill scream, followed by a ripple of laughter.

The familiar eyes gazed into Ruso's own. Instead of the determination he had expected, he saw fear.

"Come and get something to drink," he urged her, annoyed at being made to feel responsible for whatever ghastliness was going on in there. "You can tell me all about Arelate."

"If it was me," she said, "would you be there to see me die?"

"Don't be ridiculous." The words came out more harshly than he had intended. "What I mean is, you wouldn't—"

She was gone before he reached the end of the sentence, dodging around the wandering spectators and back into the shadowed entrance tunnel.

"Tilla!" he yelled, plunging after her, apologizing as he stabbed a passing foot with his stick. "Tilla, wait!"

He need not have worried. By the time he got there she had already been grabbed by an usher and was being firmly escorted back down the steps. The usher looked relieved to see him. "I was just saying," the man said as another hideous shriek issued from the arena and the crowd yelled advice and abuse, "Military veterans only in these seats. Women and slaves is around to the right and higher up." Evidently the man could not decide which category Tilla fell into and was taking no chances.

Tilla said, "I must see."

"Why?" asked Ruso.

"Because it is what your people do."

"Yes, but—"

"I want to understand."

More spectators brushed past them, voices rising and fading down the corridor. A couple of men sharing a joke. A small boy wailing and his mother demanding: "Why didn't you say you needed a pee before we sat down?"

Tilla said, "Your family come to these Games?"

"They're up there," said Ruso, pointing vaguely in the direction of the women's seats and adding, "Marcia thinks she's engaged to one of the gladiators. He'll be on later."

"So you let your sisters watch this?"

"Everybody watches it."

"That is why I must see."

"Please don't."

"If you are ashamed, why are you here?"

It was not a question he wanted to consider. He took her by the arm and led her back up the steps. "I'm a veteran," he informed the usher. "Twentieth Legion, served in Britannia." He tugged open his purse and handed the usher a copper. "Just let the lady stand at the top of the steps for a minute, will you?"

A naked man and woman were chained to a post in the middle of the arena. The man had a placard hung around his neck which read, "Temple Robber." The woman's pale rolls of fat wobbled as she caught sight of the bear. Someone in the crowd shouted an insult and laughter rippled around the stadium. The men with whips stepped forward to encourage the bear to do its duty.

The deaths he had paid for Tilla to watch were deliberately hideous. "It's supposed to discourage crime," he heard himself saying as the crowd mocked the woman's frantic efforts to burrow under the corpse of her companion. He knew now that whatever Claudia had done, he could not bear the thought of her being punished like that.

Tilla did not seem to hear him. Her eyes were fixed on the execution. Beneath the freckles, her face was an odd color and he suspected she was about to be sick.

"It's finished," he said, taking her by the arm as if she were the only one needing support. "Come down now."

As she turned to descend the steps without arguing, he glanced across at the seats of honor. Resplendent in a dazzling white toga, Fuscus was leaning sideways to chat to his companions, leaving one hand holding a silver wine cup in the air as if he were saluting the prisoners dying beneath him.

It was only as he followed Tilla down the steps that Ruso's mind registered who he had seen up on the balcony talking to Fuscus. The two men who were not really from Rome, not really investigators, and not really called Calvus and Stilo.

75

THE TWO HEAVYWEIGHTS protecting Fuscus and his guests from the common herd did not look impressed. Between them they were wide enough to bar access to the flight of steps that led up to where the great man was apparently holding a lunchtime meeting on the balcony.

"This is urgent," explained Ruso, recognizing one of the gang who had helped Stilo search the house.

"Can't be interrupted," said the second man. "Gabinius Fuscus is a busy man. Things to do, people to—"

"People to kill," put in Tilla, who had almost recovered her normal color.

Ruso shifted his stick sideways and planted it on her foot. She jabbed him with her elbow and spoke up again. "We want to stop your master making a very big mistake," she informed the guards. "Even though he does not deserve it. When he finds out that he is made a fool of because you have not let us save him, what will he do to you?"

The men looked at each other.

"My father was an old friend of his," said Ruso.

"And I am Darlughdacha of the Corionotatae, among the Brigantes," said Tilla.

"Who of the what?"

She repeated her British name and tribe.

"Dar . . ." The man frowned. "Oh, bugger it. Come up and tell him yourself."

Ruso had expected some reaction from the occupants of Fuscus's cushioned and perfumed private balcony, but the magistrate's cry of "Ruso! Just in time!" was unexpectedly welcoming.

He surveyed the row of people enjoying a light lunch beneath the cool waft of ostrich-feather fans. A scattering of bald pates and togas was interspersed with richly jeweled and colorful figures whom he assumed to be wives, and a couple of young lads who must be Fuscus's sons. Most had swiveled around in their seats and were staring at Tilla: the women with alarm and the men with interest. Nobody seemed very concerned about the proceedings in the arena below, where the bear had been recaged and Attalus's costumed men were dragging the remains of its victims away through the sand.

"Very timely, Ruso," continued Fuscus, waving a slice of melon in the direction of Calvus and Stilo and almost poking it into the eye of a bored-looking girl next to him whom Ruso assumed to be his latest wife. "Come over here and listen to this."

Calvus and Stilo were standing awkwardly at the far end of the balcony. Evidently they had not been invited to sit, and were doing their best not to turn disrespectful backs on Fuscus, his guests, or the entertainment he had so generously provided.

Ruso beckoned Tilla forward. Below them, the musicians' horns blared and a couple of tumblers performed cartwheels across the arena while the maintenance slaves scurried to rake over the sand before the next event. Ruso slipped in front of Fuscus's elegantly carved chair and perched himself on the balustrade, blocking the view of several of the dignitaries.

A familiar voice said, "Stand up, man! At least show some respect!" and Ruso realized that one of the bald pates in the less prestigious seats belonged to his former father-in-law.

Probus was looking even less pleased to see him than usual. Ruso ignored both him and the guards, who were clearly waiting for instructions to throw these interlopers out. Leaning forward, he murmured to Fuscus, "This woman has some information you need to hear straightaway, sir."

The "sir" had slipped out inadvertently, but Fuscus did not appear to be listening, anyway. "My cousin the senator's men," he announced, waving the melon in the direction of Calvus and Stilo, "have completed their investigation. They've come here to give us all a summary of the report they'll be delivering to Rome."

Tilla's "No they will not!" from behind was a surprise to everyone including Ruso, who had intended to approach the matter with more subtlety.

Fuscus, ignoring her, turned to Calvus and Stilo. "I'm listening."

The row of dignified heads turned to face the far end of the balcony. Calvus squared his shoulders, waited to make sure everyone was paying attention, and opened his mouth to speak just as Tilla cried, "He is not an investigator!"

"Control that woman, Ruso!" demanded Probus.

"Yeah," agreed Stilo, exchanging a glance with Calvus. "Shut up and listen, Blondie."

The dignified heads swiveled again, and a murmur of protest arose. Fuscus snapped his fingers and more guards stepped forward.

"You need to listen to her," urged Ruso, ducking away from the balustrade before the approaching guard could push him over it. "These two are impostors." Ignoring protests from Stilo, he pointed to Calvus. "He's a middleman who provided a rotten ship, and that's the captain who—"

"Nonsense!" cried Probus, leaping to his feet. "These men have carried out a full and fair investigation into a suspicious death and it has nothing to do with ships."

"D'you lot want to hear who done it, or not?" shouted Stilo over a growing cacophony of horns from the musicians' enclosure. One or two of the dignitaries half rose from their seats, looking around for reassurance.

"Shut up and listen, Ruso," ordered Fuscus.

One of the guards had positioned himself behind Tilla. Ruso motioned to her to be quiet.

Calvus had a restraining hand on Stilo's shoulder. "Gentlemen, ladies—please excuse my friend. He's not used to civilized company. I keep him to deal with the low and dangerous types I have to mix with in the course of my investigations."

Fuscus glanced both ways along the row at his guests, assured himself that Tilla was under control, and ordered the musicians to be toned down and a slave to refill the drinks before he said, "Carry on. We want to know the result of the investigation. We can't have poisoners running loose around the town."

Calvus bowed and began, "Magistrates, ladies . . ." He cleared his throat.

"I came to Gaul on the orders of the cousin of Magistrate Gabinius Fuscus, Senator Gabinius Valerius—"

"You are a liar!" shouted Tilla, squealing as the guard grabbed her and flung her over his shoulder.

Before Ruso could intervene the other guard seized his arm and wrenched it up parallel with his spine. As he was dragged farther away from Fuscus he was aware of Tilla yelling, "You are both liars!" as she was carried away.

"Mad bitch!" shouted Stilo as the words, "You murdered Justinus!" echoed back up the steps.

"She's telling the truth." Ruso gasped as the guard forced his wrist up between his shoulder blades. He hoped Tilla had not made a terrible mistake.

Fuscus drained his wine in one gulp. "You'd better have a good reason for this performance, Ruso."

"You need to know. They're swindlers and murderers. They killed my brother-in-law. They might have killed Severus as well."

Fuscus turned back to Calvus for an answer, but whatever denial Calvus was about to make was interrupted by Stilo's "Your Honors don't want to listen to them lies. That barbarian's protecting him."

The row of dignified heads was now turning frantically in an effort to take in Calvus and Stilo at one end of the balcony, Ruso at the other end, and Fuscus lumbering to his feet in the middle, calling for order as if this were an unruly Council meeting. The roar of the crowd said something was happening in the arena, but nobody on the balcony was watching.

"It was him what done it!" announced Stilo, pointing at Ruso. "The doctor and the wife, in the kitchen with the honey. We know about the red hair and the pink shoes!" He turned to Calvus for confirmation, but Calvus was gone. The commotion in the crowd beyond the balcony marked the point where he had leaped over the side and was now forcing his way along a row of bewildered spectators.

Stilo glanced down, thought better of it, and made a lunge for the nearest serving girl. Her tray crashed to the floor as he pulled her back against him, and a knife appeared at her throat.

Fuscus and a couple of the dignitaries clutched at the nearest women. The dignitaries appeared to be trying to protect their wives, Fuscus to use his as a shield. The guards backed away as Stilo dragged the terrified serving girl back toward the exit.

"Don't just stand there!" cried Fuscus, knocking the fan from the hand of the nearest slave. "Defend us!"

The grip on Ruso's arm fell away. Stilo reached the exit, flung the girl into the arms of the approaching guard, and clattered away down the steps.

The guard who had evicted Tilla from the balcony was returning up the steps as Ruso stumbled down. "You're welcome to her, mate. Little cow nearly had my ear off."

By the time Ruso reached the corridor neither Tilla nor Stilo was in sight but the direction of one or both was marked by a series of complaining spectators who had been shoved aside. Forcing himself to ignore the stabbing pain in the side of his foot, Ruso followed the trail up the steps, swerved around a furious vendor, and narrowly missed slipping on a scattering of pastries the man was trying to pick up. As he raced along the upper corridor he realized none of Fuscus's men was with him. He was not even sure who he was chasing. All he knew was that if Stilo decided to take on Tilla, she was in serious trouble.

An usher was trying to block his path, shouting something and holding up one hand in a "stop" sign. Ruso charged straight for him, yelling, "Where did they go?" The man faltered, leaped aside, and flapped the hand to send Ruso ahead.

Ahead, the curve of the gallery was almost empty. To his right, the open archways offered a fine view of the town, but it would be a brave man or woman who would risk the leap down to the sunlit street. To his left, on the inside of the curve, shadowy flights of steps rose and fell from the gallery every few paces.

"Where did they go?" he yelled to an old man squatting in the shade of a pillar.

The man pointed a skinny finger toward the next flight up. Ruso hopped toward it, grabbing at his injured foot. The brief massage made no difference: Every step up was a fresh wave of pain.

"Tilla!" he shouted, knowing his voice would not reach her over the sound of the crowd. "Tilla, wait for me!"

Emerging into a narrower corridor, he gasped to the usher, "I'm looking for a blond woman!"

"Aren't we all?"

"Which way?"

The usher, still grinning, pointed to his left.

"Is there a man with her?"

"No, he's in front."

The upper corridor was a lame man's nightmare: barely a few yards level at a time before more steps down into a dip, a junction with another gloomy stairway that Tilla or Stilo might have descended, and more steps back up the other side. By the third or fourth dip Ruso was beginning to feel exhausted. All those weeks of limping had left him seriously out of condition.

"Tilla!" he yelled, forcing himself to keep going. By the next dip he knew he was never going to catch up with her. She might not even be ahead of him anymore. She might have followed Stilo down any of the exit routes he had hurried past. They might have gone into the cheap seats above, with the slaves and the sailors who operated the awnings. They might have gone around to the women's area. He glanced down, and up, and ahead, and back, and did not know which way to run. Finally he leaned back against the wall, feeling his heart pounding and his breath rasping in his chest. Wherever Tilla was, he could not help her. Surely any passersby would defend a lone woman against a male attacker? Even if she was obviously a barbarian? Of course, whether they would defend a female barbarian who seemed to be attacking a local man was another matter entirely.

Outside, the crowd held its collective breath and then burst into wild cheering. Alone in the cool gloom that smelled of urine and fried food, Ruso curled up one leg and nursed his foot, trying to think past the pain. It was a moment before he registered the voice saying, "Doctor Gaius Petreius, sir?"

He looked up. "Tertius?" The youth who should have been arming himself with net and trident in the gladiators' cells was trotting up the steps toward him in military boots and a sweat-stained tunic. "What the hell are you doing here?"

Instead of replying, Tertius seized him by both shoulders. "Thank you, sir! I never thought you'd do it, but thank you! I won't let you down, I promise!"

"Do what?"

"Find the money! I can't believe it!"

"Nor can I," said Ruso, too breathless to argue.

"Are you all right, sir?"

Ruso gesticulated vaguely around him. "There's a blond woman—"

"Dressed in blue, chasing a man in a green tunic?" Tertius pointed back the way he had come. "They went down toward the animal cages."

Ruso was already racing down the steps as the words "Sir, what's going on?" echoed around him.

76

TILLA TRIED TO steady her breathing, but the stench of animals made her gasp. The row of smoky torches stretching down the tunnel ahead did little to lift the gloom, barely revealing the figures of slaves moving between arched recesses on either side. From somewhere deeper inside, beneath the middle of the arena, she heard a clang of metal, then the shout of an order and the squeak and grind of something being hoisted on a winch. An animal howl echoed down the tunnel. Tilla shuddered.

This must be where the creatures were kept before they were lifted up and thrust into the arena through trapdoors. As her eyes adjusted from the sunlight outside, she could make out the stripes of cage bars in some of the recesses.

She tightened the grip on her knife. There was no other way the man could have come. She was not far behind him, and if he had run away down that tunnel she would have seen him pass through the torchlight. He must have ducked into one of those black recesses. But even if she found him, what was she going to do?

It seemed nobody on the balcony except the Medicus had believed her. Nobody else had given chase when she ran after Stilo. She was sure the Medicus had been behind her, but even he had disappeared now. Whatever was down here, she was facing it alone.

Someone—not Stilo, it was the wrong height and gait—emerged from a side entrance hauling a trolley. As the slave approached, the eyes that glanced out of the filthy face suggested that she should not be here but that he did not dare tell her so. She said, "There is a sailor in there. He is wearing a green tunic and he has two fingers missing. Have you seen him?"

The slave's expression did not change. "No, miss." As he plodded past she tried not to look at the mangled and smeary creatures piled on the trolley.

She turned her head away from the source of the stench and took a deep breath. Then she murmured a prayer and ventured into the place where the spirits who lived under the ground were appeased with blood.

The stones beneath her boots were slippery and uneven. The first recess on each side was empty: She had been able to see that from the entrance. Beyond them, she flattened her back to the wall, trying not to think of the filth that might be crusted on it, and crept sideways. Beneath the gloomy arch opposite, she could make out the poles of brooms and shovels. Nothing round enough to be human. Nothing moving.

The roar of the crowd echoed through the tunnel, sounding like another great animal.

She slid one hand farther along the wall. Her fingers rounded a corner stone with something cold set in it. Cage bars. Down at floor level she could make out pale wisps of straw. She waited, hardly breathing, but nothing moved. She checked the tunnel and then shifted farther along toward the next recess, moving away from the bars in case there was something behind them with claws and a long reach.

What happened next was over almost before she realized it. The hand clamping on her wrist. The hopeless struggle not to be dragged in between the bars. The pain of her shoulder rammed against the cage. The screech of metal on stone tangling with the echo of her own scream: the weight of the body pressing her against the cage and the shock as the knife was knocked out of her hand. Then the smack of something hitting flesh. The grunt of pain and the sudden release. The footsteps, the shouts of "Miss!" and "Let her go!" as the two silhouettes that were racing toward her from the outside world became the Medicus and another man, both asking if she was all right.

"I think so," she said, shaking off the filth of the cage and rubbing the pain in her shoulder. The man handed her back her knife and said something about being sorry and having to go. The Medicus had already set off down the tunnel, dodging around a couple of slaves with trolleys. "Wait for me!" she shouted, running after him, ashamed to recognize it was because she wanted his protection, not because she wanted another fight with Stilo.

Beneath one of the far torches, the Medicus was shouting something at a slave carrying buckets. She heard the slave try to tell him he shouldn't be there, and the Medicus say, "Never mind. Did you see him?"

Tilla jumped over the stream of water the slave had just sloshed down the tunnel floor. "What did you just tell that man?"

The slave looked baffled. "I said the one he's chasing run out the far end, miss."

When Tilla caught up with him the Medicus had already emerged at the far end of the underground chambers and clambered up onto the end of a row of seats. He was standing with one hand shading his eyes, squinting out across the packed terraces. A couple of spectators were complaining and leaning around him to get a clear view of the arena. Tilla tried to get up onto the seating opposite. She glimpsed hundreds—thousands—of dark heads along the curving rows before a couple of men shouted at her and tried to push her off.

"Can you see him?"

The Medicus shook his head and jumped down to join her, wincing even though he landed on his good foot. "We've lost him. Are you sure you're all right?"

She said, "Where will he go?"

"A long way from here. Put that knife away, you're frightening everyone."

She looked around and saw the approaching steward.

"It's all right," the Medicus explained, taking her by the arm and steering her firmly toward an exit. "She's with me. She just got a bit overexcited. It's her first time."

The steward said, "Yes, sir." He did not look surprised.

She said, "What will we do now?"

He took a left turn. "Go back to work."

"But what about that Stilo?"

He steered her toward another staircase. "He'll leave town. Maybe the senator will send somebody after him."

And maybe not. All her effort had come to nothing. The man who had murdered Cass's brother had escaped. The Medicus was right: He could be anywhere out there among thousands of people. They would never catch him now.

His hand tightened on her arm and she noticed for the first time how badly he was limping. "You should not be walking around on that foot."

"You shouldn't be chasing a man like Stilo on your own."

She said, "Back in that . . ." She had no name for it. "Back down there. Did something hit Stilo?"

He said, "Damn. I forgot to pick it up."

"What?"

"My lunch," he said. "The army teaches you to throw stones, but I reckoned that at that distance an apple in the eye would stop him just as well."

77

"FEROX!" GASPED THE man, struggling to rise while Ruso's blood-splattered assistants tried to hold him down on the table. "Where's Ferox?"

Ruso, who dared not remove the wadding over the wound until his patient was still, said, "He'll be in later. We need to deal with you first."

"No, he's worse! Where's Ferox? What have they done with him? Let me go!"

A fist escaped and narrowly missed Ruso's jaw.

"Somebody else is dealing with your friend," said Ruso, seizing the flailing arm and glancing across at Gnostus, who looked up from washing the sand out of a nasty head wound and drew one finger across his throat.

Ruso turned back to the patient. "Lie still and let's have a look at what's going on here, shall we?"

The man continued to thrash around. "Let me go! I'll find him. I'll bring him in. He's down. He needs help."

"Somebody else will see to him."

"You're lying! You're all lying to me!"

Ruso eyed the dirt-streaked face. At least the man's lungs were in good order. "You're right," he said, too tired to lie anymore. "Ferox is dead.

Fate chose to take him and not you. Lie still and let me look or you'll be joining him."

"You bastard, you filthy lying dog! He's not dead!"

Ruso had already given the man as much mandrake as he dared, but it seemed to be having little effect.

"Ferox is with the gods," a female voice assured him. A hand, smaller and cleaner than those that were trying to force him down, reached out to rest on his forehead. "I will pray for his soul," promised Tilla, who until now had been standing in the shadows.

When she began to pray over the patient in British, Ruso was relieved. As long as nobody understood, she could—and no doubt would—rain down any number of curses on the politician who had paid for thousands of people to watch death as entertainment, and possibly on himself as well for joining in.

As the babble of British rose over the operating table, the man's arching chest sank back down. His grimace relaxed. "Ferox!" he whispered to the stone vaulting above their heads. "There you are. I didn't mean it, mate. I didn't mean it." His voice was growing sleepy. "You were supposed to go left. Up, down, left. Both left. I told you, mate, you got to . . . you got to pay . . . pay attention."

Ruso lifted the wadding from the side of the chest and began to explore the injury.

He had patched up the wound and was giving orders for the patient to be kept poulticed and under observation when another fresh and whimpering load was maneuvered in from the corridor. The bearers rolled the occupant of the stretcher onto the table, announced, "Hamstrung, can't stop it bleeding," and retreated to their station.

Tilla cried, "That is him!" at the same moment Ruso recognized the filthy and blood-streaked figure curled up in front of him.

"Tertius? How did this happen?"

Tertius groped a hand toward his own. "Is that you, sir?"

"Yes," said Ruso, lifting the dressing to peer at a gaping wound behind the lad's left knee. He said, "Who did this?"

Tertius's weak response was something between a laugh and a sob. "Sorry, sir. I wasted your money."

"He came back," said a voice from Gnostus's side of the room. "Silly bugger came back to make up the numbers so his mate didn't have to take on two men."

Ruso shook his head in disbelief.

"How bad is it?" The voice was barely recognizable as the confident youth from earlier this afternoon.

"Nothing to worry about," Ruso lied, directing the assistants to get him into a better position while he hunted for the main source of the bleeding. Tilla fetched a lamp from one of the brackets and held it close. He was finishing the first cautery when there was a commotion out in the corridor and a voice that should have been inaudible down here shrieked, "How dare you? He's my fiancé! Let me in!"

Ruso winced as the door crashed open. "It's me!" cried Marcia, rushing across to the table. "Tertius, don't die! Get out of the way, Gaius!"

Instead of getting out of the way, Ruso placed another sponge in the wound and ordered one of the assistants to hold it there. Then he gripped his sister's shoulders with bloodstained hands and said firmly in her ear, "If you want to help, shut up and wait outside. You're embarrassing me and you aren't helping him."

"But he's hurt! Oh, what did you sign up for, you stupid, stupid boy? What am I going to—ugh! Gaius, your hands are horrible, get them off!"

"Wait outside," Ruso repeated, nodding to the other assistant who propelled her toward the door.

"You can't throw me out, I—What's she doing here? You said she ran away! Get off me! Gaius, tell him to let me go!"

"And while you're out there," Ruso called over his shoulder, "think about growing up. There's a brave man lying here and he deserves better than this."

78

THE GAMES WERE over. The rows of seats were practically deserted apart from the slaves gathering up litter and lost children. Already three had been corralled near the east exit, where a plump and jolly woman was consoling them for their lack of parents by feeding them sausage fritters. Outside there were still plenty of people milling about, buying food and haggling over the price of souvenirs. Ruso made the mistake of catching the eye of a vendor. The little terracotta shapes rattled in the tray as the vendor scuttled forward to block their path and suggested that the young lady might like a little memento of her trip to the city.

"I am trying to forget," said Tilla.

No, they did not want a bronze model of a gladiator waving a sword. Nor did they want any of the terracotta portrayals of execution victims being done away with in various gruesome fashions, even if they were an absolute bargain and the man's master would be furious when he found out he'd practically been giving the stock away.

"I've got my own reminder, thanks," said Ruso, holding up his hands. He had pulled on a clean tunic to walk back to the gladiators' barracks, but he had not had time for a thorough scrub. The vendor retreated with a look that mingled respect with alarm.

Tilla said, "I think I will see this place in bad dreams."

Ruso put one arm around her shoulders. "I'm sorry," he said.

"We should have caught that Stilo man."

"Somebody will. Tell me what happened in Arelate."

After a moment she slid a hand around his waist. It was not the sort of thing one would normally be able do in public.

"At least this wretched foot is a good excuse for something," he observed, leaning on her to limp forward.

By the time they reached the gladiators' barracks the usual crowd had dwindled to a few subdued young women, two of them clutching babies. To Ruso's surprise, both gates swung open as they approached. The women rushed forward, pleading for information, only to be beaten off by the gatekeeper, who shouted, "No news! Clear the way there!" The opening of the gates was explained as the closed wagon in which Gnostus had traveled back with the wounded gladiators emerged. Ruso guessed it was returning to the amphitheater to collect their dead comrades.

"She's with me," he informed the gatekeeper, leading Tilla inside before the man had time to object, then ordering her to wait by the gate. She had seen enough: She did not deserve to be put through whatever might be waiting in Gnostus's medical room.

To his surprise, all was quiet. Gnostus was busy unloading the wooden boxes of medical supplies that had been piled on the back of the wagon.

"Eight dead, seven badly wounded, five with minor injuries," observed Gnostus, slapping down the lid on an empty box and kicking it out of sight under a bench. "What a way to earn a living."

"Us, or them?" said Ruso, glancing across the exercise yard to where one of the assistants was helping a wounded fighter wash himself over the water trough. A slave emerged from the men's quarters carrying a chamberpot.

"Both," said Gnostus. He indicated the drugged figure of Tertius, lying with his leg heavily bandaged on a bed in the side room. "Boss wants him out tonight."

"After what he did?" Ruso was incredulous. The boy had run back to don his kit after hearing the announcement that since one of the fighters had been unexpectedly withdrawn, the winner of the latest contest would stay in the arena to face the next opponent. No doubt that decision had been made by Fuscus. Ruso wondered how many people had noticed that a common gladiator had more moral sense than a magistrate.

Gnostus shrugged. "He's a free man. He chose to fight. As far as the boss is concerned, the school doesn't have to pay for his treatment. That's up to the woman who bought him out."

"What woman?"

"Just turned up, offered the boss a cash deal too good to refuse, and disappeared."

"Yes, but who was she?"

"Dunno. Never seen her before. She didn't look the type who'd need to pay for it. Not like some of the dogs we get making offers for the men."

Ruso was relieved. After Marcia's performance this afternoon there was no doubt that Gnostus would have recognized her. It had never occurred to him that she might have a rival. He suspected it had never occurred to Marcia, either. "So where's this woman now?"

"Who knows? She probably won't want him now he's damaged."

"I'll take him home if she doesn't turn up," said Ruso. "But he shouldn't travel tonight."

Gnostus glanced across to where Ruso was leaning against the wall with his aching foot resting on his sound one. "You're not looking too good yourself. Want to bunk down here for the night?"

Ruso explained that he had to take somebody home. "Just give me something to help get me there, will you?"

By the time the gatekeeper let Ruso and Tilla out of the gladiators' barracks, the supporters had dispersed. Two small boys armed with wooden swords were chasing each other in and out of the shadowed doorways while their parents strolled down the street behind them.

"Do be careful, boys!" called the mother.

"If you two don't stop fighting," put in the father, "I'll take those swords away."

Ruso waited for the family to pass, then planted the heels of the borrowed crutches on the worn stone surface and swung forward. The pain was still there, but somehow duller around the edges. Or perhaps it was his mind that was duller. Either way, Gnostus's secret painkilling potion was doing its job.

79

HIRING TRANSPORT TO get home was not easy on the day of the Games, and by the time Tilla helped the Medicus clamber up into the only carriage that was prepared to leave town at this hour, the sun had gone and the color was draining away from the day. The driver, who had insisted on payment in advance, whipped the reluctant horses into a trot. Tilla was not sorry to speed past the long rows of tombstones leading away from the Augustus Gate. The area looked distinctly unwelcoming and there was an autumnal chill in the air.

The Medicus seemed surprisingly happy now that the medicine had taken effect. He was lying across the seat with his feet halfway up the wall of the carriage and his head resting on her lap. It was not a dignified position for either of them, and Tilla was glad there were few people around to see it.

She ran a thumb along his unshaven jaw. She wished she could tell the driver to carry on into the night: to take them both away to somewhere private, far from his family and their parched land with its hideous love of cruelty. She wished they had never left Britannia. Even if he wanted her here, how could she bear to stay?

The Medicus stirred in her lap, gave a murmur of contentment, and said something that sounded like, "All home now."

She laid a hand across his forehead. "Sleep," she murmured as the carriage jolted them down the road toward the farm.

Suddenly his eyes opened. "Why did they come here?" he asked, looking up at her as if they had been carrying on a conversation. Perhaps he had been dreaming.

She said, "Who?"

"Calvus and Stilo."

"To visit their friend Severus to plan more stealing, I suppose," she said. "Or perhaps they met him on the road to your house and poisoned him. Go back to sleep."

The eyes drifted shut. The carriage jolted on. Tilla closed her own eyes and felt her head beginning to nod.

"But after he was dead, why did they stay?"

Tilla, whose mind had wandered back to other journeys in Britannia, had to remind herself who the Medicus was talking about. "To find out who killed him?" she suggested. "What did they say to that fat man on the balcony?"

The Medicus explained that a woman looking like Claudia had bought poisoned honey. "Ennia must have overheard us talking and told Calvus and Stilo, or whatever their names were."

"You see? I told you it was the old wife who did it."

"She says it wasn't, and I think I believe her."

She sighed. Even now, he could not face the truth.

"Why did they care?" he asked.

"Who?"

"Why did Calvus and Stilo care who killed Severus?"

"Perhaps they liked him and they wanted to avenge him," she suggested. "Perhaps they wanted to make some money from finding the poisoner. Why are you lying down if your mind is working and you are not asleep?"

He snuggled against her. "I can think better down here. Listen. Even if they did like him, it isn't their duty to avenge him, it's his family's. And why would they risk hanging around, knowing that somebody might work out who they were at any moment? It makes no sense. Who's to say the Gabinii would have paid them for helping, anyway? Besides, they'd already got the money Severus had helped them swindle out of Probus for the ship."

She shrugged. "Who cares? They are just bad men."

He wriggled, pulled himself up to sit properly, and peered out of the side of the carriage. "Where are we?"

"On the way back to your home."

He was upright now, leaning forward, calling, "Stop!" to the driver.

She grabbed the neck of his tunic and pulled him back. "What are you doing? This is the middle of the road!"

"Stop!" he yelled louder, grabbing one of the borrowed crutches and banging on the floor. The driver allowed the horses to slow and called, "Something the matter, boss?"

The Medicus was peering out into the dusk. "Turn around. Take the turn a hundred paces back, uphill between the vineyards."

"The senator's place? You sure about that?"

"No!" called Tilla. "He is ill. I am taking him home."

"I want to go to the senator's estate," insisted Ruso.

"Make your minds up!" came the voice from in front. "I'm not driving around all night in the dark. One or the other. Quick, or you get out and walk."

"The estate."

With some grumbling, the driver maneuvered the vehicle around in a tight semicircle and set off back the way they had come.

Tilla said, "You are going to see the old wife."

"I need to make sure she's safe."

Tilla sighed and leaned against the back of the carriage. "Still, you think you are the only one who can save her. She is making a fool of you."

"Possibly," he said, "but I don't think Calvus and Stilo ever came here for a social visit. I think they came here to find something, and they've been looking for it ever since. And if I'm right, they won't want to leave without it."

80

THE CARRIAGE WAS already disappearing into the dusk when the Medicus rapped on the gates of the big estate for a second time.

After a moment Tilla pointed out, "Nothing is happening."

He said, "There should at least be a dog."

"Why would this Calvus and Stilo come here when everyone knows they are liars and there will be men looking for them?"

The Medicus seemed to be wondering that himself. Perhaps his mind was still lost inside the pain-fighting medicine. Perhaps this really had just been an excuse to come and visit the old wife. She wished she had insisted on overruling him about the carriage. Still, if he really thought they could catch the men who had murdered Cass's brother . . . "Bang on the gate."

"No," he said, fiddling with the latch and pushing at the studded wood with one shoulder. "I don't want the whole household to hear."

She could not resist a sigh of exasperation. "Very good. The driver has gone back to town. Everyone here has locked the doors and gone to bed early and you do not want to wake them up. So now we have a long walk home."

"Not yet," he said, pushing harder at the gate. It gave way slowly, as if there were something heavy behind it. He bent to examine what he had just pushed out of the way.

"It's the gatekeeper." He was feeling for a pulse when she tapped him on the shoulder and pointed. The dog lay motionless, surrounded by a dark stain. No wonder it had failed to bark.

While the Medicus tended to the injured man she unsheathed her knife and crept out of the far end of the gatehouse.

She stopped dead.

The place was full of tall people.

She ducked back under the gatehouse. Her heart continued to thud furiously even as her brain registered her mistake. The people were not tall. They were on plinths. They were statues. She was entering a grand garden.

She took a couple of deep breaths, then moved forward again. On the left of the garden was an expanse of water and beyond it, the dark hulk of a house. She hesitated, chewing her lower lip. The Medicus had not bothered to tell her what the false investigators were looking for. All he had said was that he wanted to make sure the old wife was safe. That would be interesting. How much danger should a woman leave an old wife in before it was necessary to help her?

It was a question she would have liked to debate around the fire late one night with her own people. Instead, she had a more pressing problem. The wife would be in the house. The house was reached by the paths, and the paths were deep gravel.

She could walk quickly toward the house, or she could walk quietly. Since she needed to do both, there was only one way to do it. Tilla veered sideways, lifted her skirt above her knees, and sank one foot into the soil of a flowerbed. The scent of crushed rosemary wafted around her. She smiled to herself as she marched past the pond. The old wife would not be able to complain: The barbarian was here on the orders of the Medicus, and they were coming to save her from the murderers who called themselves Calvus and Stilo. Although why he thought they would be here was a mystery.

She crept across the gravel that separated the last flowerbed from the house and tried to peer around the shutters of a side window. Everything inside was dark. The next window was the same, and the third. It did not seem right. There should have been servants moving about. Lamps being lit.

When she returned, the Medicus had laid the gatekeeper on his side. She whispered, "There is nobody there. Will he live?"

"I think so. Are you sure?"

"No. I cannot see through walls. Do you want to go in?"

"Not yet."

When he did not suggest anything else she said, "What is happening?"

"I don't know yet."

"I am not going to stand here all night. What are this Calvus and Stilo looking for?"

"Money."

"There is plenty of money to steal back in Arelate," she pointed out. "Why come here?"

"They'd already stolen it," he said. "Or rather, Severus stole it for them."

This did not make a great deal of sense, but he seemed to have lost interest in explaining. He was pointing to the shapes of what must be farm buildings looming on the far side of the garden. "I thought I heard something over there."

"Walk through the flowers," she told him. "Not on the path."

"What?"

"Otherwise you might as well shout, Hello, here we come."

The Medicus followed her, lifting the crutches, plunging them down through the plants and swinging his feet to land heavily farther forward. There would be a fine mess in the morning, and it would be obvious who had made it.

The gate that led through the garden wall to the farmyard had been left open. Trying to peer ahead without being seen, she could make out an empty cart and the complicated shape of some sort of wooden harvesting machine under a shelter on the far side. She held her breath as something moved in the machinery, then the sleek black shape of a cat jumped down into the yard and melted away into the shadows. Somewhere, an animal snorted and stamped.

The Medicus was about to go through the gateway when there was a muffled burst of laughter from inside one of the buildings that opened onto the yard. Tilla pulled at his tunic to drag him back. "Was that what you heard?"

"No," he whispered. "That's just the slaves in the bunkhouse."

The slaves did not sound as though they knew there were murderers about. Nor did they yet know that there was another pair of intruders sneaking around the yard in the dark. Once they found out, they would have no trouble catching the one on crutches and beating him up in the name of the senator.

"This is not a good idea," she whispered.

"I know," he agreed, "but I haven't got any others."

"If we do find those men, what are we going to do?"

"I'm glad you said 'we.' "

"I have to. You are not much use on your own." She pushed past him and slipped in through the gateway. "Stay there."

She heard the crutches tap on the cobblestones as he hissed, "Wait for me!"

She was waving a hand to tell him to stay where he was when she heard the scream. Then a man's voice. Then some sort of muffled thump.

"In that building over there." She jumped when she realized that the Medicus had moved close enough to whisper in her ear without her noticing.

After what seemed an age keeping lookout with her back against the warm stone of the building while the Medicus peered through a gap by the door hinge, Tilla began to wonder if they had been mistaken. The sounds she could make out from inside the building sounded more like work than murder. The sharp crunch and rattle of earth being dug and shoveled away. Indistinct murmurs of conversation. Then a hollow clunk as if something were being smashed, the slosh of liquid, and, seconds later, the rich smell of grape juice. This must be the estate winery.

Beside her, the Medicus crouched down, trying to get a better view.

She slid down the wall to breathe in his ear, "What can you see?"

He did not seem to have heard. When she repeated the question he took her arm, pointed to the narrow gap between the door and the wall, and eased himself back to his feet.

Tilla closed one eye and pressed her face against the gap. For a moment she could make no sense of what she was looking at. She had expected an ordered winery like the one back at the Medicus's house: rows of buried jars brimming with sparkling foam. Instead she was watching an unlikely bunch of people deliberately and silently wrecking the place. As far as she could make out in the lamplight, jars had been dug up and smashed. Piles of earth and broken pottery had been dumped against the walls and inside the juice vats. The wreckers, several men and a bedraggled woman with smeared makeup and short, strangely colored hair, were squelching around in a quagmire of mud mixed with fermenting juice. It was hard to see why they were doing it, since they did not seem to be enjoying themselves. As she watched, one of the men picked up his shovel and deliberately shattered the shoulder of the closest jar. The woman stepped aside to avoid the juice that was forming a glistening pool around her feet and glanced toward the door. For a moment Tilla thought she had sensed someone watching her. Then she realized the woman was looking at something inside the winery.

"Who said you could take a rest?" The voice was familiar, and alarmingly close.

Tilla grabbed the nearest part of the Medicus, which turned out to be his knee. She was about to whisper, "Stilo!" when the woman aimed her shovel at the next jar, missed, slipped in the mud, and landed on her backside. As the woman put her head in her hands and began to sob, something moved and blocked Tilla's line of vision—but not before she had recognized the one who called himself Calvus stepping forward across the mud.

The slap and the order to shut up were followed by a third, oddly strangled-sounding voice: a girl, who seemed to be standing just behind the door where Tilla was listening. "Please!" she whimpered. "Please, just do what they want!"

"I can't!" wailed the woman.

"You can!" insisted the girl.

Tilla, still unable to see, straightened up. From inside the winery she heard Calvus say, "All right. Put your shovel down and get back in the corner. You—yes, you—move across and take over."

"Can I make a suggestion?" It was a thin, officious voice.

"No," said Stilo. "Shut up and dig."

"Only it would be more efficient if we—"

His suggestion was drowned by a squeal of pain from near the door. Tilla winced.

"See?" said Stilo. "That's what happens when you make suggestions. Just find the money. Then nobody gets hurt."

Tilla felt the warmth of the Medicus's breath on her cheek. "They've already got the steward in there," he whispered. "Go across to the bunkhouse, find out who's in charge, and get them to send a couple of sensible men into town to tell Fuscus what's going on and fetch Probus."

"Will they send help?"

"I doubt they'll get here in time. Tell the rest of the men to round up every sort of weapon they can think of—there should be plenty of scythes and things in the barns—and come over here and surround the exit to the building without making any noise."

"What if the slaves are all locked in for the night?"

"You'll think of something."

"What are you going to do?"

The Medicus straightened his crutches and hitched himself forward. "I'm going in for a chat with our so-called investigators," he said.

81

RUSO HAD INTENDED to wait until the farm slaves were armed and in position before making a move, but a long wait followed by a reverberating crash loud enough to wake the spirit of Severus and all the senator's illustrious ancestors told him that the slaves had indeed been locked in and that Tilla had thought of something.

He hopped back out of the way just as the heavy door creaked open and a head appeared.

"Calvus!" he said, guessing in the poor light.

The head swiveled around to face him.

"Sorry about all the racket," he continued. "Mind if I come in?"

"Ruso? What are you doing here?"

"Bloody crutches," said Ruso, ignoring the question. "Knocked over some old piece of farm junk out here, sorry. I'll have to apologize to them in the morning. Can I come in and sit down? This wretched foot's acting up again."

Calvus stared at him for a moment, then stepped back. The door opened wider, and Ruso swung in. Calvus closed the door and gave him a shove that nearly sent him down flat in the mud.

"Get over there with the others."

For the first time, Ruso was able to see what was going on in the parts of the winery that had not been visible through the crack in the door. As he picked his way across the slippery upheaval of the floor, he could make out frightened faces watching him from the far wall, lined up behind a pair of looming winepresses very much like the one at home. One of the faces belonged to Flaccus the kitchen boy. The one that cried out "Gaius!" as he approached was Claudia.

"You must do something, Gaius!" she urged. "They're going to murder us one by one if we don't find Severus's money!"

Ruso seated himself on the corner of the tank surrounding the first winepress. As he had guessed, Stilo had repeated this afternoon's hostage trick and was now standing behind the door with a wide-eyed Ennia clutched up against him. A knife glinted at her throat. In front of them, he recognized the slender figure of Zosimus among the half dozen wretched diggers struggling to unearth the money that Calvus and Stilo evidently believed was buried under one of the wine jars.

"Don't just sit there, Gaius!"

"What would you like me to do?"

"I don't know! Think of something."

"Well," he said casually, "I have got the building surrounded by armed men."

Stilo gave a snort of contempt.

"For goodness' sake, Gaius! This is no time for your silly jokes."

"Take a look," suggested Ruso mildly, wondering if Tilla had them organized yet.

Calvus and Stilo glanced at each other. Before Calvus could take up his suggestion he added, "I'll order them to let you get away if you give up and release Ennia now."

"Bollocks," said Stilo.

Calvus's hand was moving toward the door.

"Carefully," said Ruso. "Don't stick your head out. A slice with a scythe is very hard to stitch up."

"He's bluffing," said Stilo.

Ruso grinned. "Am I?"

"It doesn't matter, anyway," said Calvus, reaching for the bar and swinging it down to drop into the slot on the far side of the door. "When we're ready to leave, we'll have plenty of hostages to choose from."

Stilo smirked at Ruso over Ennia's shoulder. "Didn't think of that, did you, smartarse?"

Ennia whimpered as he jerked her back toward him.

"Get on with it, you lot! Keep digging!"

"They don't believe you, Gaius!" hissed Claudia. "Think of something else!"

"Find the money," he suggested. "Then they'll go away."

"How do we know it's even here?" demanded Claudia.

"Good question," agreed Ruso, turning to Calvus. "How do you know it's here?"

"None of your business," said Calvus.

"You know something?" said Stilo to Calvus. "I never liked that one. Big mouth. Always asking questions."

"This isn't a question," said Ruso, hoping Tilla really would have the slaves in position soon. "This is a statement. Claudia did not kill Severus. Did she, Ennia?"

"You know she did!" gasped Ennia, her voice sounding strangled by the effort of leaning away from the knife. "You covered up for her—ow!" Stilo had shifted his grip again.

"Keep up the digging, boys," urged Calvus as if he were encouraging them in a genteel sport. "The sooner you find it, the sooner we're off."

"Yes, keep digging," agreed Ruso. "After all, Severus did owe these two a large share of it. By the way, what did happen to Justinus on that ship?"

From behind him, Claudia demanded to know what on earth they were talking about.

"Justinus had an accident," said Stilo.

"What sort of accident?"

By way of answer, Calvus snatched a spade from the nearest digger, stepped across to Ruso, and rammed the blade up against his throat. "The sort you're going to have if you don't shut up."

"Don't hurt him!" shrieked Claudia.

Ruso leaned away from the cold metal. The mud trickling down his neck smelled of grape juice. "I can see why you're annoyed," he said, desperately trying to think what to do next. "You went to a lot of bother to earn that money." He raised one hand to indicate Ennia. "Are you absolutely sure she doesn't know which pot it's under?"

He felt a fractional easing of the pressure on his throat. Calvus was looking at him oddly as if trying to work out how much he knew.

"You can't trust her, you know," continued Ruso, silently praying that Calvus would be sufficiently intrigued not to finish him off with an angry thrust of the spade. "Did you know she poisoned her brother?"

"I didn't!" gasped Ennia.

The spade moved away from Ruso's throat. As Calvus turned his attention to Ennia, Ruso let out a quiet breath of relief and straightened up, wiping the mud with the back of his hand. He ignored Claudia's whispered, "I knew it. I knew it was her."

Calvus positioned himself beside Ennia with his back to the wall, keeping the rest of the prisoners in sight, while he said to her, "You told me the wife did it."

"She did!"

"Don't trust her, Calvus," warned Ruso, hoping this did not sound as improvized as it felt. "She's a good actress. You should have seen her weeping over the body. She had me fooled for a long time." He turned to the diggers. "Do keep working, please, gentlemen. I'm sorry I can't help, I've broken a bone in my foot. But the sooner you find the cash that Severus was planning to share with these two, the sooner this will be over and we can all go home to bed." He turned back to Ennia. "You're absolutely sure this is where he hid it?"

"Yes!" squeaked Ennia. "Somewhere in here. He said if anything ever happened to him, to look in the winery."

"You knew he had money?" demanded Claudia. "Why didn't he tell me? I had a right to know. I'm his wife!"

"I didn't kill him," insisted Ennia. "She did."

"Yes," agreed Ruso mildly, addressing Calvus and ignoring Claudia's protests. "I suppose that's what Ennia told you, isn't it? She told you she'd overheard me talking to Claudia, and Claudia had been seen buying poisonous honey. If you'd bothered to go and check with the stallholder—"

"No point," said Calvus, throwing the spade across to the digger he had taken it from, who was trying to sneak back to join the others behind the winepress. "Oy! Back to work!"

"No," said Ruso. "I didn't think you had."

"Never mind him," said Stilo, for once quicker than his partner. "We're here for the money. We don't care who killed Severus."

"Right," agreed Calvus. "Shut up, Ruso."

For a moment there was no sound in the winery but the crunch of shovels and the steady trickle of something leaking.

Ruso glanced around him, wondering what to do next. Nothing had changed as a result of his intervention. Ennia was still held with a knife to her throat. The diggers were still struggling on, weary and filthy and clearly distraught at ruining the precious vintage the farm slaves had worked so hard to produce. A call for help had—he hoped—been sent to town, but the impostors would be long gone before anyone could get here. Besides, Stilo was right: Nobody would dare to attack them on the way out if they were holding hostages. All Ruso had managed to do was add himself to their list of potential choices.

What the hell had Gnostus put in that medicine? What had he been thinking? Had he really imagined that, just because he had finally begun to understand something of what was going on, Calvus and Stilo would kneel in surrender? It was difficult to see what he could do to salvage the situation, except to distract them and hope they made some sort of mistake.

"It wasn't Claudia who bought the honey, though," he said, hoping Calvus would not repeat his threat with the spade. "It was Ennia wearing one of Claudia's wigs and her pink shoes. I didn't mention the color of the shoes when I talked to Claudia, but when you told Fuscus, you knew they were pink. You haven't spoken to the trader, so you must have got that from Ennia. She knew because she was the one wearing them. She even made sure she drew the stallholder's attention to them. If we take both women down there, I daresay he'll pick her out."

Ennia's curtailed squeak of "No—!" might have referred to the identity parade or to some new threat from Stilo.

"She poisoned her brother to get his money, and she was going to make sure Claudia got the blame."

"No!"

"Except he died in my house. She didn't plan that." Ruso turned to the diggers. "You can keep on digging if you like. At least it'll make them go away. But Ennia's not really worth much as a hostage. She's going to be sentenced to death for murder, anyway."

82

"IT WAS ZOSIMUS!" shrieked Ennia.

Everyone had stopped to listen now. Stilo, curious at last, moved the knife a fraction to let her talk.

"Tell them, Zosimus!"

The steward rammed his spade into the mud and stared at Ennia. In the silence, one of the diggers shifted position and the mud squelched beneath him.

"Tell them about my lovely brother."

"You knew all about it?" demanded Claudia. Ruso motioned to her to be quiet.

Zosimus looked at Ennia. "Which lie would you like me to tell this time?"

Ennia swallowed. "No lies. Tell them what he did."

Zosimus looked around at the faces all turned toward him in the lamplight. "Ennia was engaged to a man in Rome." There was no expression in his voice. He might have been reading a list of calendar dates. "Severus didn't think he was suitable. The man died of a fever. Ennia moved here with Severus." He cleared his throat.

"Tell them what you told me!"

"I wasn't happy about the way Severus did business here. He said that if I refused to back him up he would get rid of me like he had gotten rid of Ennia's boyfriend."

Stilo was the first to speak. "Very sad," he said, gesticulating with the knife toward the mud. "Now dig."

"Wait a moment," said Calvus. "Which of you did do it?"

"She did," said Zosimus at the same moment as Ennia said, "He did."

"Who cares?" demanded Stilo.

"Dig," ordered Calvus. Zosimus sighed and heaved his spade out of the mud. Calvus moved across to murmur to Stilo, who glanced at the door and muttered something back.

"I want to know who it was!" insisted Claudia to no one in particular. "I'm the widow. I should be told."

When nobody else seemed inclined to answer, Ruso said, "Ennia bought the honey. Zosimus must have put it in the kitchen. Afterward he went there saying he was investigating the death, got rid of the medicine, and cleared the rest of the honey out before it could do any more damage."

A voice from behind the press cried, "You made us drink that medicine!"

"You only had a little bit each," retorted Zosimus, bending to pick out a broad shard of broken pot from the mud. "It wasn't dangerous."

The voice said, "You didn't drink any."

"I had to keep my head clear." Zosimus waved the pot toward Ruso. "Everything would have been fine if he hadn't interfered."

Claudia was on her feet, one hand gripping Ruso by the shoulder. "He killed my husband and—"

She was silenced by an exclamation from Zosimus. He reached down and hauled a dripping bag out of the quagmire, resting it on the broken curve of pot. Something inside chinked as it settled in a pool of mud.

Calvus beckoned it over, peered inside, and nodded to Stilo. Then he tied the muddy bag to his belt and lifted the bar off the door. He ordered the diggers to get back against the far wall with the others. Then, turning to Ruso, he said, "You go first."

Ruso maneuvered himself to his feet and gathered up the crutches. The pain flooded into his foot with an intensity he had not experienced since the day of the accident. At least he supposed it meant his mind was fully clear now.

His eyes, accustomed to the lamplight, could see nothing out in the blackness of the yard. "Tilla?" he called before venturing out, just in case she had overheard his threat of the scythe.

"We are here," replied Tilla.

As he blinked, Ruso could make out human shapes in the darkness. To his left, the prongs of a pitchfork rose in silhouette against a light patch of sky.

"Tell those murderers," said Tilla, "that there are thirty strong men out here. All loyal to the senator."

Ruso limped out into the yard. "She's not lying," he confirmed.

From inside the winery came a fresh shriek of "Gaius!"

There was a scuffle behind him and a gasp from some of the farm slaves as a bedraggled figure appeared in the doorway with Stilo's arm around her throat. Instead of Ennia, he could just make out the cropped head of Claudia. "Anybody tries to touch us, and her ladyship's dead," announced Stilo, dragging Claudia sideways so he had the winery wall at his back. "This one's a proper hostage, doctor. Happy now?"

Calvus emerged to stand beside him. "We don't want to hurt anybody."

"But we will if we have to," put in Stilo.

"All we want," said Calvus, "is three horses. You men stand back and let us out, and once we're clear we release the hostage."

"Four horses," corrected Ennia, remarkably calm. "You don't think I'm sharing with her, do you?" She dragged the winery door shut and turned the key in the lock, leaving the diggers trapped inside.

As Zosimus shouted, "Ennia, let me out!" through the door, Tilla's voice rang out from somewhere in the darkness.

"We will give you nothing. You are trapped. As soon as you kill the hostage we will kill you."

There was an indistinct squeak from Claudia and a chuckle from Stilo. "I'm not going to kill her, Blondie. Not yet. I'll just take her fingers off. One by one." His voice hardened. "Get the horses."

There was movement out in the darkness. The pitchfork wavered.

"Do not do it!" said Tilla. The movement stopped.

Ennia called, "Acratus, are you out there?"

"Yes, miss," came the automatic reply just before someone else hissed, "Shut up, you fool!"

"Acratus, fetch the horses straightaway."

"Do not do it!" insisted Tilla.

"All of you slaves out there," put in Stilo, "are going to be dinner for the lions once word gets out you was told to do something to help this lady and you didn't do it. Who wants to catch the first finger?"

"Do not listen to him," urged Tilla over Claudia's squeal of terror. "We have them trapped."

"Just get the horses," put in Calvus, clearly tired of arguing.

"I'm in charge here," said Ruso, not sure that he was. "They're not bluffing. They've already murdered Probus's man and Ennia's poisoned her brother. Do what they ask. Fetch the horses."

In the ensuing silence, all he could hear was Tilla's sigh of exasperation.

"I think I'll take a thumb first," said Stilo. "Which d'you want to lose?"

There was a muffled shout of, "Do it, Acratus!" from Zosimus behind the winery door. "I'll answer to the senator. Go across to the stables and bring out four good horses."

There was more movement out in the darkness. Ruso took a deep breath, then reached across and gently began to turn the key in the winery door as Calvus said, "Three would have done."

"I told you," said Ennia, "I'm not sharing."

"We don't need you."

"What?" Ennia grabbed Calvus's arm, only to be elbowed roughly aside. "We had a deal!"

"Not now," said Calvus, chinking the coins. "I've got the cash."

"There is a lot more money!" she cried. "In Rome. It belonged to my fiancé. I know where it is."

The key finally reached the end of the turn. "She's lying," said Ruso, who had no idea whether she was or not.

"It's the truth. It's why I always wanted to go back there. Ask anybody." Ennia paused. "I'm the only one who knows how to find it. Get me out of here, Calvus, and I'll make you rich."

83

RUSO AND TILLA stood among the bewildered household, staring into the darkness after the four figures who had ridden away toward the gatehouse: one horse's reins in the hand of another rider.

Tilla was complaining about him giving way and handing over the horses, but the pain in his foot was making it difficult to concentrate. He wished it would also take his mind off what might be happening to Claudia. Calvus had repeated his promise that she would be released unharmed, but that could have been a lie to ease their escape. No matter what excuses he made for himself, the truth was that he had failed her. This was how things had always been with Claudia. No matter how hard he tried, he could never quite—

Shouting. Coming from the gatehouse. Screams. Everyone else rushed toward the sound, leaving Ruso slow and exasperated, swinging dangerously far forward on the crutches as a horse whinnied and there was a yellow flare of torchlight beyond the wall. Moments later he heard the thud of hooves cantering away down the track toward the road.

By the time he pushed his way to the middle of the melee, two bodies were being held down with hoes and pitchforks while jubilant slaves jeered and shouted encouragement and argued about what to do with them. Calvus and Stilo had not escaped after all.

He said, "Where are the women?" but the only answer he got was from a delighted Flaccus. "Nobody can say we didn't defend the family now, sir, can they?"

Tilla appeared at his elbow. "We have did this because I expect you will let them go," she announced, confusing her tenses as she did when she was excited. "So I send some men to wait for them on top of the gatehouse."

He said, "What have they done with the women?"

"Are you not pleased?"

"I'm impressed. I'm amazed. I'm very tired. Where are the women?"

She said, "I think the horses bolt."

Ruso sighed. Claudia was not a practiced rider, on the grounds that horses had sharp hooves and big teeth. If her horse had stumbled or swerved, she would probably have fallen off in the dark. He glanced across to where one of the recovered mounts was being led back in through the gates. "Ask them to light me a torch, Tilla. I'll go and have a look."

Somewhere ahead of him along the darkened track a voice was saying, "Nice horse. Nice horse, *please* . . ."

"Claudia?"

"Gaius! Is that you? Have those men gone? Oh Gaius, I thought I was going to die out here!"

"You're safe now."

The torch picked out the shape of the animal steadily munching on the dry grass at the side of the track. He could make out the line of a rein as the figure on its back was trying to haul its head up. He moved alongside, bending down to take the bridle. "Did you see what happened to Ennia?"

"Oh Gaius," she sobbed. "It's all been so horrible. Ennia just rode off and left me on my own in the dark. First it wouldn't stop, and now it won't go! Why did you let them take me on a horse?"

84

"IT'S ALL RIGHT," said Lucius, shuffling back across the hot tiles in his bathing shoes. "I've locked the door. Not even the bath boy can get in now."

"Excellent." Ruso stretched out on the bench and closed his eyes, relishing the peace and quiet before he had to ride back into town to visit Tertius. The hoped-for relaxation did not come. Instead he remembered something else he needed to do.

"I ought to warn Tilla to keep quiet about the Christians."

"Are they really a problem? Cass seems to think they're harmlessly eccentric."

"As far as I can make out, it's a religion full of women, the poor, and the ignorant. I don't think Tilla will stick with it for long. She's not very keen on loving her enemies."

"But we're definitely in the clear over poisoning Severus?"

"Ennia admitted it in front of witnesses. And Fuscus turned up and had his men arrest Calvus and Stilo and the steward. I'd imagine he's planning something ghastly for them at the next Games."

Lucius said, "Ouch."

Ruso shifted to get comfortable, and flinched as his arm came into contact with the heated wall. "You know, even after everything she did, I almost hope they don't get their hands on Ennia."

Lucius said, "I'd like to. If she's got a pot of gold stashed away down in Rome, she ought to give it to us."

"At least the senator will be too busy sorting this lot out to bother with the bankruptcy case."

"Good. I knew once I'd rescued the girls and worked out who those investigators were, I could leave the details to you."

"I see," said Ruso. "Actually, I thought it was Tilla who worked that out."

"I let her think that," said Lucius. "Women like to think they're needed."

Ruso had expected Lucius to ask more questions, but evidently all he wanted to know was that whatever other threats were out there, his big brother had dealt with them. The monsters were safely back in the cupboard.

He sniffed and opened his eyes. "What the hell are you putting on your head now?"

"Something I picked up in Arelate." Lucius was massaging a thin brown dribble into his scalp. "It's the latest thing. I'm surprised you didn't know about it. Burned hooves of she goats in vinegar."

Ruso, who could think of nothing to say, sank back onto the bench and closed his eyes again.

"Now that we've got a minute," said Lucius, "I suppose I should mention something. It's a bit embarrassing but Cass says if I don't tell you, she will. We tidied up the study and had another run through the accounts last night. When we came to balance them—oh, what now?" He waited until the thumping on the outside door had stopped, then shouted, "We're busy, come back later!"

"But Papa," came a small voice, "there's a cross old man come to talk to Uncle Gaius."

The brothers exchanged a glance.

"Name, Polla!" shouted Lucius. "Go and ask the cross old man what his name is."

Before she could reply, a familiar voice demanded, "Are you in there, Ruso? This is Probus. Doesn't anyone in this family have any manners?"

Ruso considered asking Lucius to pretend he was out, but then thought better of it. He would have to face Claudia's father sooner or later. No doubt the man had come to complain about last night's events.

Leaving Lucius to stew under his hair tonic, Ruso offered his former father-in-law a bench in the warm room next door. "There's towels if you want to bathe," he offered, feeling at something of a disadvantage since Probus was fully dressed while he was wearing nothing but a hastily grabbed towel around his waist and a bandage around his foot.

To his surprise, business was not the very first thing on Probus's mind. Neither was Claudia.

"The sister's dead. I thought you'd want to know. Found at first light, about five miles out on the Arelate road. Earrings ripped out, most of her clothes stolen. They took the horse, of course."

Ruso shook his head. "So she never got to Rome."

"It's some sort of justice, I suppose."

Ruso wondered if Ennia had really had the misfortune to run into robbers, or if some of the estate staff had slipped away and taken matters into their own hands. Even so, it was a kinder fate than she would have suffered in the arena had she been convicted of murdering her brother. "Claudia was right," he said. "She said it was Ennia. I didn't believe her."

While Probus was speculating on the gruesome end that awaited Calvus, Stilo, and Zosimus, Ruso was wondering whether Severus really had done away with Ennia's fiancé down in Rome, or whether that had just been a boast to keep Zosimus in line. And whether there really was a hoard of cash in Rome that nobody now knew how to find, or whether that had been another lie. He said, "How's Claudia?"

"She's over at my house, confined to bed. I've been across to the senator's place. The winery looks as though there's been an earthquake. I've never seen such a mess."

"And the gatekeeper?"

"I don't know, Ruso. I'm not here to give health reports on all the staff."

For once, Probus had a good excuse for being bad-tempered. "Now that I can speak freely," he said, "I'd say Severus got what he deserved. He was implicit in the murder of my steward, he was unfaithful to my daughter, and he tried to swindle me out of a very considerable sum of money."

"And your investors."

Probus cleared his throat. "Naturally, now that the truth about the sinking of the *Pride of the South* has been brought to my attention and a proportion of the stolen money has been recovered, my investors will all be fully reimbursed and compensated. Under the circumstances, it's the honorable thing to do."

It was the only thing to do if Probus was to salvage his business. For a moment Ruso almost felt sorry for him.

"Of course, I still don't condone you allowing your sister-in-law and that woman—"

"Tilla," prompted Ruso.

"I don't condone your allowing them to go to Arelate when I had specifically asked for the whole business to be kept quiet."

"Cass was making inquiries about the loss of her brother," said Ruso, not pointing out that they had not sought his permission, anyway. "You gave her reason to believe he might still be alive, and then told her nothing more. What was she supposed to do?"

"I was doing everything I could to trace him!" snapped Probus. "I'm not inhuman, Ruso. Justinus was a good man."

"You did give the appearance of only being interested in your cash flow."

Probus's eyes met his own, and for a moment Ruso almost thought he caught a hint of contrition.

"Now, about this business last night."

"There wasn't time to get reinforcements," Ruso explained. "I did my best, but—"

"No need to be modest. I've come here to thank you. You've been loyal to Claudia all along. Last night she tells me you saved her life."

"It was Zosimus who finally got the staff to cooperate. By the time I got to her she wasn't in any danger. The horse had stopped."

Probus's brief moment of vulnerability vanished. His face hardened. "Are you suggesting that my daughter is not telling the truth?"

"I think she's a bit confused. I think everybody was."

"Hm." For the first time Ruso could recall, Probus seemed unsure what to say next. Finally he offered, "I have been giving Claudia's situation a great deal of thought."

Ruso, not sure where this was leading, tried, "Of course."

"I've come to the conclusion that I may not always be the best judge of what is good for her."

Not knowing whether he was supposed to agree or disagree with this, Ruso cleared his throat.

"Frankly, Severus was a disaster."

"He certainly was," Ruso agreed with a fervor that he hoped made up for the prevarication.

"You've proved a loyal friend to her, and although I have very grave doubts about the wisdom of this, I have agreed to bring a message saying that she would be prepared to consider a reconciliation."

There were many things Ruso could have said in reply to this, but none of them occurred to him until several hours later. While he was waiting for a set of coherent words to assemble themselves in his brain and make their way to his mouth, he found himself scratching one ear until it hurt.

"Is it the hair?" demanded Probus. "Rather a shock, poor girl. But it will grow back, you know."

"It—it's not the hair," stumbled Ruso, adding truthfully, "In fact I think it suits her short. Perhaps not green, though."

"Financially, we are still very secure," Probus assured him. "And I suppose you could master some sort of rudimentary business skills?"

"I really don't think—"

Probus got to his feet. "Well, you don't have to give her an answer straightaway. But it would cheer her up."

"Not for long," said Ruso. "I'm flattered, but I'd be hopeless in business and she'd only get exasperated again."

"Yes," agreed Probus, surprising Ruso with a smile. "That's exactly what I told her. Well done, Ruso. It seems you do have some sense after all. I take it you're still hugely in debt?"

"Of course."

"Come and see me sometime next week and we'll work on rearranging your loans. Oddly enough—"

Whatever Probus found odd was lost in the sound of more hammering on the door. Ruso apologized and went to see what the latest crisis was.

To his surprise, the interruption was caused by Flora. Seconds later he was pulling on a clean tunic and apologizing again to Probus. With a strong sense of foreboding, he stepped out into the garden and braced himself to deal with, "Gaius, Mother says you've got to smarten yourself up because Lollia from next door's turned up with Marcia's gladiator and his aunt, and Marcia's hiding in the bedroom."

85

RUSO RAN BOTH hands through his hair, buckled his belt, and opened the door of the bathhouse. As Probus strode away toward the garden gate, Arria was hurrying down from the porch. Across in the yard, Lollia Saturnina scrambled out of the back of a cart and an anxious-looking woman who was presumably the aunt hurried forward and opened the yard gate for her.

Lucius said, "I need to leave this on my hair for another half hour," and made to retreat back to the bathhouse.

"What was it you were going to tell me about the accounts?"

The tone of Lucius's "Ah" suggested that he had been hoping his brother would forget to ask. "We seem to have a bit more money than we thought."

"How much more?"

"About two hundred." Lucius coughed. "Exactly two hundred, in fact."

Ruso slumped against the door frame.

"It was in a bag that had slipped down behind the trunk."

As Ruso said, "I don't want to hear this," a chorus of petitions rang out.

"Will somebody tell me what's going on?"

"Can I have a word, Ruso?"

"Gaius, go and tell Marcia she's got to come out!"

"In fact," said Ruso, "I think I haven't heard it. Use it to pay the wheelwright." He stepped forward and closed the door behind him. "Did somebody say Tertius is here?"

Ruso climbed up into Lollia's vehicle and knelt beside Tertius on the straw. The lad was still horribly pale, but there was no more hemorrhaging and the wound did not seem to be inflamed or excessively swollen. Neither, according to Tertius, was it very painful. "Gnostus gave me some of his potion, sir."

"Yes," said Ruso, reaching across to take his pulse. "I'm going to have to find out what's in Gnostus's potion. Tell me, Tertius, how is it you keep turning up unexpectedly like this?"

The lad managed a smile, although he was too weak to lift his head. "Now that I'm not a gladiator, sir . . ." He paused for breath. "I'd like to ask your permission to marry Marcia Petreia."

"I still don't understand why."

"Because I love her, sir."

Ruso released the pulse. "I meant, why aren't you a gladiator?"

The lad shifted to get more comfortable and winced. "My aunt prayed to Christos for me, sir."

Ruso was tempted to ask the aunt how Christos had come up with the huge sum of money that would be required to induce a gladiator trainer to pull a fighter out in the middle of the Games. "I don't know about Marcia," he said, recalling how Gnostus's potion tended to addle the brain, "but I'd imagine that whoever paid for you has plans for you herself."

"Do I look like the sort of woman who fawns over gladiators, Ruso?"

Ruso wished he had checked behind him before speaking.

"Our relationship is purely business," continued Lollia. "I've come to ask you to take care of this young man until he can work."

"I see," said Ruso, not entirely sure that he did.

"I had some spare jewelry," she said, as casually as if she were speaking about a spare pair of socks. "His aunt told me about Tertius's situation and said he was a good worker."

Still baffled, Ruso said, "You could have bought an ordinary slave for much less."

"Our Lord gave his life to redeem us," said Lollia. "All I needed to give was a few colored stones. And I'm certainly not looking for a man for myself. Not this close to the final judgment."

"I see," repeated Ruso, now wishing he didn't. "So you're another one?"

The gap-toothed smile that had so impressed him a few days ago reappeared. "I was still thinking about it when you took the trouble to warn me the other day," she said. "Your attitude helped me make my mind up."

"Which lord is that, Lollia, dear?" asked Arria, who had evidently been listening over the garden wall.

While Lollia was cheerfully confirming that she had decided to join the followers of Christos, Ruso was deciding that he was going to keep his mouth shut about religion in future. And he was going to have proper arrangements for visitors, with a waiting area and servants to usher people in and out of the study, instead of holding this sort of free-for-all where anybody could wander up and barge into his conversations.

"Gaius is very interested in Christos, aren't you, Gaius? Would he have to do that circumcision thing, do you think, dear, or don't they do that these days?"

"I am not doing the circumcision thing!" snapped Ruso. "And I am not going to turn into a Christian. Somebody has to keep their feet on the ground around here. Sorry, Lollia."

"Oh, but Gaius, dear, you could—"

"No he couldn't, Mother," insisted Flora. "And besides, Lollia's given loads of her money away now, so what's the point?"

86

HOW CAN YOU possibly lecture me about what love is?" demanded Marcia, planting both hands on the study desk and glaring at Ruso. "What do you know about it?"

"Not a lot," agreed Ruso. "But how many girls get the chance to nurse a hero?"

Marcia wrinkled her nose. "I don't like ill people."

"I'm only asking you to like this one," said Ruso. "Especially as he's not out of danger yet." He leaned forward, resting his elbows on the desk. "I'm not saying you have to marry him tomorrow. But if you get up those stairs right away, smile at Tertius and convince him he's got something to look forward to, I'll fix your dowry by the end of next week."

Marcia paused to consider this. "Will you cancel those awful music lessons?"

"Agreed," said Ruso, who had never seen the point of spending money on them, anyway.

"And I want my own bedroom instead of sharing with Flora."

"You can have that upstairs room after Tertius has recovered and gone to work at Lollia's."

"What? That's not a room, it's a cupboard!"

Ruso folded his arms. "That's my final offer."

Marcia grinned. "All right, then. I would have looked after him, anyway, you know."

He decided to let her enjoy her triumph. Nursing Tertius back to health would be a long slow job. "You don't happen to know where Tilla is, do you? I can't remember what she said she was doing this morning."

Marcia extended a finger to poke him in the chest. "That, Gaius, is exactly why you have no right to lecture me about love."

87

THE DOOR LATCH dropped with a click. Over in his bed, Tilla stirred and opened her eyes. He supposed she had crept in here to sleep off the exhaustion of all the chasing about last night. "Sorry to wake you."

"I am not asleep. I am thinking."

This was ominous.

"In my country," she said, "women can be warriors."

"Well, in my country, they can't."

She said, "There is something I did not tell you about what happened in that bar in Arelate."

"Do you want me to know?"

She thought about that for a while, then said, "No."

Outside, two figures were making their way down between the tall rows of the vineyard. Watching Cass slip an arm around Lucius's ample waist as he paused to inspect a vine, Ruso said suddenly, "What makes a marriage happy?"

"I do not know. I have never been married."

Should he ask directly, or hint? Allude to his last proposal, or begin afresh? He should have practiced. In the absence of rehearsal, it was best not to try to be clever. He took a deep breath and sat down beside her on the bed. "Tilla, I have something to ask you. Will you—"

"Those insects are not screeching today."

He swallowed. "It's the end of the summer."

"Soon the ships will stop crossing the seas."

"That'll be a few weeks."

"Then I should go now."

He said, "I can't take you yet. I've promised to look after Tertius."

"And you have Lollia Saturnina and that old wife with the strange hair," she said.

"They're just friends."

"The nephews and nieces have their mother," she continued. "Cass and Lucius have each other. Marcia has her gladiator, Galla has Christos, your stepmother has Diphilus—"

"What?"

"Oh, open your eyes, Ruso!"

They both stared at each other in surprise. She had never called him that before.

"I need to visit Claudia this afternoon," he said, and watched her mouth tighten. "Just to see how she is, and irritate her enough for her to remember why she can't live with me."

"I see. And then what will happen?"

He said, "Ennia said there was a stash of money hidden away in Rome. If that's true, it would help me shift the family debt. I could go down there and try to track it down—"

"I am not going to Rome."

"Or we could—"

"I have seen enough greedy people who like to show murder to their children."

"I—"

"If this is what you call peace, it is not worth it."

He said, "Have you finished?"

She thought about that for a moment, then said, "Yes. For now."

"Or, Valens is bound to know some unit in Britannia where there's a medic's job out of the reach of the rebels, or warriors, or whatever they're supposed to be called."

"They should be called people of honor."

"Please don't start that now."

She said, "I am not the one who is starting."

He lay back on the pillow with his hands behind his head. "You asked me once if I was ashamed of you."

"Are you?"

"I'm the one who should be ashamed. I should have introduced you better."

"And what would you have said?"

He paused. "I would have said, This is Tilla. She is the bravest and most beautiful woman I know, and I don't deserve her."

She smiled. "All these things are true." The smile faded. "I will want children," she said.

He thought about that for a moment. "I shall expect them to read and write and speak Latin and Greek and be properly brought up."

"I will teach them to sing the song of my ancestors."

"Do you have to?"

"All six of them."

"What is this, a competition?"

He slid his hand into hers and their fingers intertwined. After a moment he said, "You really think Arria and Diphilus are serious?"

"You should encourage him. Then perhaps he will clean out the drains for free."

"We might not need him," he said. "Feel that breeze?" He lifted his head to look out of the open window and squinted at the clouds forming in the distance. "I think it's going to rain."

Author's Note

Readers who are familiar with modern Nîmes will know the amphitheater, the temple, and the other fine remains that inspired much of this novel, although neither Ruso's family temple to Diana nor the gladiator barracks survive among them. Fortunately for the good citizens of Nemausus, there is also no record of Fuscus, nor of his cousin the senator.

It occurs to me that at some points in this story there may be readers wondering, Why didn't they just call the police? The Roman Empire was equipped with neither an investigative police force nor a prison system in the sense that we understand them, so unless someone was prepared to step up and bring an accusation, there was no case.

Furthermore, there will be readers who would offer Christians to lions without hesitation. However, the reigns of Trajan and Hadrian were a period of relative calm for the early church: a lull between the persecutions of the first century and the gruesome martyrdoms which took place in Lyon only a couple of generations later.

Anyone seeking a more reliable source than fiction may be interested in:

Roman Medicine, by Audrey Cruse

Pagans and Christians, by Robin Lane Fox

Religions of Rome (Vol 1), by Mary Beard, John North, and Simon Price

Gladiators, by Michael Grant

The Bankers of Puteoli: Finance, Trade, and Industry in the Roman World, by David Jones

Textbook on Roman Law, by Andrew Borkowski and Paul du Plessis

Voyage en Gaule Romaine, by Gérard Coulon and Jean-Claude Golvin

But of course the best way to discover Gallia Narbonensis is on foot, armed with plenty of time and a copy of *The Roman Remains of Southern France: A Guidebook*, by James Bromwich.

Acknowledgments

Grateful thanks for their help in bringing order to chaos go to Mari Evans, Benjamin Adams, Peta Nightingale, and Araminta Whitley, and by the time this manuscript reaches print, unsung but invaluable copy editors will have tidied away many infelicities.

For suggestions and sources on medicine ancient and modern, Roman law, and the Roman remains of Provence, I am grateful to Professor John Scarborough, Carole Page, Dr. Paul du Plessis, and Stephen Young. Any errors are of course mine.

Fellow scribes Chris Allen, Carol Barac, Kathy Barbour, Caroline Davis, Maria Murphy, Jan Lovell, Sian Parrett, and Guy Russell read and reread versions of the early chapters with enormous patience, and Andy Downie put up with lots of grumbling and some very strange and hastily concocted offerings for dinner.

KEEP READING!

More intrigue and bad luck lie ahead for Gaius Petreius Ruso.
Turn the page for a sneak preview of the next installment
in the Medicus series,

CAVEAT EMPTOR

Ruso and Tilla have moved back to Britannia, where Ruso's old friend and colleague Valens has promised him a job. But it's unusual work for a man with experience as an army doctor: He's tasked with tracking down a missing tax collector named Julius Asper.

Of course, there is also something else missing: money. And the council of the town of Verulamium, Asper's home, is bickering over what's become of it. What's more, anonymous letters have begun to arrive, warning Ruso to run for his life. Now Tilla and Ruso, despite their best efforts to get fired from the job, are being pulled deep into a murder case that may be more complex—and dangerous—than they bargained for.

The new novel by Ruth Downie

CAVEAT EMPTOR

Hardcover U.S. $24.00
Bloomsbury USA
Available wherever books are sold

1

THIS CLOSE, EVEN Firmus could see that she was the sort of woman his mother had warned him about. Six feet tall, red hair in a mass of rats' tails, and a pregnant belly that bulged at him like an accusation. The only thing that separated them was a folding desk, and even that wobbled when he placed both hands on it. He sensed a movement behind him. Pyramus's breath was warm on his ear.

"Shall I call the guards, master?"

Firmus opened his mouth to say yes, then realized what a fool he would look if she proved to be harmless. He gestured the slave back to his place. Perhaps, beyond the boundaries of Londinium, this was what all the Britons looked like. He squinted at the sweat-stained folds of her tunic and hoped the guards had at least checked her for weapons.

"Are you the procurator?" she repeated.

Of course not, he wanted to say. *Do you really think Rome would send a short-sighted seventeen-year-old to look after all the money in Britannia?* Instead he straightened his back, pushed aside the wax tablet on which he had been compiling a list of Things To Ask Uncle, and said, "I'm his assistant."

"I must talk to him."

Firmus swallowed. "The procurator's not available."

She took another step forward so that her belly protruded over the desk. He forced himself not to flinch. She smelled hot and stale.

"I have traveled twenty miles to ask for his help," she announced. "Where is he?"

Outside, the relentless clink of chisel on stone rang around the courtyard. Someone was whistling. The world was carrying on as normal, but the woman was between him and the door that led to it. Pyramus, crippled with rheumatism, would be no help at all. Should he have called the guards? How fast could a woman in that condition move?

"The procurator won't be here all day," he said. This was not strictly true, since his uncle was only two rooms away, but the thought of interrupting him while he was with the doctor was even more terrifying than facing the woman.

"All day?" she asked.

"All day," he said, wondering how he was supposed to manage if the Britons were all like this, and why no one except his mother had warned him.

"If you put your request in writing," he tried, "I'll pass it on to the—"

"Writing is a waste of time. I must talk to him."

"But he isn't here," Firmus insisted, ignoring a roar of pain from the direction of the procurator's private rooms.

"I will go to find him."

"He's ill." It sounded better than admitting the great man had fallen off his horse. "You can talk to me."

He could see her eyes narrow as if she were assessing him. She glanced around the chilly little room, taking in the one cupboard and the triangular blur on the back of the door that was his cloak, hung on a rusty nail. "You are very young to be assistant procurator."

It was what they all said. Usually he explained about his eyesight and the army and how grateful he was to his uncle for finding him a post where he could get some overseas experience, but after a taste of that experience, Firmus was not feeling grateful at all. His uncle gave the impression of being perpetually annoyed with him and the staff seemed to think he was a joke. The one with the front teeth missing had practically laughed out loud when Firmus had explained that, as part of the emperor's tightening up on the Imperial transport service, he had personally been put in charge of the Survey of British Milestones. They were probably listening in the corridor now, and snickering.

Firmus decided he might as well tell the truth. "I'm only here because the procurator is my uncle."

To his surprise, this seemed to reassure her. "So, you really are his assistant?"

"Yes."

"And you will help me?"

"I don't know," he said. "Who are you?"

Her breasts lifted in a distracting fashion as she took a deep breath to launch into her speech. "I am Camma of the Iceni," she announced, "I am wife of . . ."

Firmus had no idea who she was the wife of, because although he tried to pay attention, all he could see was the swell of the magnificent breasts, and all he heard was one word.

Iceni.

Several of the things he had read about Britannia before leaving Rome had turned out to be misleading—where were the woad-painted wife-swappers?—but he was fairly certain that the last time a tax official had annoyed an Iceni woman, it had been a very big mistake indeed. Especially since his own grandfather had been one of the officers killed in the ill-fated attempt to rescue the people of Camulodunum.

The books said that the Iceni had been crushed years ago, but this one did not look crushed. This one looked tall and fierce and none too clean: exactly how he imagined the raging Queen Boudica at the head of her savage hordes.

When future histories were written about Britannia, Firmus did not want to appear in them as the man who had been fool enough to upset the Iceni *again.*

He cleared his throat. She stopped talking.

"Sorry," he explained, making an effort to look her in the eye. "I'm having trouble following your accent." He reached for the stylus and picked up the tablet. "Could you say all that again, a bit slower?"

"I said," she repeated, louder rather than slower, "something has happened to my husband."

"We don't deal with husbands and wives here. This is the finance office."

"I know it is the finance office! I am not stupid!"

Firmus gulped. "No! No, of course not." He recalled the advice of a distant cousin who had served here as a tribune: Half the challenge of dealing with the natives was working out what the problem was, and the other half was deciding what other poor bugger you could pass it on to.

"This is why I have come to you," the woman explained. "My husband is a tax man."

"Your husband works in the tax section?" he asked, wondering how that had been allowed to slip through security.

"His name is Julius Asper."

"Julius Asper," he repeated, scraping the name into the wax. "What's happened to him?"

"He is missing."

"Missing," he repeated, then looked up. "I see. Thank you for coming to tell us. We'll look into it. If you could leave your details with the clerk—"

She folded her arms and rested them on top of her belly. "How can a boy like you assist the procurator when you do not know anything?"

"I've only been here a week," he said. "You'll have to explain a bit more."

"My husband collects the taxes in Verulamium."

"Ah!" Firmus felt a sudden wave of relief. He was on safer ground now. According to his research, Verulamium was a relatively civilized town just a few miles up the north road. For reasons he could not begin to guess, this Camma had married a tax collector in one of the places her tribal ancestors had burned down. "If he works for the council at Verulamium," he said, seeing a way out, "you should go to them."

"I spit on the council!" To his relief, she did not demonstrate. "They will lie to you," she said. "That is why I am here. Whatever they tell you about stealing the money is lies."

"Stealing the money?"

"The tax money."

"Your husband has gone missing with the tax money?"

"No, that is a lie."

Firmus put down the stylus and got to his feet. "Wait here," he ordered. "I'll be back in a—" He stopped, because the woman was no longer paying him any attention. Instead, she had pressed both hands into the small of her back and was staring at the floor with an air of intense concentration.

As he watched, her mouth formed a soft Oh! She stepped to one side and slid a hand down to lift her skirt. He followed her gaze, peering around the desk in an attempt to make out what she was looking at.

Pyramus was at his side, whispering, "There is liquid trickling down the inside of her leg onto the floor, master."

For a moment Firmus had no idea what his slave was talking about. Then he said, "You can't start that in here, madam! This is an Imperial office!"